PRETENDING TO WED

ALSO BY MELISSA JAGEARS

FRONTIER
VOWS

PRETENDING TO WED

MELISSA JAGEARS

UTMOST
PUBLISHING
www.utmostpublishing.com

To my mother,
who is not the inspiration for all the parental drama my characters go through! She's one of the most generous people I know, and I've never once thought she didn't believe in me.

CHAPTER ONE

Wyoming Territory ~ Summer 1884

This couldn't be happening. Not unless he'd stumbled into one of those silly romance novels his aunt used to read.

Nolan Key had only read the one that summer he'd lost his leg, but what else could explain the ridiculous stipulation in his father's will? How could the town's interim lawyer have rattled off those sentences as if they'd made sense?

Yet he'd gone and thanked Mr. Wright like an imbecile, taken his leave, and stared at the building across the street for who knew how long until his brain finally kicked in.

He had to find the lawyer again. Surely he'd misunderstood the terms.

As Nolan rushed past Doctor Ellis's office, he was glad to see the old man wasn't on his porch. Doc likely would've hollered at him, reminding him for the hundredth time he wasn't supposed to run, hop, skip, or jump with too much vigor, lest he rub his stump raw in his artificial leg.

But then, the doctor hadn't been the one who'd just received such preposterous news.

Perhaps Dad had once read a whole stack of Aunt Edith's dime novels, for where else would he have gotten such an absurd idea? To keep the ranch from his only son just because he wasn't married? And to leave it instead to his nephew Matt?

If only Matt's younger brother were still alive and could have inherited. Though Lionel hadn't had any Key blood in his veins, he would've realized he had no business running a ranch and would've handed it straight back to Nolan.

Matt, however, was another story.

Why had his father let him work his tail off to prove he could handle the place if he'd never planned to give it to him? It would've been better if he'd just shipped him off to live with his mother when she'd been alive.

Upon seeing the lawyer walking into the laundry, Nolan rushed around a group of ladies and doubled his limping tromp. "Mr. Wright!"

The dark-haired young man didn't appear to have heard him and stepped inside.

Eric Wright had to be intelligent considering he'd obtained his law degree at such a young age, but he'd surely misunderstood what the last lawyer had written in his father's will. No man should lose his livelihood because his dead father decided he ought to be married. Perhaps Dad's brain had been addled at the end of his life and no one had realized.

Nolan shoved his way through the laundry door. The bell announcing his presence barely registered as he worked to catch his breath.

"Mr. Wright," he breathed heavily. "I need you to explain my father's will."

Eric turned from the empty counter and frowned. "I'm sorry, I thought I had."

"But you said if I didn't get married in three months, my cousin gets the ranch."

"Correct."

"But that's ridiculous."

The young man's expression was sympathetic, but he only stood there watching Nolan gulp air.

He pressed a hand against the stitch in his side. If Dad's posthumous demands hadn't befuddled his brain, he would've ridden his horse instead of running halfway across town. "My father must have been suffering from dementia—either that, or the last lawyer was crazy. Who'd include such a thing in a will?"

"Someone who really wanted you to get married?"

Nolan tried not to scowl. How many times had he told his father he'd never marry, and Dad had told him, "never say never?"

"Do you have witnesses who'd attest to his not being of sound mind? Without that, the last lawyer drew up the paperwork believing he was. Therefore, the will is valid."

Nolan pulled at the front of his shirt and swiped at his clammy skin. He could probably scrounge up a few people who'd say his father was cantankerous, but not loony.

"Here you are, Mr. Wright." The laundress, Miss Stillwater, walked in from the backroom. The tight lines around her mouth didn't match her cheery tone. "I'm sorry it took me so long to wrap, I just—" She stopped and winced.

Had she hurt herself?

She smiled wider, but not brighter, and pushed the twine-encased package forward. One damp blond curl clung to her cheek.

Maybe it truly was hot in here, and not just because he'd hobble-run across town.

"I'm grateful for your business, Mr. Wright."

"No problem, Miss Stillwater. Thank you." Eric began pulling change out of his pocket and turned to Nolan. "I'm afraid if you don't have a legitimate case against your father's sanity, we'll have to follow his wishes."

"But I can't." Nolan shook his head, as if doing so could make this situation go away. "It'd be like admitting this made sense."

He turned to Miss Stillwater and patted her well-oiled countertop. Surely he could get Eric to see how absurd the will's terms were. "Miss Stillwater, do you read those dime novels the mercantile sells?"

"Um, no." She gave him a strange look. Her blue eyes appeared weary, but there was a sparkle in them.

"Why not? Because you find them ridiculous? Contrived? Their plots nothing like real life?"

"I simply don't have the time, Mr. Key."

"I should've known you'd not waste hours on drivel. You *are* one of the more sensible women in town." He turned back to Eric. "But surely you see how completely bizarre his stipulations are? A novel's mustache-twirling villain would be the kind to force his son into this, not a sane, flesh-and-blood man."

Eric pushed a small stack of coins toward the laundress and picked up his package. "Actually, I'd think the twirling-mustache kind of villain would do much worse. I've read a dime novel or two." He headed for the door and held it open for Nolan to pass through.

Nolan frowned at having the door held open for him. Long ago, he'd given up informing people a wooden leg didn't stop him from using his arms, so he stepped through without a fuss.

Eric let the door slam behind them.

"All right, fine. My father evidently wanted to leave earth in a wake of drama, but that doesn't mean I have to participate. How can I save my ranch without going through wedded nonsense?"

Eric stopped on the porch's edge and rubbed at the hint of beard growing along his jaw. "You could ask your cousin to relinquish his claim."

And that was even less likely to happen outside of a dime novel than the current predicament he was in.

"I'll let you know if I think of anything, Mr. Key." Eric tipped his hat and headed west, likely toward the McGill mansion on the outskirts of town where his friend lived.

Nolan dropped his hands to his sides and looked up at the

clouds looming over the dusky blue mountain ridge surrounding town.

God, I'm nowhere near as godly as Job, so my questioning you about this won't come as a surprise, right?

So, why?

You got me through the loss of my mother and my leg, but how am I going to survive without my ranch?

Corinne counted the change in her cash box, as if the young lawyer's coins might have magically multiplied and she'd find more money. But unfortunately, there was barely more there than before. Glancing out the window, she could see Mr. Key standing outside, face upturned toward the chaotic, cloud-filled sky hanging heavy over the ridge.

What had all that fuss been about with Mr. Wright? Mr. Key had always been the quiet type, his father, too. She couldn't recall the elder Mr. Key speaking a word to her beyond asking what they owed, and she'd certainly had never seen the younger so animated.

Earlier, he'd been sweaty, and his eyes wide and round, flinging his hands around as if he were rearing up like a spooked horse.

Mr. Key's father had never given her the impression of being a soft-hearted man, but what could he have done to make his son think him a villain?

She rubbed at the space between her thumb and forefinger where it'd been throbbing since she'd awakened. Though the younger Mr. Key had been nice to her the two years she'd lived here, he'd never complimented her—and she'd been glad he hadn't. Though having a man call her sensible was likely the best compliment she'd ever received.

But the cherry on top was that his compliment hadn't been followed by a request for her to consider his court.

If men weren't ignoring her because her position in town wasn't much higher than a servant's, they seemed to believe she'd bow down at their feet, thankful they'd offered her an escape from laundry in exchange for a lifetime of arduous work by their side.

Of course, most of the men doing the asking were either ancient, toothless, or made her skin crawl.

Now, if one of them had been of Nolan's caliber ... He wasn't particularly striking, but he did have a decent face upon broad shoulders.

No, what was she thinking? Corinne shook her head and placed the cash box back under the counter. He'd called her sensible, and she needed to be so. She was no dime novel heroine who did ridiculous things to capture a man's attention.

Not because she hadn't been that way before. Oh no, she'd been plenty naïve years ago, undone by charm and seduced by the promise of security.

Never again.

She scooped up a solitary stocking sticking out from beneath the counter and stood. Now whose was this?

Mrs. Tate bustled in. "Miss Stillwater, you must take care of my tablecloth at once. The Ivenses have agreed to come to supper, and look what I've found." She heaved a wad of fine silk fabric onto the counter and pointed to a smattering of grease stains.

Despite the numbness in her fingers, Corinne pulled the fabric closer and spread it out for inspection. "I have several jobs in front of you. I don't think I can get to it until—"

"But they're coming tonight! You have to get this done right away." Though the woman was on the heavy side, her nose was thin and she was adept at looking down it.

"I don't—"

"Did I tell you it was the Ivenses?"

"Yes, you did." Now that the McGill family was practically

disgraced, the Ivens family was not only the richest in Armelle, but also the most important.

"I'm sorry, I can't—"

"I'll pay you triple."

How could she pass up that offer? Even if she did have to work past closing time.

All she'd wanted to do since waking this morning was return to bed. Though her hands would likely continue to ache, she couldn't let go of the hope that one day, sleep would once again be a respite from pain. Despite the warmth rushing to her eyes, Corinne nodded.

"Thank you, Miss Stillwater. I'll put in a good word for you." And Mrs. Tate left.

Where was the old woman planning to put in a good word for her? Or did that just mean she'd refrain from tittle-tattle and say a kind thing or two about her for the next few weeks?

Corinne gathered up the tablecloth and forced herself not to drag her feet on the way back to the washbasins.

If only being a damsel in distress—and having a hero sweep in and save her—were a sensible plan.

But it wasn't, so she must rescue herself. She'd done it before; she'd do it again. Though it would be nice to be carried off to some castle and be waited upon by servants. A shame she hadn't the time to read any of those dime novels and pretend for half an hour each night such a possibility existed.

Romantic, charming heroes, however, could not be trusted.

She dropped Mrs. Tate's tablecloth onto her worktable and took up her special mix of chemicals and rubbed it into the stains, noting how low her canisters of caustic soda and powdered limestone were.

Even if she could find the time to read, she'd not waste her money on a novel. She needed more chemicals. A pregnant friend of hers was breaking out in a rash when doing her own laundry, and every soap on the mercantile shelf caused a reac-

7

tion. Corinne had yet to figure out a mixture that would clean well and not irritate her friend.

Women didn't need knights to swoop in to save them—if any could. Their real hope lay in inventions that would cut down, if not eradicate, the backbreaking work required to survive. Then they'd all have time to read as many outlandish dime novels as they wished.

After pretreating Mrs. Tate's tablecloth, Corinne sat to allow her hands a rest. She reread the advertisement she'd clipped from the newspaper yesterday for a special set of irons.

Would she ever be able to do what this woman had—or at least before someone else beat her to it? She glanced over at the washing dollies she'd built and abandoned, for none had worked better than the one she'd bought from the Montgomery Ward catalog. Her thoughts for a special iron had not made it past ideas on a page. Before she'd had time to make a prototype, this Mrs. Potts had invented and was selling something even better than she'd dreamed up. Two of the irons in the set could be heated while the other was being used, all double pointed, so they could iron both ways. Plus, they retained their heat longer than average if the advertisement was to be believed.

With enough timesaving inventions like this, maybe one day, the life of a laundress wouldn't be such a pitiable position.

Flexing her stiff fingers, Corinne pulled the small vat of lace she'd started soaking closer, and her heart skipped a beat. Had she gotten the stain out?

She wrung the water from the fabric then hurried to the window to inspect the fancy needlework in the sunlight. Were the rust stains gone? After inspecting one side, she glanced at the other. Her grin grew until she pulled on the lace and noticed the weakened threadwork.

Her eyes slammed shut and her shoulders sagged. So close, but she couldn't sell a stain remover that ate through fabric.

She trudged over to the washboard and started working

despite the nerves that ran from her fingers to her elbows protesting vehemently.

The only kind of knight she could be tempted to daydream about was one who ordered his squires to wash Mrs. Tate's tablecloth for her. And since that would never happen, laundry, for the time being, would be as painful and drudgery-filled as it had always been.

CHAPTER TWO

Nolan tapped his pencil as he reviewed the words on the telegram form. Was it really a good idea to ask Matt if he'd be willing to forfeit his claim to the ranch? There were still three months to find a way out of this.

Slumping against the telegraph office's counter, Nolan closed his eyes, shutting out the tap-tap-tapping of Mr. Udall sending a message along with the chatter of his wife visiting with Mrs. Tate.

God, could you keep Matt from fighting me? I mean, if he doesn't know I'm more deserving of this land already, nothing in a telegram will change his mind. Convincing him somebody could be better than him at something is a task I've yet to see anyone win. I can't let him have—

The bell above the door clinked.

Nolan moved to the side and leaned against the wall so Bo McGill and Eric Wright could get in line. The lawyer did nothing more than lift his hat toward him before turning to nod at the women. Seemed Eric hadn't come up with any new ideas on how to circumvent Dad's will.

Bo walked over and held out a hand. "Long time since I've seen you."

Shaking hands, Nolan tried to smile back, but the weight of

the past few days hung heavy. "I haven't been in town much lately. I hear you've been busy, too."

The young man's smile slumped, and he took his hand back to shove in his pocket. "There's been a lot for me to clean up, but I'm trying. You don't suspect my father stole anything from you, do you?"

Nolan shook his head. It was his own father doing the stealing right now, attempting to take away what he'd spent his life to build up.

"Good." Bo's posture straightened. "I wouldn't want any bad blood between us."

"There wouldn't have been. I understand how a father and son can have totally different aims in life. So whenever you want to come out to the ranch and hunt coyotes again, let me know—of course…" He sighed. If Bo didn't have time to hunt within three months, what good was the invitation? Though Bo was dealing with a setback in finances—trying to figure out what property actually belonged to the McGills and what his father had stolen—his family was still wealthy, they'd…

Wait, what if he didn't have to surrender everything to his cousin?

Nolan knocked an anticipatory beat on the wall with his knuckles. "You know what? What would you think about buying my cattle? I know it's a strange time of year to be asking, but—"

Eric forcefully cleared his throat. "I'm afraid you can't do that, Mr. Key."

"Of course I can. It might not be the wisest—"

"But they're not your cattle."

Nolan narrowed his eyes at the young man. "Yes, they are."

"They're your father's."

He narrowed his eyes even more. "They were *ours*."

"Do you have written records delineating which percentage is yours?"

Nolan clenched his fists to keep himself from lurching over, grabbing the lawyer, and shaking him. "We ranched together. It was my head for numbers and business that got us what we have."

"But it's your father's ranch."

"It's mine."

"For now, but until you've met your obligations, the property and its assets need to remain intact."

"Are you trying to tell me nothing's mine?" Nolan's heartbeat rose clear up into his throat. If Matt got wind of this, he might not allow Nolan more than the clothes on his back when he showed him the door.

"Any assets you can prove were purchased under your name alone are certainly yours. However, until everything in the estate is settled, nothing should leave it."

But it was the Key Ranch! They'd bought things together as Keys! Even if his father had done more physical work, he'd not have denied that his son had run the show for the last five years.

"Are you ready, Mr. Key?"

Nolan jolted and turned to Mr. Udall, realizing the man's wife and Mrs. Tate had been silent for quite a while from where they sat behind the counter.

"I suppose, yes." He pushed the paper toward Mr. Udall, slapped his telegraph money down, then tipped his hat at Bo and his useless lawyer friend. "Excuse me while I go check on things."

He mumbled a goodbye then shoved his way out the door. He stalked across the street toward the bank, not caring that he was tramping through mud puddles.

What did I do to deserve this?

Could you berate a dead person through prayer? Would God relay his disappointment and frustration to his father? Seemed unfair that Dad could leave him in such a lurch but be safely tucked away in a place he couldn't be made to regret treating his son so badly.

Though maybe Dad wouldn't feel remorse, even if he were alive. He'd never mentioned regretting leaving Mother behind.

Nor had he ever been pleased with Nolan after he'd lost several inches of his leg above the knee—as if the accident in that horse stall had been Nolan's fault.

Everyone else had agreed he'd not been careless, he'd simply been in the wrong place at the wrong time.

And though it was true he'd been left physically incapable of doing as much as his cousin could, why had his father been more pleased with Matt? He was a braggart who did nothing but live off the trust fund his late mother had set up for him and pretended he was worthy of his sales manager title. Surely the only reason Uncle Matthias hadn't fired him from his catalog business was pride.

After staggering up the bank's stairs, Nolan took a deep breath before shoving his way inside.

The silence of the lobby warred with the rushing in his ears. He needed to calm down.

Yet what if all the ranch's accounts included his father's name? Would that mean he didn't possess a single cent?

Nothing could bar him from providing for his own needs for the next three months, but would every non-consumable purchase be considered the ranch's assets and not his?

He unclenched his fists. If what he feared was true, he had to get a hold of himself lest he make a scene.

"I need more time." A young woman's fervent whisper pulled him from his panicky fog.

"I'm sorry, miss, but he said you couldn't have another extension." The teller's voice was full of compassion, yet his face appeared set in stone.

"May I speak with Mr. Rice?" Miss Stillwater's skewed blond updo lost a wavy tress as she leaned closer to the opening in the metalwork running down the middle of the counter, creating an intricate wall between the waiting area and the tellers. "Please." Her voice was a strangled whisper.

"I'm afraid the answer I gave you came straight from him."

"He could change his mind."

"Perhaps." The teller glanced over Miss Stillwater's shoulder at Nolan and gave him an apologetic look before looking back to his customer. "Why don't you sit, miss?"

Mr. Rice came up from behind the teller, a grimace on his face. "I heard you were asking for me, Miss Stillwater."

"Yes." She lowered her voice even more. "You can't rent the laundry out from under me. If you do, how else can I pay you what I owe?"

Nolan took a step back and looked for somewhere else to stand. She was clearly distraught and probably embarrassed to know she could be overheard. But the waiting area was quite small.

Her predicament was surprising though. With the amount of work he'd seen piled up at her place, she ought to be doing well.

"Miss Stillwater, I'm afraid you're already two months behind. How can I be assured you'll be able to pay for three months altogether?" Mr. Rice lifted one shoulder. "I can rent your place out tomorrow and have my losses covered. I have children and employees to think about."

"I understand." Miss Stillwater's voice held tears while she wrung her hands in a rather strange manner. "Though if you kick me out, no one around here will be willing to rent their place to me, and I—"

"You've been dependable until now, Miss Stillwater. Is there no one from whom you could borrow money?"

"No," she said, nearly crying the word.

Nolan backed away as quietly as he could to sit in the farthest chair.

"You have a contract that needs to be adhered to."

"Maybe I could take out a loan? It'd only be for twenty-four dollars. That'd cover three months, and then—"

"I'm afraid we wouldn't be able to do that, but you have the rest of the week to get caught up." Mr. Rice frowned and rested a hand atop hers. "Do you have unpaid accounts you can call in? I'm happy to keep you as a tenant if you meet your contractual obligations."

A silent tear rolled down Corinne's cheek as she stood staring at a spot on the polished counter between them. Then with a huge inhale, she wiped her face, nodded, and bid the banker good day before walking away, head down.

"I'm so sorry to keep you waiting, Mr. Key." The teller stepped back to the counter as the bank president returned to his office.

"Not a problem." He glanced at Corinne before pushing himself to stand. He wriggled his leg to put it back into a better position since sitting had turned it askew. "I've come to check on how we set up the ranch's accounts. Are any in my name only? I know the main account isn't, but what about the savings?"

"Let me check." The teller headed for the shelving at the back of the bank.

Nolan turned to look through the front door windows. Corinne was leaning against the porch post, her hands tucked up against her chest, pressed in a ball as if praying.

"Your savings account is in your name only, sir. Do you have a transaction to make?"

"Yes, but with the ranch's account." He shouldn't touch his savings since that might be all he had in a few months. Though he likely couldn't transfer money directly from the ranch account to his savings without a lawyer's censure, he couldn't be stopped from using the ranch account within reason. "Sixteen dollars please, and apply it to Miss Stillwater's debt. That'll cover the two months she's behind if I did the math correctly, right?"

"Sir, I'm afraid I can't discuss—"

"I don't need a discussion. That's two months, yes?" He lifted an eyebrow.

The teller's head tipped forward.

"That's all I'd like to do today."

"And if she asks?"

"My identity is between you and me."

"All right, sir. I'll thank you on her behalf, for I know she'll be grateful."

He nodded and waited for the teller to give him his withdrawal slip.

After that was settled, he headed outside and found Miss Stillwater sitting on a bench in the shadows. Her face was puffy, and silent tears were coursing down her cheeks.

He cleared his throat. She had to know he'd overheard. "I'm sorry about your struggles."

She shrugged and turned her face away.

He stepped closer. "I could bring you a few extra loads of laundry this week."

Did she just laugh and whimper at the same time?

She pulled out a handkerchief and blotted her eyes. "I—I thank you, but no. I can't." She stood and fumbled her handkerchief. Once she retrieved the dainty square, she shoved both the handkerchief and her hand into her pocket and walked past him with barely a nod farewell.

Had she just rejected work? Maybe his act of charity had been in vain. Perhaps she wasn't the most sensible female in town.

However, there wasn't much else he could do for her. In three months, they might both be homeless.

Three months?

No. The time frame was coincidental. From what he'd seen, she had plenty of work to keep her afloat. She'd figure things out in time to save her business.

He, on the other hand, had no such work to rescue him. What could he do to save himself that didn't require marrying?

CHAPTER THREE

Corinne stepped inside the laundry, took one look at the dirty piles awaiting her, and sat down and ripped open her letter. She usually delayed reading mail until she retired, but bedtime would take forever to arrive today with how often she had to rest her hands between scrubbing.

Corinne's heart rate stuttered. The page was covered in her brother-in-law's handwriting. He never communicated with her unless absolutely necessary. Thankfully, a quick skim proved her sister was still alive.

Though he loved Yvonne far better than Corinne had ever thought possible, she still didn't enjoy talking to him. Because when a boy breaks up with his "secret" girlfriend in order to take her younger, prettier sister to the spring concert instead—well, can anyone blame a girl for not being keen on talking to such a boy ever again?

But before Corinne had bucked up enough to tell Yvonne what he'd done, she'd overheard his best friend ask him why he'd switched sisters. Gerald had shrugged and said he couldn't "get serious" with a girl who kissed worse than a fish gulping for its last breath.

Mortified, she'd chosen not to tell Yvonne anything. She'd

figured her little sister would soon enough discover what a louse he was.

Except, within weeks, he gazed at Yvonne as if he would die if he couldn't breathe the same air that she did. And Yvonne constantly sang, flitting about the house, happier than Corinne had ever seen her.

And in regard to what she'd overheard Gerald tell his buddy … well, nothing since that day had proven he'd lied about how badly she kissed.

Corinne forced herself to get back to reading before she started thinking over memories that only got worse.

> …*I'm afraid the panning's not going well. I've seen no flakes for weeks now. I know you're wondering why I'm telling you this and not Yvonne, but she's been really tired lately and I don't want to worry her.*
>
> *What I'm writing to say is, I'm going to have to ask you to make extra payments, preferably double.*
>
> *I know Yvonne told you about being in the family way in the last letter, but that was before the midwife predicted twins, seeing how fast she's growing and being so tired. If it wasn't for that, maybe I could get by with what you're sending, but…*

Double the payments? Corinne tilted her head back with a sigh. It'd been hard enough to humble herself to request the loan in the first place when her laundry had burned down in Rapid City. With how things were going now, was it even possible?

This morning, she'd been both relieved and embarrassed to learn somebody had anonymously paid two months of her rent when she'd gone in with only a third of the money needed. The bank president had most likely forgiven her debt but didn't want anyone to know. Otherwise, everyone might expect him to write off overdue balances.

Just like last week, she'd left the bank in tears, but happy tears this time.

She rubbed the corner of the stained letter. Seemed there wouldn't be much of a reprieve to her toil though, for how could she say no to Gerald's request when it meant her sister's children would suffer if she did?

Corinne tried to slip the letter back into its envelope, but her fingers were too numb to cooperate. She stared at Gerald's slanted handwriting instead. How could she possibly double or even triple her workload to pay him and keep up with her rent if she couldn't tuck his letter back into its envelope without wincing?

Was it possible to wash clothes with your feet?

Hmmm, not a bad idea.

Potential contraptions started whirling about in her mind, but she shook them away. She might be able to figure out a way to power a washing machine with her feet, but there was no time to build, test, and tweak such a thing now. She had to get all this work done quickly if she had any hope—

Knock, knock.

The front door whined open, and she turned to present her customer with the best smile she could muster—hard to do, since all her facial muscles had settled into a perpetual grimace lately. "Can I help you?"

Leah Whitsett, a petite brunette with a puckered scar running through her brow, stepped inside. Hands folded in front of her, she offered a smile which looked off center below her drooping left eye.

Corinne froze the half-smile on her own face to keep from letting any pity show. Only a few months ago, Leah's outward beauty had matched her kind heart.

"I was hoping you could help me." Leah's voice was rough, no longer the clear, feminine lilt it used to be.

"Do you have laundry for me to bring in?"

"I'm sorry, no. I'm not dropping off anything. I need work."

Corinne couldn't help her frown. This poor woman

shouldn't have to ask for work. "Unfortunately, I can't offer you any."

Leah scanned the piles of unfinished laundry, but when she turned to look back at Corinne, her gaze held no accusation, rather, resignation. "I understand. Good day, Miss Stillwater."

"I'm sorry, Mrs. Whitsett."

The lady frowned, gave her a nod, then turned for the door, a slight limp to her gait.

Corinne exhaled. She could've used Leah's help, of course, but she couldn't pay her. She stared down at her throbbing hands. If only she'd already invented something to circumvent the majority of her manual labor, she might not be in such a poor financial position right now. Might have been able to hire a woman who needed help paying bills while her husband was imprisoned.

But at least the townspeople loved Leah. As soon as people found out she was asking for work, surely others, especially the former marshal and his wife, would make sure she didn't lose her home and had enough to eat until her husband returned.

Corinne pushed herself out of her chair, dropped the letter onto her desk, and forced herself back to work.

Unlike Leah, she didn't have a town full of friends to save her. Since arriving in Armelle, she'd been too busy to socialize. Even if she had been able to leave work more often, she couldn't hold a candle to Leah—the nicest woman she'd ever met.

And she couldn't count on the bank president to bail her out again either, for he had a business to run.

Her right hand pinged with pain, so she gritted her teeth to keep pushing her hands through the motions of rubbing Mrs. Ivens's blouse against the washboard.

What if a month wasn't enough to get caught up and her hands got worse like the doctor predicted? Yvonne would probably beg for her to come live with them and help with the babies, but she couldn't do that to herself. She was over Gerald, but she just couldn't live under the same roof with him.

Besides, they lived too far from any town for her to find work while staying with them, and if she couldn't make a go of things here…

She stopped to huff a sigh. She had to find a way to pay them.

A few people in town had overdue accounts, but collecting them wouldn't cover half a payment to her brother-in-law.

The bell above her door tinked again, and Celia Hendrix, a tall, lanky girl of sixteen, marched in. Her hazel gaze locked onto Corinne. "How come you didn't hire Mrs. Whitsett?"

Corinne took her hands out of the water, sighing with the relief her hands felt, but that didn't make answering the young woman any easier. "Unfortunately, I can't use her."

Celia took a long look around at the piles and then pinned her glare back on her.

The young woman had worked for her last summer when a bunch of surveyors had come through. Celia knew exactly how long washing everything in this room would take.

Corinne glanced at the walls of laundry closing them in. "Yes, I've got work, but I can't afford—"

"I thought you were better than everybody else."

"Pardon?" What did everyone else have to do with laundry?

"Just because Mrs. Whitsett's speech is all gravelly now and her hip didn't heal perfectly, you act as if she's no use. She's got hands and can stand, that's all she needs. There's no reason for any of you to think she's no longer a good worker. Why, she volunteers for everything!"

"I'm just—"

"She won't slow you down. She'll work hard. If she gets behind, I'll come in and catch her up."

"Celia—"

"You won't have to pay me nothing."

"But you have chores at home and the sidewalks—"

"I'm done with the sidewalks."

As part of Celia's punishment for the part she played in

21

Leah's accident this past spring, she and a few other boys had been sentenced to build boardwalks for Armelle residents who'd yet to construct any despite city regulations.

Celia crossed her arms. "Plus, my mother can do without me. She did while I was working for the city."

"It's not that I don't believe you'd help. I just can't afford to pay someone right now."

"But Leah's been all over town, and no one's hiring her." Celia flung open her arms. "After all she's done for everybody, people should be bending over backwards for her—like she's bent over backwards for everyone in Armelle at some time or another. So I don't believe you. You're all thinking that because her speech is slow now, her brains must be slow, too."

"I'm so sorry, Celia. I understand your frustration and your desire to help." The girl really had been working hard to help Leah lately. "I'll pray she finds the work God's prepared for her."

Celia scowled. "That's what Leah's been saying. That God has something for her, and we gotta pray to find it. But if someone like you who obviously needs help won't hire her, she's expecting a miracle." The young woman turned on her heel and stomped out, the door shutting behind her just short of a slam.

With a lump in her throat, Corinne lowered her hands back into the murky water and started scrubbing again, wincing at the stiffness in her fingers.

If only she could run after Celia and tell her she could hire Leah. She was exactly the type of woman Corrine wanted to help, a woman like she'd once been, thrust into an untenable position by a man who'd done her wrong.

Yet she couldn't.

Corinne sucked up the moisture threatening to leave her face. She'd done enough crying this week, over finances, over her inability to sleep because of pain, over the piles of work she couldn't get ahead of. Though the stinging in her hands was the worst it'd been in three weeks, the fact that Leah now suffered because of them seemed even more unfair.

After taking twenty minutes longer than necessary to wash Mrs. Ivens's clothing, Corinne hung everything up and then cradled her hands. If her body didn't start cooperating soon, she'd be begging for a job as well.

And she'd probably fare worse than Leah.

Closing shop, she trudged to the doctor's. She couldn't afford more medicine, but now that she faced eviction, she'd use what little money she had to see if the doctor could help. Hopefully he wouldn't tell her the same thing he'd told her the last two times she'd visited.

Her hand slipped off the office's doorknob, and she tried again with a stronger grip and a grimace, finally making her way into the empty waiting room.

"I don't want to see you back in here again for something like this. You know better than to wear your leg so long. One of these days, a salve won't fix it."

Corinne grimaced at the doctor's condescending tone, but he would likely talk to her in that same manner soon enough. He'd already told her several times she had to quit the laundry —as if that were a possibility.

"I understand, Doc, but I wasn't in a position to go back for my crutches. My men needed—"

"Then don't get into such a position again. You have to take care of what you have or you'll lose it. And you shouldn't have come into town on your leg. Stay off it for a few days."

"I'll try." A few moments later, Nolan stepped out of an examination room, air hissing through his teeth with each step. He looked up and stiffened upon seeing her. The sharp lines around his tightly pressed lips deepened, but he started walking past her as if he hadn't been limping. "Good day, Miss Stillwater."

Attempting to keep her face blank so he'd not think she

pitied him, she nodded as he moved past her toward the door. She likely wouldn't fare any better with the doctor than he had.

"Miss Stillwater? What can I do for you?"

Holding out her hands, she gave him a half-hearted shrug.

Doctor Ellis shook his head and pointed her toward an exam room. "I suppose you're still laundering from sunup to sundown."

She crossed in front of him, sat on the table, and laid her hands on her lap for him to examine. "I can't do anything else if I want to survive."

"Nonsense. I've already told you your best course of action is to get married so you can stop doing the same things over and over with your hands. If you don't, you could permanently damage them."

"But getting married won't get me out of laundry."

"True, but that's not all you'd do."

She suppressed an irreverent chuckle. Men seemed to have no idea how long the laundry process was. And then there was the ironing. "If I were to give birth to baby after baby, I'd have just as much washing as I do now."

"All those kids could help you with the washing."

"Not until I've suffered through years of boiling diapers. Plus, I don't see how churning butter, mending, and kneading dough would be any better for my hands."

"It's different movements. Though it'd be best if you took a few months off. A honeymoon holiday would do you good. Then you could ease yourself back into work."

Did he expect her to marry a rich man? She might be able to find a homesteader willing to wed a random woman who promised to clean up after him, but if the doctor thought such a man would give her weeks off for a holiday and then let her ease into chores, well, Doctor Ellis was well-off enough to hire a maid and had likely never observed his wife toiling all day washing linens.

Even Nolan, on his fake leg, had it better than a woman hunched over a washboard. "I have to work, Doctor."

"And if you don't take my advice, you could permanently injure yourself. Then where would you be?"

A question she couldn't think about if she wanted to sleep at night—not that she did much of that lately with her tingling fingers. "I understand."

But understanding didn't help much.

Jesus had said His followers were supposed to let tomorrow worry about itself since each day had enough trouble of its own. And though the doctor was insistent she worry about tomorrow, God knew she'd never look to marriage to rescue her, no matter how bad the future seemed.

All she could do was survive today.

CHAPTER FOUR

SORRY FOR YOUR LOSS MUST BE HARD TO
HANDLE RANCH ALONE-
LOOK AFTER IT FOR ME YOU CAN STAY IF
DESIRED-

Crumpling up the telegram, Nolan resisted the urge to pitch it across the telegraph office. He should've known Matt would act as if the ranch was already his, not worrying that Nolan might marry to keep it from him.

Of course, he couldn't exactly fault Matt for not thinking he'd go through with a wedding. He'd told his family often enough he had no plans to marry.

But to have the gall to tell him to "look after" the ranch?

If his cousin were in charge, he would not remain on the ranch, no matter how magnanimous Matt thought he was to propose he stay on.

Nolan forced himself not to punch the wall beside him. He'd still been a boy when Dad had brought him to Wyoming. In an attempt to impress his father, he'd thrown himself into ranching, working sunup to sundown. But within two years, he'd lost his leg.

Dad was known for his daring feats on cattle drives, his ability to wrestle nearly any man into submission, and the sheer amount of backbreaking work he could squeeze into a day, but he'd been terrible at managing money. He should've been proud of a son who'd managed his books well, even if he couldn't physically do as much as most ranchers.

"Was there anything else you needed?"

Nolan startled.

Mr. Udall stood behind the telegraph counter, his eyebrow arched as he looked from Nolan to the people lined up behind him.

"Sorry." He backed away from the counter, nodding his head to the others. "I'm not in line. Forgive me."

Outside, he stuffed his hands in his pockets and walked slowly. Since he hadn't brought his crutches into town, he needed to be careful not to aggravate the abrasion on his leg.

What should he do now?

Nolan stopped and stared down the main road in the direction of his ranch. He couldn't stay and submit to Matt's orders. Though his father hadn't acted as if he valued his management abilities, he had given him free rein to run things as he saw fit.

Matt wouldn't.

Across the street, Miss Stillwater stepped out of the mercantile. Her hunched shoulders likely mirrored his own.

Despite her slumped posture, she was a decent-looking woman. Probably more than decent if he thought about it. He'd always admired the way she did business, even if her work ethic had declined recently.

If he had to marry…

No, he'd not change his convictions for material reasons. But double checking to be sure Miss Stillwater didn't want his extra laundry would be a good thing—neighborly even.

His heart kicked up an unusual rhythm as he followed far, far behind her. It wouldn't do to make her believe he'd followed her across town.

Minutes later, he paused in front of her door, then just shook his head and plowed in before he—

"Oh!"

A thud registered before he frowned down at Miss Stillwater, who was scrambling about on the floor by the window. Several glass bottles were strewn about in a mess of puddles.

Of all the clumsy things to do. He shut the door behind him. "I'm sorry, I didn't mean to make you drop—"

"Of course, you didn't." She looked up at him for a second before scooting over to pick up another bottle. "It was my fault. I just…" She picked up a glass vial and brought it up to eye level before audibly sighing. "Doesn't matter."

"It does if I caused it." He leaned over to retrieve an empty bottle which had broken at the neck. Nothing on the faded label indicated what it once contained. "I'll buy you more."

She took the jagged jar from his hand, wearing a pained expression. "They can't be replaced."

"Sure they can." It couldn't be too expensive.

"Well, *you* can't replace them. It's not something you buy. It takes time." She glanced up at him, then shrugged. "They're at different stages of evaporation."

"Oh." So maybe he couldn't replace them, but why care about evaporation stages?

"And it wasn't your fault—not directly anyway. I was turning over the sign, but missed the hook. You startled me, but I'm the one who knocked them over." She leaned over to pick up her closed sign. Her face paled, and she seemed to be gritting her teeth while lifting the placard up to the window.

He knew that look, or at least, he'd seen it on his own face occasionally. On mornings when the weather wreaked havoc with his amputated leg, or when he'd worked too hard the day before and caught a glimpse of himself in the mirror above his washstand.

The look he'd likely sport now if he weren't in town and anxious to keep people from asking him if he was all right every few minutes. After a while, no one wanted to hear about your chronic pain, and it was hard to lie and say everything was fine when your face told a different story.

Glancing down the length of her, he searched for signs of blood where broken glass might have cut, but all he saw was her hands curled up tight, holding nothing.

But he wouldn't ask what was wrong. She had likely seen the same look on his face the other day at the doctor's and refrained from asking. A woman who didn't nag… "So why haven't you married?"

All right, so that question was even worse to have blurted out.

Her eyes nearly popped out of her head. "Why…"

"I'm s—"

"…I'd rather die."

"Die?" Perhaps one person in this world was more adamantly opposed to being wedded than he.

"I'm sorry. That just—" Corinne put a hand across her mouth, "—slipped out."

"No need to apologize. It's none of my business. I shouldn't have asked."

She eyed him. "You mean, that's all there is to it?"

Her piercing gaze made it hard not to squirm. "I'm not sure what you mean."

"Any time a man asks me that, there's always a proposal following, if not immediately, then soon after. No matter how clearly I've hinted I'm not interested, the question comes anyway." Her face colored, a nice change from the ashen tones from earlier. "Though I suppose the 'hint' I gave you was a bit harsh."

"'I'd rather die' is hard to miss."

Her mouth wriggled to one side. "So then?"

"I was, uh, just wondering." He reached up to run a hand through his hair, but stopped short of knocking his hat off. "Like you, I'm always trying to thwart people from attempting to marry me off. Why can't they stop badgering us when it's clearly a strongly held conviction?"

She relaxed a little, but not enough to release the tension in the fine lines around her mouth.

"I knew better than to ask." He reached past her to straighten her sign. "I understand how it is—well, maybe not as well as you do since I'm not fending off unwanted proposals. But it's obvious why I've remained single. I guess I'm just curious as to your reasons."

"And why are you single?"

He frowned. "I thought that was self-evident."

She shook her head slightly, though he wasn't sure she'd meant to do so.

"My leg." He pointed.

She blinked. "What about it?"

His frown deepened. "A woman doesn't want a husband without one."

"That's a sorry excuse. You're walking around just fine, and your ranch is doing well from what I've heard."

He opened his mouth to explain why a woman ought to think twice about marrying a man who could one day become more of a burden than an asset out West, but then shrugged. She could think it through if she wanted to figure out why wedding him was unwise. "What about your reason?"

She shook her head.

He bit his tongue to keep from pressing her. It wasn't as if she'd started this interrogation. "Well, if you don't mind then, I'd appreciate it if you don't tell anyone why I'm opposed to marriage."

"Why not?"

"Since you found it lackluster and not as obvious as I believed, if you let others know, I might have to fend off a stampede of proposals." He grinned, hoping to pull this conversation out of the quagmire he'd put it in. "I'd rather leave that mess to you."

She rolled her eyes, but he heard the hint of a chuckle. Glancing down at the broken glass near her feet, she sighed and turned to look around the room.

"Looking for your broom?" He pointed behind her, but then sidestepped to retrieve it himself. "I'll take care of it."

Though she was biting her lip, she didn't stop him, even when he started to lower himself onto his good knee. Of course, his fake knee's hinge chose now to protest his attempt to get down far enough to sweep up glass fragments.

She stepped forward, but he shook his head. She better not stop him when he'd already gotten down this far. Since something was wrong with her hands, it wasn't as if she were better off sweeping.

After all the shards were collected, he rested his elbow on his wooden leg socket, summoning the strength to get back up without making an awkward show of it. Considering how much difficulty he was having getting up and down—as if he were seventy already—how would he survive the coming years if he hadn't the ranch to support himself? He could labor, yes, but not as well as other men his age. And who'd believe he had a good head for numbers if they found out he'd lost his ranch?

Any woman desperate enough to wed him within three months likely had problems of her own, and marrying a mess of a woman could make him more miserable than he would be landless.

And considering Corinne was tight-lipped about her reasons for not marrying, they were likely bad enough he'd rue marrying her—if she ever got desperate enough to agree, which seemed unlikely.

"Um, do you need help up?"

Heat spiraled up his neck. "No, I'm just gearing up to it." He put out his hand to have her back away and tried to get up in one fell swoop. He teetered when his false leg didn't quite cooperate but he held it together. Then he glanced down and realized he'd left the dustpan on the floor.

"I'll get that." She swooped down without looking at him. "Thank you."

"Of course." Perhaps witnessing his complete lack of grace would make it clear why no young lady would choose to marry him.

So maybe he ought to look for someone old.

The laundry door's bell jangled as Celia Hendrix charged in. She didn't spare him a glance before stopping in front of Corinne. Her messy auburn braids were uncharacteristically coiled atop her head, though it did appear she'd pinned them up without looking. "Have you thought any more about helping Mrs. Whitsett? No one's hiring."

Corinne got up off the floor, and he took the dustpan from her hand.

Celia glared at the laundry piled up around the room. "You can't tell me you don't need help."

Corinne looked at him for a second before clearing her throat. "As I said, it's more that I can't afford it. Though I'm trying to think of a way Leah could help me, I don't—"

"You're going to help her?" Celia's brows shot up.

Corinne nodded with a slight shrug. "I'm not sure I can do much, but I want to—"

"Thank you!" The young lady grabbed Corinne by the shoulders. "For whatever you're going to do, thank you. Don't worry about anything. I'll help out. I'll do whatever."

"I know you will."

"I've got to tell—"

"Don't." Corinne grabbed Celia before she escaped. "I can't promise I'll be able—"

"Fine, fine. Will you know by tomorrow?"

Corinne rubbed her forehead but stopped with a hiss, dropping her hand back down. "Have her come talk to me after supper, and maybe—"

"Thank you so much." Celia slipped back out the door, leaving the bell clattering in her wake.

Corinne seemed lost in thought, enough so she probably forgot he was there.

He cleared his throat. "Are you certain you don't want me to bring in more laundry?"

She turned, her expression not as hopeful as Celia's had been. "You can if you'd like, Mr. Key, but I'm afraid it'll be a while before I get to it."

Didn't she plan to hire Leah? His extra laundry wouldn't help her financially if she couldn't get it done by the end of the month. "Would it be done by next week?"

"I believe so."

He stayed silent, wondering if she'd explain what was going on, but she didn't seem interested in filling him in. "Well then, once again, I apologize for the mess I startled you into making, but I hope you have a good rest of your day, Miss Stillwater."

"You, too."

Please, Lord, let me walk out of here without too much of a limp.

Once he made it onto the porch, he heaved in the clean mountain air.

While he owned the ranch, he could pay Corinne's rent anonymously if she was still floundering, but if Matt took over, she'd be on her own.

Corinne could save her place without marrying someone she didn't love, but could he?

I'd do most anything to keep Matt from kicking me out of my house, but waiting at the end of an aisle for a woman who'd rather march toward a firing squad than me—well, that can't be one of those things.

CHAPTER FIVE

"So, I heard Frank's selling piglets. You want any? I was thinking of buying them all, but … I'm not sure I can handle … pigs with nine legs that can snort fire."

"Huh?" Nolan blinked up at his friend Jacob Hendrix. "What're you talking about?"

Jacob's lips cocked with amusement as he stood on the boardwalk in front of the mercantile. "I'm surprised you heard. I lost you several minutes ago, I think."

"Sorry." Nolan shook his head. He was the one who'd initiated the conversation, but when Jacob had mentioned his wife—as any happily married newlywed would—Nolan had started wondering what percentage of convenient marriages turned out well. "I was just thinking about things I've never bothered thinking about before."

"Who's the lady?"

"Huh?" Had his mind wandered off again?

"Either it's a lady who's got your attention or you're in a heap of trouble."

"More the latter. Though it may have to turn into the former."

"What?" Jacob screwed up his eyebrows.

Nolan blew out a breath. "Do you mind if I ask you a rather invasive question?"

Jacob shrugged, but the confused lines in his face didn't smooth out much. "I guess it can't make this conversation much stranger."

"It's just that..." Nolan shifted his weight off his fake leg, though it didn't do much good. "Why'd you marry Annie?"

Jacob frowned as if he were stupid.

"I mean, I know about saving her land and all, but what drove you to it when nothing was on the line for you?"

"You know I've always wanted to ranch, and Anne's a hard worker, so—"

"Be honest. How much pity was involved?" Because that's what he was afraid of.

Shaking his head, Jacob looked up as if searching for an answer in the wispy clouds. "Sympathy played a part, but I wouldn't say I pitied her. Did I come across that way?"

"No."

Jacob narrowed his eyes. "Then why'd you ask?"

"I was only wondering. No real reason. I—"

"So it's true? You need to marry to save your land?"

Nolan blinked and stiffened. "Who told you that? Mr. Wright? If so, people need to know he can't be trusted with—"

"No, it was Mrs. Tate."

"How...?" Nolan frowned. She was the biggest gossip in town, but how would she know? "Surely Mr. Wright wouldn't have—oh!" He gritted his teeth. "I should've known better than to leave a telegram unattended anywhere near her."

"I have no idea where she got her information, but there's truth to it?"

He sighed. "My land's in jeopardy unless I marry, yes."

Jacob rubbed his chin. "Well, Gwendolyn McGill's probably your best chance at money."

"Miss McGill?" He huffed. His own father would've believed such a match was beyond him. If Miss McGill couldn't abide wearing dirty gloves, she'd be unwilling to stand beside a legless man. "She's never even flirted with me, and she flirts with everybody."

Jacob shrugged. "She's not as flighty as she looks."

Nolan crossed his arms. When had Jacob turned into a matchmaker? "She was gunning for you for years and you were never tempted."

"I've learned she's not as bad as she seems." Jacob looked toward the McGill mansion, which sat outside town on a small rise. "She still has her own money from what I've heard, and her brother would help you save your land if it's going to be his sister's place."

"Thanks for thinking Miss McGill would even contemplate marrying me, but I'm not after money."

"You're not?" He scratched his head, messing up his dark hair. "Then how is your land in jeopardy?"

"In the most ridiculous way possible. My father's will says I have to get married or the ranch goes to my cousin."

"Matt? The one who comes up every summer?"

Nolan nodded, gratified to hear the same disbelief coloring Jacob's voice that had overwhelmed him when he'd first read the will.

"I've never heard of such a thing."

"Exactly." Nolan glanced up at the heavens, wishing his father could be dragged down to explain himself.

"There has to be a way to appeal."

"Evidently, you can put anything you want into a will, no matter how ridiculous. If there *is* a way around it, by the time I find an affordable lawyer who's willing to fight it—because Mr. Wright sure isn't—the land will be in Matt's possession. Then if I try to take it back … well, if I lost, I could dig myself into an even deeper hole. You know of any way around a will?"

He shook his head. "My time as marshal was busy enough enforcing laws I knew. I didn't have time to study the ones I didn't. So what lady are you thinking of?"

36

"I'm not thinking of any lady."

"So no one's ever caught your eye? Someone in your past you could write and ask if she ever felt the same?"

He waved his hand. "I'm not contemplating marrying for love. If I were looking for anything in particular, it'd be desperation. Why else would a woman marry me on such short notice?"

Jacob pointed down the street with his thumb. "Then what about the laundress?"

Nolan tried not to physically react to that suggestion. Maybe one woman had crossed his mind. "She's dead set against marrying."

Literally.

"That's common knowledge, but everyone knows you don't want to get married either. Perhaps you two could strike up a deal. Anne seems to think she's in a lurch..."

Jacob's words faded as Nolan turned to look in the direction of the laundry.

A deal.

If any woman in town would be more interested in a business deal than a wedding ceremony, it was Miss Stillwater.

Here he'd been thinking about how impossible it'd be to ask a woman to give up wedded bliss to save him from poverty, when maybe he didn't have to offer a real marriage at all. Just two names on a piece of paper—a business deal. Maybe they wouldn't even have to live together.

"Nolan? Do I have to talk about fire-breathing pigs again?"

Nolan grabbed Jacob's shoulder. "No. But thank you. I think I've come up with a way I can live with this now. Doesn't matter who I marry."

"Now, hold up. I'm thinking you need the same advice Bryant once gave me. No matter who you choose, don't marry a woman who'll make you miserable. You might not be marrying for love, but don't rule out the possibility."

Nolan tried hard not to chuff. Business deals didn't result in love. "I'll keep that in mind, but I've got to visit the lawyer before he closes for the night."

"We'll be praying for you." Jacob reached out and squeezed his upper arm. "And don't be rash."

Getting married within three months to stay financially solvent was the epitome of rash—but his father hadn't left him any other choice. "Thanks for the prayers and the advice."

Nolan marched toward the law office. Hopefully Mr. Wright hadn't left early. He'd not be able to sleep tonight unless he knew if this would work.

Why, he might not even have to know the woman at all—he could marry by proxy. Some old lady who didn't want to upset her life but could use some money. Neither of them would have to be involved with the other, and they'd both financially benefit. His steps took on a bit of a swagger.

Once at the lawyer's, he knocked and at the call for him to come in, breathed in deep. "Good afternoon, Mr. Wright," he said as he walked into the stuffy room.

The lawyer turned from the filing cabinet he was riffling through. "What can I do for you, Mr. Key?"

"You know of any spinsters back in your hometown who'd marry me by proxy? She'd not have to move here, she could stay with her family, and I'd send her money on occasion. That'd be good enough to keep my land, right?"

Eric tilted his head and rubbed his chin.

Nolan's heart sank. He'd been expecting immediate confirmation.

"Problem is, you're to follow the intent of the will. If your cousin protested, it could be shown in court you were trying to skirt the law. Like when a couple's denied a divorce on abandonment grounds if it can be shown they set out to do so together—there's potential for you to lose. Then without land, you'd be stuck with a wife you promised to care for. Are you willing to gamble on either your cousin not caring or receiving a favorable court decision?"

The odds of his cousin fighting for the land over a technicality were high, if not absolutely certain. As to the court…

And here he'd been excited he'd found a way around his father's demands.

Seemed not only would he have to find a woman willing to change her name to Key, but one who was actually willing to live as one.

"Miss Stillwater!" Spencer Hendrix burst through the laundry's front door, red-faced and out of breath. "Doc needs his bandages now!"

Corinne pulled her hands from the hot water and frowned at the pile of bandages the doctor's wife had dropped off three days ago. "I haven't started them yet." She should have, but Mrs. Ellis hadn't told her it was urgent.

"Then what do I do?" The nine-year-old looked about with wide brown eyes as if clean bandages would appear out of thin air. "Doc's got two guys who stabbed each other. One's bleeding real bad."

Corinne winced and looked around, hoping clean bandages would indeed materialize if she looked hard enough. Laundry wasn't supposed to be a life and death situation.

So not only had she been unable to come up with a way to help Leah support herself beyond letting her know Mr. Hutton's clothing needed mending, but she'd now be responsible for someone's demise? "I don't know what to tell you, Spencer. I haven't got them done. I don't know what to do, either."

"Mama will." Spencer rushed back out the door, sending the bell to clanging.

Scanning the full washbasins and piles of laundry around her, she estimated she could get the bandages washed and dried within an hour or two, but that wouldn't help. She'd have to buy the doctor some bandages. Would the mercantile have enough

—or any? But Mr. Owens had already told her he'd no longer sell to her on credit.

She slumped against the counter. How many more times could she fail before the townspeople started sending their laundry elsewhere?

The door whined open, and Spencer and his mother, Annie, rushed in. The redheaded woman came straight toward her and pulled her to stand upright. "Come on, we've got work to do."

Corinne shook her head. "It'll take too much time to wash—"

"You've finished my sheets, right?"

"Yes." But what did that have to do with anything?

"Where?"

Corinne led her behind the counter. "I don't think this is the time to—"

The moment Annie spied her linens, she pulled off the top sheet and handed it to Corinne, then grabbed a second one and unfurled it. "Scissors?"

"What?"

"You have scissors?"

"Oh, yes," She turned to get them. "You aren't going to cut these up, are you?"

Annie grabbed the scissors and started making snips along the top. "Yes, and you'll help me rip them."

Corinne forced herself not to grimace. Tearing up sheets would hurt her more than Annie suspected, but she deserved more than pain for failing at her job. "I'll pay you back for these."

"Don't worry about it."

How could she not? They wouldn't be destroying the Hendrixes' linens right now if she'd been on schedule or had come up with a soap that wouldn't break Annie out in a rash. The doctor had said pregnancies sometimes caused strange symptoms and Annie would likely be able to wash her own clothes again when the baby came, but that'd be a long way off considering Annie's waistline was still trim. "Well then, I'm doing the rest of your laundry for free until you can do it yourself."

Annie chuckled, ripped the fabric, and handed both Spencer and Corinne a third of a sheet. "If I needed my laundry done for free, I'd have Celia do it. But I figure it's a blessing for both you *and* me if I don't have to fight with her to get it done to my standards."

Annie had started on her second strip of cloth, so Corinne grit her teeth and pulled faster.

"Celia has been pretty good lately at helping without a fuss, but she can't stand washing clothes. She only worked with you last summer because she wanted the money."

"I'm so ashamed I'm the reason we're ripping these up." It wasn't like the Hendrixes were rich.

"Worry about that later. We've got to get these to the doctor." She ripped off her last strip, grabbed another sheet, and quickly cut snips along its top before ripping more sections.

"Regardless." Corinne winced as her hands protested starting another strip. "The rest of your laundry will be free."

Annie set a torn strip on the counter, taking a glance around the shop. "Looks like you've got more than enough to keep you busy. You don't need to be volunteering your services. Celia will have to buck up and do it."

"Now I feel even worse. Won't that keep her from helping Leah?" Annie's daughter had been that woman's shadow for months.

"Leah won't mind." Annie started piling up the strips she and Spencer had finished as Corinne worked on her last two. "Okay, son, run these to Doc Ellis."

He swooped in to grab Corrine's last strips and ran out the door.

Corinne let her tingling hands dangle at her sides. "I'm so sorry, Annie. I've been swamped—"

"I can see." The redhead gave her a smile, then unbuttoned her right cuff and flipped it up. "So let's get to work."

"Oh, no." Corinne reached out to stay her. "My soap irritates your skin just like yours does. You shouldn't—"

"It's all right. Spencer's supposed to be helping the doctor for another hour, and with the mess in his office right now, he'll be happy to have him longer. Besides, the rash doesn't hurt the baby, just annoys me." Annie had rolled up her second cuff and immediately dipped her hands into the water of the nearest tub full of soapy water.

"But you shouldn't."

"You likely shouldn't either." She pointedly glared down at Corinne's hands. "If you can work despite the pain, I can deal with a rash."

"How did you—?"

"Anyone who takes more than a few seconds to look at you would know."

Corinne stared at her hands. How quickly she'd become an object of charity when she'd had such high hopes she'd be the one helping others.

She'd been homeless and abandoned twice now, and so she'd set out to work harder, make wiser decisions, and rely on God more fully, so she'd never be in that position again.

Yet, here she was, days away from being destitute again, in need of assistance.

Oh, God, where did I go wrong?

"So what's the matter with your hands?"

Annie's voice pulled Corinne from her prayer, and she sighed while stooping to grab a washboard. "Doctor's not sure, but he believes repetitive motion is causing the tingling and numbness."

"What can you do about it?"

She shook her head. "He tells me I should quit laundry and get married."

"Get married?" Annie chuckled. "Never thought I'd hear a doctor prescribe such a thing."

Corrine took up the pants she'd set to soaking early this morning. "I wish he would prescribe something I could actually do."

"Why not get mar—"

"Never. Never will I do that."

The sloshing of water stopped behind her. Once the silence grew long enough, she turned.

Annie's mouth was scrunched as if trying to figure her out. "I've never pried, but I've always figured a man broke your heart. But, honey, one man is often far different than another. My first husband was good to me, just like my second, but he was a different sort of man. It took me a while to understand Jacob since I expected him to act like Gregory. Not all men behave the same."

"Though you've had two great relationships, that's no guarantee for me or anybody else. In fact, I could fall for someone who'd treat me even worse."

"I'm so sorry."

"Don't be." Corinne kept her eyes on the grass stain she was trying to rub out. "I was responsible for getting into a relationship I knew was less than ideal. The other ones ... well, I guess I've learned my heart cannot be trusted to choose men."

"How old were you?"

"The first time? Sixteen."

"Why, that's no older than Celia. Don't be so hard on your younger self. I've often told Celia if you can learn from your mistakes, then you're better off for it. It might not be something you can look back on proudly, but you can use what you've learned to make your future something to be proud of."

"But I didn't learn. Or maybe I finally have."

"Finally?"

"After the second man who ... devastated me, I moved to Rapid City. I did the wash for the railroad workers. One partic-

43

ular worker kept flirting with me, but I kept myself from responding because I knew better than to trust a man. However, he was insistent and charming, with eyes the color of clover."

When her heart couldn't take it any longer—yet knowing he'd no longer be interested if he knew the truth—she'd told him everything, bracing herself to watch him walk away. But he'd only smiled and returned the next day with wildflowers.

She cleared her throat. "Once I decided to give him a chance, within weeks, we were talking of the future. He insisted on having enough money to buy a house outright before we married to be sure I wouldn't have to work when children came along. I did his laundry, cooked him dinner—everything to help him save."

Yet the week her laundry had burned down, he'd been nowhere to be found. Though he hadn't yet saved enough for a house, she'd hoped he'd agree to move up the wedding so she'd have a place to stay. When she'd finally found him, he was ducking into Margaret Chase's. The pretty widow had just started taking in laundry to support herself. Corinne had walked into the house in time to hear Randolph thank Margaret for taking care of his clothes, call her 'sweetheart,' and tell her he'd be back for dinner.

When he'd turned, his face had blanked and he'd walked past her without a word.

That day, she'd decided to never allow a man to shatter her heart like that again. Seemed Randolph hadn't cared about her past mistakes only because he'd been after what he could get from her for nothing.

She'd been right all along. A good man wouldn't be able to overlook her past.

"And?"

Corinne startled and looked at Annie. Seemed she'd relived all that in her head—good. "And then he left me, so I no longer waste my time hoping a good man will ever want to spend the rest of his life with me."

Annie wrung out a chemise. "Only a year ago, I thought there weren't many eligible, respectable bachelors living around here, but that's what happens when you're swamped with work and don't get to know people. I'm sure others could have warned you about those men. Ask people you trust to be honest with you if you're worried about someone. I could name a handful of men that I'm sure are decent, now that I know them. There's Frank Dent, Abel Jones, Nolan—"

"I'm sorry, Annie, but I know good men exist. I have no doubt your husband is one of them, but unless there's a man out there who simply wants me to change my name in exchange for letting me lounge about and rest my hands, I'm not interested."

Annie kept her eyes trained on hers.

If Annie was expecting her to recant, she'd be disappointed.

Finally turning, Annie went back to scrubbing the nightwear in her hands. "Seems as if your heart wasn't just broken but smashed to bits."

Going back to her work as well, Corinne stayed silent, allowing Annie to believe what she wished.

It wasn't that her heart had been broken beyond repair; rather, she knew for certain she could never make a man happy.

She wouldn't doom someone to being as disappointed as she'd been three times over.

CHAPTER SIX

Setting buckets under the well pump, Nolan started to fill them and squinted at the wagon coming down the road. Did he have visitors, or was another newcomer roaming about looking for a place to claim?

After he hauled the water to the coop, the wagon was close enough he could make out Annie's red hair. He waved to welcome his neighbors.

He knocked the dust out of his hat then walked over to meet them. "Ho! What brings you over today?"

Jacob only nodded as he pulled his horse to a stop. He jumped down and helped his wife to the ground.

Annie gave him a tremulous smile. With the way she held her hands to her stomach and took hesitant steps, it seemed as if she were a girl afraid to go up front and sing her first church solo more than a neighbor on a friendly visit.

And had Jacob just pushed her forward?

"Good morning, Mr. Key."

Nolan took his hat back off. "Morning, Mrs. Hendrix."

He also greeted Jacob, whose face was a touch frozen—except one cocked eyebrow, which twitched.

What were these two up to?

"I uh…" Annie inhaled sharply, exhaled just as forcefully, and then gave herself a nod before taking a more decisive step toward him. "We thought we'd come for a visit."

"All right." Normally he would've invited them into the house, but they were acting strange. "What's the visit for?"

Jacob's lips wriggled with what seemed to be a smile trying to get loose.

"Last night," Annie began, "Jacob and I were talking about your situation."

Oh, no—matchmaking. He'd expected Jacob to interrogate him at church every Sunday, but he'd not expected personal visits.

"And we think—"

Jacob cleared his throat.

Annie rolled her eyes and shook her head. "All right, *I* think —though Jacob doesn't disagree—that we know who'd be the best woman to help keep your land."

Nolan braced himself by leaning against the hitching post. Part of him wanted to stop this conversation, but if anyone might know who'd—

"We think you should consider Miss Stillwater."

Guess they wouldn't be much help after all. "I'm afraid you don't realize how opposed to marrying she is."

Both of Jacob's brows shot up. "You mean you've already asked?"

"Well, no, but—sort of." He tugged on his collar. "I asked in general, and she has no reason to reconsider her situation like I do."

"Oh, I think she does." Annie nodded decisively. "Especially if what you said to Jacob was true, that you don't expect love."

He'd told Jacob that, but hearing someone rule it out for him … well, what did it matter? He'd decided against marrying for love years ago. "What do you know of her situation?"

She shrugged. "Not everything, but enough. I know some men didn't treat her right. More importantly, she said she'd only

47

consider marrying if all she had to do was give up her name in exchange for not having to run the laundry anymore."

That … that was exactly what he'd told the lawyer he was looking for. A woman who was willing to marry him for nothing more than an allowance to live on. "But she told me she'd never marry."

"I believe what she meant is she isn't interested in everything marriage entails. She's worried about picking another man who'll hurt her or leave her. We know you wouldn't do that. We'd also recommend you not rule out falling in love, but if love never came, we think you two could work well together."

With how pretty Corinne was, he could be in danger of falling in love, so he ought to marry her opposite. Someone who'd not be easy to fall for, like the widowed Mrs. Tate.

No, that wouldn't work. Old might work, ugly might work, but Jacob was right that marrying someone who'd make him miserable wouldn't work at all. Not only would people pity him for marrying someone so unsuited, he'd have to deal with all her old lady gossip.

Of course, he didn't know much about Corinne. She certainly seemed to mind her own business, but what if her flaws were better hidden? She was a hard worker, yes, but she didn't socialize much. Did anyone know her well?

"I'm grateful you two want to help…" His attention wandered down the road where another horse and conveyance cleared the rise. This one was a fancy buggy with what looked like three passengers. Who'd be driving out here in one of those?

"It wouldn't hurt to ask Miss Stillwater." Jacob grinned and wrapped an arm around Annie. "You never know how things will work out."

He glanced at the two of them, but shook his head. He'd talked to Jacob just days after he'd married Annie when their life had taken an unexpected tumble. They may not have married for love, but they'd not expected to live as anything but husband and wife.

"I do thank you for your——" He blinked hard and swallowed. It couldn't be...

He took a step to the left to look past Jacob, his chest constricting.

Annie and Jacob turned to look behind them, and Nolan took another step and tightened his jaw.

The massive shoulders, the elaborate muttonchops...

What was Matt doing here? Before Dad died, he'd written to let them know he wasn't visiting this summer, and Nolan had praised God full out for such a blessing.

Slamming his hat back on, Nolan scanned the two women seated next to his cousin, one stiff and starched, encased in velvet finery, the other clothed in drab, coarse gray.

Jacob stepped beside him. "Is that...?"

"Who else spends that much time on his facial hair?" Nolan held in a curse—not that he had a habit of cursing, but if there was ever a time.

Nothing good could come from Matt being here.

"Hallo!" Matt called when he turned through the open gate. He lifted his tall felt hat and then slapped the reins harder to speed up the team he must have rented from the livery.

A dust cloud rolled in ahead of the buggy, but the bellow of dirt couldn't be blamed for the dry condition of Nolan's throat. He did not need this complication—he was supposed to have at least two and a half more months before he had to deal with his cousin.

Matt pulled on the reins with a flourish, whipped the straps around the hitching post beside Jacob's wagon, and hopped down to the ground. He held up his hands, arms wide, as if he were a circus master about to thrill them with a spiel on all the extraordinary acts that were about to perform. "Good morning, everyone."

Nolan didn't even bother to conjure up a smile.

Matt's, however, didn't fade in the slightest. He turned back to the buggy and helped the finely dressed woman to the ground. She wore a riding suit that was the darkest red color Nolan had ever seen with gold braids ornamenting nearly every seam. Her hair was curled and piled beneath a matching hat, as if she'd prepared to go to a dance rather than on a drive through the empty countryside.

Without a glance at the other young woman scooting across the seat, Matt and the fancy lady marched arm in arm toward Nolan. Her eyes were narrowed as if she were unimpressed by what she was seeing as she scanned the land—and yet, the fine features of her face, the creamy texture of her skin, and the rosy hue in her high cheekbones kept her shrewd glare from stealing too much of her beauty.

"To what do I owe the honor of this—" *unwanted* was the word he wanted to spit out, but he swallowed it, "—*unexpected* visit?"

"Lilith, let me introduce you to my cousin, Nolan Key. And these two are…" He waved his hand dismissively at the Hendrixes. "Your names?"

How he wanted to smack the haughtiness right out of Matt.

Nolan stepped forward. "This is our former marshal, Jacob Hendrix, and his wife, Annie. They ranch to my north."

"Right, and this is my fiancée, Miss Lilith Mortimer." He patted her hand on his arm. "We've come so I can show her the property. She wants to see everything."

A fiancée would explain why he'd chosen not to visit this summer.

"Congratulations on your engagement," Nolan gritted, though he'd rather have called Matt out for why they'd really come up—to count the silverware.

"Lilith here couldn't be convinced of the charms of this place back in Denver. Of course, it's more rustic than we could ever live in permanently, but we have money enough to fix that.

Though she seems to think I don't know what I'm talking about."

Not hard to imagine, since Matt always weaseled his way into any conversation that seemed important whether or not he had actual knowledge of the subject. "I'm afraid—"

"Don't worry about us redoing anything while you're here. We'd not ruin your last weeks with renovation, but we do need to know what to purchase before we return."

Annie's and Jacob's expressions were frozen, though Annie chanced a side glance at him.

Dandifying a ranch house was about the stupidest use of money Nolan could think of. If comfort and luxury were Matt's first order of business, that did not bode well for the ranch continuing to prosper if he took over.

Nolan ungritted his teeth. "Things aren't settled yet."

"No, but you're the one always complaining I don't plan things out, so you should be happy about this." He patted Nolan's shoulder as if they were best buds.

"Mrs. Hendrix." Nolan turned sharply toward Annie. "You once lived in a big city, correct? If you enjoy city life, would you find anything out here appealing?"

"Oh, uh…" She turned to Miss Mortimer and gave her a stiff smile. "I'm afraid ranching is nothing like what I knew growing up on the East Coast. Life wears you down out here, though hard work has its rewards."

Nolan glared at her.

Annie shrugged and then turned back to Miss Mortimer. "You'll find only a few fine ladies on big ranches living like those in the city. It's a lot of work to keep a ranch going, so one often gives up the more refined aspects of life."

"Which is why we ought to sell, Matthias." Lilith's voice was cultured, southern sounding even.

"Nonsense, if one has money, one doesn't have to do that much work—that's true anywhere. Let me give you a tour. You don't mind, do you, Nolan?" Without waiting for an answer,

Matt walked past him while sweeping his other arm out to show off the house. "The bones of the place has its charms. It'll take nothing more than a new paint job, some gingerbread, a bigger porch, an indoor washroom, of course…"

Oh, why had his father not allowed him to forfeit the ranch to someone who'd be more concerned about the water access and the health of the herd than how the house appeared?

The woman in gray, sporting small round spectacles upon a pert nose and likely only a few years older than Miss Mortimer, came up beside them. "How cold does it get in winter?" She looked around, her eyes shrunk to half the normal size behind her lenses. "It seems too flat and the mountains too far away to block the wind."

"It's indeed cold." He turned toward Matt and Lilith who were skirting the well pump and nearly shouted across the lawn. "It gets incredibly cold here in winter. It's hard to keep warm from October to May."

Matt shrugged and smiled back at him. "If the winters don't suit, we can just summer here, as I've always done."

This wasn't a holiday home!

The two of them started toward the barn, and the woman in gray hustled after them.

"Don't worry about what he says, dear." Matt's voice faded as they walked farther away. "We'll fix everything that's wrong with it, and you'll be the envy of all the women in the county."

Annie and Jacob stood with him in silence as his cousin herded the women into the barn.

It took all Nolan had not to go after them and order them out. Marrying Mrs. Tate couldn't be all that bad if every night he went to bed knowing Matt would never own this ranch.

Jacob cleared his throat. "As I said the other day, the most important thing about marrying a woman you barely know is to make sure she won't make you miserable. Best indicator is if your worldviews match. If you agree on the major things and you're patient, everything else will follow. Patience is key, though." He smiled down at Annie. "Impatience only makes you agonize more while you wait for her to come around."

Nolan couldn't keep from shaking his head. "I don't need anything beyond a legal way to keep him off my property."

The house was large enough to be a boardinghouse. Perfect strangers, even those who hated each other, could live together in a boardinghouse without driving each other insane, right?

And if they found out they couldn't stand each other, they could always "separate." Who didn't know of an estranged married couple living apart?

Surely once his cousin married and settled somewhere other than here, he'd not bother to check up on his marital happiness —which shouldn't matter anyway. Dad hadn't stipulated he be blissfully wed.

Other than Mrs. Tate and Miss Stillwater, the only other likely candidate was Miss McGill. But she was always husband chasing, looking for all the things girls dream about.

Miss Stillwater, however, was not.

He would ask Corinne.

His insides jittered at the thought of living with her for the rest of his life, which was unreasonable, considering she'd likely turn him down flatter than the day he hadn't asked her to marry him.

CHAPTER SEVEN

Outside the laundry's window, the steady, albeit irregular thump of footsteps passed by once again. She'd thought the pacer had been waiting on someone coming to town, but the stage had left ten minutes ago. Corinne sighed and dropped the garment she was washing. Her hands needed a break, anyway.

Pretending to straighten her new bottles of starch water on the windowsill, she took a glance outside.

Few people walked along the boardwalk, but the one with the stiffest posture and the most determined march looked like Nolan from behind, and did he have…?

She squinted.

Flowers. He had flowers in his hand.

Oh, no.

Surely he wasn't pacing in front of her laundry convincing himself to come in and ask to court her despite her more than obvious hint she'd never say yes.

He had to be pacing for some other reason. Their talk had been days ago, and he'd said he didn't want to get married, either.

Though perhaps she shouldn't have been so adamant that

his missing leg was a sorry excuse for not marrying. Maybe she'd inadvertently encouraged him.

She shook her head at herself. How vain was she to believe every single man would eventually try for her hand?

Nolan turned on his heel and tossed the flowers into the street, where a passing cart and horse smashed them into the dirt.

Well, now. What *was* he doing?

She scooted back from the window in case he glanced her way. She didn't want him to know she was watching, but what direction would he go? Seemed he'd made some sort of decision when he'd thrown the flowers.

His marching—as much as a one-legged man's gait could be called a march—tapped along quicker and more decisively as he neared. His forehead was furrowed as deep as a newly plowed field despite his face looking harder than a rock.

Reaching her door, he abruptly turned again and strode away.

Whatever he was doing, his stern expression was likely driving away her customers, along with the milliner's and the butcher's. Not that she needed more customers, but she did need those who owed her money to come in.

Moving to the door, she opened it and nearly melted with the breeze. She should've opened this door sooner with how hot and muggy the washing made it inside. She propped the door open and glanced down the boardwalk to see if Nolan was going to about face or finally storm off.

He turned, head bent, and she waited, arms crossed.

When he was about five feet away, she stepped forward. "Mr. Key?"

Jerking as if startled, he lifted his head.

"I know you're free to do as you please in this territory, but would you mind not pacing so decisively in front of our businesses? I'm afraid people will be worried about crossing whatever line you seem to be guarding."

"Sorry."

His face didn't soften, but now he seemed to be fidgeting—and staring at her. Was something bothering him?

Of course something was, considering all his marching.

"Uh…" They weren't exactly friends, though he'd always been kind enough to ask about her day when retrieving his bunkhouse's bedding.

Had she ever asked him how his day was going?

She breathed in deep and let her questions out in a rush. "Is something wrong? Do you need to talk to someone?"

She looked diagonally down the road toward the church. If Pastor Lawrence was in town, maybe she ought to encourage him to go there. Or—

"I probably should just spit it out. Though I'm not really sure I should." He moved to open her door wider, swinging his arm to indicate he intended to follow her in.

He wanted to talk to her? She ought to be flattered that he thought her "sensible" enough to speak with instead of searching out a man. But at the same time, those limp flowers lying in the dirt made her wonder how personal and uncomfortable this might be, especially if he wanted advice on wooing a woman.

She crossed in front of him and turned to flip the closed sign. Her fingers seized, and the sign slipped through her hand yet again, this time sending the sharp wooden corner into her foot. She hissed. Her work-worn boot had done little to protect her toes.

Drat her luck at having him see her do that a second time.

He stooped to pick up the sign, hung it, then abruptly turned. "There's something wrong with your hands, isn't there?"

She pressed her lips together, but then, Annie had said it didn't take a genius to see she was in pain. "Yes."

"What exactly?" He took a brief glance down at her hands. When his eyes came back up, they seemed to be probing her for a confession, as if she were obliged to give him one because he asked.

"None of your business, I'm afraid."

"They look as if they're causing you a great deal of pain, and in the last few weeks, it's become apparent they're getting worse. Are you afraid you'll lose the use of them?"

She turned to shield her hands from him, but if he'd figured all that out, what point was there in concealing her fate?

"I won't," she whispered. "Well, not necessarily."

"Not necessarily?"

A part of her hoped the throbbing would simply go away, but what if the worst happened? What if he told others and they took their business elsewhere? Any number of homesteading women might welcome extra cash. She couldn't lose her only source of income quicker than she already was. "There's no reason to worry about me. Everything will be fine."

Nolan still stared at her, a quizzical tilt to his lips.

She clasped her hands together and walked away. "The doctor says I only have to do things differently. Even if they get worse, there's no reason to take your business elsewhere. I can hire help."

"My laundry has been late two times already, yet you've not hired help."

She kept her back turned and grabbed the pencil off the counter, but then immediately wished she hadn't, considering the jolt of pain. Forcing herself not to grimace, she tapped the writing instrument a few times before setting it down. What answer could she give that wouldn't be a lie, yet keep him from going elsewhere? "I'm sorry for that, but I've been ... busy. It won't be late this month. I promise."

Hopefully her voice had sounded convincing instead of desperate. But after the Ivenses pulled their account yesterday, if she lost the Key Ranch, would she be able to make her rent payment? Should she pray for anonymous charity to land in her lap again?

Nolan cleared his throat. "I know it's personal, but could you tell me why you're so determined to hang onto this place when it's obvious you're overwhelmed?"

"Money." Did he think she worked for fun? "Isn't that the only reason a woman would work until her hands fell off?"

He moved back, as if her words had physically pushed him.

She *had* been a bit forceful. "I'm sorry. I didn't mean to snap at you."

"I understand how it feels to be losing something you desperately need."

To her relief, he didn't keep pestering, but he did go back to pacing.

The irregular clomping was even more disconcerting done in the small space in front of her counter. His steps scraped against the boards every other step as if he wasn't lifting his fake leg enough to clear the floor.

Didn't he realize pacing in here was not helping her get work done?

But she wasn't about to start working with him here either, not if he, like Annie, decided she needed help. "I need to get back to wor—"

"Hiring someone won't earn you more, unless Armelle's population increases."

He'd been trying to figure out how to save her business? That was sweet, but there wasn't anything he could do. "That's true, but I'll hire someone if I must. However, we came in here to talk about what's bothering you. I don't wish to discuss my problems."

He pivoted to face her. "But your problems are my problems."

"I told you I'd not be late again."

"I'm not worried about my linens." He took in a quick breath. "What I need is a business partner."

How did he consider that her problem? Or was he thinking of offering help in exchange for a share of her business to pretend he wasn't giving charity? "I'm grateful for the work you've given me, but it's obvious I can't handle more. There's no profit worth splitting."

"Unless I've missed my guess, if you don't stop working with your hands, you'll lose your profit entirely."

If both Annie and Nolan had divined how bleak her future was just by looking at her, how many others had? Was that why the Ivenses had pulled their account?

"When you lose the laundry, and I lose the ranch, we'll both be out of luck."

She frowned. Was his ranch in trouble? From what she'd heard, he had one of the more successful ones in the area. Perhaps he was in debt. "I can't imagine how partnering with me would help."

"I'll lose everything if I don't marry."

She tensed, afraid he'd get down on one knee, but no, if he needed money, she wasn't in the running to be his bride. "So, how would partnering with me help?"

His body deflated. "My father's will states that unless I'm married, I'll lose the place to my cousin."

She scrunched up her face. "That kind of thing only happens in books."

"Exactly." He smiled, and his eyes turned soft.

Oh, no. If he wanted a wife, she didn't need to be encouraging him in any manner. Though why had such a comment earned her that look? She shook her head. She was imagining things.

He shifted his weight, and suddenly snatched his hat off his head, evidently just realizing he still had it on. "I'm not looking for a marriage in truth because, like you, I'd rather die than saddle a wife with me, but what else can I do? I've sunk all my money into what I thought was mine, and now I've been denied the proceeds from its sale. Without the ranch, well, I'll be working as hard as you, in a job I'm not physically capable of."

"I—" She wanted to negate him, but could she honestly? She swallowed hard and looked away.

"I know how it is to lose the use of your limbs. So if you and I are both going to lose our places separately, why not save one of them together?"

"I'm flattered, but—"

He jerked up a hand. "It's not flattery. It's desperation."

She narrowed her eyes at him.

His face reddened, and he waved his hand vigorously. "I didn't mean a man would have to be desperate to marry you, but unless I miss my guess, you're desperate, too. I can offer what you need—time for your hands to heal. In fact, you don't even have to work if you don't want to."

Not work at all? If he thought she could be reeled in by a man who spouted off things that were too good to be true, he had another think coming. "That's too much to believe."

"You told Mrs. Hendrix you'd consider marrying if the only thing required of you was a name change, did you not?"

So that's why he'd chosen her. "Uh, I—yes, that's what I said, but you have to realize I never believed someone would offer that."

"Well, it's an offer you have now. Please consider it. As for what I need from the marriage, your name is it. I have an old cabin on my property that could be yours. Though according to the lawyer, you might not be able to move into it right away. There has to be a show that I'm following the intent of the will. As long as we're amicable toward each other for a while, take some trips to Denver to show my cousin we're committed, and you don't disappear on me, no one has to know we won't be getting any closer than living behind the same four walls."

She pressed her lips together against the vehement 'no' clawing its way up her throat.

He was offering her a cabin of her own? No need for a true marriage? Time for her hands to heal?

"If you wish, once the deed appears secure and my cousin

has lost interest in my property, we could act as if we've had a falling out. I promise not to divorce you. I've seen enough divorcees and widows to know how hard it is for a woman to be on her own. I'd owe you forever for saving my land, so I'd commit to providing for you for your whole life in honor of that. I'll take care of your room and board and pin money—"

"You'd allow me to sit back and do nothing?" No man this far west would want so little from a wife.

"I'd prefer you help, but if the doctor says you shouldn't— well, there's no other way to keep the ranch. So as long as you didn't create extra work, cleaned up after yourself—"

"There *is* another way. You marry someone else."

"But you don't want to be married, correct?"

She scrunched her eyebrows. "True."

"Neither do I, so it's a business deal. What other woman could I offer marriage to like this and not ruin her hopes of family and love? You're a good businesswoman, you must see—"

"That you're not offering me a true business deal? Yes. What you're offering is a position of eternal indebtedness. You say I could do nothing—"

"But I realize you're too hard of a worker to lie around all day and eat cake. On my ranch, you won't have to do anything that will injure your hands—I won't question what you're capable of. Believe me, Dad questioned me every time I told him I didn't feel physically comfortable doing something, so I won't do that to you. Besides, I'm making you the same deal— I'll be eternally indebted to you. Though it's more like we'll be tied to the land together."

"I don't know about this." She needed to suppress the flutter that had just flitted around inside her before hope left her worse off than it ever had before.

"You have no obligation to help me, of course. But I'm offering a much lighter yoke and more security."

Everything—from her hands to her insides—was shaking. "Are you truly offering a business deal?"

"Yes."

"Then if it's an actual business deal—if two people are required to save your property—then a portion of the profit should be mine. I don't want room and board and pin money."

He blinked.

Maybe he deserved *some* credit for calling her sensible and hardworking, but he'd only talked business to flatter her. "See, you weren't truly offering—"

"No, wait." He fiddled with his hat as he looked her in the eye.

She lifted her brows, and he started pacing again.

So they were back to this? The poor man truly was in a dilemma. And though his offer wasn't—

"All right." He turned and marched back toward her.

She held up a hand, not only to stop him from continuing, but to stop herself from agreeing. She'd learned the hard way that a man's promises rarely held up in the wash. "Don't let desperation make you offer something you'll regret following through with."

He stood, staring at her as if lost.

The poor man was in a terrible spot, but with enough time, he'd figure out something to save his land that didn't require her involvement. "Pray about it."

He nodded. "Good idea." He looked out the front window and sighed before tipping his hat to her. "I'll leave you to your work."

With that, he left, sending the door bell to jangling.

Feet heavy and throat thick, she trudged over to her next pile of laundry and started scrubbing. Heat flooded her eyes, but not because of pain.

Nolan wouldn't return.

She'd turned away the best offer she was likely ever going to get.

CHAPTER EIGHT

Two days later in front of the laundry, Nolan took the deepest breath of his life and forged inside.

Corinne looked up and froze.

Was that a look of terror?

Surely his offer would be much more appealing than death. "I—" He cleared his throat, hoping to make it work. "I've thought it over. I'm willing to make you a true business deal, as long as you don't take me up on my 'do nothing' offer. In order to share my profit, I'll need you to do your fair share."

She straightened. "Your profit?"

"That's what you asked for, right?"

With a blank expression, she stared at him while her hands remained submerged in gray, soapy water.

He pulled out the contract he'd drafted, his heart thumping. "We can talk over terms. Once we agree, we could get our agreement witnessed if you'd like—we'd just have to be careful about who we chose."

The front door opened with a sad whine, hitting the bell halfheartedly.

Why, oh why, did someone have to come in now?

Leah Whitsett hobbled in. She hadn't yet learned how to

disguise her limp as well as he had. She glanced between the two of them. "Am I interrupting something?"

He looked to Corinne to see if she thought his offer was indeed "something" worth turning away business for.

When Corinne did nothing but stand there blinking, the older woman stepped forward. "I'm sorry to return after you told me no, but I need work, even if it's only for a few hours. I…" Her voice petered out.

Though Leah's timing was awful, perhaps he should step outside so she didn't have to beg in front of him.

Corinne finally extracted her hands from the water and wiped them on a towel. "Would you excuse me a moment, Mrs. Whitsett, while I take care of Mr. Key?"

His heart beat all the way up into his throat. Was she going to turn him down in front of Leah?

"Of course." Leah slid onto the bench Corinne's customers sat on while waiting.

Corinne was pale, but there was steel in her jaw as she walked toward him. The smell of lye and starch grew stronger as she leaned close, her voice coming out in a soft whisper. "Are you willing to pay Mrs. Whitsett to work so we can have a business meeting?"

His breath left him in a rush. "Certainly."

She gave him a nod and walked over to Leah. "It seems I could use someone to take over for a few hours so I can attend to other matters."

Leah's expression relaxed. "Thank you so much."

As Corinne showed Leah what to do, Nolan's heart only beat half the time.

Could he truly go through with giving this woman a say in how he ran his ranch?

Though how would he survive if he didn't?

In a corner of the hotel's restaurant, Corinne squirmed in her seat, hoping no one was paying attention to them. If Nolan's business proposition went nowhere, they could still stir the gossip mill if they ate together in public. She'd rather not deal with that.

Nolan reached into his pocket and pulled out his paper, smoothing it open upon the table and spinning it toward her. "You should read this before we start. It's nothing more than a skeleton of a contract, but I figured it'd be best to come up with exact terms together. This isn't—"

"I'm not sure a contract is what we need." She skimmed his neat paragraphs.

He lifted his gaze to hers. "You don't want to negotiate?"

"As nice as this is, if we have to marry for this to work, we won't be able to dissolve our partnership if one of us doesn't fulfill our obligations." She tucked back a loose tendril of hair. "It comes down to if we can trust each other."

Frowning at the contract, he started refolding it. "I suppose this wasn't necessary, then."

"Oh, no." She put a hand atop his, but slid it right back off in case someone was watching. "It proved you were serious— that you intend to follow through. I'd not have discussed the possibility without it."

He nodded, but didn't seem reassured. "What do you want to discuss, then?"

"Our expectations of one another. If what I'm willing to do is enough for you to give me a percentage. Besides, stipulations like 'no unwanted romantic gestures' would look silly on a business contract."

"'Unwanted romantic gestures?'" He blinked, his face confused. "Are you saying there will be wanted ones?"

Heat filled her face. She worked hard not to lower her gaze like an embarrassed school girl. "No. But we have to face the possibility of complications."

"What sort of complications?"

"That you fall in love with me."

Nolan took in Corinne's serious, no-nonsense expression.

She said nothing more. Seemed she didn't think falling in love with him was a possible complication.

He closed his eyes for a second, chastising the sudden pang in his chest. This wasn't a romance. He didn't want her to fall for him. "All right, how would you want that handled?"

"In normal situations, if someone gets rebuffed, the pair could keep their distance. The disappointed party could move on, but we'd not be able to do so."

"So what's the plan?" It seemed she'd thought this through. Perhaps the likelihood she'd agree to this was higher than he'd thought.

"If either of us feels attracted to the other, we'd need to ask permission to court, as if we weren't married. If the other said, 'no,' we'd have to concede."

He leaned back and rubbed his jaw. He'd never heard of a woman asking a man to court, so she likely meant this stipulation solely for him. "So if the feelings aren't ever mutual?"

The hostess approached, and they both remained silent as the young woman set Corinne's ham and fried potatoes and Nolan's pork chops on the table.

Corinne laid her napkin in her lap and looked back at him once the hostess left. "You'll have to decide whether you could endure being married to someone you're attracted to, knowing you could never move on. Or, if you fell in love with someone else, never being free to pursue her."

He blew out a breath. Complications, indeed.

Silence grew as neither of them moved to start eating. Oh! She was likely waiting on him. "Would you mind if we said grace to ourselves?"

"Of course not." She folded her hands to pray.

He shut his eyes.

God, she's right. I'm more likely to fall for her. As a man… I can't deny I'm susceptible to urges—married or not. Will I be able to have her near, but never have her? I've already chosen not to entertain any attraction I've felt for women—but this would be different.

He'd have to guard his heart against romantic nonsense, as she'd said.

The clinking of her silverware startled him into finishing his prayer, thanking God for the usual things and begging for discernment.

He picked up his fork and straightened. Time to discuss business. "So, what do you intend to do to earn your control of the purse strings, and how much are you thinking?"

"I haven't given that much thought, considering you've only now convinced me you mean to follow through. Maybe thirty-five percent?"

He nodded. Considering that number was only five above what he'd written up, he'd not quibble. Even if she ended up doing nothing, sixty-five percent was a heap better than zero.

She took a bite of her potatoes and looked up contemplatively. "I'm willing to do all the typical household duties, of course. Feed your workers, clean the house—unless you have someone already doing that. I'd also want to learn how you run the place in case something happens. I can ride—or at least I used to."

"I've always taken care of the meals since I work from the house most of the time. Nothing fancy, though. And I don't ride for lengthy periods anymore; my missing leg makes me feel off balance. I hire hands for that."

"How many men do you have, and how old are they?"

Why did she need to know their ages? Was she trying to decide if his men could be another 'complication'—that she'd fall in love with a cowboy and be unable to do anything about it? Having her fall for someone else…

He rubbed his chest where a strange sensation clenched

inside him. "I have three I keep year round and a foreman. The youngest, Tim, is nineteen. Abel is in his early thirties and splits his time between my ranch and his brother's. Rascal is upper fifties—he's worked for my father since before I can remember —and Sal is almost fifty, I think."

What if one of the hands fell for her?

Even if he had no hold on her heart, he'd fire that man in a heartbeat. Making eyes at the boss's wife was not a quality he wanted in a ranch hand.

"Can you get on with only four?"

"I hire more for cattle drives and any other times the five of us aren't enough."

She took a bite of her potatoes while sporting a faraway, worried look.

"You can have a say in who we employ if you wish. If any of them make you uncomfortable for any reason, we can talk. Though I hope you'll agree to most of my choices. Half the reason I've done so well is because of who I hire."

She nodded, looking relieved. "What if I want to check your books? Will you let me inspect your figures whenever I choose? Are you willing to give me straight answers when I ask questions or will you patronize me by saying I don't have to worry my 'pretty little head' over numbers?"

"If I didn't consider you sensible enough to handle business matters, I'd not have drawn up a contract. I'm willing to discuss whatever you wish."

Her expression turned less guarded, eager even. "I'm obviously unfamiliar with ranching. How often do you sell cattle?"

"In the fall. All other income is incidental: stud fees, equipment rental, hay surplus, and the like. Since the bulk of our money comes but once a year, I have to be careful. One of the reasons we've prospered is because I follow a strict budget. I spend only what we have, rather than what I expect to bring in."

She scooted her potatoes around on her plate, staring out the window behind him. Seemed she needed time thinking things through. He started working on his own meal, which had grown cold.

Beneath the table she knocked his leg once, twice. Did she realize that was his false leg or did she think she was kicking the table leg?

Maybe he should write a list of things he wouldn't want her to do that wasn't business-related, like rushing over to help him if he was struggling to stand, or—

"All right, I'll marry you."

He swallowed hard. Had she said what he thought sh—

"But I'll need you to front me a hundred dollars."

He swallowed harder. "A hundred dollars?"

CHAPTER NINE

If Nolan's eyes could have gotten any bigger, they might've fallen out of his head.

For a moment, she contemplated taking back the request for money. Her brother-in-law would probably be happy with half a hundred, but she had no idea how much Nolan would bring in come fall. And she'd have little time to learn enough to help him bring in more.

If he didn't agree, would he renege on the whole thing?

In a way, her heart had already latched itself onto everything he was offering: a home, partnership, rest.

However, if he only got paid once a year, could she be sure she could pay her sister and brother-in-law what she owed anytime soon?

"Why do you need a hundred dollars?"

"It'd prove you're serious."

"I could see that, but at the same time, I want to know what you're using it for. If I'm giving you part of my profit, I need to know you're the kind to spend it wisely."

She pressed her lips together, but then, she'd want to know the same about him, too. "I owe my sister and her husband money."

"A hundred dollars?" He whistled, a high tone that swooped straight into a low note. "For what? No wonder you've been troubled lately."

How long had he been paying attention to her worries? "Actually, I owe them a little over three hundred. My brother-in-law loaned me money to purchase the building I used in Rapid City. Then the place burned down. What I had in savings had to cover starting over. I only had enough for supplies and equipment, hence why I'm renting."

"He needs a hundred now?"

"He's got a baby, possibly two, on the way, and his panning isn't going well. He asked me for more than I usually give him. If you don't get paid until fall…"

Nolan nodded absentmindedly and stirred more sugar into his tea.

Thankfully, he didn't seem curious about why her first laundry had burned down. She'd moved to Armelle because no one would rent to her in Rapid City after finding out an experiment had started the fire. If she'd burned the place down cooking, people probably wouldn't have been so opposed to letting her set up shop again. And of course, she'd wanted to get as far away from Randolph as possible.

Their hostess showed up and took away Corinne's plate. When the young lady reached for Nolan's, he stopped her and started again on his abandoned pork chop. He chewed in silence, looking off into space.

Was Nolan considering giving her the money? Could she marry him if he didn't? It wasn't as if she was sure she could pay her brother-in-law as it was now.

"I'm afraid a hundred dollars is a lot."

Her buoy of hope sank like a rock. Maybe it had been too much to ask, but if he couldn't afford it, then where would she get the money—

"Could you wait until after we married?"

She stiffened. Though she trusted him more than most men

in town, she needed to know he'd follow through on his promises before she got stuck with him. She knew that for a fact. "I'm afraid not. They need it."

He squirmed. "All right."

Her mouth fell open, but then she snapped it back shut.

The rock that had settled in the pit of her stomach expanded into a happy bubble intent on lifting her out of her seat. How merciful was God to give her better than she'd ever hoped for after she'd messed up her entire life!

And her past wasn't even a factor.

Nolan pushed away his now empty plate. His face didn't appear as jubilant as she felt, but the lines of tension around his mouth had eased.

She folded her napkin and gave him a smile. "I'll do my best to be worth taking on, *partner.*"

She held out her hand, and he shook it.

The pain caused by their handshake barely registered.

Hours after he and Corinne had ironed out what she would do to earn her thirty-five percent and the hundred dollars she was asking for, Nolan waited for the customer Leah was helping to leave before he approached the counter.

"Back so soon?" Her eyebrows lifted, though one didn't move up as far as the other.

He refused to squirm. It wasn't as if he were a young man asking permission to take Leah's daughter on a walk. "May I speak with Miss Stillwater?"

Leah pointed behind her, just as Corinne walked in through the doorway.

"I—" Maybe he shouldn't come right out with the fact he'd already withdrawn the hundred dollars. "May I speak with you?"

She turned sideways and gestured for him to precede her into the back room.

Stepping through the doorway, he stumbled over a haphazard stack of crates and into some metal pipes jutting from a crowded workbench. Thankfully, he caught himself.

The whole room was full of tables overflowing with scraps. What a mess. The banker should be ashamed of himself for forcing a renter into storing all this junk.

"Come with me. I have to keep working." Corinne grabbed a basket of wet clothing, deftly zigzagged through the maze of stuff, and walked out the back door.

He followed her outside and frowned up at the contraption attached to the corner of the building where she'd stopped. Several long wooden rods were screwed into the siding on hinges, which she had fanned out like a spiral staircase.

She pulled a pair of trousers from her basket. "I hope you don't mind if I hang clothes while we talk."

"Of course not." He took a step closer and pushed a wooden bar back and forth, testing its movement.

"I don't advise making one of these for your ranch unless you intend to start a laundry. It's handy, but costs more than a clothesline. I just didn't have enough room for another."

Her yard—if leveled dirt could be called a yard—ran only a handful of feet before smacking up against an uneven sandstone walkway separating it from the next backyard. Linens were already waving on the short, doubled line that filled the space.

"Would you want to start a laundry on the ranch?"

"Goodness, no." Grimacing, she flicked out another pair of trousers. "For the household wash, several clotheslines will suffice, which I assume you have."

"Yes. Along with some stiff bushes to drape things over." She so easily spoke of chores on his ranch. Would she actually be hanging up his clothes soon? He picked up a pillowcase and flicked it before draping it over one of her rods. "So I—I went to the bank."

She stilled.

"I've got the money." He reached into his pocket and wrapped his hand around a large portion of his savings.

Her chin crunched into a disbelieving frown. "Already?"

Did that frown mean she'd hoped he'd changed his mind? "I do need to make something clear before proceeding, though. If you run with the money, you'll get nothing more from me."

Her frown wriggled up slightly. "No need to worry about that. Thirty-five percent of a ranch? I'll be sticking around and doing what I can to help. If your bank account prospers, so does mine."

A businesswoman through and through. Even if she murdered him in his sleep, the ranch would be in better hands than his cousin's. "I know you told me earlier it was none of my business, but perhaps it is now. Are you sure you want to give up marrying for love?"

"I already have."

"What if the right man came along?"

She looked away, smoothing out the nightdress she'd hung. "I was once betrothed to a man who could've fulfilled all my dreams. Another who said he couldn't wait to be with me forever. Both were not who I thought they were." She stopped to hang up some stockings. "If my dreams had come true, I would've been stuck with men I now wish I'd never met. I know better than to trust myself in finding the 'right man.' With that being said…"

Turning to face him, she tilted her chin up. "I will not tolerate abuse of any kind."

His heart kathunked at the thought of any man laying hands on her. "And you shouldn't have to."

"If you mistreat me—agreement or no—I'll leave, and you'll lose your ranch."

"And I'd deserve it."

She stared deep into his eyes and must have found the assurance she wanted, for she nodded and dropped her gaze to his hand, which was tightly clenched around a small roll of twenty-dollar bills. "I intend to work hard for you. You'll make that money back in no time."

She didn't know how long "no time" could take considering ranching success depended on nature's mercy, but he certainly believed she'd work hard once she was able.

Was she really agreeing? Was he in his right mind to give so much to a woman he barely knew?

"However, why don't you think about it longer? I won't hold it against you if you decide against marrying me." She put a hand on the side of his arm and looked at him as if he were a scared jackrabbit.

Perhaps he was. The closer he got to her, the harder it was to breathe. Could he truly go through with this?

"We should pray more, yes?" She nodded, causing even more blond waves to fall out of what was always a messier updo than what the other women around town sported. "Neither of us will lose our livelihoods in a couple of days. Why don't you take the weekend to decide?"

"All right." The feel of her hand lingered on his bicep, though she'd let go of him already.

She blinked up at him with eyes the color of strong coffee.

"I, uh, … I'll just leave then." But his feet stayed stuck. If any other man was taking leave of the woman he planned to marry, there'd be a kiss goodbye.

Would kissing always be off the table?

"Uh, Nolan?"

He blinked. And found himself leaning. A few more inches and she'd be up against the wall.

He'd not even have to tilt—

"Nolan?"

He shook his head and pushed away, then patted her upper arm as if she were a chum—or worse, his horse.

"Sorry." He snatched his hand back and clenched it at his side. "I should go now. I'll be back after the weekend."

Turning, he hightailed it down the back alleyway, not wanting to go through the laundry in case Leah would wonder why he flew past her like he'd been set on fire.

He might've thought he was willing to do most anything to keep from losing his ranch, but was he only trading one type of trouble for another?

CHAPTER TEN

"Not another one." Lilith lifted one of the saucers she'd insisted everyone use for breakfast, even if they were drinking from clunky coffee mugs. She ran a dainty finger along its edge as if it were covered in filth rather than chipped. "They may not be good quality, but honestly, how can you be trusted with finer dishes if you can't treat what you have with respect?"

Nolan glared at his stove instead of his future cousin-in-law. He could inform her there was no need to worry about fine china in this house, but if Matt inherited the ranch, of course she'd drag in hoity-toity stuff. "If you don't trust someone with china, don't give it to them. But don't waste time worrying about these. They were chipped when I got them."

She blew out a breath and muttered to herself, "So many things just need to be gone."

He stuffed his mouth with three large bites of egg to keep from responding.

Matt came downstairs with one of Lilith's trunks on his shoulder. Under his arm was a beat up satchel, possibly Lilith's companion's.

Nolan couldn't help but sit taller in his chair.

After dropping the luggage by the stairwell, Matt scanned

77

the place settings, then tromped toward the plate piled high with extra bacon which Miss Flower had prepared for him before heading back upstairs. "Excellent. I'm starving."

"So." Nolan wiped the corner of his mouth with a napkin and shot up like a jubilant firecracker. "You're leaving today? Can I help bring something down? Have you got your train tickets?" He'd pay for first class if it'd get them out faster.

"Oh, we're not leaving until tomorrow," Matt said after swallowing a mouthful of eggs. "It's just the ladies realized they didn't need everything they brought. With how small your rooms are, they decided to get stuff out of their way."

Tomorrow was better than he'd hoped. "So you've got your tickets?" They hadn't visited town for several days with how busy they'd been inspecting the ranch, writing down every deficiency.

"Not yet, but we won't be gone long. We'll be back in a few weeks to see how things are going."

Without any eggs left to stuff in his mouth, he bit his tongue instead. He needed no more of Matt and Lilith's "supervision."

If his talk with Corinne went well this afternoon, he'd have the pleasure of telling them they only needed to return if they wanted to personally deliver a wedding gift. "Are you sure you shouldn't spend more time in Denver? If country life doesn't suit, you'll have to have a job to go back—"

"No worries there, plus I'm looking forward to returning. The country is so much more relaxing than the hubbub of the city."

Nolan snorted. "Ranching is not relaxing. You might've been under that impression since Dad coddled you, but my ranch hands did all the wor—"

"The person who got spoiled was you." Matt spoke around a mouthful of biscuit and jam. "Ever since your leg came off, you've been given the easy tasks. I was the one out riding and roping—"

"Being given certain types of work because of a physical

limitation is not coddling; however, having chores modified to match your irresponsibility is. No telling how many hours my ranch hands spent fixing everything you messed up."

"They didn't." Matt's scrunched face turned high pink. "Your father—"

"Didn't know. My men wouldn't have wasted time complaining about the work you caused them. They're too mature to gripe about a temporary inconvenience."

"Keep telling yourself that." Matt smeared the napkin across his face, then dropped it onto his empty plate. "But your dad knew which one of us could handle this place, and it wasn't you."

"Now, gentlemen." Lilith speared them with her gaze, jabbing her fork at them. "I won't stand for arguing at my table."

Her table? His body nearly shook to keep from snarling at her.

Jesus likely would've encouraged Matt to overcome his faults instead of pointing them out at breakfast, true. But he just couldn't help his cousin become good enough to take over a ranch he'd done nothing to earn.

Especially since he was the one who'd literally lost a leg for it!

Nolan let out a slow, shaky breath. He was a long way from being Jesus—that was certain. "Excuse us, Lilith. We'll take this elsewhere."

"No need." Matt stood and shoved in his chair. "I'd thought to let you stay once the land became mine, but I've changed my mind now. I won't employ someone who doesn't know who's boss."

That right there signaled Matt's unsuitableness more than anything else. "To run a successful ranch, you can't surround yourself with toadies. You have to realize where you're weak and hire people to take over those areas for you."

Even if it did make a man look pathetic.

"I know. I'm not stupid."

However, knowing the truth was far different than applying it.

"I don't think you're stupid, Matt." He had a whole list of alternate adjectives he could suggest, but he didn't want to turn one of his last living relatives into an enemy—any more than he already was. He grabbed his hat. "Now, excuse me. I've got to leave."

"Where're you going?" Lilith gave his Sunday suit a quick perusal.

"To town. Are you sure you don't want me to pick up tickets?"

Neither of them answered with more than a glare, so he turned his back and focused on walking away without stomping. He'd never been so happy to leave his own home.

After checking on the men, he saddled his horse and galloped out of the gate despite how unstable he felt riding at such a quick pace. The more yards he put between himself and his unwelcome houseguests, the easier his breathing grew. When his place was nothing but a speck behind him, he finally slowed. No reason to rush into town. He could stand to be away from his cousin for a good long time. Plus, Corinne's answer might not be what he wanted to hear.

She had allowed him time to think rather than take his hundred dollars immediately—a sign she'd not try to take him for all he was worth, but that meant she'd had time to think, too.

God, please give me favor in Corinne's sight.

But with every mile he put behind him, the more his stomach flopped.

This weekend had only strengthened his resolve to save his land from his cousin, but what if Corinne had decided against him?

Perhaps he shouldn't have fought with Dad so much about the ranch. Maybe if he'd been less assertive with how money was spent or less adamant about how his plans were better, Dad would've written the will differently.

He'd always insisted Nolan would need a wife to care for him, as if he were a weakling, as if he were his mother, who'd been left behind because Dad had thought she'd slow them down because of her ill health.

So Nolan had worked harder and longer than anyone else to be sure his father wouldn't see him as a burden, too, but when his leg came off…

Wyoming wouldn't have been the best place for his mother, true, but neither was it for a cripple.

He'd done the best he could though, with a grin to boot so his father wouldn't send him away. But he'd never been able to work as hard as his father had. Nolan had always known he'd likely have to pay a nurse to attend him at the end of his life, and he wouldn't change that plan. Corinne was not signing on to care for him when he got old. He'd simply have to work harder to save his money since thirty-five percent of the profit would no longer be his.

As he rode into town, a few passersby gave him strange looks. Did he seem as if he were about to climb onto the gallows?

His gut sure roiled like that was what was about to happen.

At the laundry, he tried to swallow whatever nonexistent thing was blocking his airway before forcing himself inside.

"Oh! Don't touch that." Corinne caught a toddling girl who'd run behind the counter, while the frazzled mother juggled two babies on the other side.

Corinne waved her hand in front of a washbasin. "Hot."

The girl's little blond ringlets bounced as she nodded and pointed at the basin. "Hot!"

"That's right, hot."

"Hot! Hot! Momma, hot!"

"Yes, Jemma, hot." The poor, skinny mother amazingly fixed her skewed shirtwaist while cradling an infant in each arm.

Jemma hopped on alternate feet as she circled her mother,

sing-shouting the word 'hot,' as if it were the most interesting word in the world.

Corinne smiled as if the girl's tuneless crowing was pleasant. She then hefted a bundle onto the counter, a painful expression contorting her face. "Let's get this into your wagon."

He stepped forward and held out his arms. "Allow me."

She gave him a look—as if she suspected ulterior motives.

"Something more unruly needs you to lug it outside." He tilted his head toward little Jemma, who'd slipped under a bench with a squeal.

"Right." Her smile reappeared, and she moved over to Jemma, hushing the mother's attempt to keep apologizing. "I've got her, no worries."

"After you," he said to the mother.

Corinne cooed to the little girl to come out and nearly got knocked over when Jemma threw all her weight into Corinne's open arms.

He walked outside accompanied by the precious sound of two sets of giggles.

His heartbeat, which had been galloping since reaching the town's outskirts, turned sluggish.

How sad that a relationship gone wrong could take away a woman's desire to have a family.

Yet maybe Corinne could still have children. What would stop them from adopting?

He plopped the basket into the back of the woman's wagon, and Corinne literally skipped out of the laundry hand in hand with the little girl.

Corinne swung Jemma up onto the bench seat, but the little urchin kept hold of Corinne's collar. "Come play wit' me!"

"Let go of Miss Stillwater, Jemma."

Laughing, Corinne tried to extricate herself. "I wish I could, baby. Maybe another day."

The little girl's eyes turned dewy and her lip quavered. "No, no. Play."

"Now, Jemma." The mother pulled her daughter off Corinne like a spiked bur. "I apologize, Miss Stillwater."

Corinne only smiled and waved at the little girl until their wagon was several lengths away. She sighed and headed back onto the porch without a glance toward him.

Had she forgotten he was there? "Corinne?"

She startled.

So she had. What daydreams had she been lost in? Of the babies she'd given up having?

"I'm sorry, I forgot you were there."

He tried not to let that hurt too much. After all, what man could compete with gold ringlets and huge dimples? He tipped his head toward the laundry. "Why don't we go inside?"

He followed her in, and she flipped the closed sign over, spun around, and stared at him.

"I suppose you've decided." She sounded more breathless than that short burst of activity should've left her.

He pulled off his hat and pointed it at the bench. "Sit beside me, if you would."

She nodded and waited for him to sit before perching herself on the opposite end.

"I'll go first." He cleared his throat. "I'm willing to follow through with what I offered. A hundred dollars, thirty-five percent of my profits, and no romantic nonsense—as long as you don't treat me as if I don't exist. Though I'm not asking for a wife in every sense of the word, our futures will be tied together for a long time, so I'd like us to get along."

She nodded, then a look of alarm crossed her face and she shot up and rushed toward the backroom.

He'd expected her to bolt the first time he'd proposed, but…

Then the faint odor of burning hit him. And not the smell of a wood fire, but chemical-like. He hobble-ran after her.

In the far corner, Corinne was using the end of her apron to flick away the steamy vapor enveloping her.

"Of all the careless things," she muttered. "What was I thinking?"

"Are you all right?"

She startled and whirled about. "I'm fine, just fine." With a clatter, she pushed a bunch of junk behind her as if hiding it from view. "Just forgot something. Burned it."

A beaker charred black rolled to a stop on the counter. What was she doing with a beaker? He'd only seen those kind of jars at the druggist's.

"Anyway, no harm done. Shouldn't have left it going when Mrs. Stout came in, is all."

"I—"

"Don't worry about it." She gestured for him to head back to the front.

How could he get back to asking her if she'd marry him? "Anyway—"

"No need to go through the spiel again. If you have the hundred dollars, I said I'd follow through."

That was likely the least exciting answer to a proposal in all of history, but beggars couldn't be choosers. "Thank you, Miss Stillwater."

Once they returned to the front counter, he opened his billfold and counted out the money despite the sudden jitters filling this stomach. "Would you mind if we get the license today so I don't have to return later to—" He stopped himself short. Though she wanted everything to be business like, that had sounded cold. "I mean—"

"Of course, we can. We should get things over with."

He flinched.

She'd agreed to save his land, for Pete's sake. Nothing she said reflecting the true nature of their arrangement should have made his heart seize like it just had. "I owe you much, Miss Stillwater."

"You don't owe me anything more than a tour of your ranch."

"*Our* ranch." His insides did a sad little flop with those words, but he bucked himself up. Sharing with Corinne had to be better than handing it over to Matt.

"Yes." She looked up at him and swallowed hard. "Our ranch."

CHAPTER ELEVEN

Less than a foot of space separated her from Nolan as he drove the livery's wagon, yet he felt far away. Corinne tried not to fidget, but the silence hung heavy. He'd been solemn at the courthouse when they'd asked for a marriage license, and then he'd looked ill as he watched her send his money to her brother-in-law.

He'd wanted this marriage desperately considering how he'd gone about obtaining it, so how badly had that hundred dollars put him out?

As his business partner, she ought to ask. Yet, until they married, prying might not be the wisest thing unless she wanted to pay him back—which she couldn't do.

Gazing out over the paintbrush-covered land, she pretended she was on the lookout for his ranch. She'd seen it months ago when she'd been invited to the Hendrixes'. From what she recalled, his place would be over the rise.

Nothing felt different. The sun was still hot, horses still stank, her hands still hurt, and yet, everything about her life had changed.

Taking a surreptitious glance to her left, she noted Nolan's gaze was cemented ahead of him as it had been for miles.

Maybe getting the license had made it feel real to him, whereas she was still shaking her head in disbelief.

They cleared the rise and a small puff of cheery smoke rose from one side of a barn that was still far off in the distance, likely where a forge was set up. One of his hands was a metal-worker, considering the state of the bunkhouse bedding she washed for Nolan. The distant ting of hammer against metal confirmed her suspicion.

With a huge inhale, Nolan sat up straighter.

The ridge that surrounded town was farther away, and cattle huddled under trees on nearly every dip and rise. The grasses rippled in front of them as if beckoning them toward the two-story gray house still a quarter mile away on the gently rolling plain. A windmill beside a well house turned with the steady breeze.

Squinting, she tried to make out what type of vehicle was parked next to the barn. It was finer than any buggy she'd expected Nolan to own.

Could all these beautiful acres and that large house be hers? She'd recalled it being smaller. "Is this it?"

"Yes." He smiled. "*Our* ranch."

She frowned. With how he'd acted the past couple of hours, she'd have thought he'd sound much less happy about that.

He urged his horse to speed up.

She lifted a hand to keep hold of her hat. "You seem excited to give me that tour all of a sudden." She'd wondered for half the trip if he was going to turn around and drive her back.

He grinned, his eyes bright. "I just realized you won't be making me pull out silverware to count. Or saucers—do you mind if I have chipped saucers?"

"What?" She couldn't help but chuckle. "Why should I care about chipped saucers?"

"Why, indeed?"

She laughed at his overly satisfied expression. "Though perhaps I should?"

"Please don't. Lilith cares more than enough for the both of us."

"Lilith?" Something fluttered inside her at the mention of a strange woman's name.

"My cousin Matt's fiancée. I guess I forgot to tell you they showed up. They're here, I'm sorry to say."

Her insides didn't stop flopping.

This was it. Within a half hour, someone other than the two of them would know they were engaged.

Despite the pain in her hands, she clamped onto her seat.

Now, it felt real.

"They've been acting like they already own the place, despite two more months left to fulfill my father's will. They've counted the silverware, chastised me about chipped dinnerware, wrote a list of 'improvements' they intend to make. Treated me like *I'm* the guest—an unwelcome one, at that."

"They sound delightful."

He rolled his eyes. "Yeah. They've only gone to town once since they've arrived, but when they did, I found myself praying for their quick return. I felt sorry for the townspeople."

"Wait, does this Lilith have a beauty mark on her cheek right here?" She pointed to a spot below her eye.

"Yes."

"And a lady friend who walks behind her as if she's royalty?"

"Seems you've already had the great misfortune of meeting Miss Mortimer and her companion."

"They came into the laundry the minute I opened my doors and dumped their bags on the counter. This fiancée cousin of yours demanded I have her clothing done before they returned from shopping."

"Wait a second. When I saw the wash on the line, I'd actually thought she'd done something useful."

"I only had time to do a wet wash since others were ahead of them. When she returned, I told her she'd have to hang it herself."

"I bet she thanked you warmly and gave you a generous tip."

"Or gave me a dressing down through gritted teeth and had to be encouraged to pay by her companion. Same difference."

"I wish I'd been around to watch her scowl at each piece she had to hang up."

"I doubt she was the one who did it."

"True, Miss Flower likely did."

"Who is that unfortunate woman?"

"A poor relation from what I gather. She's snapped at and pointed to and dismissed with a wave of a hand, as if she were a puppy—yet she doesn't cry foul."

Corinne recalled the luxurious riding habit Lilith had been wearing. "Why would a woman like Lilith want your ranch?"

"My guess is she likes the idea of owning as much property as possible. She wouldn't last a summer out here."

"And they just assumed the ranch would be theirs?"

"Yes."

What a kick to the ego to have them move in and make themselves at home, certain he'd never find a woman to marry him.

As they neared the main gate, she took in all the buildings, the new fencing, and the fine horses in the side paddock. Even if he couldn't attract a woman with his person, his land would've been enough.

He'd told her no woman would marry him because of his leg, but he must have another reason to believe so. One glimpse at his ranch demonstrated he could succeed despite his missing limb.

Had some woman jilted him on account of his leg? Had his mother been ashamed of him? Considering her disappointing relationships had ruined her desire to wed, she couldn't blame him if he couldn't trust a woman after being failed by one.

Though it wasn't as if she believed no men were worth marrying. But knowing how unlikely a good man would want to marry her after hearing about her past, it'd been saner to choose to never love again.

Nolan was a man worth marrying, yet he'd chosen to marry her without asking about—

"Hey, Rascal," Nolan called to an older man twisting wire around a post.

The man looked up with a greeting that died on his lips. Upon spotting her, his silvery, bushy brows bunched.

She looked away, uncertain how to react. Nolan wasn't bringing her home because he was in love with her, but most would assume so.

What if he did end up falling for her? If things changed...

Unfortunately for him, if he ever asked her to court, she'd have to say no. Being rejected by men who weren't worth marrying had hurt enough. Once Nolan recited his wedding vows, she'd be unable to flee humiliation and heartache if he cast her aside. So, she would lock her heart up tight.

As they maneuvered through the main gate and slowed, her body started jittering. If that old man had been confused upon seeing her... "Does anyone know I'm coming?"

"No. I didn't want them to know I was looking to marry. They might've tried to stop me."

"You think they'd try to cheat you out of the place?"

"Not cheat, exactly, but Matt's father is rich. Lilith's father, too. The wealthy can pull a lot of strings to get what they want."

"Should we marry sooner rather than later, then?"

He pulled to a stop. "You'd be fine with that?"

"We've already agreed to the stipulations. Bringing them about faster than expected won't change anything."

"All right, I can go in tomorrow and see when the judge will be in town."

"The judge?"

"To schedule a time to marry us."

"Do you have something against marrying in the church?"

He sat up as if affronted. "No, nothing. I've been going since I was little. Accepted Jesus as Lord when I was twelve. You?"

"I was eight." Although God hadn't done much for her since, she still believed He'd saved her from ultimate suffering.

"Good, but since this isn't going to be real. Vowing before God and all ... Well, I thought maybe the church wouldn't be a good idea."

"So you don't want to be held to your vows?" He wanted to cavort with other women?

He tilted his head. "I thought since you told Annie you were only willing to change your name in exchange for financial security, you'd be more comfortable treating this wedding like a legal ceremony."

The horse stomped and huffed, clearly eager to get back to moving.

How could she live with a man who'd... who'd... She dropped her gaze, unable to look at him. "Maybe we shouldn't do this. What I'm asking of you—if you wanted to seek out a woman willing to ... well, I couldn't face the town if..."

How ridiculous was every word spilling out of her mouth? How could she even be talking about such things with a man she hardly knew?

"I—" He cleared his throat and slapped the reins gently, allowing the horse to walk. "I don't need to say vows inside a church to pledge not to sleep with a woman who's not my wife. I realize this arrangement is even more constricting since we're likely never going to be more than business partners. But I've counted that cost."

She tried to look at him, but couldn't. How had she not realized she was taking more than thirty-five percent of his ranch from him? She knew men found great pleasure in intimacy. Her first fiancé had—or at least said he had. Enough that he'd pressured her into more than she'd ever been willing to give in her attempt to keep him tied to her—but she'd found out quickly that giving in had done little to keep him faithful. In fact, it had worked against her, driving him away.

Even if he'd been true to her, sex had certainly not made their relationship better. She hadn't responded as he'd liked; he'd compared her unfavorably to his late wife.

She'd given more, only to receive less.

Which made her demands on Nolan quite hypocritical now, didn't it? What right had she to get testy over his faithfulness when she was not a virgin bride?

She shook her head. Her lack of innocence should have no bearing on a business relationship. Her old fiancé was long gone and cared not a whit about what she did.

"If you want to say our vows in church, I'm not opposed."

"I'm sorry." She held to her seat as they neared the house. "I was being unfair. I'm sure you'll keep whatever vows you say in front of a judge as well as a preacher."

"Just so you know, I wasn't planning to ask the judge to take anything out of the ceremony. Our vows are still made before God, no matter where we say them."

She swallowed a few times so she could speak. "I don't mind a judge, but could we be married in the church with the pastor?" So much for not asking for romantic nonsense.

"Whatever you wish. Are you settled, then?"

She let a ghost of a smile form. "Yes, settled."

However, her stomach wasn't. Especially not now that Lilith was riding toward them. Even across the spacious yard, her condescending air was thick. This introduction would likely not go well.

Though she couldn't give Nolan everything a man might want, she could certainly do her best to keep this woman and her fiancé from wrenching away his land.

CHAPTER TWELVE

Corinne stiffened as Lilith pulled her horse up beside their slowing wagon. The woman's deep scowl didn't detract too much from her finely chiseled face. She wore the fanciest riding habit Corinne had ever seen, its velvet skirts draped artfully over the side saddle.

"Good afternoon?" Lilith's groomed eyebrows arched high beneath her glare.

What kind of greeting was that? Did the woman expect her to answer a question?

Nolan tipped his hat toward Lilith. "Indeed, it is." With a smirk, he pulled to a stop.

It took all she had not to smirk along with him, considering how bright his face had lit. Hopefully he wouldn't enjoy the upcoming battle too much—if he were a man who got pleasure from fighting, that wouldn't bode well for her.

Oh, the things she should've found out before agreeing to this marriage. But then, neither of them had the luxury of time.

Nolan set the brake and slid to the ground.

Without waiting, she climbed down, startling when she felt Nolan's hand upon her back. She should've known he'd help her down despite his own lack of coordination.

A man with golden hair and perfectly groomed, voluminous muttonchops exited the barn. His questioning scowl matched Lilith's.

The thin woman in gray who'd accompanied Lilith to town scuttled behind him in an attempt to keep up with his long strides.

"Your cousin, I take it," she whispered to Nolan as he held her steady now that her feet had hit the ground.

"Yes."

The blond man looked at her with narrowed eyes. "What is she doing here?"

"Good afternoon to you, cousin. Seems you've forgotten your manners."

"You didn't tell us you were bringing home a guest."

"That's because I'm not. She's no guest." Nolan squeezed her shoulder and pulled her close. "Even if she was, I'd expect you to receive my guests with better decorum."

"I apologize, ma'am. A pleasure to meet you." Muttonchops pulled off his hat and tipped his head like a gentleman, but his jaw was stiff.

"Miss Stillwater, this is my cousin, Matt Key, and his fiancée, Miss Lilith Mortimer, and her companion, Miss Ernesta Flower." His arm squeezed hers. "I'm happy to introduce you three to my fiancée, Miss Corinne—"

"The laundress?" Lilith's green eyes snapped fire as she turned to glare down at Corinne from upon her horse. But in an instant, her gaze cooled.

Corinne held the woman's gaze which was thick with condescension.

"A laundress no longer." Nolan forcefully cleared his throat. "As I was saying, this is my fiancée, Miss Corinne Stillwater."

Lilith gave her a perfunctory nod and reined her horse around to ride back to the barn.

"If you'll excuse me." Matt turned on his heel to follow his fiancée. Miss Flower gave them an apologetic shrug and scurried off as well.

"I admit," Nolan leaned close, "I found that more satisfying than I probably should have."

Corinne relaxed, but truth be told, she'd itched for Nolan to say more. Something ought to be done to swipe away that woman's arrogance. "What say you to calling off our ban on no romantic nonsense?"

He frowned deeply. "I don't—"

"Only for an hour or two." She smiled up at him and fluttered her lashes, though she felt quite silly doing so. When was the last time she'd felt free to relax around a man? She could do so now—at least enough to help Nolan convince his cousin they were in this together. "You think you could endure being called 'pudding pie' in front of Lilith for that long? Seems she'd enjoy hearing me call you that."

He laughed full out. "Enjoy it, indeed." He smiled down at her and winked. "What am I to call you?"

She swallowed hard at how quickly he'd flirted back with her. He wasn't Randolph. He wasn't plying his charm to get what he could take.

Besides, she no longer had to discourage light-hearted behavior in an effort to keep men from thinking she returned their interest. Nolan knew their banter wouldn't lead to anything other than what they'd already agreed to. She took a deep breath. "Something gaggingly sweet, of course. How about 'sugar dimples'?"

"No good—unless you have dimples."

She pointed to her right cheek. "I've one when I smile big, or so I've been told. It doesn't always show."

"Sugar *dimple* it is then."

At that roguish grin, she had to break her gaze from his. She could be playing with fire right now. But if she couldn't have a little fun with her business partner, what a miserable partnership this would be. And he had asked that they treat each other amiably, considering how long they'd be together—for life.

Her heart tripped more than she'd expected. Forever was a long time.

"So, for a quick tour." He walked her toward the side of the house, both of them pretending to ignore the heated argument occurring in the barn. "Here's the well and the storm cellar."

Without much to say beyond complimenting him on the upkeep of the place, Corinne found it difficult to keep her thoughts focused on the layout of the yard while Matt and Lilith's muffled exchanges rose and fell in intensity.

Moments later, Matt stomped off across the yard and into the house.

Nolan winked. "Are you ready for a tour of the inside?"

"If you are."

"I'm more than ready." He led her toward the house.

Despite her earlier bravado at offering to act like sweethearts, her heartbeat sped up at the upcoming confrontation.

At the table, Nolan's cousin was lighting a pipe, his mud-encrusted boots propped upon a chair, dirt crumbles scattered upon its seat.

"Good afternoon again, cousin." She hoped her greeting hadn't sounded as stiff as it'd felt.

He grunted some indiscernible reply, glaring over the top of his now smoking pipe bowl. He flicked his hand to extinguish the match.

Nolan entwined his arm through hers. "If you happened to be worried about me having a full set of silverware, Corinne, you'll be happy to hear Matt and his fiancée were kind enough to count that for me only days ago."

"Oh? That's wonderful…" She tried to push the words 'pudding pie' out of her mouth, but couldn't. Maybe she should've chosen a term of endearment that was less saccharine. She did want to be believable, after all.

Matt's boots hit the floor. "I don't understand." He

narrowed his eyes at Nolan. "I mean, I get that you'd—but why stoop so low?"

Nolan dropped her arm to jam his hands on his hips. "I don't ever want to hear you degrade my future wife again."

Matt shrugged and leaned back. "I didn't mean it like that."

"Oh, yes, you did."

Matt's barb had stung, but she couldn't muster up too much ire. Nolan *had* stooped to make a laundress a rancher's wife. Working women often became the wives of homesteaders out here, but in whatever big city these three were obviously from, she doubted many laundresses rose up in society.

"Well, it's not what your father would've wanted."

"You know nothing about what he wanted or what it takes to live out here."

"I know enough."

"You only think you do. Women from every walk of life out here are working ranches, from well-born English aristocrat types to lowly immigrants. The land doesn't play favorites. It treats us all with equal disdain and occasionally shows a few of us mercy."

She tucked her arm back around his. "Honey … pie, I'm sure he meant no harm." She turned to Matt. "That's one of the things I love about Nolan. He sticks up for everybody, even if they don't deserve it."

Nolan gave her a squeeze. "Don't lump yourself in with people who don't deserve to be defended. I expected hostility toward you, but not in front of you."

She patted his upper arm and turned to nod at Matt. "We can let bygones be bygones, right? Now, Nolan, tell me where you got this lovely wallpaper. Do you have any left to cover this blank wall over here? Other than that, I can't think of how one could make this kitchen any cozier."

Letting himself be led off to what appeared to be a pantry, Nolan leaned to whisper into her ear, "You may be laying it on a little thick. We don't want Matt suspecting this is just a game."

"But it is just a—" She stopped short as she turned to whisper back. She'd nearly brushed her lips against his.

He didn't move. His breath fanned her cheek, her nose, her mouth. "A dangerous game," he whispered.

Her chest almost caved in with how hard she pulled in her breath.

His soapy, bergamot sort of smell jammed up any words she might have formed.

She took an abrupt step back to clear the air.

Glancing behind her, she noted Matt watching them. She mustered up a smile and some words. "I'm sorry, cousin. I should've kept my decorating thoughts to myself. I know what it's like to lose what you thought was yours. But wherever you find yourselves, I do hope you and Miss Mortimer will be as happy as I'll be here with Nolan."

And that was no lie, for she would indeed be happy with Nolan.

He hadn't asked her to surrender her heart, and yet he'd offered her the world.

And if she unwittingly fell for him?

No. Nothing good would come of that. Nothing but disappointment for them both.

CHAPTER THIRTEEN

In front of the church doors, Nolan paced, wiping his sweaty palms on his Sunday slacks. He pulled out his timepiece again. Ten past the hour.

If she'd traveled from outside of town, he might not have been worried, but she lived down the street.

He'd prayed the whole way into Armelle that God would stop them from marrying if they weren't doing the right thing. Maybe Corinne not showing up was the answer.

"You're going to drive us crazy if you keep pacing." Jacob sat on the church's lone outdoor bench, his arm around his wife. "Stop worrying. She'll come."

"I'm not so sure."

What if she'd realized he'd been attracted to her when they'd played lovey-dovey in front of his cousin and decided to call this off?

Maybe that was the smartest thing to do.

"You're making me nervous." Annie's smile faded.

"I might have reason to be."

Annie gave him a sympathetic look. "I can't say I blame you. I wanted to run for the hills right before I married Jacob." She snuggled in closer to her husband. "I'm glad I didn't though."

Surely Corinne hadn't run. But what if Matt had gotten to her and paid her to back out?

Matt and Lilith hadn't left as planned, and Nolan had made it clear they were not invited to the wedding. However, he couldn't order them not to visit his bride-to-be. He walked to the edge of the church's porch, though he knew he couldn't see the laundry from there.

When his cousin hadn't followed him into town, he'd breathed a sigh of relief. Perhaps he shouldn't have.

A trail of smoke billowed across the horizon, and the imperceptible shaking of a locomotive rumbled beneath his feet. Could Corinne be on the departing train, bribed to leave him behind?

Maybe she'd not needed a bribe. Maybe she'd realized she could do without him. Or Matt had given her money to help save her business—no potential romantic complications to even worry about.

Down the street, Matt appeared a block away and marched in their direction. So he had followed him in.

Nolan descended the front steps, arms crossed, scowl at the ready.

His cousin looked up, a tic in his cheek ruining what seemed to be an attempt to keep from smiling. "She got cold feet, huh?"

Had Matt just given her those cold feet?

"Nolan?" Jacob came up beside him and frowned at Matt.

"Aren't you the marshal?" His cousin swiped off his hat.

"I was," Jacob drawled as he stepped forward.

"Do you know where the lawyer's at?"

"Mr. Wright?"

"No, the other one."

"You mean, Mr. Grayson?" At Matt's nod, he shook his head. "I'm afraid he's in prison. Why?"

"I don't like the new lawyer."

God bless Mr. Wright. He must not have caved to whatever scheme his cousin had tried to finagle the lawyer into.

Jacob shrugged. "Mr. Wright doesn't intend to stay long from what I've gathered. We'll likely get a new lawyer before the year's end."

"That won't help me." Matt pierced Nolan with a glare. "I've talked with him about the will. About everything…"

Why was he pausing? To make him nervous? He was certainly succeeding. Where *was* Corinne?

"He told me you have to follow the intent of your father's request."

Nolan fought against fidgeting. "I know. Mr. Wright informed me of the same."

It'd been a mistake to move the wedding up so soon, making it more than obvious this was not a love match. Yet "love match" had not been what his father demanded. A convenient marriage was enough.

What if his cousin stuck around to prove that they'd not married in truth?

But what could he do to prove it? Peek in their windows at all hours? Maybe Matt was simply hoping to intimidate him into changing his mind.

Behind him, Pastor Lawrence cleared his throat. "Has the lady arrived?"

Nolan wished he could make the heat in his face disappear. "Not yet."

Matt's smirk widened. "I'll be on my way, gentlemen." He turned on his heel and strode off.

Nolan couldn't help but take out his timepiece once more. "Do you think he's done something?"

The pastor clasped his shoulder. "Do you need to check on Miss Stillwater? Perhaps we should reschedule?"

Down the street, Nolan caught sight of a flutter of shimmery green.

Head down, Corinne walked toward them in an emerald dress made of iridescent fabric that shone wherever it captured the sun.

She glanced up, but quickly looked back down at her feet, one hand twisting a loose curl that framed her face and spilled down her neck. The white flowers behind her ear quavered as she tugged on the ringlet.

She was more beautiful than he'd ever seen her.

"Seems we've got a bride, Pastor." Jacob patted Nolan's shoulder before turning to walk up the stairs and head into the church.

The bloom in Corinne's cheeks and the dangling white earrings that caressed her neck kept him from following them in.

Where had a laundress gotten a dress like that?

Stopping in front of him, she peeped up, her mouth scrunching to the side. "You don't have to look at me like that."

"You mean I shouldn't look at you as if you're beautiful?"

Shrugging, she dropped her gaze again, picking at the minuscule white flowers tied to her wrist.

He tugged the curl by her cheek, making it bounce. "I thought you outlawed romantic nonsense?"

"Evidently one's not allowed to get married in work clothes —not according to Mrs. Whitsett, anyway. You can blame her."

Taking into account Corinne's blush and slight grin, it seemed she wasn't too upset at being forced into wearing something other than her usual plain blouse and nondescript skirt.

"After learning why I was asking her if she'd take over my laundry, she practically dragged me to her daughter's." Corinne fussed with a skirt pleat. "It's Ava's dress. She's a bit fuller than I am, so it took time to alter. And I couldn't help much, considering—" She held up her hands. "Pain kept me up all night."

He reached for her curled fingers and gently raised them to kiss the back of her hand.

She pulled away, her eyes wide.

"I'm sorry. I didn't mean to hurt you."

"It's all right." But she turned her face away.

Were her cheeks pinker or had Mrs. Whitsett and her daughter insisted on rouge, along with whatever it was that was darkening her eyelashes? But even if her blush wasn't natural, that didn't explain why she avoided looking at him. "I'm sorry I teased you earlier. A woman wanting to look her best on her wedding day isn't romantic nonsense."

"Thanks." She pursed her lips. "But I think it might be a bit much."

"Not at all. Perhaps when you pay off your loan, you can buy some expensive fabric like this so you can feel beautiful on more days than today. You're gorgeous in green."

She looked up at him sharply.

He smiled and lifted his hands. "I'm breaking no promises. You being beautiful is simply the truth."

She scrutinized him in such a way he could almost imagine she was thinking him handsome, desirable even.

But then she huffed and hooked an arm around his. "Pastor Lawrence has likely given up on us. Let's go."

"Yes, yes. We should do that." He walked with her up the stairs, trying not to let her nearness do things to him it shouldn't.

He'd told the pastor earlier that they wanted the ceremony to be bare-boned. But with how her dress brushed up against him, her heightened color making him wonder if her skin was as warm and soft as it appeared, and the way she smelled of powder and lavender, it was a shame he'd asked Pastor Lawrence not to include the ceremonial kiss.

Years from now, he'd likely regret not kissing her when he'd had a legitimate reason to do so.

Oh, who was he fooling?

He already did.

CHAPTER FOURTEEN

Back in her normal clothing after returning the lovely green gown to Leah's daughter, Corinne took the stairs up to her bedroom slowly, but not too slowly lest Nolan realize she was climbing leisurely for his sake. She glanced over her shoulder to check if Nolan was still behind her—he was, of course, and her heart sped up yet again.

There was nothing untoward about taking one's husband up to her bedroom to bring down her luggage.

One's husband.

Hers.

But since he was more a business partner, having him up to her room didn't sit quite right. Even if Leah had smiled at them as they made their way upstairs.

She'd tried to tell him she didn't need help, but he'd insisted since her hands were hurting.

After blaming her hands for lost sleep and being late to her own wedding a little over an hour ago, she couldn't insist they were fine. She *had* been up all night, but not because of pain—she dealt with that most nights—nor was it because she'd worried Nolan wouldn't follow through with what he offered.

She'd been unable to sleep because she knew he'd follow through.

It'd been a mistake to make eyes at him the other day in front of his cousin as if they were in love.

It had almost felt real.

Stopping at her door, she swung it open and stepped back to let him in. "This is it."

He frowned at her two carpetbags at the foot of the bed, then scanned the room.

There wasn't much to see. A narrow mattress, a washstand, five hooks on the wall.

She hadn't been lying when she'd said she didn't need help getting her things from upstairs.

"Are you wanting to take the washstand?"

She shook her head. "If you have one for me to use, it's nothing special."

Without saying more, he crossed the room to pick up her bags.

Leah didn't need this apartment, though she could sublet it to help pay rent. Hopefully, she'd only do so if she trusted the tenant—Leah shouldn't be hurt any more than she had been.

At the bottom of the stairs, Nolan turned to wait for her as she took the last set of steps. "I'd thought we'd be busy moving all afternoon, but seems I was wrong. Would you like to eat at the hotel?"

She frowned. Did he think those two bags were all she had? "We have lots to pack and haul out." She wouldn't have bothered giving Ava back her dress already if she'd only had two bags to carry away.

He turned to peer through the doorway that led to the front of the laundry. "Aren't you leaving the equipment for Leah?"

"Of course, but the rest goes." She beckoned for him to take a look around the room where he stood. "I've got all this."

She crossed over to a nearly full crate and wedged in another glass container filled with chemicals. "I don't have enough boxes, however. Though some things would be awkward to pack, like those split barrels and wagon wheels. I figure it'll take us most of today to get what we can, considering we'll have to make multiple trips."

He scanned the room as if seeing it for the first time. "I thought this stuff belonged to the banker."

"No, it's mine." She bent to lift a bucket full of metal odds and ends, bracing for her hand's inevitable protest. "The heavy items should probably be stacked as close to the wagon bench as possible."

"Wait." He grabbed the handle which had bent with the weight of the material.

Maybe she shouldn't have filled it so full.

His other hand wrapped around hers, and despite the fact they'd married this morning, her hand tingled as if touching were inappropriate.

"You shouldn't lift this."

"I figured I'd have to, considering." She glanced down at his leg.

His jaw worked, and his eyes shuttered.

He'd told her earlier that saying she was beautiful was truth, not romantic flattery, so she wouldn't allow him to hurt himself in some chivalric demonstration that ignored reality. "There're plenty of things you can help me carry out, but these—"

"My leg is missing, not my arms." Nolan didn't unwrap his hand from around hers.

"All right." Maybe she shouldn't have assumed what he could and couldn't do—as he'd promised not to do to her.

She let go.

He looked around and sighed. "I should ask Jacob to help."

"But he's already on his way home."

"He and I can come back later this week."

And now he was assuming she would be of no help. "We can do it now."

"No—"

"Either this goes with me," she set her hands on her hips, "Or I stay with it."

His forehead wrinkled, as if trying to gauge if she'd actually follow through with the threat. "Why does it matter? It's just junk."

Her head snapped back. "Junk?"

"I'm sorry." Though a glimmer of amusement danced his eyes. "But you can't fault me for thinking it is what it looks like. What do you need it for?"

She scanned the tables laden with what indeed resembled rubbish. Would he be too proud to let her earn patents in her own name? Would he steal them from her as her father once had? "Uh, just … tinkering."

His expression indicated he didn't believe her.

"You remember that wooden clothes rack on the back of the building? I can't make stuff like that without materials. And if we don't have money until you sell cattle, it's not wise to spend money to replace all this."

He exhaled slowly, but turned to scan the room. "I don't have anywhere to put it."

"What about that cabin you said I could have one day?"

"It's small. If all this were in there, and you wanted to move in later, it'd be cramped."

"We can decide what to do then if necessary. In the meantime, we'll work to raise your profits enough to build something else to store my things."

A ghost of a smile showed up on his face, and she had to turn away. Something about that grin had made her breath grow short.

She picked up another bucket and turned toward the back door, but not before she saw him shake his head at her. "Bring the wagon around back, Nolan."

"Aye, aye, boss."

She couldn't help but roll her eyes, and yet, his good-natured sarcasm made her breathe easier.

Two hours later, she wiped sweat from her forehead with her sleeve, wincing despite her attempt not to use her hands. The pulsating ran clear up past her elbow. "Nolan," she breathed.

He stopped in the middle of shoving a crate into the wagon to look at her.

If only she could've held out for a half hour more.

She tried to voice that she couldn't continue, but she'd lost her breath calling out to him.

After giving the crate one last shove, he came toward her, his gaze probing. "I let you do too much, didn't I?"

Now that her hands were no longer busy, they tingled with needle-like pinpricks.

She couldn't look at him. Earlier, she'd basically accused him of ignoring his physical limitations, but she'd been the one who hadn't stopped when she should have.

Once again, he reached for her hands and she inhaled sharply—this time because of the pain.

He let go and wrapped his arm around her shoulder. "We can get what remains another day."

She nodded, trying not to let the warmth in her eyes turn into tears. Thankfully, he seemed to realize she didn't want to talk—or rather, couldn't.

There wasn't much left anyway. All junk, as he'd said.

If things didn't work out between them and she had to leave, what did she possess that could save her?

She struggled to climb up to the wagon's seat, attempting to keep weight off of him, unsure of how much he could bear.

Once his hand left her back, she slid onto the bench and tried not to think about what the future might hold. But there was no denying she'd made herself completely vulnerable to a man yet again. The stuff they were hauling was worthless, and the laundry was now in the hands of the banker and Leah.

But Nolan's vows this morning were words no man had ever said to her. He'd sworn to protect her until death—as if he'd meant it.

However, Kurt and Randolph had said many things just as convincingly, and she'd fallen for their every line.

Nolan cleared his throat. "You ready?"

She nodded weakly, and he flicked the reins to start the team.

Whether or not she was ready, there was nothing she could do now. Hopefully marrying Nolan was a better decision than all the one's she'd made before.

CHAPTER FIFTEEN

Once they left town, Nolan had given up trying to engage her in small talk. The panging in her hands and arms had made it difficult for her to formulate logical responses.

Leaning back, Corinne allowed herself to sway with the wagon, willing the pain to leave with each exhale.

If her hands weren't better soon, would she be of any use in bringing in enough money to keep them afloat this fall? Maybe asking for a profit split had been too much. She was no cowgirl, and no rancher paid their housekeeper a percentage of his profits. What if she couldn't do enough work to be worthy of her share? Perhaps taking his offer to do nothing would've been smarter.

But how to ask? She didn't want him to think she had no intention of following through with what she'd promised.

Nolan cleared his throat. "I'm afraid our arrival will not be a happy event. Matt and Lilith chose to stay. I don't think they believed I'd go through with it. Lilith especially since, well—"

He cut himself off again with the clearing of his throat.

"I know," she whispered. A laundress was worth less than the mud on Lilith's dainty kid leather boots.

He patted her leg as if to assure her but then snatched his hand away.

"I'm sorry my acting skills were so bad they didn't believe we'd marry."

He chuckled. "Even if we weren't acting, I'm not sure they would have believed it. Matt's heard me tell my father often enough that nothing would persuade me to marry, hence why they showed up at the ranch, sure they'd inherit. It wasn't your acting skills. Besides, I had too much fun watching them writhe. You made me laugh."

She tried to come up with something witty to make him laugh again, but stopped. If she enjoyed her time with him too much, would her heart attach itself?

She glanced at the plain gold band on her ring finger. "Maybe I should drop the fake flirting this time and act like an anxious wife, ready to have the house to myself, claim it like a dog—uh, wait. That metaphor wasn't going anywhere flattering fast."

He laughed full out.

Goodness, he was handsome when he was amused. Another reason not to have too much fun with him.

"I'm happy you're dedicated to making this appear real, but I think once we show them the license, if that's even necessary, they'll concede defeat. Unfortunately, they've made no travel plans. I don't exactly want to kick them out though, considering they're family."

"I understand—" Oh, wait. "Are … are they staying in the house?"

He nodded solemnly. "I can't put Lilith and her companion in the bunkhouse with my ranch hands."

"So that means … we'd…" Suddenly her throat was stiffer than her fingers.

"If they don't leave tonight, I'll sleep on the floor."

Her throat relaxed enough to swallow. That wasn't too bad, him being on the floor.

But she'd be in his bed.

She closed her eyes and concentrated on the pain in her hands. Who knew pain could come in handy for something?

When they traversed the main gate, she could see Matt on the front porch, glaring at them as they drove closer.

She scooted toward Nolan. Not for appearance reasons, but because she had no idea what kind of man Matt was. How would he react?

Nolan's body tensed. Was he worried marrying her wouldn't be enough?

Best thing she could do was act happy, which should require no acting at all. What woman in her position wouldn't be thankful to have a spacious home, freedom from debt, and no worries about surviving tomorrow?

She forced herself to give his cousin a carefree wave. "Good afternoon."

Matt didn't reply. He really was quite the ogre.

Nolan called for the horses to stop, climbed down the side of the wagon, and came over to help her. Once she hit the ground, he tried to release her hand, but she held fast despite the pain.

He frowned at their hands clasped together, but then took a deep breath and gently squeezed.

Placing her other hand on her chest, she inhaled deeply, letting the exaggerated movement bring attention to the ring on her finger. "Is Miss Mortimer nearby?"

Matt's jaw worked as if he were chewing a cud, but then he tilted his head toward the front door, making his muttonchops appear to stick out even farther. "She's inside."

"Good. I heard she made a list of improvements we could make to the place. I was hoping to hear her thoughts before you left."

Matt turned to scowl at Nolan.

He pulled her closer. "My wife and I would love to have you stay for supper."

"Stay?"

"Oh." Nolan shrugged nonchalantly. "I figured you'd spend the night at the hotel, since you're likely leaving tomorrow."

Matt shook his head, his jaw crooked out. "We'll leave tomorrow, yes, but the hotel is too crude and cramped for Lilith. Your guest rooms barely suffice."

"I apologize. I suppose." Nolan's voice took on a hard edge.

Jiggling his arm, Corrine encouraged him to relax. Matt could claim the house wasn't worthy of stray dogs, but that didn't mean he could take it from them.

Matt fixated on their clasped hands. "I guess I should offer you my congratulations."

"Thank you," Corinne responded before Nolan could point out how uncongratulatory his tone was.

Matt shrugged then marched inside.

"I'm so sorry to put you through this." Nolan fidgeted as if he wasn't sure he wanted to follow his cousin into his own home.

"It's temporary, right? Could be worse."

He nodded and led her into the house.

At the kitchen table, the women were drinking tea. Lilith didn't even turn to greet them.

Miss Flower fidgeted and kept glancing between her, Nolan, and something nonexistent by the door.

Extricating her hand from Nolan's, Corinne stepped forward. When neither lady made a move to acknowledge her presence, she hesitated. She ought to treat them as her guests, but they knew where the teacups were and she didn't.

After throwing back her shoulders, she strode straight to the table and sat beside them. Whether she knew where the dishes were or not, they were her dishes more than they were theirs. It seemed Lilith needed the reminder. "Good afternoon, ladies. How was your morning? Are you enjoying your tea?"

Lilith gave her a short nod, and Miss Flower nearly flipped her saucer while setting down her cup.

"Thank you for asking, Miss Stillwater. Lilith makes the best

113

tea." Miss Flower glanced at Corinne, then stared back down into her milk-laden drink.

"It's Mrs. Key now." Trying to hide her nervousness, Corinne pulled the tea service to her side of the table. She'd serve the tea.

"Would you like a cup, hon?" Rising, she cast a wide-eyed glance toward Nolan. Would he save her from looking like a fool by somehow indicating which cupboard held the teacups?

But he seemed intent on glaring at the back of Lilith's head.

"Hon?"

Nolan didn't respond.

Corinne huffed. "Nolan?"

He shook his head as if waking from sleep. "What?"

"I asked if you would like tea."

"Oh, you were talking to me?"

"Yes, honey … pudding … pie."

Nolan's mouth pinched in an attempt to keep from laughing. At least he was done glaring a hole in their guest's head. "I'd take a cup, yes."

"Then…" She widened her eyes again and tilted her head toward the cupboard. "Any particular cup you'd like?"

He shrugged as if he couldn't care less, but then with a jolt, he seemed to figure out what she needed and crossed the room. "Oh, it doesn't matter, but I'll pick one."

"Good." She turned her back to the women and let out a sigh.

After opening a cupboard to his right, he handed her two cups. "Do you want tea, Matt?"

"No, thank you." The man stood in the shadows by the cookstove. "May I have a word with you?"

"Sure." Nolan placed a quick, awkward kiss against her temple before following Matt down the hall.

With a prayer for success, she opened the drawer to her right and nearly melted to see silverware inside. She selected a teaspoon and returned to the table.

"How was the wedding?" Miss Flower asked. When Lilith shot her a glare, the wilting woman actually shrugged her off and turned to face Corinne. "It's a lovely day for a wedding. Not too hot."

"Yes, the rain last night was welcome. Were you comfortable here in the … our guest rooms?"

"Your rooms leave much to be desired." Lilith picked up her tea and took a sip, glaring over the top of her cup as if she'd delivered a death blow.

"Oh?" Corinne straightened and forced herself to look directly into her future in-law's eyes, though she'd never be able to match Lilith's ability to look down on a person even when she was in truth looking up.

Better to heap coals of kindness on her head than try to play her game. "What exactly are your complaints, so we might—?"

"You can't do anything about their abominably small size, but the mattresses are old, musty even. You could try airing them out more often. I'd discard them and buy new. Miss Flower's washstand bowl has a chip in it, and a few of the sheets have stains. I'm supposing that's your fault, since he takes his laundry to you."

Oh, this woman was going to make maintaining good manners hard. How likely were those stains nothing more than faded smudges? "I'm sorry, but I believe none of the household laundry was ever brought to me. Perhaps it would've been better to ask, rather than assume."

Lilith huffed, shoved her teacup away, and somehow, with both grace and haughtiness, exited the room.

The moment Lilith disappeared from view, Miss Flower turned, her shoulders nearly up to her ears, as if preparing for an anticipated beating. "I'm sorry about that, Mrs. Key. Congratulations on your good fortune. *Your* Mr. Key is a good man."

"Thanks." Corinne might've said more, but her voice had barely worked for that one word.

Miss Flower slipped out of her chair and trailed after Lilith.

Closing her eyes, Corinne cupped her hands around her teacup, hoping the heat might relieve the ache in her fingers.

A cold hand slid onto her shoulder and she nearly jumped out of her skin.

Nolan leaned down to whisper in her ear. "I'm afraid they're staying the night. I'll take your bags to my room."

She nodded and listened to his footsteps receding behind her.

Was it strange that her stomach flip-flopped more over the thought of spending the rest of the day in Lilith's presence than a night with a man she hardly knew?

•

CHAPTER SIXTEEN

Lilith's tea was indeed good, but not good enough to be drinking a fourth cup. Nolan poured himself another anyway.

The crickets had started their nightly chorus, and the candle was about to splutter out. Nolan leaned back against his parlor chair, taking a covert glance at his cousin, hoping for some indication the man would turn in soon.

He looked quite engrossed in the paper, not one sign of weariness upon his face.

Which was no surprise since his cousin hadn't helped him unload Corinne's possessions or do the evening chores with the men. The moment Corinne had arrived, Matt had decided to take a holiday.

During dinner, the tension between Lilith and Corinne had been palpable. The entire night remained stressful until the women retired. It was as if the air Lilith exhaled spread out like a heavy blanket, trying to squash them all down to the level she believed they ought to be. Poor Miss Flower had barely been capable of sitting up straight in her chair.

Why Lilith hadn't dragged Matt to the hotel was beyond him.

The rustle of Matt folding his paper nearly made Nolan's

heart jolt. Once Matt retired, it'd be time for him to do so as well.

"Why didn't you tell me in your telegram you were marrying? You asked me if I was willing to give up my claim to the ranch, but why bother if you were getting married?"

Nolan tried not to let the question fluster him. "I hadn't asked her yet."

Matt simply stared at him.

"I didn't want a wedding to be forced by a timetable set up in a will."

"You were always so adamant you'd not marry. Hasn't your complaint about me always been I don't follow through with my word? That I don't say what I mean, or do what I say? Why did you change your mind suddenly? Just to deprive me of the ranch?"

"I never promised anyone I'd stay single," Nolan gritted through clenched teeth. "Convictions change."

Why was he being chastised about taking something from Matt when his cousin had been born with more assets than Nolan currently possessed?

"What do you even know about this woman? I hear she showed up out of nowhere two years ago. Everyone I asked was surprised to learn you two were getting married. A few men told me how adamantly she'd turned down *their* suit. A couple of them were well-to-do. All of them had their limbs. Are you sure she isn't going to poison you in your sleep and claim the ranch for herself?"

"First off, that's preposterous. Second, if she did kill me, she'd at least run this ranch better than you."

Matt's eyes narrowed dangerously.

"Besides, I could ask the same of you. How well do you know Lilith?"

"I've known her long enough to know she'd not kill me for my property."

"I'd say the same of Corinne. Stop grasping at straws and accept that the ranch is, and always will be, mine."

Matt spent a few seconds staring at him, but then shrugged and set his paper aside. "I suppose I should wish you well."

"Yes, that's what you should do."

Matt smoothed his muttonchops with a hand down his face. "I'm not sure I can though, considering I have no idea why you're still down here on your wedding night."

Nolan gave him a granite glare. "Having overnight guests puts a damper on things."

"I suppose there's no reason for me to ever return for a visit?"

Nolan wanted to be the type of person who loved his blood relations enough to ask them to visit whenever they liked, but what was the point? "As family, you're welcome if you have a strong desire to visit, but don't you think sharing news through letters would be enough for us?"

Especially if Matt's future wife was going to treat Corinne as if she wasn't worthy of breathing the same air.

Matt drummed his fingers on his armrest. Was the man truly without words? That'd be a first.

Though he had hoped Matt would cease coming to the ranch one day, it didn't bring him as much joy as he'd expected. Making someone feel unwanted wasn't something to revel in. He'd dealt with such feelings plenty after losing his leg. He didn't wish it on anyone.

"We'll be out of your hair tomorrow." Matt pushed himself out of his seat and walked out. "Goodnight."

Nolan forced himself not to call his cousin back to smooth things over. It was best for both ladies, if not themselves, for this to be the end.

After Matt's footsteps faded, the tree branch scratching against the window grew noisier in the silence. Nolan picked up the pillows, straightened the newspapers, wound the clock.

Eleven twenty-eight.

Corinne ought to have had plenty of time to get changed, burrow under the covers, and fall asleep by now. Staying out of the room until she was solidly ensconced in dreams had been the only privacy he could offer her with their unwanted guests still here.

As quietly as a man on a wooden leg could climb stairs, Nolan inched his way upward, checking for light under each doorway as he passed. Matt was the only one burning a lamp. Good.

Wishing he'd thought to grease his hinges, he gingerly opened his bedroom door.

No light, but she wasn't asleep. Muffled sniffling sounded from the bed.

How long had she been crying? A weeping bride was not the best thing to have in the house if they wanted Matt to believe this marriage would be long-lasting.

After clicking the door shut, he let his eyes adjust. On the bed, Corinne was lying atop the quilt, still dressed in what she'd worn that afternoon. How many hours had it been since she'd come up?

"I'm sorry," he whispered. "Do you need more time to get ready?"

"An eternity maybe," she whispered.

His heart seized. Was she that overwrought having to sleep in here with him? Perhaps they should be the ones to go to the hotel, not that they could have separate rooms there either.

She scooted up in a funny inch-by-inch wriggle until she reclined against the headboard. "What if the doctor's wrong?"

"The doctor?" He took a step closer.

"What if they don't get better?" She tucked her hands up against her chest.

He felt an urge to cradle and comfort her, but what good would that do? "Have you taken any medicine?"

She nodded, emitting a sound that was a cross between a

hiccup and a sigh. "I've done no laundry today, yet my fingers hurt too much to undo my buttons."

"Did you forget you picked up more stuff than you should have?"

"He only said I had to differentiate activity."

"Likely after your hands got better."

She moaned. "We only packed for a few hours. It's the least amount of work I've done in a day for an entire year."

"Shhh, shhh, shhh." He couldn't help but cross over to her now. He perched awkwardly on the mattress's edge and cupped her face. He didn't want her to turn hysterical. Less because others might hear, and more because the cracks in her voice were stabbing his heart. "They'll get better."

"But I've rested them all afternoon and evening and—and they're not." Her voice had softened into an emotion-laden whisper. "What if I'm always in pain? I'm too young to always be in pain."

Knowing how devastating it was to face decades of pain in one's future, he smiled sadly. "What did you take to alleviate it?"

"The medicine Doc's given me, as much as allowed."

"What about whiskey?"

"No!"

He startled. "I'm sorry, I—"

"No, I'm sorry. I never touch the stuff. You don't drink, do you?" Her eyes widened as if she just realized a wild animal had her cornered.

He rubbed her arm. "It's only in the house for medicinal purposes."

"And you're in pain how often?"

He couldn't help his chuckle. "All the time, but whiskey's only for emergencies."

"Oh." She leaned back against the headboard. But then her breath sucked in sharply again.

"You sure about the whiskey? What about a small glass?"

She shook her head.

"What if I help you…?" Surely he couldn't offer to help her undress. "Would you like me to take off your boots?"

A muffled moan escaped her, but by the sound of it, she'd agreed.

"All right." He stood and frowned at them. Those buttons were awfully tiny, but she'd gotten a few undone. Hadn't his mother had some sort of contraption for this?

She pointed behind him. "The hook's on the nightstand."

He turned to find what he might've mistaken for something women used for needlework. He snatched it up and moved to the end of the bed. Gingerly, he sat down, then lifted her right foot onto his lap. "I apologize ahead of time for how terribly this might go. I'm afraid I've never had reason to practice this skill."

"A good thing," she whispered with a hint of amusement.

Seemed the pain hadn't sunk her all the way into despair. He wriggled the hook under the loop and pulled, slipping the leather over the tiny button. Not so hard after all. He did a line of them in quick succession.

"Are you sure you've not done this before?"

"Seems I've discovered a hidden talent."

After he finished the row, he slipped her foot out, noting the harsh creases in her stocking, as if the material were embedded in her skin. Once he'd freed both feet, he pulled the creases from her stockings and started rubbing his thumbs along her soles, trying to knead the stiffness away.

The stockings were too slippery, so he peeled those off, and began with her right foot. He hoped to have heard sounds of contentment, but she was crying again. "Does this hurt?"

"No," she whispered.

She didn't tell him to stop, so he continued.

They might not ever become husband and wife in truth, but he couldn't come up with a reason not to help when and where he could. In the past, he had wished he wasn't single on occasion when an out of reach itch or anything requiring more than two hands presented itself.

Now that he'd married, he'd make everyone suspicious if he called in one of the men to assist him with a splinter.

How many other ways had marrying changed what he could do?

Though feet weren't the prettiest things on the planet, he couldn't recall ever seeing a woman's bare foot before. He definitely had never held one, and her skin against his...

He closed his eyes. *Stop thinking, Nolan.*

When the first foot relaxed, he glanced up at Corinne to see if he should move to the next.

Her face was more solemn than peaceful.

"What are you thinking?"

"I'd rather not say."

He stopped rubbing her feet. Was she afraid to tell him to stop?

He was in a position of power right now, on her bed, at night, when she was obviously in debilitating pain. But when she said nothing more, holding his gaze as if she were simply curious, he moved to her other foot.

Once those muscles relaxed, he gently lowered her foot. "Let's—"

She'd fallen asleep.

Lifting himself off the mattress as gingerly as he could, he took hold of the edge of the quilt she was lying on and wrapped it around her. He pressed his lips against her forehead before he realized what he was doing.

He stilled and pulled away slowly. Her expression remained peaceful.

Seemed a kiss on his wedding day hadn't been entirely out of the question. "That wasn't so bad now, was it?" he whispered to her with a grin.

He pulled the quilt farther over but was met with resistance. He frowned. She was on top of *all* the blankets. He gently tugged on the quilt beneath her, but she was sleeping hard and he hated to wake her.

But leaving the room to gather blankets on a summer evening could clue his cousin into the fact he wasn't sleeping with his wife.

One good thing about her sleeping heavily was he didn't have to worry about her watching him take his leg off. He'd not figured out how to do that modestly in front of her or how he could do so elsewhere without arousing suspicion.

Taking coats and sweaters out of his trunk, he made a makeshift pallet on the rug that stuck partway out from under the bed. Probably not enough padding to keep him from waking up sore, but he hadn't anything else to sleep on.

Groaning, he unstrapped his leg, massaging the spots where the padding had sunk into his flesh like Corinne's stocking had wrinkled her feet. Taking the liniment from his bedside table, he stopped and frowned. He should've massaged this into her feet —or offered it for her hands. Had the doctor given her something similar?

Rubbing the pungent oil into his leg, he noted a raw spot and hopped over to put salt water on it, careful not to hiss too loudly lest he wake her.

After getting ready as best he could, he settled down on the narrow strip of rug. He groaned at the feel of the unforgiving floor beneath him, then arranged the sweaters to cover most of his body.

At least this was only for one night. And knowing he'd be waving goodbye to his cousin first thing in the morning would make all the aches and stiffness worth it.

CHAPTER SEVENTEEN

Every joint in her body ached, and not just her hands. Corinne fought to stay asleep, knowing mornings only intensified every single sting and prick.

Her eyes fluttered open, but it was still dark. Only a blessing if she could get back to sleep, but her throat was dry. She needed water.

She tried to roll out of bed, but had to wrestle herself out of the cocoon she'd twisted herself up into. Her first foot hit the floor, but the other hit a large bump, throwing her off balance. She reached for the wall, but it wasn't there. Something clamped around her middle and she yelped.

Her head hit the side table hard, and stars exploded. She whimpered and fell to the floor. When the world stopped moving, she pressed her hands against the hot pain in her head despite the jabbing pinpricks tingling through her fingers. She growled to keep from saying bad words.

"Shhh, shhh."

Was she shushing herself? Then all of a sudden, she realized what had grabbed her.

She wasn't home. This was Nolan's room. His nightstand. There'd been no wall to keep her from falling, and now she was sprawled out on a pile of whatever he'd been lying on beside the bed.

The pounding increased above her brow. She shut her eyes tight and tried hard not to cry.

Harried thumping sounded in the hallway.

"Is everything all right?" a masculine voice called through the door.

She couldn't stop the next whimper that escaped. Had she gashed her head open?

The doorknob rattled, and suddenly she was encased in warmth as blankets were thrown around her.

Nolan jerked her toward him, and she groaned again since the sudden movement made the stars dance.

The door whined open a crack. "Is everything all right, Miss —uh, Mrs. Key?"

"We're fine," came Nolan's rough voice. "We uh—" He cleared his throat. "We fell out of bed. She hit her head."

"For Heaven's sake, you two haven't gone to sleep yet?" Matt's voice was full of derision. "I thought you would've worn yourselves out hours ago."

Her tender forehead was already hot, but now her whole body flushed.

She glanced around trying to orient herself, then realized her top wasn't under the blanket so she pulled the covers up.

Matt was barely visible in the couple of inches the door was open. Had he noticed she was in her shirtwaist buttoned clear up to her neck? Surely he couldn't see much, but the moonlight...

She held her breath, gritting her teeth against the lessening ache in her head.

"Just uh, keep it down, would ya?" The door closed with a click.

A jerky shudder against her left arm drew her attention away from her mortification.

"Are you laughing?" She hissed at Nolan.

He sputtered out, "Sorry."

"You don't sound sorry."

"I don't, now, do I?" And then he lay back on the floor and laughed, muffled only by the hand clamped over his mouth.

"My head doesn't think this is funny." But even as she said so, she couldn't keep the amused embarrassment from her voice. "What he must think..."

Nolan laughed harder and clamped a second hand over his mouth. "Imm orree."

His muted apology only made her give in to her own chuckle, which she immediately regretted. "Oh, my head." She halfheartedly smacked him with her free hand despite her fingers aching about as much as the throbbing above her eye. "You're not helping."

He reached up, making a noticeable effort to curb his amusement. "Here, let me check."

His laughter died. "That's quite the bump already."

Pushing himself up to sit, he pulled her over, his fingers probing gently despite her groans of protestation. "We need light."

He scrambled awkwardly onto the bed, then leaned over to snatch a blanket from the floor to cover himself, allowing her only a moment's glimpse of the odd picture of a one-legged man. He lit the bedside lamp then pulled her up to sit beside him.

"I'm so sorry," he murmured as he pushed the hair gingerly off her face to take a look. "I'd figured sleeping on the rug might put me in danger of being stepped on, but I'd not realized you'd get hurt."

Corinne couldn't answer, choosing instead to breathe through the pulsing ache in her head.

"At least you're not bleeding. I can get ice, but you'll have to be patient. I've got about ten minutes of putting myself back together to do so."

"No." The word didn't jolt her head as badly as she'd expected. "I can do it, just tell me where."

He shifted. "In case Matt didn't go back to bed, you shouldn't go down fully dressed. You'd need to—"

"Oh…" She held her hand against her forehead. The pangs were abating, but ice would reduce the swelling. How was she going to explain this to anybody? Would Matt tell the women?

Her flushed body turned frigid.

"I guess I could use my crutches to go get some ice. They're under the bed, I think." Nolan groaned as he slid to the floor, dragging the blankets with him.

"All right." She curled up on the mattress.

"I'll return soon and then you can get back to sleep. We've got hours before dawn."

The door clicked shut before she recalled she needed a glass of water. But she'd not holler after him.

How on earth could she possibly fall asleep now? More pain wracked her body, her thirst had grown, and the countless places Nolan had touched her felt cold and warm all at the same time.

And far worse, she'd have to face Matt in the morning.

CHAPTER EIGHTEEN

Somehow, Nolan kept up a steady stream of banter at the break-fast table as Corinne tried to gag down the porridge she'd prepared. She concentrated on putting spoon to mouth, keeping her eyes from meeting anyone's.

When Matt had come down while she was stirring oats, she'd sensed exactly when he'd caught sight of her. She could still feel his cold gaze despite her refusal to look at him all morning.

Miss Mortimer and Miss Flower had shown up next, and they'd been unusually quiet. Matt surely wouldn't have been so crass as to share with the ladies what had happened last night. But since her falling out of bed had made enough noise to cause Matt to come check, what might they have overheard?

Corinne reached up to ensure her hair lay across her fore-head. She hadn't been able to completely hide the greenish-purple knot over her right eyebrow.

Neither woman had asked how she'd acquired her goose egg.

"Pass me another apple, Miss Flower." Lilith had refused porridge, sighing loudly over having to make do with fruit.

Not that Corinne could blame her. The gloopy mass had congealed into something wholly unappetizing.

"So," Nolan said. "How's Uncle doing?"

She felt Matt's probing gaze lift off her to answer Nolan.

Corinne sprinkled more cinnamon onto her breakfast, then slid the shaker toward Miss Flower. The mousy young woman seemed to be having a hard time forcing down her breakfast as well.

"Can I get you more milk?" Corinne whispered to Miss Flower.

The young lady shook her head, but smiled her appreciation for the offer. Corinne took her own cup and headed to the ice chest, needing something to do other than stir her unpalatable porridge again.

Matt pushed his half-eaten breakfast to the center of the table. "I doubt Father will believe the news of your wedding. When did you two become interested in each other, exactly?"

Corinne fumbled her cup, the clatter loud against the countertop.

"Uh, it's hard to say." For the first time this morning, Nolan's voice wavered. "We've known each other for some time."

"But how?" Lilith scoffed, shaking her head, muttering something that might have included the word *riffraff*.

Matt's eyes narrowed at Corinne. "Do you know how he lost his leg?"

She turned to face him, but what should she say? If they'd been in love, they would've discussed it. She forced her chin to stay up. "I, uh, never asked."

"So you don't know?"

She threw a wide-eyed look at Nolan. Was she stepping into some sort of trap? "No, cousin, I don't."

"But why wouldn't—"

"That's enough, Matt." Nolan's chair screeched against the planks as he pushed away from the table. "Don't badger my wife."

A thunk of metal against wood startled them all.

"Oh, I'm so sorry!" Miss Flower snatched both her and Lilith's napkins. On the floor beside her chair was the creamer, glugging its thick cool contents onto the floor.

"How could you be so clumsy, Miss Flower?" Lilith frowned as she scanned the table. "Now what am I going to do for a napkin?"

Corinne crossed back to the table, trying to keep herself from glaring at Lilith. She grabbed Nolan's napkin and her own.

"Please, don't worry about it, Mrs. Key. I'll get it." Miss Flower had rescued the creamer and was now blotting the floor. "I'm so sorry about all this."

Corinne kneeled beside her and laid a hand on Miss Flower's back, hoping to stay her frantic movements. "You don't need to be sorry. Accidents happen."

"Of course, of course." She sniffled, but then, as if her brain had a snap of clarity, she gave Corinne a soft, yet intense look.

So she'd dropped the creamer on purpose?

"I'm *so* sorry, Mrs. Key," she whispered.

Corinne nodded to let her know she understood. "I'm sorry, too." More for how financially bad off this woman had to be to put up with Lilith's treatment.

Picking up the now empty creamer, Corinne fortified herself with a deep breath, happy to hear the men's conversation had returned to the trite chatter they'd started out with. Pushing off her knees, she stood and took the soggy napkins from Miss Flower.

"I'm afraid what I told you yesterday about our plans has changed," Matt said. "The women are still going on the afternoon train, but I'll be staying."

Nolan dropped his fork and it clattered off the table. "Might I ask why?" Her husband's teeth barely parted to ask that question. A vein on the right side of his forehead popped up.

Corinne wanted to disappear, but instead, walked to the sink to deposit the sopping wet cloths. How much longer must she endure his presence and frigid glares?

"As you know," Matt's voice was cool. "My heart's always been set on ranching. Your father knew that, hence why he was going to leave me the place. So I intend to inquire after land. I've plenty of money to buy a ranch outright. I don't need this one."

"You should check for places closer to Denver." Nolan's tone was barely civil.

"Considering the debacle with your former mayor, I think I can find a good ranch around here for cheap."

"Why not go home with your girl and let me keep an ear open for you?"

Matt patted him on the arm. "Thank you, but I can see to it myself. Plus, I won't force Lilith to stay here with—" He coughed and looked away. "Well, she'd be more comfortable back home."

Nolan's eyes narrowed dangerously. "Bowen's taking his time, trying his best to get the land his father stole back into the right hands. It's not as if any of those places are up for sale right now."

"I'm sensing you don't want me to stay, cousin. Why's that?"

"Stay as long as you like—in the bunkhouse. I'm only trying to save you from wasting time." Nolan's chair screeched back. "Corinne, would you like to take a walk?"

Her hands stilled and she blinked at how he was scowling at her, though the scowl couldn't be meant for her. She nodded and washed her hands—she'd do anything to escape, too.

"Come." Nolan held out his hand, and she slipped her clammy one into his.

As soon as the door slammed behind them, Nolan released her and stalked off toward the barn as if he'd forgotten her the second he let go.

"Nolan?"

He turned but didn't stop. "I'm sorry. I couldn't take him anymore."

"I understand." She scurried after him. "Do you think he'll actually stay in the bunkhouse?"

"I won't give him a choice. Hopefully that means he'll change his mind about staying. If he doesn't, he'll still be in the house more than we'd like him to be, I'm sure."

Nolan was practically shaking. If they survived this morning with Matt around, they'd survive a few more. She placed a gentle hand on his arm. "Maybe you could walk me out to the cabin you put my things in? I could work on setting it to rights while you go for a ride."

He exhaled forcefully. "A ride wouldn't help me, but I can take you to the cabin. My desire to strangle him should fizzle out by the time we get there." He gave her a lopsided grin and held out his arm, as he had the day he'd walked her to the hotel's restaurant. Though this time, her heart wasn't about to burst out of her chest at what she was contemplating doing, but what she'd already done.

Surely once Matt left, things would settle into a routine that would feel more normal. What she needed to do was forget all about the dynamics of how this unusual partnership should play out and get to work. "Do you have any books on ranching I could read? I don't want to end up as bad at it as you say Matt is."

"I think you'd have to try really hard to accomplish that." He started them down a path that wandered away from the back of the house. "I don't have any books, though. Most learn by doing, but I have some battered copies of *The Prairie Farmer* in the rolltop desk if you'd like to flip through them. There's not much on ranching, but I'm sure you could glean something from them."

"Thank you." And there'd be no flipping about it. She'd study them front to back, and if they didn't explain enough, she'd purchase a subscription.

Over by the fence line, a familiar-looking, gangly young man ambled along. Nolan's dog followed at his heels.

She squinted. The dark, limp hair. The worn clothing. "Is that Timothy O'Conner?"

After his involvement this past spring with the cattle rustlers, she'd only seen Timothy once after he'd graduated. She'd overheard Mrs. Tate say no one would hire him. She'd assumed Timothy had been sent off to live with relatives.

"That's him." Nolan waved at Timothy who turned to head their way. "If you're worried about him working for us, don't be. He's grateful for the job, so much so, he's like a completely different person. Much less sullen. And before you think I pay him so poorly he can't dress himself, he gives most of his money to his mother."

"Maybe we could gift him a new set of clothes."

"He might accept that at Christmas." Nolan leaned closer. "Take care not to stare at his face. He's self-conscious."

"I wouldn't." How she could empathize at the moment with his blemish-covered face. She touched the bruise on her forehead and turned to look at Nolan, stopping short when she realized how close he was.

He reached up and gently pulled down her hand. He then smoothed the hair she'd left out of her simple bun to lay more fully across her forehead.

She stilled as his thumb skimmed over her eyebrow. His fingers, calloused, yet gentle, brushed her hair back to anchor it behind her ear.

He looked down at her—his gaze entirely too soft. She took a quick step back but his arm was still looped around hers so she didn't get far.

"I'm sorry," he whispered.

She started to shake her head, but stopped so as not to mess up her hair. "Nothing to be sorry about."

"It doesn't look that bad."

She couldn't help rolling her eyes. "Now you're lying to

make me feel better."

Nolan stiffened. "I wouldn't."

The young man stopped in front of them and grinned wide. He needed to shave off that scraggly mustache. It did little for his appearance.

"I'd heard you'd married, boss." He looked toward her, shoving away the bangs hanging over his eyes. "Even heard it was Miss Stillwater, but I wouldn't have believed it without seeing her."

His eyes glimmered and he reached out to shake her hand. "You must be something. The men said he was dead set against anybody even mentioning a woman they thought would be good for him. Should've known he already had his cap set on a lady pretty enough to rival an angel. Took a while to convince you, eh?"

Corinne couldn't allow Timothy's smooth talk to puff her up. He likely would've said that to any woman Nolan brought home.

Though after Matt and Lilith's treatment of her this morning, maybe flattery wasn't so terrible. "I bet you say that to all the women on the dance floor."

"Naw, I only try flattering the young ones. Mature ladies don't fall for my lines."

Nolan snorted. "You do realize you just completely ruined the compliment you gave her?"

Tim's face scrunched in confusion.

"You called her old."

"No, I called her mature."

"'Bout the same, I reckon."

Timothy swiped off his hat. "I'm sorry, Mrs. Key. I meant those younger than myself. I don't ever try dancing with anyone—"

She waved at him to stop. "I think I appreciated the second observation more than the first. I can trust someone who tells me the truth without thinking whether or not they should."

"Yes, ma'am, but my mama told me to be kind as well, and I—"

"What you said wasn't mean. Sometimes it's good to be reminded of the unflattering truth."

"I've not made my mama very proud my whole life." Tim dragged the brim of his hat through his hand, his eyes now downcast. "I've been aiming to try harder."

She shook her head to show him there were no hard feelings. "What do you do around here, Mr. O'Conner?"

"Whatever you or the others tell me to." He plopped his hat back onto his head. "As pleased as I am to meet you, Mrs. Key, if I'm to keep my job, I better shut my trap and get back to Sal."

"Goodbye, Tim."

"Ma'am."

She couldn't help but smile as he walked away. The young man's lowly upbringing, troubled past, and uncomely exterior might have kept others from hiring him, but she'd rather have him around than Matt. The thought of whom made her frown as they started back down the path. "How long do you think your cousin will stay?"

Nolan's arm tensed beneath hers. "Not long."

"Do you think he'll find a place near here?"

"I hope not." He pointed to a building with a collapsed lean-to barely hanging on to its side. Rolls of fencing, posts, and farming implements were stacked nearby at haphazard angles. "This is it."

Her frown deepened. She'd assumed they were going to walk past this building.

"Sorry about everything piled up. We wanted to build a paddock over here, but haven't had the time. And we had to pull out our junk to put in your j—I mean, your things. It's not clean either. I hadn't expected to—"

"No more apologies." She held up her hand and assessed the place. Considering the crumbling chimney bricks, the fireplace might very well be unusable, and was that a hole in the roof? At least it wasn't as bad as the old barn in the east pasture that was half collapsed. "I had been hoping to work out here."

"You can. We'll do repairs."

"I see." She quickly made a tally of what needed fixing. No wonder he'd been reluctant to part with that hundred dollars.

He climbed the porch stairs and leaned against the railing. His leg had to be hurting if he was trusting that sun-bleached, splintered wood to hold him up. "We'll fix the roof first thing so nothing inside gets ruined."

"If I can do anything to help, let me know, but I realize the ranch comes first." On her first tour of the place, he'd told her some of the chores he hoped she'd take over. "I know I've agreed to take turns cooking for the men and doing all the household chores—"

His throat clearing made her hold up a hand to stop him from giving her the "take it easy" lecture again.

"Yes, yes, I'll rest enough not to damage my hands, but I'd like to work on improving the chicken and egg production right away—seems like something I could handle. How can I get those hens you told me about to lay in the coop instead of the yard so I don't have to chase down eggs?"

He chuckled. "I doubt that's possible."

"Your father thought it wasn't possible to see you married, and yet here you are."

"Yes, here I am."

She'd expected to hear some bitterness in his voice, but he seemed pleased.

Her neck warmed at the soft look he was giving her, the same as earlier when he'd tucked her hair behind her ear. And last night when he'd massaged her pain away.

If she wanted to survive, she had to stop reacting to him like this.

She *would* corral her feelings. Just like she would round up a few headstrong chickens. She must if she didn't want her heart to be crushed again.

CHAPTER NINETEEN

When Corinne went back to scribbling in her notebook instead of gazing out at the passing landscape as they rode into town, Nolan resituated his leg.

He'd pushed himself too far this past week.

If only Corinne had taken it easy, he'd have rested some. But it was as if she were afraid he'd deny her the profits he'd promised if she didn't do all the chores.

When she'd asked to go into town, he'd hoped that meant he could sit on the bench outside the mercantile and visit with whoever was in town as she shopped. But then she'd informed him she wanted to get her things from the laundry.

The wagon thumped and bumped over a huge rock, and the groan he'd been holding escaped against his will. He needed to watch where he was going.

He tried to catch a glimpse of what Corinne was writing. "What are you figuring up?"

She gave him a quick glance. "Oh, just what to do with the chickens."

"Would you like my help? I do have some knowledge of livestock."

She smiled—a soft smile he hadn't seen before. She continued to scribble, keeping the paper tilted so he couldn't see it. "Thanks, but I'm just coming up with possibilities right now."

A few agonizing bumps later, she quit writing and stared off into space.

By unspoken agreement, they'd been pleasantly, but purposely, avoiding talking to each other beyond what was necessary. She couldn't be a more pleasant houseguest—unlike his cousin. Except he'd never had a guest who slept in his bed. After her disastrous fall, she'd insisted he sleep beside her. Hence why they'd neatly avoided each other, especially in the evenings. For as long as Matt was there, they'd have to room together. He might've been banished to the bunkhouse to sleep, but Matt wasn't leaving the main house until late evening—likely to minimize the amount of time he had to spend with the 'help.' And they weren't too certain Matt wouldn't show up in the house early in the morning and knock on his bedroom door for any number of stupid reasons. If only he'd leave sooner rather than later.

But surely Corinne wasn't working so hard to exhaust herself so she'd fall asleep immediately—afraid he might ask her for something she'd explicitly told him she wasn't going to give him just because she was in his room.

Did she not trust him when he said he wouldn't require that of her? He'd agreed to the "no romance" part of this deal, but it wasn't his fault Matt was still staying with them.

Well, perhaps it was. But if he could keep Matt from being an enemy by helping him find a ranch, then maybe his cousin wouldn't look into ways to take his. Matt would likely sell the place within a year anyway once he realized he hadn't the work ethic to keep a ranch going.

Though Matt wasn't his favorite person, once Lilith left, the man had turned back to his normal self. Still arrogant, but now more interested in puffing himself up in Corinne's eyes than tearing her down. Lilith's presence had made him extra unbearable.

He glanced over at Corinne. The bruise above her brow was now a pale yellow that could be seen every time the breeze ruffled her hair.

Though everything between them had been platonic—he'd only kissed her forehead that once—there was something comforting, yet unsettling, about falling asleep to the soft breathing of a woman.

He'd looked forward to it every night.

How had he not realized how lonely he was? As boss, he'd not let himself get too close to his men. And of course, his father had always been cold. Uncle Matthias visited occasionally, but Matt had been their only regular guest. And though Jacob was his closest neighbor now, their friendship was new.

But going from lonely to a woman in his bed?

The last two nights, particular thoughts he tried to suppress kept him from falling asleep.

Maybe Corinne had the right of it. He needed to work much, much harder so he'd enter dreamland the second he lay down.

He winced as he tried to readjust his leg. "Corinne?"

"Huh?" She startled as if awakened from a dream of her own. Had she been sleeping sitting up?

He held the reins out toward her. Timothy had shown her how to drive the team two days ago. Apparently, she was a quick learner. "Take these for a second, would you?"

"All right."

He stopped short. "Hold on a minute. What's that?"

He took her hand and inspected the bright red oval of raw skin that lay between her thumb and finger.

"Oh, nothing." She slipped her hand from his grasp and took the reins.

"The doctor told you to rest your hands. If you've got broken blisters—"

"He said to differentiate movement. Next time, I'll wear gloves."

"And how is your pain?"

She shrugged. "It's supposed to go away. Doc said it would once I stopped doing repetitive motions."

"Mucking's the epitome of repetitive motion." Timothy had chastised her twice this week for doing his job instead of finding him.

She shrugged again.

He pressed his mouth shut. Considering he wasn't following doctor's orders either, he had no right to order her to stop. He grimaced as they thumped hard into a hole.

Perhaps Timothy's boast about her being a natural driver had been more kind than true.

Once they reached the laundry's backyard, Nolan helped her down. "I have a few things I need to do before I can help."

He waved to Leah, who'd opened the back door, and took his leave, walking off slowly so as not to stress his leg. But with each step closer to Doctor Ellis's, he had a harder time keeping the grimace off his face.

The doctor took one look at him from behind his desk and shook his head. "Go straight into an exam room, Mr. Key."

Nolan limped inside and let loose a hiss as he climbed onto the table.

Doctor Ellis came in, without his ever-present clipboard, hands planted on his hips as if he were about to lecture a child.

"I know you're not going to be happy with me." Nolan stripped off his trousers—he'd been through enough examinations to know Doc wouldn't take his word for the state of his leg. Though it had been nearly eight years since he'd come in with a sore this bad. "I know I'm supposed to take my leg off the minute the flesh gets raw—"

"Then why'd you come into town? You could've sent your wife in if you needed a poultice." He gathered up his bottles and bandaging cloth.

"I have to help her load the rest of her things from the laundry."

He set his iodine bottle down with a clatter. "You will do no such thing."

Nolan kept his mouth shut.

Doc rolled back the leg of his linen drawers and pulled off the wadded bandage Nolan had stuck to it this morning. "Not good."

Nolan sucked air through his teeth. The gentle cleaning he'd expected felt as if the doctor was purposely scouring in order to express his disappointment. "I promise I'll take my leg off once I get home."

"Pearl!" Doctor Ellis walked away and called out the door. "Bring Mr. Key the crutches we have in the supply closet."

"I don't need—"

"Yes, you do, Mr. Key."

Mrs. Ellis walked in with a pair of crutches that looked six inches too short for him.

"Those crutches are worse than the ones I have at home."

"Which you should've used for your trip in." He started applying something so pungent Nolan's head began to ache.

"I'll be fine."

The doctor gave him a narrow-eyed stare. "Don't make me carry you back to your wagon."

Nolan scoffed. "You're too old to do that."

"I'm more capable than you."

Nolan couldn't help the sharp inhale at the insult. The man was in his mid-seventies.

"Sorry." The doctor's face softened a touch. "But I don't give orders for no reason. Do you not remember I told you it's entirely possible for you to lose more of your leg if you let it get bad? You can't play with infection. I know the soldiers thought I got some macabre pleasure from sawing off legs, but I never want to do it again."

"I understand." Nolan moved to grab his artificial leg. He might cave to using the crutches, but he wasn't going to do so with an empty pant leg.

Doc pushed him back onto the table. "I'm not done with you yet. Lie down, please."

Nolan tried to comply without scowling at the old man—or the pain.

Doc frowned at Nolan's other leg, and with a hand to his shoulder and the other pressed against his shortened leg, he pushed down.

Nolan flinched. "That hurts."

"That's what I was afraid of. You're not stretching it enough. How are you sleeping on it?"

Lately? Definitely not in any of the positions Doc had advised—not with Corinne in his bed.

"You need to work your hip back to full extension. It's also going to need deep massaging."

"Fine." Though considering the last time he'd endured this, he wasn't looking forward to it. "How often do you want me in?" When Matt was gone, he could go back to sleeping appropriately.

"Do it at home."

"I can't do it myself." Even if he could, he'd not be as merciless to his muscles as Doc was.

"Have your wife do it."

"She—" No way was he letting her put her hands on his bare skin, with him stripped to his drawers. "She doesn't know how."

"I'll teach her."

"She doesn't have time. She's got too much to do."

Doc gave him a funny look.

"I mean, I don't want to burden her with more work. Besides…" He narrowed his eyes at the doctor. "Her hands."

"She can do the stretches and massaging well enough to get

you by between visits. Coming into town every day will take more time away from your ranch than her taking a break from her chores." He moved back to the doorway. "Pearl! Get Mrs. Key from the laundry."

Why did Doc have to keep sending his wife for things Nolan didn't want? He scooted to the edge of the bed and reached for his leg, but the doctor snatched it before he could.

"I'm going to add padding to this, and I'm not done dressing your wound."

Nolan scowled at the doctor's retreating back.

Wait—Corinne was coming.

He grabbed his trousers and began to wriggle them back on.

"Keep them off." Doc turned before heading out the door.

Nolan's fingers curled into the fabric. Mrs. Ellis had seen him in his drawers when she helped her husband. However, Corinne was different.

Not that they'd know.

Gripping the edge of the padded table, he steeled himself for her getting a good look at his mangled stump.

Ten minutes later, a flurry of anxious women's voices filled the waiting room. What had Mrs. Ellis told Corinne to get her that worked up?

His wife came into the room, her brown eyes wide. Her cheeks were flushed beneath the dirt marks on her face, her blond ringlets mussed. "Is it true you could lose the rest of your leg?"

"No."

"Yes." Mrs. Ellis looked out the side of her eye as if he were a child caught in a lie.

"No. It's not."

"Not if he takes care of it," Doc said.

"Thanks, Doc." Nolan gave a sharp nod to Mrs. Ellis.

"Which is not what your husband is doing." The doctor pointed at his leg. "When he's in pain, put your foot down and tell him to rest."

Corinne looked to him with surprise, then scanned him from head to toe. "What signs and symptoms am I to look for? How much rest does he need?"

"Any pain's too much. Discomfort is to be expected, not pain. This open sore…" He pushed back the end of Nolan's drawers over his thigh.

Nolan forced himself not to yank his leg away or tell them both to get out. How could they talk about him like he wasn't there?

"I shouldn't ever see an abrasion this raw. Before it gets like this, he needs to be off his leg."

She picked up his artificial one.

Nolan looked away. As if he didn't feel emasculated already, having Corinne hold up his lifeless limb certainly made him wish he wasn't in the room.

"Is his leg causing it? Is he wearing it incorrectly?" She ran her hand inside the shell that cupped the end of his leg as if fascinated.

"I've added more padding to the interior but what was there should've been sufficient. No amount of padding will keep him from getting abrasions if he wears it too long. Sitting around doesn't matter as much as standing and moving, of course."

Doc turned to him and put a hand on his shoulder. "Lie back, Nolan."

Figuring it would make him look like a petulant schoolboy not to, he lay back, keeping his protest swallowed since they both seemed intent on dismissing him from this conversation.

"He needs his muscles stretched to keep them from permanently contracting. Like so. Without his leg…"

Doc had certainly gotten his wish. He would never again let his leg get this bad. He'd not endure this humiliation a second time.

After the two of them left the room discussing how the padding was secured inside his leg, Nolan yanked on his trousers.

How could Corinne take Doc's side and leave him to hobble through town with an empty pant leg?

She was his wife, not the doc's nurse. Well, more business partner, but partners didn't force personal decisions on the other. She should've asked him what he wanted.

He slid off the bed, grabbed the crutches, and forged into the waiting room.

"Wait, Nolan."

Ignoring Corinne, he kept going.

"Thanks, Doctor Ellis. I'll make sure Nolan rests."

He struggled to get out the door, but thankfully got through before Corinne opened it for him. He stabbed his crutches into the boardwalk and swung forward at a quick clip.

She rushed up to him. "Why don't you stay here and I get the wagon?"

"I don't need the wagon." He kept thumping forward, refusing to look up at anyone passing.

Maddeningly, she kept pace beside him in silence.

A few moments later, she leaned toward him and whispered, "People are staring."

"Of course they are. I've never come into town without my leg. Since you and the doc took it from me—"

"It's not that. I think it's because I'm carrying your leg, and it's glaringly obvious you're refusing my help."

He stopped and huffed. "Sorry. You're not the reason I'm stomping through town one-legged. I shouldn't have let it get this bad."

"How often does this happen?"

Tilting his head up to the sky, he neatly avoided anyone's pitiful gazes. "Not often. It hasn't been like this since I was young."

"What caused it this time?"

"Don't worry about it. It won't happen again."

Him and his blasted desire to keep his new wife from

146

outshining him. Maybe he shouldn't have married such a hard worker. His ego evidently couldn't handle letting a woman outperform him.

And yet, why was he so compelled to be sure Corinne didn't think him a weakling when he knew full well he wasn't?

CHAPTER TWENTY

"More coffee, please."

Corinne frowned at the top of Matt's head. He hadn't even looked up from his reading, only pushed his mug toward her.

Though he had said please.

Gingerly, she picked up the pot and poured him another cup. Her hands had been getting better, but packing at the laundry yesterday had taken its toll. Nolan had balked at how much she'd done, but with the doctor telling him to keep his leg off for a week or more, he hadn't been able to help.

Last night, she'd fallen asleep before he'd come up, so she hadn't massaged his leg as the doctor ordered.

How effective could she be though, if her hands seized up? Yet, it had to be done.

After putting down the coffee, she walked to the stairwell and listened. When would Nolan stir? Or should she abandon Matt, go upstairs, and take care of things?

She'd been embarrassed at the doctor's yesterday—less because of Nolan's state of undress, and more because she'd felt like a fool. The doctor had told her when she saw Nolan hurting that badly, she should put her foot down and make sure he stayed off his leg.

But she'd not noticed. Not until the doctor had forced Nolan to lie back, and in that unguarded moment, she'd caught a glimpse of pain in his eyes.

Perhaps she should insist he rest whenever he snapped at someone. He'd certainly been testy at the doctor's office when he wasn't bothering to cover up the pain, and there'd been that dull look in his eyes. She'd have to peer into his eyes more often —or start anyway. It wasn't as if they'd taken up gazing at each other like lovers.

"Nolan still sleeping?" The paper rustled behind her.

She turned but decided not to answer. She didn't want Matt interrogating her about their morning routine—which by silent agreement was done as separately as possible.

Matt reached for the sugar bowl and doctored his coffee. "He's working too hard. I don't recall him ever sleeping as late as he has this week. It's a shame this ranch has become too much for him to handle."

"I think he handles it well." She dried the last of the ranch hands' breakfast dishes—they'd been in for breakfast and back to their chores an hour ago.

"You know, maybe you should convince him to give this place up for his own good—for your good, too."

"Right." She couldn't keep the sarcasm out of her voice.

"I'm not as bad as Nolan has made me seem. He squawks when I come to visit, yes, but I'm a good rancher. His father thought so." Matt sighed. "I understand Nolan's dislike for me —I was his dad's favorite. Nolan has had a hard time seeing me as anything other than the enemy."

She started putting away the dishes. Nolan's father *had* willed his place to Matt.

Yet, even if Nolan were wrong about Matt's inability to ranch, it didn't mean her husband was incapable.

"Though the will states the place isn't mine if Nolan's married, it can still change hands. You could convince him he doesn't need to keep up the bravado. I saw him hobble in yesterday." He tsked before taking a leisurely sip of his coffee.

"He won't give it up."

"I realize he's got a lot of money in it. But if you convince him to relinquish it to me, I can offer you a nice parting gift—I have loads of cash, you know."

She kept her back turned so she could roll her eyes with as much exaggeration as she wished.

"I could give you enough to live on for a year or two. You should consider moving to Denver or another big city where he can use that head of his for mathematics. That's why this place is doing well." Matt's voice held less haughtiness than usual. "But the manual labor he's doing to make up for his father's absence will catch up to him. My father could talk to a dean at the University of Denver, maybe get Nolan a break in tuition. You see, Nolan's dad might have preferred me, but my father has always preferred him…" Matt's voice caught, and she glanced over her shoulder.

He was staring into his coffee, looking genuinely gloomy.

She shook her head. "I don't think he'll ever give the ranch up. He's attached."

"As am I." He looked up and gave her a wan smile. "I know it's hard for Nolan to admit I'm better than him at something. But it's as if we were switched at birth—our fathers and the vocations we were raised to take over were meant for each other. If he needs help going in a direction that better suits him, know that my father will do whatever he can to help."

Even if this whole spiel was just an attempt by Matt to get the ranch back, it was somewhat nice—in a condescending sort of way. "I'll let Nolan know."

"Be sure you don't mention I advised it. It's best when advice doesn't come from someone you dislike."

"I'll take that into consideration." She scanned the table. "How much cream is left?"

His eyes dulled at her change of topic, but he turned to

glance over at the wall clock. "Enough for two. Is Nolan coming down at all?"

Nine-thirty *was* extremely late for him. Matt still lounging about wasn't surprising, but Nolan hadn't left the house later than eight since she'd been around.

She dried her hands on a towel. "Doc said he should stay off his leg for a few days, so maybe he's following orders for once."

Matt tsked again and stood. "As I mentioned, there's no shame in admitting when you're in over your head. If your husband didn't practically seethe whenever I'm around, I'd have proposed a partnership, but some men can't be reasoned with." He grabbed his hat and overcoat. "Be wise, Corinne. If you need to liquidate this place, you'll have to figure that out before I buy my own. I don't need two ranches."

She watched Matt head outdoors, whistling.

Matt couldn't really be putting Nolan's desires above his own, but did that mean nothing he'd said had merit?

Regardless, what was best for Nolan right now was to get his leg back into shape.

After sweeping the floor, she headed upstairs. At his room, she pushed the door open slowly as not to wake him if he were asleep.

Nolan was sitting up in bed, reading his Bible, fully dressed.

"Oh, I hadn't heard you stir. Were you waiting for Matt to leave before coming down?"

Truth be told, it had been a much more pleasant morning without the two men together.

"No, just resting like I'm supposed to. Told Sal yesterday what I wanted done. They're working already, I assume?"

"Yes, they were in and out quickly. I don't think they enjoy Matt's company any more than you do."

"I don't doubt it."

"But maybe we shouldn't disregard everything he says."

Nolan stilled, his eyebrows rose as if she'd just frozen him in place by tossing a bucket of ice on him.

"I mean, though he rubs you wrong, maybe he isn't out to get you."

Nolan relaxed a little. "I don't believe he's out to get me, but I do believe he's out to get whatever he can for himself. If that hurts me, well, he just might convince himself it wouldn't."

She chewed on her bottom lip. Did Matt have no redeeming qualities deep down?

"Did you need something?"

She stepped into the room. "Yes, or well, you do. I'm here to do the massaging—"

He lifted his hand to stop her. "Not necessary."

"Huh? But I thought…"

He looked out the window. "Doc's high-handed. Treats me like a child in need of a nose wiping just because I don't follow his every order."

"I know that's true." She stretched out her aching fingers and frowned at them. "But considering how he was talking about your leg, it seemed serious."

"Don't worry. From now on, I'll take care of myself like the doctor wants."

"Promise?"

He shrugged, but then nodded.

Her chest lost its tension. "All right. If you're going to be up here today, do you mind if I go into Armelle and get the last of my things?"

He shifted on the bed. "I don't need the wagon, so that's fine."

"Good, I'll finish my chores, then—"

"No need. My men can handle your chores. So if you need to stay in town all day, feel free to do so."

"Oh, well, all right." She tried not to let his words make her feel worthless. Had none of the work she'd done this past week been helpful?

"I'll be on my way then."

Nolan dragged his open Bible back onto his lap. "Say hi to Leah for me."

"Of course." She backed out of the room.

After heading outside and getting Timothy to hitch up the horse, Corinne took her time driving into town.

The little pit that had started forming when Nolan said he didn't need her help grew as empty as the wide open space surrounding her. Which was ridiculous. She knew he didn't need her. He'd initially offered her the freedom to do nothing.

Though it wouldn't hurt to feel a bit appreciated.

But if they really didn't need her, maybe she could go back to tinkering.

The swirl of thoughts she'd had at the doctor's office bombarded her again. Ways to make the hinge of Nolan's fake knee work more efficiently, give him a smoother gait. Ways to better pad the socket of his false leg so he wouldn't get an open sore again. Ways to make the leg less heavy.

If she could make things better for him that way, she could prove she wasn't just a warm body bearing his name and eating his food.

Behind the laundry, she unhitched the horse. But before she could walk her over to the sole patch of grass in the dirt yard, the sound of a wail pierced the muggy air.

Dropping the reins, Corinne rushed inside. "Leah?"

"No, no, no!" A muffled sob and then a groan.

In the washroom, Leah stood with her head bowed, with most of her brunette hair fallen out of her bun. Her hands gripped the side of the tin tub as if she'd fall in if she let go.

"What's wrong?"

Leah didn't look up, but pulled wet fabric out of the water and plopped it on the counter next to several other soggy lumps.

Corinne glanced at them and frowned—too much bluing. "It'll likely come out. But it's best to work on it right away. The longer you let it set, the harder it is to remove."

"I don't know what I was thinking." She frantically gestured at the wet clothing. "Mrs. Turner wants all this done by the time her husband arrives on the train, but I went and ruined them all."

With a hand to Leah's shoulder, Corinne gave her a reassuring squeeze. "They can be fixed."

"Not in time. They live so far out of town, it's not as if she can return for them soon—and that's not taking into account everything else that has come in." She gestured to the bags against the wall.

Yesterday, Leah had been close to catching up. "It's normal to make mistakes when you're rushing. Mrs. Turner will understand."

"I don't have time for mistakes." Leah sniffed.

If it wasn't for the fact that bluing was difficult to get out, she'd have told Leah to go home and rest.

She completely sympathized with wanting to curl up under the covers and cry but having to tackle piles of work instead. "The two of us can do it."

Leah looked toward her with sad eyes. "Are you sure? You gave me this job so you wouldn't have to do it anymore. I know how to do laundry, I promise, but I was woolgathering. I should've—"

"I know you know what you're doing." She started pulling out the rest of the clothing Leah had ruined, bracing herself so Leah wouldn't see her grimace when she wrung the water out. "What happened, happened. But now's the time to make something else happen."

"I'm sorry you're having to help me instead of whatever you came in for." Leah sniffed, but pulled out more wet fabric. "But I appreciate it."

"Don't mention it. I wasn't needed at home." She could come back tomorrow for her remaining items.

Doctor Ellis walked in and frowned at the two of them, stopping midstride. "I thought you were putting laundry behind you, Mrs. Key—and becoming a wife."

When would the man realize marriage didn't mean a woman could shun difficult chores? "Mrs. Whitsett needed my help today, but don't worry. Once I finish helping, and then packing the last of my things, I'll go back to regular ol' household laundry."

The doctor looked around. "Who's going to help you load your wagon? If Nolan's here, I told him—"

"No, he's at home resting like you ordered. I came alone."

Frowning, the doctor clicked his tongue. "You two are quite the pair, never asking for help, suffering like martyrs instead of obeying doctor's orders."

"That's not—" Well, maybe it was true. When was the last time she'd sought help?

The man sighed and leaned his wiry frame against the counter. "Spencer's supposed to clean my office today, but I don't have much for him to do, so I'll send him over once he takes out the trash."

"I can't—" Well, even if Nolan hadn't much ready cash, Spencer might accept something from the ranch in exchange, like a carton of eggs—though what nine-year-old boy wanted that? "I guess if Leah can't pay him, I could."

"You don't have to pay anyone for me." Leah turned to the doctor and gave him a nod. "I could use him."

"Good." The doctor pulled out his money clip. "I came for my suit coat. Is it done?"

"Yes." Leah shook the water from her hands and crossed to the clothing rack.

"How did working on Nolan's leg go last night?" The doctor turned to Corinne, awaiting an answer.

She quit wringing the shirt she was washing, afraid Doc Ellis might notice how stiff her hands were and order her to stop. "He went to bed too late to do anything last night."

The doctor scowled. "What about this morning?"

"He assured me he did it."

"*He* did it?"

"Yes." Why was he so upset?

"You need to do it."

She blinked. "I thought—"

"I wouldn't have brought you into my office yesterday if Nolan could do it himself."

Corinne's jaw hardened. How dare Nolan make her look like she'd pawned off her responsibilities. "Sorry, I didn't know."

Well, she did know, but she'd taken Nolan at his word. "I'll take care of things once I get home."

"You need to stretch his leg every day he doesn't see me, Mrs. Key." And with that, the doctor took his coat from Leah and walked out.

Plunging her hands back into the water, Corinne started scrubbing.

"Are you all right?" Leah's voice was soft and worried.

Looking down, Corinne realized she was strangling a delicate chemise. She forced her fingers to loosen and slow, ignoring the tingling she'd aggravated. If she had to massage Nolan's leg tonight… "I'm fine, yes. Let's get to work."

Seemed Nolan *did* need her help—but didn't want it.

Unfortunately for him, he needed to be at full capacity to run their ranch profitably—and she intended to make sure he was.

CHAPTER TWENTY-ONE

In the barn, Nolan poured fresh oats into a bucket while trying to keep his crutches beneath him.

Blacky sneezed multiple times. "Goodness, girl, what's gotten into you?"

He hobbled over and patted the mule's neck. She put her muzzle in her oat sack and started sneezing again.

Opening the gate, he led her out into the fading daylight, thankful she wasn't a spirited youngster anymore. The pack animal sneezed a few more times, but soon enough, she changed back to her normal self as she ripped up grass.

Nolan headed back inside, looking for something out of the ordinary. Had Corinne hung a bouquet of ragweed from the rafters?

He examined every corner of Blacky's stall, then stuck his hand into the oats and recoiled. Pulling out a handful, he ran his fingers through it. Was it his imagination or were they wet? He looked up to the roof, but saw no pinpricks of fading sunlight— not that it would've mattered if there'd been a gigantic hole, considering it hadn't rained in a while. He grabbed another handful and smelled them. They sure didn't smell good. Had a critter relieved itself in the oats? Taking out the bag, Nolan dumped the ruined grain outside.

Wagon wheels crunching on the road made him look up.

Corinne. With an empty wagon. Surely she hadn't come back earlier today, unpacked, and returned to Armelle without him noticing.

He started toward her, but stopped short. Was she glaring at him or squinting against the dying sun?

Circling around him, she pulled into the barn, and he followed her inside. Letting his eyes readjust, he was surprised to find she'd already jumped down and was unhitching the horse. What fire was driving her?

"I'd thought you'd have a load of—"

"Are you supposed to be out and about?" She swished past him and started unbuckling the horse.

"I'm not an invalid." He moved to help her unhitch.

She narrowed her eyes at him over the top of the horse. "And *I'm* not a sluggard."

He flinched at her vehemence. Had someone in town said she was? "If anyone thinks you're lazy, they're addled."

Her dress was wrinkled oddly in places, and a few tendrils of her hair hung undone—not too unusual for Corinne. She'd obviously worked hard all day—yet at what?

She didn't look bad, though—the glow in her cheeks made her a touch prettier. Though with the way she was yanking off straps, the attractive flush in her cheeks might be from whatever was annoying her. "Be careful. Don't—"

"Do you know who lectured me for not doing as I ought?" She stomped over to the wall to hang up tack.

It'd been a long time since he'd lived with a female in the house, but he remembered well enough this tone meant he was in for it. "Whoever it was, it doesn't matter."

"The doctor. He's the one who got onto me for shirking duties." She turned to glare at him, her hands jammed on her hips. "You can't massage and stretch your leg by yourself—and you knew it."

"I, uh—"

"And I had to do laundry all day." She grabbed Buttermilk's curry comb. "You thought my hands hurt earlier? Well, they're worse now, but that doesn't matter. I told him I hadn't stretched your leg, repeating what you'd said about doing it yourself. I took your word for it."

He'd not said he could do his stretches on his own, but it was likely best to keep that to himself right now. "Why were you doing laundry?"

"Leah needed help, but that's not what matters." She shook a finger at him. "You're getting a massage whether you want one or not."

The sparks in her eyes and her exaggerated expressions were adorable. An angry woman likely wouldn't cotton to being called adorable, though. Even if it was the truth and not romantic nonsense.

"Why are you grinning like that?"

He pressed his lips together.

"You heard me? You're not avoiding this again."

He couldn't help but loose a chuckle. "All right, you win. But then, I don't think any man would fight too hard if a woman like you so vehemently wants to get her hands on his body."

The anger drained from her face like water from a washtub. She opened her mouth but then closed it.

He winked and then hobbled out. Without a doubt, she wouldn't pester him again after that.

But goodness, for a second there, he'd wished...

No, he'd not start thinking about how he could enjoy an actual marriage, because she'd been clear she didn't want one. He was and would remain content with the partnership.

And with how exhausted he was after hobbling around the ranch this afternoon, he should fall straight to sleep tonight.

Which was the best thing for the both of them until she was out of his room.

The mantel clock chimed ten and Corinne kept up a steady, unhurried stitch as she mended the last item from Nolan's pile. She would triple stitch his nightshirt if necessary to keep from going to bed before he did.

Matt glanced up again, looking between both of them and the clock, before straightening his paper with a shake and going back to reading.

The satisfied grin Nolan had sported throughout dinner had waned the later she'd sat up with them darning and mending. He was still reading his book, but his page turns were slower than when he'd started this evening. He'd only attempted to remind her of the time once, to which she'd responded with a smile and a 'yes, dear' before returning to her sewing.

Shockingly, Matt had chosen to read the county paper to himself rather than ponder aloud every article, filling the room with nonstop, pretentious chatter. Seemed he knew there was a showdown going on.

And she was going to win it.

During dinner, Nolan's self-satisfied smile had made it known he'd somehow believed he'd gotten the upper hand. After he'd left the barn, while the heat alternately drained from and returned to her cheeks, she'd worried Nolan was like his cousin, thinking he was irresistible to women. Not that Matt outright flirted with her, but he certainly preened and flattered himself when talking about the women in his acquaintance, as if he couldn't help but attract feminine admiration.

Nolan had never struck her as an overly confident man, despite his decent looks and being a man of property. She'd definitely never heard him say anything so shocking as what he'd said to her in the barn—with a rakish grin to boot.

She pulled out a knot and contemplated throwing a pillow at him.

Talk to her as a business partner? Sure, she'd hear him out.

But what he'd said in the barn was not how one talks to a business partner.

She frowned at her empty teacup and glanced at the clock. She shouldn't have more to drink, but she was running out of things to do. How long did the men usually stay up anyway? "Would anyone like more tea?"

"None for me." Matt stayed immersed in his paper.

"Don't you think you should turn in, darlin'?" Nolan's expression looked halfway worried, halfway exhausted.

She shot him a sly smile. "I'm waiting for you." She headed for the kitchen but stopped by his side. She leaned down to whisper in his ear. "As you mentioned earlier, I can't wait to get my hands on you."

He fidgeted uncomfortably, the tips of his ears turning crimson.

Good, that ought to teach him to embarrass her in an effort to get his way. She straightened and swished past.

Behind her, Nolan's throat clearing sounded almost like he was choking. "Uh, I hope you don't mind if I turn in before you head out, Matt. Good night."

Without waiting, she stomped up the stairs, knowing it'd take him plenty of time to follow on crutches. She needed the time to sit on the bed and breathe before he arrived. Just because she was miffed at him didn't mean she should lay into him. She'd gotten her point across—she hoped.

The door eased open minutes later, pushed in by one of Nolan's crutches. He looked straight at her as he swung his body inside. "Good job."

"Good job?"

"Yeah." He awkwardly shut the door behind him. "If Matt harbored any doubts about us, they're likely gone now."

"That's not why I said that."

161

"I guess I had it coming."

"Correct." She stood and pointed to the spot she'd just vacated. "Along with this. You may not want a nurse, but you're getting one."

He stilled.

All right, so maybe she hadn't sat and breathed long enough. But snapped or gently worded, he wasn't going to avoid the command.

"I don't need a nurse."

"If you don't get better, then we don't make money. The doctor explained if you lost more of your leg or its mobility—if you don't die of infection first—it would take a while to readjust, and we don't have time for that."

His face didn't soften, but he did nod. However, he didn't move.

She took another step away from the bed so he could pass by her more easily. "Don't make me take your clothes off."

His eyes widened and then he suddenly lost all his coloring.

Her ears grew hot. She likely looked as silly as he had downstairs with red ears. But he still didn't move. As if he were … more afraid than embarrassed.

"Nolan, I've seen your leg at the doctor's office, remember?" She could understand not wanting to be vulnerable in front of a near stranger, but they hadn't much choice. "If the doctor or I don't do this, then a nurse would. Think of me as a nurse."

He shook his head adamantly. "I didn't ask for you to be that."

"I know, but we're stuck." She took a step toward him but stopped. He'd likely consider an encouraging shoulder squeeze from her a sign of pity.

"I can—"

"No, you can't. And don't you dare try to embarrass me again in an attempt to avoid this." She patted the bed. "I'm your business partner, remember? No romantic nonsense. If this is necessary to ensure our ranch runs smoothly, we push aside our 'rather nots' and forge on."

He let out a sigh before trudging over to the bed, as much as a man on crutches could trudge. Once he leaned his crutches against the footboard, he took a deep breath and then moved to undo his belt.

Good.

She turned her back. "I'll get the salve and whatever else we might need."

Slipping out the door, she prayed Matt had left for the bunkhouse. She'd rather not have to talk to him again tonight.

The parlor was thankfully dark. From the linen closet, she gathered up towels, soap, and water.

Upon her return, Nolan had propped himself up against the headboard, his arms crossed over his chest, a quilt thrown across his lap.

Corinne arranged her things on the bedside table, then reached for the quilt.

Nolan's hand grabbed hers. "I'll do it."

He pulled the corner of his blanket higher, uncovering just the end of his leg's stub. "That's all you need to tend to."

She eyed him, but decided to keep her words to herself for the moment. The doctor had been clear that she was to hold onto both of his legs while putting his shortened one through its full range of motion. After squeezing out the excess water from her rag, she unwrapped the bandage and began to bathe the wound that was slightly weeping, though the scab looked good.

The crickets' chirping and the clock's ticking mixed in with the swishing of water and Nolan's controlled breathing. She patted his leg dry and lathered on the salve. Once she cut off the end of the new bandage and tied it, she rolled up the excess. "I need you to slide down now."

He stared straight ahead. The muscles in his arms bunched even more where they were crossed tight across his chest.

Was he in pain? The doctor had made her realize she wasn't

good at noticing such. Somehow she doubted he wanted to talk about it, so she moved herself off the bed and with a firm hand, nudged him to comply.

He wriggled down to lie flat and closed his eyes.

Without asking, she tugged up the blanket and set to work.

At his low growl, she stopped to look at him. His lips were screwed up as if he'd just eaten the most disgusting thing he'd ever put in his mouth.

He must be hurting, but he hadn't asked her to stop. If what she was doing was making things worse, surely he'd tell her. She turned back to her task and worried her lip over how stiff and quiet he was.

Though the time felt short, her hands couldn't take much more. With gentle movements, she pulled down the leg of his drawers, noting the bandage was damp where it was still seeping. Neither of them likely wanted to go through the process of re-bandaging though.

The second she pulled the quilt over his legs, he turned his back to her.

"I'm going to get ready for bed now," she whispered.

If only Matt weren't still around, she could've let Nolan sleep in peace.

CHAPTER TWENTY-TWO

"Nolan."

Corinne's voice whispered to him from somewhere in the darkness.

Her hand pressed against his chest, and his eyes flew open. He blinked hard in the gray light.

"Sorry." Corinne took her hand away, leaving a cold spot above his heart. "I didn't mean to scare you awake."

With his pulse rushing at a chaotic clip, he closed his eyes and dropped his head back onto his pillow with a thump.

"You sure wake up hard." Corinne sat beside him, the mattress dipping to his left. "In case Leah needs help again, I'm going into town early to get the rest of my things."

"That's fine," his voice grated out. He let his body sink back into the dark of sleep.

"So I'll need to do your leg now."

His warm quilt moved. He yanked it back. "No."

"We talked about this."

"I'm not in control yet."

The quilt moved again.

He forced his eyes open and pushed himself into a sitting

position, dragging the covering with him. He glared at her. "I said no."

She studied him. "What do you need to be in control of?"

"Myself." Sleeping next to her was hard enough—she needed to keep her hands off him. He yawned and tried to rub the sleep from his face. "And I don't want to explain to an innocent like you."

"Oh." Her cheeks flushed.

He dropped his hands. "If you want to get to town early, you'll have to do so without attending to me."

She sat there for a minute and then let out a noisy exhale. "I think I ought to tell you something." Her gaze anchored to his chest. "What's your opinion of me?"

He rubbed his face again. Sleep was not giving him up easily. "I'm sorry. I don't understand the question."

Her shoulders rose and fell with a sigh. "How would you describe me to someone if you weren't trying to be polite and was assured I'd never hear? The unbridled truth."

Corinne certainly knew how to start a day. "I'd tell them you were beautiful, smart, curious, sensible, hardworking—" He interrupted himself with a yawn. If his brain was more awake, he might've been able to add to the list.

"Well..." Her voice cracked and she cleared her throat. "That was nicer than I'd expected."

He pushed himself up straighter. "Which do you disagree with?"

She played with a loose thread on the quilt. "None, though I'm not sure about the smart thing."

"I shoved enough of your contraptions into the wagon to know you're smart."

"None are any good."

Where had the Corinne who spoke so decisively gone? "If you weren't smart, you'd not be drawn to tinkering, regardless of whether you've made something you like yet."

She raised one shoulder. "Thank you, but still, nothing you

said would be how people would've described me back in Chicago."

"Maybe you misjudged them, because though we were only acquaintances weeks ago, I saw all those things."

She just sat blinking at him.

He clenched his fists to keep from reaching over to cup her face, look deep into her eyes, and repeat his list. Why didn't she believe those things about herself? "How old were you when you accepted Christ?"

"Um, eight."

"I can't imagine you lived such a wicked life before then that you've had to struggle to overcome it."

"I accepted God's forgiveness when I was young, yes. But I didn't realize how much I'd need it until later." She looked back down at her lap. "When I was almost seventeen, I fell in love with a man."

He stiffened, preparing himself for whatever she was about to reveal.

"My life was drudgery at home, so I hired myself out to a widower with a young son."

She paused, looking out at the barely lit sky. "Kurt's late wife left him lots of money, so he didn't need to marry for security. After a few compliments from him, I became enamored. I told myself I could see loneliness in his eyes—that all he needed was love—my love."

She sighed and shook her head. "Do you recall asking me if I read novels?"

"Yes."

"Well, I didn't lie. I've never had much time to read any, but I'm sure the fantasies my seventeen-year-old self dreamed up could rival those stories. I'd not felt loved in a long time, not since my mother died when I was young. A boy I'd grown up with had recently humiliated me, and though my sister is only a year younger than I am, we were so very different and things had changed between us."

She turned to stare back out the window. "Anyway, once I thought Kurt found me as charming as I found him, I failed at keeping my feelings concealed. I was desperate to be accepted, though scared at the same time because, well, let's just say, boys never really liked me. My sister Yvonne was prettier and well…"

She swallowed hard and closed her eyes.

A part of him wanted to tell her she didn't have to continue, but it'd probably be best to know this at some point. Despite uncertainty, he reached over and squeezed her hand.

She squeezed back halfheartedly then let go. "Sorry. Anyway, when Christmas Day came and went without a letter from anyone in my family, Kurt wished me a merry Christmas, and I broke down, telling him I hadn't had one in a long time. He sat and listened to my struggles as if he really cared."

She thumped her chest, as if her heart was aching with that feeling once again. "From then on, he talked to me every day, asked how I was, lamented about his own problems. I'd never felt so special.

"But one day…" Her voice disappeared for a moment and she closed her eyes. "One day, in the middle of a heart-to-heart, I told him no one cared for me." She turned to glance at Nolan, tears gleaming on her lower lashes. "That no one wanted me…"

She cleared her throat and stared out the window as if the cloudless gray sky riveted her. "I suppose when a young woman throws herself at a man after revealing she hasn't a tie in the world, that proves more than a little enticing."

Nolan pressed his lips together to keep from cursing a man he didn't know. Regardless of what she'd done, he'd been the adult.

"We engaged in what you'd suspect following such a story. Over the next few weeks, my fear of never finding a man who'd love me melted away because he spent his every spare moment with me. I was sure he was going to marry me." She turned to give him a sad, self-deprecating smile.

Nolan shook his head. "I'm sorry, he——"

168

She cut him off with her hand. "Whatever his faults may have been, I was reveling in those heady feelings and not thinking clearly. I wasn't prudent and told everyone we were to be married, but the longer we played husband and wife…" She stopped and swallowed hard. "When I'd first started working for him, a single look would warm me all over, his touches made me shiver."

Maybe she did understand what a touch could do. Did she feel that way at all about him?

She straightened and her gaze turned steely, though it wasn't directed at him. "But those fluttery feelings amounted to nothing. Once the newness of our relationship wore off, he became frustrated with how I responded to him—or rather, how I didn't. Considering we weren't married, I couldn't ask any women for advice. All I'd ever overheard was how a wife was supposed to submit to her duty, and I did, despite saying no vows. But evidently what he'd experienced with his first wife … well, I didn't measure up. I wasn't enough. That's always what I've been."

Nolan pinched the bridge of his nose instead of reaching out to her again. He could sympathize with not being enough, doing his utmost to make someone happy but have them yank away what was promised.

"Our love soured once intimacy became a chore. At first, he blamed me because I'd let others know we were together. He thought their negative opinions were affecting me, so he moved us to a suburb where we could start over with new staff. He said we had to be sure we were compatible."

The desire to pull her close was nearly overwhelming, but he kept his arms folded across his chest.

She gave him a quick glance. "As you can guess, we never became physically compatible, and he decided we should take a break. Within three months, right in front of me, he introduced his son to a woman he'd met through a co-worker. The look on his face told me everything I needed to know."

The silence grew along with the sunlight spilling in around the curtain.

After a few more ticks of the clock, she glanced at him, but broke eye contact immediately. "As I said, God had to extend more forgiveness to me than I'd ever thought I'd need, and hopefully will ever need again. My sin had given me insight into what marriage to me would be like though. I swore I'd never allow myself, or anyone else, to be disappointed again, and yet I met a man in Rapid City who I thought was good and trustworthy. I let hope grow. I did everything properly with him, but it wasn't enough. Attraction, love, infatuation—they all give you hope that everything will be all right. But sometimes, you're just not enough."

He closed his eyes, his body aching, knowing he couldn't pull her to him to comfort her. Knowing if he told her she was mistaken, she'd not believe him. But then again, what did he know? Her experience far exceeded his own. Yet at the same time, he just couldn't believe she'd been as disappointing as these men made her feel. Were they even worthy of her? Had they actually loved her?

If he were in love with her, would knowing what had happened in her past change how he felt? He just hadn't any idea. "So that's your reason against marrying?"

She nodded. "Those men have moved on, happy with who they chose. I figured it'd be wrong to steal anyone else's chance at getting everything he hoped for by attaching himself to me. I thought it best I no longer waste my time or anyone else's."

Nolan retook her hand, thankful she didn't pull away. "I want you to know, I don't think you're a waste of my time. I still think you're all the things I listed when you asked me what I thought about you. Plus now, I'm adding strong to the list."

She sputtered while shaking her head. "My story shouldn't have given you any reason to add to my list of good qualities."

"I'll add conscientious, too."

A derisive snort escaped her. "I wish I were that, for if I was, I'd not have gotten into those messes to begin with."

"Sometimes the trials we bring upon ourselves are the worst we face, but you learned from yours. So I'll add that you're a good learner, too."

She rolled her eyes. "I certainly did put myself through disaster, but it took a long time to learn anything from it. Anyway..." She started playing with the quilt's loose thread again. "I thought you ought to know I'm no innocent. That I understand that my being here, well, I understand you've been robbed of what men desire. I realize you're trapped, too, in a way, and that if you know there will be no romance between us, if you have no illusions about things being ... good. Well, if you need me to submit—"

"No, no. Stop right there." She was not going to offer that. "It's business partners or lovers. I won't live in the in-between."

She stared at him for a moment as if she didn't understand what he'd said, but then nodded and patted his knee. "Then as your business partner, you need to let me help you. Like I said, I've been far more intimate than this with a man before. If you're uncomfortable with me for some reason, then you need to find someone else, because I'm depending on you to make this ranch flourish. Perhaps Timothy could help? Tell him my hands aren't strong enough, pay him extra, find a way."

She stood. "I'll go now. And don't count on me to be back at any particular time."

Then she slipped out the door.

His breath rushed out and he sunk back under the covers.

This convenient marriage had just gotten much harder—or maybe more permanent. With such a dismal outlook on marriage, would she ever let herself fall in love with him if he fell in love with her?

How had he ever convinced himself this was a good idea?

CHAPTER TWENTY-THREE

Nolan tried to concentrate on the book in front of him, but the words may as well have been in Greek. He leaned back against the sofa and stretched his arm out to push aside the parlor curtain. The clouds were thick, but the silence in the house was thicker. The clock said it was only five past six.

At least Matt was gone.

When he'd asked his cousin when he intended to leave, Matt had said he'd find a room in town and packed up. Seemed he truly was determined to buy a ranch.

Though he'd always complained Matt never kept his nose to the grindstone, did this have to be the project he stuck with? They might be family, but didn't his cousin realize he'd rather not be neighbors?

Well, at least he was off the property—and no longer at his dinner table from morning until night.

And Corinne? He'd watched her drive straight back to her cabin around three-thirty.

The clock's tick echoed in the quiet.

Too quiet. Quiet allowed him to think—and after what Corinne had suggested this morning, thinking was not what he wanted to do. His thoughts kept wandering to that which he'd told Corinne he'd not entertain.

She had said she'd explained her past so he'd know she wasn't a woman ignorant of men—and yet, it seemed she didn't realize the mere mentioning of being intimate with him would drive him absolutely insane.

A man didn't have to be in love with a woman to have difficulty keeping his mind from imagining her in his arms and in his bed, especially if she seemed willing to go there. With them being married, there was nothing wrong with doing such.

He shook his head hard and flipped the book's pages back to the last place he remembered what he was reading. He'd been far better off when he'd thought her definition of romantic nonsense was giving her flowers and calling her "sugar."

None of the words in front of him looked familiar. What was he reading, anyway? He flipped the book to read the spine, frowned at the unfamiliar title, then tossed the book onto the sofa beside him.

He had to get out of this house and do something. He growled at his empty pant leg before snatching up his crutches.

Sal and the men were in the barn, and when he'd gone out earlier, they'd refused to let him help. He moved to the back door and squinted against the overcast light, spotting the wagon behind a tree near the cabin. He couldn't tell if it'd been unloaded.

He pivoted and stared at his artificial leg in the corner. Doc had told him not to wear it until his sore was completely healed. But walking to the cabin on crutches was too much—riding, overkill.

He turned to look at the clock. Two whole minutes had passed.

After snatching up his leg, he worked to put it on, and winced only slightly with his first step. He'd just force himself to walk slowly.

When he stepped out the front door, a billow of dust caught his attention.

Please let it not be Matt.

Within seconds, the wind swirled enough that he could make out Annie's red hair beside Jacob's black hat. Good, he could use a ride to the cabin, and now he wouldn't have to wait until his leg healed to ride over to talk to Jacob.

He stepped off the porch and waited for his friends to pull up. Spencer was poised to jump off, and once they passed the well, he took a flying leap.

Oh, to be able to do that again.

Jacob stopped the wagon. "We've come to invite you and your wife to dinner next week."

"That's kind of you. I doubt there's a reason to say no, but we should check with Corinne to be sure. I was about to go out to the cabin to see if she needed help unloading. You mind giving me a ride?"

"Get in."

Spencer climbed back into the wagon as if he were a monkey. "I'll help, too."

Nolan hoisted himself onto the bed beside the young man, and Spencer scooted closer as Jacob turned the team.

"Does your leg still hurt you?"

Nolan stilled his hand—he had started massaging his leg without realizing it. "If you mean from when I got it cut off, no. But sometimes it hurts from having to use it."

"What about phantom pains? You have those? Old Mr. York —" Spencer jabbed his finger to the south where the man lived with his brother, surrounded by twenty miles of nothing. "He told me his missing leg feels like it's still there sometimes. Hurts, too."

"I'll occasionally feel something like that. Sometimes I reach down to scratch my leg and realize I can't."

Spencer's eyes widened. "You mean you can't make the itch go away? Is that why Mr. York's so grumpy?"

"I don't know. Do you think I'm grumpy?"

"Not most of the time—or at least, I don't think so."

Spencer poked his wooden leg. "Can you feel that?"

"I can feel you move my leg, but no, I don't feel it."

"But you have an itch there?"

"On occasion, yes."

"Are you worried you'll go crazy since you can't itch your itch and get sent to the madhouse?"

"Spencer." Annie's voice held a warning tone.

"It's all right. He can ask me what he wants." He patted Spencer's leg. "Next time you get an itch, try ignoring it. Itches go away on their own after a while."

"Did your leg get blown off like Mr. York's?"

Seemed Spencer had swallowed a curiosity bug that was desperate to escape. The boy had never asked him about his leg before. "No, though I sometimes wish it had, because then the government might help me buy a better leg. I was only a few years older than you though, nothing more than an accident while tending my horse."

Spencer frowned and threw a quick glance up to the front of the wagon.

Nolan patted the boy's arm. "Don't you worry it'll happen to you. Just listen to your parents and do what they say to keep safe."

"So you disobeyed your parents and got hurt?"

"No. Mine was a complete accident, but it sure taught me to respect the power animals have over us, even if they're big ol' softies."

And women held a similar power—no matter how uninterested in romance they were.

In seconds, one horse's decision had changed his entire life, and Corinne? Everything she did and said from now on could change his life completely—he'd been stupid to think otherwise. She'd turned his world upside down this morning, and they'd only been married two weeks.

Before the wagon stopped, Spencer jumped off again.

"If you don't want to lose a leg like me, you might want to stop doing that."

"You listen to Nolan." Annie blew out an exasperated breath. "He's off and over and into everything these days. Why, yesterday, he jumped out of a tree and onto our roof—liked to scare the life out of me."

Before he could respond, the boy rushed into the cabin.

"Spencer, no!" Came Corinne's panicked voice.

"Oh, boy." Nolan hopped off the back, but Annie was faster and disappeared inside.

Once he caught up, Corinne was standing between Spencer and a collection of bottles on the makeshift table behind her. "You can't touch or knock over anything. These are chemicals. Some could eat into your skin."

Spencer was undaunted. "What are you doing with them?"

Corinne straightened and took a deep, ragged breath.

Had Spencer scared her that badly? What *did* she have in those bottles?

She turned to Annie. "I'm sorry I snapped at him, but one wrong move and—" She froze as if she'd about said something she shouldn't. "Well, it's bad."

"How bad?" Spencer craned his neck to peer around her.

"Bad enough you don't want to find out." Turning, she pulled a white cloth out of a bowl with tongs. "Right now, I'm trying to get rid of this stain. See? It's axle grease. The new livery man isn't careful when it comes to his clothing, so I'm hoping to make it easier for Mrs. Whitsett to clean."

"What's that one?" Spencer pointed to the bowl next to the first.

"Another linen square with axle grease but in a different solution." She plopped the first one back into its bowl. "I haven't had time to play with these before now." She snapped her head up and pulled out her pocket watch. "Goodness, I didn't realize how late it was."

Nolan stepped farther into the cabin and noted the haphazard piles, just like at the laundry. Maybe she was like Timothy who insisted he couldn't clean up after himself because he'd not know where anything was.

Jacob ducked into the doorway behind him. "Nolan said you might need help moving things in?"

"No, I finished earlier."

Nolan frowned at the big barrels in the corner. They'd hardly budged when they'd brought the first one home. "Did the men help?"

"I didn't want to bother them."

"Was that wise? You should ask for help rather than endanger yourself." Nolan walked over to the barrel closest to the door and surreptitiously bumped it to see if it was empty. It didn't move a millimeter. He'd known she was a strong woman, but—

"With mechanical advantage, you can do almost anything. I made myself a ramp and lever." She smiled down at Spencer and beckoned him toward a pile of stuff on a rickety table in the corner. "Have you ever played with a buzz saw? Simple machines make fun toys, too."

At the promise of a dangerous-sounding toy, Spencer lit up. "No, ma'am, I haven't."

Corinne pulled out a circular piece of wood with string passing through two drilled holes in the middle. "I saw a child playing with one of these back in Chicago, and I like to make them to give away. Watch this." She squatted down in front of Spencer and showed him how to wind up the string to make the wooden circle spin in a mesmerizing blur.

Did Chicago schools teach kids more than the territory schools, or had Corinne paid better attention than he had? He looked over at a crate half filled with books. Of course. Maybe she didn't read dime novels, but she likely read more than he'd assumed.

He'd always learned by doing. Never thought to order books on ranching, yet that had been the first thing she'd asked about.

While Spencer busily made the wooden disk whirr, Annie gestured toward the linen squares swimming in bowls. "Have any of these worked?"

"I've not forgotten your soap if that's what you're wondering."

"Of course not. And even if you did forget, I'm sure I could use whatever this is, too. Jacob does his fair share of mucking up clothes."

"Well, I don't hold out much hope for these. They're mostly concoctions using pantry items—vinegar, lemon juice, oils. I have some chemicals in mind that might work if these don't, but I have to save up for them."

"What chemicals might those be?" Annie picked up a cloth with the long metal tweezers Corinne had used earlier, squinting at the fabric as if to inspect it.

Corinne shifted uncomfortably. "A handful of different things, but I'm not ready to share yet. They might not work either."

With a small splash, Annie dropped the wet cloth back into its solution. "Have you ever heard of the Centennial Exhibition? The women's pavilion?"

Corinne's face contorted. "I don't think so."

"We were in Denver not too long ago." Annie gestured between her and Jacob. "We met a woman at the telegraph office there. She was wiring her mother because she'd just been awarded a patent for a new style of washboard—told me all about it. I didn't realize I had an inventor friend back home."

Corinne shrugged. "I wouldn't say that."

"I would. And she told us her washboard was nothing compared to what she'd seen at the fair. Seemed they had a whole tent full of women-invented gadgets. Said some smaller fairs showed off women's accomplishments, too." Annie's face brightened. "Maybe one day you'll be there."

"I *was* working on an iron with a removable handle, but a lady beat me to it." She scurried across the room and pulled something out of a file box. "See this? It's close to what I was imagining, but hers is better. Read it. Doesn't it make you want one?"

Annie fingered the newspaper clipping. "I've seen this ad once or twice. It would be nice if it worked as claimed. Do you think it would?"

She nodded and when Annie put down the advertisement, Corinne mouthed the word "birthday" to Jacob, and the man gave her a slight nod back.

Nolan made a mental note to put that iron on the birthday list for Corinne as well...

When was her birthday? And did their relationship require the exchange of gifts?

Hopefully his birthday came before hers and he'd do whatever she did.

"Can I take the buzz saw home with me?" Spencer gave the toy another good spin. "I'll give it back when you come next week."

"Next week?" Corinne frowned at Annie.

"We came to ask you two to dinner. You're my closest woman neighbor now, and I'm excited to have you over."

"Oh, well..." She looked to Nolan.

Considering how her face had brightened, he wouldn't have said no even if the Hendrixes were his mortal enemies. "I believe any day of the week would work for me."

Corinne turned back to Annie, happier than he'd ever seen her—which sort of stung. "How about next Friday?"

"Great." Annie reached out to squeeze her hand. "Since you don't need our help, we best get back home. We've got a cow about to give birth and a sick cat Spencer was loath to leave."

The women walked out side by side, discussing what Corinne would bring for dinner next week.

The Hendrixes seemed to have forgotten about him, so he leaned against the table to take the pressure off his leg.

Maybe it had been too early to put his leg back on.

Oh, who did he think he was lying to? He shouldn't have put it on at all, let alone walked on it. He closed his eyes against the pain of what was surely his scab rubbing off.

In seconds, Corinne stomped back into the cabin and shot him a pointed look. "You shouldn't be walking on your leg."

"I know."

"You're supposed to take care of yourself, find someone to help you, not make it worse."

Shoot. He'd been so enthralled with Corinne telling Annie about her tinkering he'd forgotten to ask Jacob about helping with his stretches. He'd just have to ride over tomorrow to ask because he wasn't going to ask Timothy or any of his other hands to help, no matter Corinne's suggestion. If he was going to maintain authority, no employee of his would be seeing him in his drawers.

"You need to take your leg off."

"I will."

"I mean now."

He narrowed his eyes at her. Being his business partner didn't make her his boss. "I'll take it off at the house."

"Or you can take it off now." She put her hands on her hips and held his gaze.

He readjusted his stance. If she thought he looked like he was in real pain—this was nothing. "How would I get back home?"

"I'll help you hobble out to the wagon."

"It's not that—"

"Are you going to make me take it off?"

He snapped his head up. "What?"

She shook her head at him, a touch of a smile on her upturned lips. "Seems to me if someone doesn't make you obey orders, you won't do as you ought."

"You're as bad as Doc Ellis."

"So the sore is completely healed?"

He kept his mouth pressed shut.

"I think the doctor and I just know something you don't—that you're too stubborn for your own good."

"Neither one of you know me well at all."

She flinched, but her gaze quickly turned back to steel. "Regardless, I know you aren't doing what you're supposed to. Besides, I'm not necessarily looking out for you—I'm looking out for me. If you get gangrene and die, I won't know how to run this place. So if you're determined to go against medical advice, you need to stay around long enough for me to learn."

He only harrumphed.

"You need to leave your leg here, anyway. I have an idea about a modification that might help you avoid getting a sore like that again."

He glanced around at the gadgets and junk she had lying around. Could she improve his leg? With the knowledge she'd spouted off to Spencer, and the fact she'd unloaded the heavy things from her wagon without help...

She might need him to teach her the ins and outs of the ranch now, but it wouldn't be long before she didn't need him at all.

Which was a very good reason not to play around with physical fire. The more he grew attached to her, the more he'd be inclined to yearn for some "romantic nonsense"—however they chose to define it—and he didn't want to be yearning alone.

CHAPTER TWENTY-FOUR

Corinne shoved the half-formed artificial leg away and hung her head in her hands. It wasn't coming together as she'd imagined.

A few days ago, when Annie had mentioned the Centennial Fair, she'd gotten her hopes up that with the time she now had, she could make something worthy of a women's exhibit. But she was kidding herself. Ideas could be so promising—but she hadn't the talent.

She glanced over at the bowls of wet cloth—all of which had a grease stain that wouldn't budge. None of these were soaking in chemicals she'd hoped to use, but she'd expected a few to have helped a little.

The cabin's door creaked open and the cool evening air wafted in. Nolan's unsteady gait as he tried to come through the door on crutches while carrying a lantern made her want to jump up to help, but considering how stubborn he was being about his leg, she remained seated. "You shouldn't have hobbled all the way out here."

"I was checking on you." He got himself through the door and set the lamp down, his voice breathy. "I'd wondered if you'd fallen asleep. You worked hard earlier."

She smiled a bit at his noticing. She'd taken over all his

chores and had helped the men with the fencing—not that they had let her actually do anything with the fence, but she'd insisted on helping carry things since Nolan wasn't available. And since she couldn't have her bedroom light on at night to keep the men from realizing they slept in separate rooms now, she'd decided to work out here until she was ready to turn in.

"You're not tired?"

She pulled out her timepiece and took a second look. Ten o'clock was far later than she'd been up in a long while. As if her body only needed to know the hour, a yawn overtook her. She rubbed at her eyes. "Seems I lost track of time. I'll clean up and come in."

"If you're going to stay out this late, I'd feel better if you encouraged Mickey to come with you. The coyotes have gotten closer the past few weeks."

Her heart warmed at his desire to look after her, though she wasn't sure how much protection an old dog would be against a pack of coyotes. "I admit their singing's making me nervous, but I figured you'd roll your eyes at me if I told you how unsettled they make me feel."

"They're closer than even I'd like." He readjusted himself on his crutches. "Not worried about us much, but the animals, certainly."

She started reorganizing her piles. How did they get so unruly in such a short amount of time?

"Are you finished with my leg yet? The sore's healed, and I was hoping to have it back." He reached across the table and dragged the new leg she'd been working on toward him. "Where'd you get this?"

"Made it."

His brows rose. "You made this?"

"Out of the barrel staves."

He picked it up and examined it. "Looks like one a man I know got from the army."

She rubbed her eyes. Of course someone else had already

made something like this. Just like Mrs. Potts' handle-swapping iron. "Did you try it on?"

"Uh, that's like asking to try on someone's drawers."

She smiled at the twinkle in his eye. His sense of humor always came as a nice surprise—though he had been more serious this past week.

"If I gave you the catalog that has an illustration of the leg, could you replicate it?"

"Maybe." Not that building something someone had already invented would earn her a spot in a women's exhibition. "Though it'd probably be better to just save up money enough to buy one since this leg isn't turning out like I'd hoped."

And there was probably some catalog out there that had a soap powder for sensitive skin Annie could order as easily as Corinne could order chemicals that may or may not work. "I should just stick to tinkering with what will benefit this ranch. Like healthier chickens and plentiful eggs."

She handed him the sketch she'd drawn up earlier to redo the coop.

He didn't even look. "One failed attempt does not mean you can't do it."

She frowned at him. "I've had more than one failure."

"Doesn't matter." Nolan kept his gaze steady on hers. "You should invent things because you enjoy it."

"I do, it's just … it's silly. Don't worry about it."

"I can't imagine a woman who can replicate a Hanger leg without knowing it exists could want something silly."

"I don't know about that, considering I didn't even think to ask if there was a catalog of false appendages I could peruse to see what's available. I had thought I had an idea that might get noticed, but the hinges aren't working. I do think I've improved your old one, however." She crossed to the corner where she'd left his leg in hopes she'd be able to hand him something better.

Walking back, she pointed inside the leg's cupped socket. "I added contoured padding. Considering the shape of your leg…"

She didn't look up at him in case he'd be embarrassed that she'd studied his leg while cleaning it. "I figured this might improve your comfort. I'd have to take a look with your leg in it to determine if there's any more I could do."

"Thank you." He looked at her for a few seconds before closing his eyes. "Do you want me to put the leg on now so you can check?"

He'd let her? With how he'd gotten Jacob to agree to do his leg stretches and how he'd waited until she was asleep or out of the room to strap on or remove his leg when Matt had been there, she'd thought he wouldn't. "Yes, if you're willing. If there's something that could be done to make it better, I could work on it tomorrow."

"Or you could rest." He set aside his crutches and shrugged one suspender strap off his shoulder. "I don't begrudge my men their evenings. You can relax, too."

She turned her back to give him privacy, though it seemed silly since he couldn't cover himself up while she examined his leg. "I like to keep busy."

"I've noticed."

She rummaged through her pile to find her measuring tape. "Thank you for believing I can do something to help you."

"Why wouldn't I believe that?" The creak of a chair indicated he'd sat.

"Not everyone has."

"Do you talk about the things you make with everyone?"

She chuckled. "No. When I've tried, most tell me I'm wasting my time. I don't bother anymore. You ready?"

"Yes."

She turned to find he'd taken off one pant leg and had rolled up his drawers. His arms were locked against his chest and he stared straight through her.

"I'll just be a minute." She took measurements, made a quick sketch, then made another once he'd slipped the leg on. "I'm done. Why don't you wear the leg home and tell me how it feels? Give it a few days and then I can adjust things, if you'd like. Or maybe I should start making that other leg."

Once she turned, shuffling indicated he was putting himself back together. "I'm not sure I'll like a new one better. I got that Hanger brochure a few years ago, but decided against purchasing one. Figured I might end up spending all my money searching for the perfect leg, but end up with a closet full of disappointment. Though with all the odds and ends you keep, perhaps you would've found a pile of junk legs useful. Why's that?"

"Why's what?"

"Why do you collect so much stuff? You seemed busy at the laundry and strapped for cash. Even if most of this was free, you've spent a good sum on those chemicals."

She scanned all her stuff. She'd not realized how much she'd had until she moved. She would've had even more if she'd not lost her last collection in the fire.

Nolan waited as if the clock hand wasn't moving closer to an absurd time of night for them both to be up.

She shrugged. If anyone should know everything about her, it might as well be him. "My stepmother never attached herself to me, neither did my father. I don't think he blamed me for mother's death, but he never seemed interested in me after that."

"Maybe you reminded him of your mother."

She shook her head. "Actually, I think it was because I wasn't like my mother. He always said she was sturdier stock than me."

"If anyone's 'sturdy stock,' I'd say it's you. I know plenty of women who'd wilt under the amount of work you do."

"Thanks, but it's more a description of how we're built." She waved her thin fingers at him, wondering if her mother would have had the same hand trouble she'd had doing laundry. "Since I was skinny and sickly when Mom died, I wondered if he resented that I'd survived and she hadn't. Whatever the reason, he lost interest in me. He was warmer toward Yvonne, but not much. The only time he seemed to talk to me was to chastise me for wasting time whenever I tinkered. So I sort of gave it up."

"Sort of?"

"I'd catch Daddy looking at Momma's paintings and thought maybe learning to paint could get his attention, but I ended up more interested in creating colors than using them. I was also fascinated by my stepbrother's bug collection and the iridescent blue of the dragonflies. My father was originally a pharmacist, and when he expanded into chemical supply, I had access to what he sold. I knew bug paintings likely wouldn't endear him to me, but I wanted to replicate that metallic color."

"Were you able to do it?"

"Almost." She smiled at the memory of sneaking into her father's warehouse to steal teaspoons of chemicals. The risk of punishment hadn't diminished the excitement of being on mission. "I read through my father's books to see which traits each chemical had, and mixing a few with the paints I owned, I got close. A lustrous color you couldn't buy at the store. It shimmered like a dragonfly, even if it wasn't the blue I was going for. He was astounded, and I thought my father was finally proud of me."

"I sense a 'but' coming."

Her smile died. "But he was interested in my iridescent paint —not me. He sold the formula to a company he worked with."

"That didn't make you happy?"

"He didn't tell them I created it. When I got angry, he asked what did I expect. No one would believe a twelve-year-old girl had come up with it."

"So what's the name of your color?"

She let out a sad sigh. "Never asked. Didn't want to know. If I found it in a store, what was I going to do? Hold it up and tell everyone I'd invented it? People would've thought me delusional."

"Not all. That fair Annie mentioned—"

"Those women weren't stupid enough to share their inventions with someone who'd sell it out from under them."

"You weren't stupid. If children can't trust their father, then who should they trust?"

"We have that in common."

Nolan furrowed his brow.

"My father took away what I'd worked hard to create. Yours, too."

He rubbed a hand though his hair. "I've been thinking about that lately. Wondering if Dad may have been right. By marrying you, I'm far better off than I was. Not only do I have my ranch, but the perfect wife."

"'Perfect'?" She scoffed. "I thought you agreed to no romantic nonsense."

"If the truth sounds like nonsense to you, I can't help it. You should hear my men sing your praises. Their feathers were ruffled at first when you poked your nose into their business, but they're impressed with how hard you work—even if they won't let you do everything." He shook his head. "I certainly picked a better wife than Matt."

"You didn't pick me. You were forced." She stared at the messy counter in front of her and fiddled with a wood scrap. "If you'd known my past beforehand, I suspect you'd not have chosen me."

His silence went on long enough she couldn't help but look up. Though she'd expected to see pity, his expression seemed more confused. "I think you've forgotten lots of men marry widows with an intimate past."

"Sure, but they pursued them knowing so. A man in love with a woman he believes is a virgin bride would recoil once the truth came to light."

"The light changed nothing." He shrugged. "You're the same woman."

If he'd been in love with her, his tune would've been different. The fact that they meant nothing to each other was what kept him level-headed—which was good. So why was she arguing with him about it? She took a deep breath and dropped the wood scrap. "Well, thank you, and also for how you treated me before and after knowing."

"You're welcome, and if you enjoy tinkering, don't give it up because you're worried it's a waste of time. You don't have to spend all day making things that will benefit the ranch. I want you to make things that make you happy, too, all right?"

She swallowed against the lump in her throat. "Thank you. I ended up with a pretty perfect pretend spouse myself."

The soft look in his eyes faded, and he cleared his throat. "Well, then. Let's get back to pretending we're together and head to the house. Having you out here burning the midnight oil so soon after our wedding might set the men to talking." He scooted off his seat, and after adjusting his newly padded leg, he headed out the door.

She frowned at his retreating back. If he'd wanted to put on a show of them being together, heading off without her wouldn't do it.

And why did that sting? He'd not meant *together* together, just that they shouldn't be apart so much.

But after feeling like someone was listening to her for the first time in a long time...

She reached for the experimental leg, but stopped short. Ranching should come first, like the chicken coop among other things.

This leg was nothing special. Just like all her washing dollies, stain removers, and clothing irons.

She leaned over and blew out the lamp.

CHAPTER TWENTY-FIVE

Bang!

Nolan startled awake, his heart pounding. Was that a gunshot? Swinging his legs over the side of the mattress, he stumbled forward and hit the floor.

Growling, he picked himself up. How many years had to pass before he'd stop waking in the middle of the night and falling because his brain still thought he had two legs?

The hum of men's voices called his attention to the open window. When they continued with no hint of panic or distress, his heart slowed. Why were his men up at this hour?

Mickey's low growl rumbled somewhere outside.

His men were responsible enough he didn't have to put himself together to go check, so Nolan hauled himself back into the bed.

Lying down, he tried to drift back to sleep, but the men kept talking—though not loud enough he could figure out what was going on. Hopefully Corinne hadn't been awakened.

He refolded the pillow under his head and closed his eyes. He'd pray himself to sleep again if possible, and he needed to begin with his wife.

Last week, he'd thought encouraging Corinne to invent to

her heart's content would've made her happy, but she'd abandoned her projects instead.

Lord, give her peace. Cover her in a supernatural ability to sleep through—

His eyes flew open. A woman's voice. Outside.

He swung his legs back around and reached for the shirt hanging on the footboard. She must've heard something was amiss to have gone out at this time of night. Had he been awakened by them pounding on the door?

The voices faded as he searched for his crutches. When everything went quiet outside, he stopped. By the time he could make it downstairs, they'd likely be back in bed.

He attuned his ears, waiting for the sound of the back door, but never heard it.

Was she being exceptionally quiet so as not to wake him? Or was she not going to inform him of what happened?

He shook his head and settled back into bed. She'd likely tell him over breakfast, and not having her in his room, in the dark, in her nightdress … a good thing.

He was getting worked up over nothing.

Just when his breath began to slow enough to return to sleep, his door creaked.

"Nolan?" Her whisper floated over.

"Hmmm?" He likely shouldn't have muttered that as if he'd just awakened, but he didn't want her to know he'd been fretting for fifteen minutes either.

A scratch, and then a flame filled the room with light.

He sat up and rubbed at his eyes. Why was she lighting the lamp? "What's happened?"

"Something got the chickens."

Why was she still whispering?

"Killed all of them." Her face contorted as she turned the flame down. "Took the men too long to figure out what Mickey was whining about to save any. We gathered up the bodies before he was tempted to chew on one, but the eggs…"

She made some sort of frustrated whining noise. Why would losing eggs make her sadder than losing animals?

The lamp light flickered as she turned to walk toward him. She thrust both hands in her dressing gown pockets, and then pulled them out, eggs in both hands. Why would she have brought them up here?

"These three are the only one's left. They're supposed to hatch tomorrow, according to what I learned in *The Prairie Farmer*. We can't let them die." She thrust one of the eggs toward him. "So here."

He took the egg but frowned. Maybe he needed to have a talk with her about not getting attached to farm animals. "Honey, when you live on a ranch, you're subject to the whims of nature. Wild animals, the life cycle, disease—"

"I know all that." She scoffed at him. "We don't make friends with food, but look, this one is already cracking."

She put the speckled egg to her ear. "I can hear it scratching."

Without warning, she crawled over his legs and scooted herself into a sitting position on her side of the bed.

Of course, she didn't really have a side. But that hadn't stopped him on occasion from turning over in the middle of the night and wondering why she wasn't there.

Her cold hand cupped his and lifted his egg toward his ear. "Do you hear anything in yours?"

Listening to eggs in the middle of the night seemed more than a little absurd, but he held his laughter. "I don't think so." He took a glance at her but quickly looked elsewhere—she was entirely too close. "I've seen gadgets in the catalogs for hatching motherless chicks. We could order one if you'd like for future mishaps, but this is what happens—"

"We're not going to let it happen." She snatched the egg from him and laid them all in her lap. "We're going to hatch them."

He shook his head. Maybe he'd fallen back asleep and was dreaming. "You think we're going to sit on eggs?"

"No." Her voice slid down in timbre, as if he'd been the one to propose something silly. Then her cold hand landed on his chest and slipped under the unbuttoned yoke of his nightshirt.

Seemed it was entirely possible to forget how to breathe.

She slipped an egg under his arm and patted his shoulder. "We can keep them warm like a momma bird though."

His eyes widened. She wanted him to hold the egg in his armpit? The desire to laugh fled as her hand slid back across his chest.

Stopping her hand atop his rapidly beating heart, she glanced up. Was he imagining things, or had she stopped breathing, too?

A few ticks of silence passed before she snatched her hand away. "You only have to take care of one. I'll hatch the other two."

She sat back and stuffed the other two eggs inside her night-dress. "It shouldn't take long." The warble in her voice had changed, now clearly colored with embarrassment. Was that because she'd dragged a hand across his bare chest or because she'd asked him to hatch an egg in his armpit?

And yet, she'd come to him for help in the middle of the night. "You do realize we'll have to stay up to be sure not to crush them. Why not put them next to the lamp? Either way, they probably won't make it."

"Oh, I forgot to prepare the crate." She handed him her two eggs.

She wanted him to stick these in his armpit, too? With a sigh, he tucked one under his opposite arm and cupped the third in his hands.

She'd crossed the room and started setting up another lamp next to a crate he'd thrown on the burn pile the other day.

"Do you expect me to sleep with cheeping chicks?"

"If they hatch, I'll move them out in the morning." She

turned to him. "You told me you didn't want a light on in my room."

Surely burning lamps to keep chicks warm in the guest room could be explained, though did he really want her to leave? "This might not work."

"I'm fine with that, but I need to try."

With all his insistence that she do whatever tinkering she wanted, why stop her? "You sure you don't want to ask one of the men to do this so you can go to sleep?"

She crawled back onto the bed, took the third egg from his hands, and slipped it beneath her nightdress's top. "I didn't think it appropriate for me to stay up all night with one of them."

Chewing her lip, she held out her hand, and he gave her back the second egg.

An awkward silence descended as he adjusted himself to sit beside her, yet not touch her.

It was inappropriate for her to stay up with one of their men, but he wasn't sure sitting up all night with him was a good idea either. And yet, he couldn't, or maybe his brain refused to, come up with a reason to send her away.

With eggs under her arms, Corinne tipped her head back until it thumped the wall behind Nolan's bed.

This was ridiculous. What had she been thinking? Hatching eggs in their armpits! She should've just chosen to try to save two and cover the cracking one with lamplight and prayer, and yet, she was pretty sure this would work. The eggs only needed to be kept warm a few more hours.

Designs started flying about in her head on how to make an incubator with lamps, though this time, she'd find the catalogs Nolan mentioned before building anything. If what she came up with wasn't better, she'd buy something more promising, so they would be better prepared for a next time.

As silly as it was having an egg tucked under each arm, how had she found the nerve to march into Nolan's room, set up a nursery, hand him an egg, and crawl into bed beside him to spend the night together? She'd not even given it a thought. She'd simply barged in—as if one chick was worth asking him to skip a night of sleep.

With the way he was silently sitting there, staring at nothing, he was probably wondering how he'd ever talked himself into marrying such a crazy woman. Maybe she should pack up this silly setup and head downstairs.

His hand landed on her thigh, sending a delicious jolt through her. "I hope this works for your sake. But if they aren't hatched by morning, you'll need a different plan."

She blinked hard, trying to make sense of what he'd just said. But her brain was far too focused on the pleasant feeling of his hand—just like earlier when she'd realized hers had been flat against his bare chest. She scooted away, pretending to readjust her gown.

When he took his hand back, she closed her eyes and breathed out forcefully.

Nolan scooted farther up against the headboard. "Would you mind handing me that book on your table?"

Her table? She turned to look at the items beside her, but it was as if she couldn't see a thing. The feel of his hand was no longer distracting, yet now, wishing his hand would return made it impossible to think.

He pointed across her lap. "That one."

With arms tucked against her, she fumbled the slim green volume. "Sorry, didn't want to drop the eggs."

He took the book, his fingers skimming hers. Gooseflesh formed up her arm, and when he fumbled to light his lamp with one hand and knocked into her leg, every nerve in her lower half prickled. Her body's reactions were nothing short of trouble.

She remembered these anticipatory feelings all too well—

and once the anticipation was satiated, everyone wound up disappointed. Feelings were just that—feelings, and she'd promised herself if she ever experienced them again, she'd do nothing about it.

Nolan turned. "Would you mind getting—"

"What are you—" She'd turned at the same time, and his warm breath brushed across her lips causing her to shiver.

His eyes dropped to her mouth.

None of her muscles seemed capable of scooting away, and yet, she found the ability to lean…

A tap under her arm made her jump. "Oh."

"What?" He blinked.

She swiftly slid off the bed. Thankfully something had made her do so!

"I think it's hatching." She rushed the egg over to the crate and turned up the flame, illuminating a small chipped-out hole. "It worked!"

Or maybe the chick would've hatched anyway, but she'd take credit for doing something right this once. Because what she'd almost done a second ago would've been a mistake. "How much oil do you think I'll go through with it turned up high? Do you think I should put in some batting—or wool? Good thing it's not winter. Or maybe it would've been better if it had been, because then we'd have a fire going."

Was all her babbling distracting him from what had almost happened? Hopefully he hadn't realized she'd been about to kiss him.

The eggshell buckled, starting a crack. She handed her other egg to Nolan and rushed out to bring in a second lamp.

Her feet echoed in the stairwell as she muttered to herself, "You are not going to play the fool again, Corinne. Screw your head back on and get a hold of yourself."

Grabbing the parlor's smallest oil lamp and some scrap wool, she returned upstairs. Back in the room, she tossed the fabric in with the egg, picked up the crate and the other lamp, and headed out the door.

"What are you doing?"

She didn't answer, just blew out a breath as she made her way to the parlor and set the stuff down. What *was* she doing? Getting herself out of that room, that's what. As far from him as possible.

She started a fire in the fireplace and stoked it until it burned bright. The heat would not be good for sleeping, but she'd be chastising herself all night, anyway.

Once she had the sofa set up for her and the egg's top had nearly cracked all the way around, giving her a glimpse of wet yellow feathers, she returned to Nolan's room. She walked in, keeping her gaze fixed on his forehead, not sure it'd be a good idea to look him in the eyes. "I'm sorry I interrupted your sleep. I should've realized I needed a fire, even if it is summer. So I'll take the eggs now and let you get back to sleep."

She reached over, but he didn't seem willing to hand them to her. She waggled her fingers. "Thank you for humoring me."

Head tilted, he looked at her for a second, but then pulled an egg out. "I hope I didn't give you the impression I was upset with you. In fact, I'm happy to know what lengths you're willing to go for the ranch. I don't—"

"No need to thank me. I'm obligated to help."

He opened his mouth once, then twice, but then pulled the other egg out from under his nightshirt. "All right."

Cupping the eggs, she turned for the door.

"I'm still thankful, Corinne." His words were softer and more gracious than she deserved.

She hesitated at the door. She didn't want him thinking she was mad at him, but she couldn't go back over and talk to him either, nor explain why she had to leave. "Good night, Nolan. I'll see you in the morning."

CHAPTER TWENTY-SIX

Nolan was pretty sure he was being ignored. All week, whenever Corinne had sat down to eat, she had immediately pulled out her notebook and started scribbling.

He'd tried not to ask much of her since she'd hatched those three chicks, ecstatic that she was coming up with all kinds of absorbing ideas. However, he'd caught her joking with his men earlier, yet the moment he'd walked in the door, she turned frantic in her need to get everyone their supper. Once she'd handed out the plates, she'd opened her notebook and refrained from joining in with the evening's banter.

Now that the men had left, she was still glued to whatever it was she was drawing.

He cut his pork into tiny pieces. "What are you sketching?"

She looked up at him blankly, as if she'd forgotten he sat across from her. "Not sure, actually."

"Are you not drawing with a goal in mind?"

"No, just..." She took a sip of water, then picked up her pencil again, twirling it between her fingers. "I'm searching for an idea worthy of a patent. After I told you about the paint the other day, I realized I wanted to show people my tinkering is worthwhile. I want to come up with something better than what my father took credit for."

He let out a chuckle. "Revenge inventing, huh?"

She shrugged. "I bet some of the best inventions didn't have altruistic motives behind them, but they still changed the world. So I'm going to ride my emotions as far as they'll take me and hope to discover something impressive."

She went back to her scribbling, her plate still full beside her. Maybe the success she'd had after saving those chicks last week had inspired her and she didn't realize she was ignoring him. "I like how honest you are."

She glanced up.

"And how free you are with your thoughts. I've come to expect that of you. I've missed it this past week, actually. You're really intent on what you're working on."

"I'm sorry." She shut her notepad and pushed it away. "I've been rude."

"That's all right. Could you tell me what you've come up with so far?"

"I'd rather not. I'm not certain they're any good yet."

"Maybe I can help you figure out which ideas have potential? I could at least tell you if I'd be interested in buying them."

"Perhaps." She pulled her notepad back toward her. "But I don't think it'll help me at the moment." With that, she ate a spoonful of beans and took her plate to the sink.

Was she not going to eat the rest of her supper? "Won't you wait for me? I'll walk you to your cabin."

"No need to inconvenience yourself. I'll take Mickey with me." She wiped off her hands and made for the back door. "Check on my chicks if you would."

Then she shut the door behind her.

He sighed at what was left of his food.

Why was she shutting him out? They'd talked so freely before. Maybe she was worried she'd told him too much about her past, but he couldn't think of anything he'd done to push her away.

He stared at Corinne's empty place setting, shook his head, and ate the rest of his beans. He'd given her permission to invent to her heart's desire—he'd not told her she could only do so if he wasn't feeling lonely.

After finishing his meal, he cleaned up. Picking a piece of notebook paper off the floor, he checked it before throwing it away. The page had three sketches and a lot of scribbling. He squinted at the words, clearly not written for others to read. Funny to find a woman's handwriting worse than his.

In the upper right-hand corner, he made out enough words to figure out he was looking at a chicken waterer. He stared at the sketch again. The way the cover was drawn, he could easily imagine it would keep chickens' dirty feet out, yet wouldn't hinder them from drinking. Ingenious. Chickens could muck up water as fast as a pig.

He glanced at the next drawing. A wire basket with hay? Studying the slanting words, it seemed she thought it'd keep nests from getting moldy. Would that sell? It was easy enough to swap out nasty straw with new.

Even if it wouldn't sell, she should get a patent on both. Beyond that, should they do anything with her ideas? He hadn't the money to put her inventions into production or buy advertising to sell it. And even if he did, doing so would take time away from the ranch. But what if...?

Uncle Matthias could help. Or at least he could tell them how successful each product might be. What if this chicken waterer could bring in more money than he could ever hope to make ranching? Since Uncle was in charge of sales for most of the Northwest Catalog's salesmen, he'd have plenty of people to ask whether this would be worthwhile to produce. And he'd know which factories would be the best to approach. And unlike Matt, Uncle Matthias was trustworthy.

But Uncle likely wouldn't give these inventions a second look if he knew they were Corinne's. Taking her paper to the parlor, Nolan noted the three chicks were huddled in the corner of the crate farthest from the fire, so he pulled them several inches away. Crouching down, he reached in to feel how warm they were, then pulled them back another few inches. He picked up the striped one, which was quick to wriggle from his grasp and rejoin the others trapped in the corner because of the heat.

"I know how you all feel." He grabbed one of the yellow ones, which was much calmer, its eyes droopy with sleep. "I'm sort of stuck in a corner, too."

The chick's eyes opened and closed rhythmically as Nolan petted its downy head with his thumb.

"Do we ask Uncle Matthias about these inventions? We should. But with Corinne thinking they're not good enough, I doubt she'd agree. What do you think?" He pulled out the drawing, but then shook his head at the absurdity of asking a chick for advice. He set the chick down, but continued talking. "Uncle knows business, and he's not responsible for Matt's incompetence—not directly, anyway. Poor parenting doesn't mean he can't help us."

Unfortunately, Uncle Matthias would look down on these ideas simply because they were a woman's. One of the things he had in common with his son was his opinion that males were superior to females.

What if…?

Grabbing another piece of paper, Nolan worked at copying the sketches. He could ask if these might sell and whether investors would be interested without letting Uncle know who these inventions belonged to. If he didn't think anyone would be interested, he could tell him how much they'd have to put toward these projects in hopes of seeing a profit.

If Uncle could advise him on these inventions' potential, he'd know if he should push Corinne to patent these or just let her continue inventing for the joy of it. He'd hate to get her excited about selling something only to learn it wasn't as good as he thought. He didn't want to pile more discouragement upon her than what she already heaped upon herself.

He'd certainly buy one of these chicken waterers if it worked though, and surely others would, too. And if Uncle agreed they were good, he'd help them know how to proceed.

CHAPTER TWENTY-SEVEN

Rubbing her temples, Corinne tried to relax her jaw. She'd been sitting at her cabin's worktable for hours. Her headache was likely from too much reading, or maybe lack of sleep. She dragged out her timepiece. Not as late as she thought.

The past two weeks, she'd hustled to help the men after finishing household chores. Then after feeding everyone dinner, she ran out to the cabin and tinkered until she was certain Nolan had turned in. Except for meals, she'd found every reason to be somewhere Nolan wasn't—even if it meant she stayed out later than her normal bedtime.

She flipped through her notebook and folded down corners, marking projects that held promise. She double-folded the page detailing her improvement to the stepladder. She'd already made a rough prototype. Timothy had been impressed, trying to swap her ladder with his every time she wasn't looking as they hammered shingles onto the newly extended coop roof.

She made a note to ask the mercantile owner if she could flip through his catalogs to see if stepladders with similar folding abilities and safety latches already existed. She'd waste no more time reinventing things if she could help it.

Closing her notebook, she looked at the leg replica she'd

finished for Nolan yesterday. Though it looked nearly the same as the one in the brochure, appearances weren't everything. What if Nolan put it on and abandoned it the next day?

She shook her head. It either worked or it didn't. Prototypes were made to show whether an idea had merit or not. Failure happened.

And yet, she didn't want to fail him. But no new ideas were coming to her on how to improve it. Time to give it to him.

Whether it ended up making walking easier for him or not, he'd be grateful. He'd likely show it off proudly, just like this morning when he'd taken an unexpected visitor to see the improvements she'd made to the coop. He dropped compliments about her in front of others without the slightest hint of flattery or patronizing.

He acted as if his pan were overflowing with gold because he'd married her, but he wasn't the richest one in this partnership. When had Randolph ever made dinner so she could spend an extra hour on her own projects? Nolan wasn't even exasperated with her—like Kurt had been—when she spent time tinkering instead of cleaning.

When had her father ever excused her from a chore because he could tell she needed a rest? Granted, she had a doctor's excuse now, but even if she didn't, Nolan would probably still take over the evening cleaning to give her a break if he thought her tired.

He was the type of man who'd voluntarily take every other dirty nappy.

Corinne rubbed against her itchy eyes.

She liked to tell herself her disastrous relationships had been a godsend because she'd not gotten herself stuck in a marriage that would eventually turn cold. But why didn't that knowledge make her feel better right now?

Oh, to dream about what it would be like with Nolan—but those dreams could only be dreams. She could not survive being found disappointing again, especially now that she was actually married. Oh, they could "separate," but she just couldn't live with taking money from a man who didn't want her. They would be happier in the long run if they remained business partners.

She needed to subdue these impossible longings, but she'd forgotten how strong attraction could be. She stood and shook her hands, as if she could rid herself of her desires by shaking them out through her fingers.

After tidying up, she grabbed Nolan's leg and marched out the cabin door and toward the house. The sun was setting, making the horse tied near the well house a fuzzy black silhouette.

A visitor? That could be good. She could sneak inside, zip upstairs, and put Nolan's leg on the bed rather than endure his praise in front of their guest. And if she acted at all like she wasn't worthy of being thanked, he'd peer into her eyes in an effort to convey his sincerity. He'd likely gaze long enough that the gold webbing behind the intricate green lacework of his eyes would steal her breath away.

She pushed the back door open slowly, which only made the whine last longer. She should have greased the hinges.

Unfortunately, Nolan's guest was in the kitchen with him —Matt.

No escape.

Nolan's face brightened. "Have you finished?"

She resisted the urge to hide his leg behind her back. "I think so."

Matt glanced between the leg Nolan wore and the one she held. "Did you buy another?"

"No, Corinne made it." Nolan's relieved countenance likely had nothing to do with her project being completed, but getting out of his conversation with Matt.

"She made that?" Matt's expression was more like what she expected of men—disbelief, suspicion.

"I told you she was talented. You should see what she's doing with the coop."

Which was harder to endure? Matt's spitefulness or Nolan's pride? She could *not* let herself like her husband any more than she already did.

Nolan handed Matt the replica leg as if presenting a prized gun or knife.

Matt frowned as he turned it over in his hands. "So this is what she's been wasting her time doing in that cabin?"

She blinked. Who'd complained to him about that? Not Nolan—at least not in such a dismissive tone. And though the men knew she was out there a lot, why would they have talked to Matt? They all seemed to share an aversion for Nolan's cousin.

"What's so special about this leg that it wouldn't be easier to order a new one?" Matt handed Nolan the leg, not even glancing at her.

"Well, it's—"

"It's a replica." She stepped between the two men, arms crossed. "An attempt to save money."

Matt's usual smirk settled into place between his ostentatious muttonchops, fluffed to their fullest this evening. "I'd gotten the impression people thought you were an inventor."

"She practically did invent this." Nolan pointed the leg at his cousin. "Before I showed her the illustration, she'd created one almost like it. And she has a whole notebook full of ideas neither one of us has enough imagination to dream up."

Matt's brows rose as if Nolan was spinning yarns. He gave her a sidelong glance, then spied the notebook in her hand.

She put her work behind her back. The desire to shove illustrations under his nose and dare him to dismiss her ideas had to be resisted. If any man would steal an idea of hers and try to pawn it off as his own, it'd be Matt.

"I consider myself more of a tinkerer," she breathed, congratulating herself for sounding civil.

"But—"

"Go." She gestured for Nolan to head upstairs. "Put it on and show him how well it works." So much for being a humble tinkerer.

As he headed for the stairs, she crossed the kitchen and pulled down the tea service to put some space between her and their visitor. "You want tea?"

"Nolan already offered."

Guess that meant no. "Hope you don't mind if I make myself a cup."

He didn't respond, but instead, tipped his head as if inspecting her. She turned her back to him. Maybe he'd take himself off to the parlor.

"So you're spending a lot of time in that cabin inventing."

Since he wasn't asking a question, she acknowledged him with a shrug, and poured hot water over her strainer.

"I find that odd."

"I realize most men believe women's brains are incapable of thinking of anything other than babies and housekeeping."

"That's not what I meant. Rather, I find it strange a newlywed bride spends most of her time doing something other than making her new husband happy."

She forced herself not to react to what he couldn't know was more perceptive than his usual self-serving observations.

"What kinds of things are you inventing other than legs? Teacups that hold your pinky out for you? Pretty curtain rods?"

She swallowed her sigh. "Projects that would appeal to both sexes and would actually be useful."

"Like what?"

Even if she listed off her most promising ideas, he'd still mock... And yet, she kept her face turned from him so she'd not give in to the desire to sneer at him. "Things like a coal lamp incubator, an egg candler, a stepladder."

He scoffed—as she knew he would. "Those things exist already."

"I hope to improve them."

Nolan's thumping down the stairs would soon prove her abilities or make Matt scoff all the more.

Her husband's smile when he stepped into the kitchen made all the tension in her chest float away.

The jaunty way he walked was a bit unnatural, but his steps seemed smoother. He paced the floor, demonstrating the knee joint's bending ability. "It's definitely better than my other one."

Matt's muttonchops wriggled as he seemed to be gritting his teeth. "New things often hold appeal, but the test of time will show—"

"If anyone's qualified to decide if one artificial leg is better than another," Nolan huffed, stopping to glare at his cousin, "It's me."

Matt shrugged. "Well, if it is, I'm glad of it. Your wife can help pad the coffers by giving you things to patent. My father—"

"No man will patent my inventions, thank you very much." She let her sugar spoon drop onto the counter and glared at Matt like her husband was.

Matt looked to Nolan, his brows raised, as if to ask if he was going to allow his wife to speak for herself.

Nolan didn't say a thing.

"Well, I've got to get back to Armelle before the sun sets. Good night." Matt snatched up his hat and left.

The minute the front door shut behind him, Corinne let out a long exhale. "Why did he come out here? Just to pick a fight?"

Nolan crossed over to peer out the window. "He'd heard about my oats going bad and had the gall to come out and advise me to fire my men. Said that's what he'd do if he were running the place."

The oats had gone bad? "So should you fire someone?"

Nolan shook his head. "If one of my men were responsible, I'd give them a second chance since it isn't a recurring problem. But I have a feeling." He put a hand to the back of his neck. "Though it makes no sense, I think Matt's behind the oats, along with the fence cutting, though I have no idea why."

"How else would he know what happens around here unless he's behind it?"

"Rascal goes to the saloons on the weekends to chat. Matt might have overheard him say something." Nolan came back to grab the tea tin. "I'm going to ask around town tomorrow if Matt's been looking for land or just hanging around poker tables. I can't think of how sabotaging the ranch would benefit him other than the thrill of punishing me for keeping the land from him. And if he thinks I'd sell because of a string of bad luck, that only proves he shouldn't spend a dime purchasing his own place."

"Perhaps he's doing it so he can point out to others how he would've run the place better?"

Nolan pursed his lips as he poured his tea. "Possible. The man can't stand not being better than everyone else—at least in his own eyes."

"Are you sure you don't want to make him mad enough he'll leave you alone?"

"I can't say I don't occasionally think of doing so, but no. I respect his father enough not to punch his son's lights out." He gave her a silly smile, then stuck out his new leg. "This is extraordinary. Don't let Matt's derision make you doubt your abilities. He's probably just miffed a woman can do something he can't."

"Well, thank you. Though he's right about taking time to test something before making a final judgment. Don't shy away from telling me if it causes you pain or is difficult to maneuver. I've scrapped plenty of things I thought were perfect only to realize later they wouldn't last."

"Fair enough. But the leg is certainly better than what he or I could've done." He leaned casually against the counter with his cup of tea. "Did I hear you say you've designed a stepladder and an incubator?"

"Yes." She stared down into her cup. How awful he must feel that she'd told his puffed-up cousin more about her ideas than him. But as always, he didn't appear ruffled.

"Do you think your things might be worthy of that fair Annie mentioned?"

She took her first sip of tea and winced as she forced herself to swallow the too hot liquid. "The stepladder maybe, but I'd want to build one to test it out."

"Shouldn't you get a patent right away? I don't know how any of that works."

"I'd rather not. I want my first patent to be the best I can offer, not some crazy idea no one wants. Besides, it costs money. Fixing the chicken coop comes first."

Turning, she stopped at the bright smile he was directing at her. "What?"

He smiled even bigger. "You said the *first* thing you patent. I'm glad you're not giving up."

She leaned over to kiss him on the cheek. "Thank you."

His smile disappeared. "For what?"

She froze. Why had she kissed him? The impression his stubble left on the soft skin of her lips felt hot. "For letting me spend a ridiculous amount of time in that cabin," she whispered.

"No problem." His voice was raspy, and his gaze riveted to hers.

Their warm breath mingled and she couldn't help but wonder what his lips, rather than his beard, would feel like against her own.

He didn't move, but his eyes did. Down.

Seemed he was thinking the same thing. Leaning toward a fire wasn't the smartest thing to do, but she let herself lean, and when he did likewise, she closed her eyes.

His mouth landed gently upon hers, but instead of pressing hard against her, his lips moved tenderly, achingly slow. His hand came up to cup one side of her jaw, and ever so slightly, he pulled her closer. Warmth pooled somewhere in her middle, sweet and decadent, and she let herself kiss him back.

Needing a breath, she pulled away. "I…" Her heart was beating too fast and she couldn't remember what she was going to say.

His features were screwed up as he looked at her. Was he confused … or dismayed?

He certainly wasn't pulling her back in for another kiss.

Well, of course he wasn't. Who was she fooling? Just because he was a good man, that didn't mean he'd find her kisses any more enjoyable than the others had. She looked down, unable to meet his eyes again. "Good night."

Plunking her teacup onto the counter, she didn't stay to clean up what she'd just spilled.

She couldn't remain in his presence any longer without letting feelings grow that shouldn't.

Tonight, she'd pray for it all to go away.

CHAPTER TWENTY-EIGHT

Nolan walked out to the cabin where Corinne had remained all evening once again, likely in an attempt to avoid him. He swung his lamp in a wide arc to make sure he was still on the path. The overgrown patches were getting worn down now, but it wasn't easy to follow in the dark.

He shouldn't have kissed her last night. He'd promised if he wanted to change their arrangement, he'd ask—and he'd certainly not asked.

But he'd not thought to do so when she'd looked so willing, and with the way she'd melted into him, he'd lost all awareness of anything other than her lips...

He'd wanted to kiss her again but wasn't sure he'd be able to contain himself.

He'd reveled in the sparks of awareness. He'd soaked up the delicious warmth. He'd immersed himself in the sensation.

Sensations he replayed every few seconds.

He'd been jittery waiting for Corinne to come down for breakfast this morning. Partially because he knew how awkward it would be, and partially because she'd not been opposed to his kiss in the moment, even if she had run afterwards.

She felt something for him. Even if she wasn't ready to admit it.

But she hadn't come down before he'd left for Armelle, and then she'd skipped dinner, sequestering herself in the cabin. With every quarter hour past sunset, his worry grew. Was she talking herself out of whatever she was feeling for him, or had she had an accident doing an experiment?

If she wasn't in trouble, should he apologize for last night's kiss or pretend it didn't happen? Assure her he'd never let it happen again?

He certainly didn't want to do any of those things.

But she'd said if he asked to court her and she refused, he'd have to concede. He couldn't let this end so soon.

With the cabin looming in front of him, he hadn't much time to decide—

A rustle to his left made him stop. He turned and held up his lantern, narrowing his eyes to peer into the shadows.

Other than worrying about Corinne staying out so late, learning that his cousin wasn't searching for property had made it hard to concentrate on anything once he'd returned from town.

Someone at the bar had mentioned Matt talked of property, but no one knew if he'd visited the courthouse, the lawyer, or Bowen McGill. Those three would've been where he'd have started to inquire after land.

The lure of the poker table likely accounted for Matt's lack of searching though. Evidently, plenty of newcomers had been willing to bet against him, and he was raking in dough every night.

Talking instead of doing had always been Matt's way, so maybe the annoying problems plaguing the ranch had nothing to do with his cousin. Matt was too lazy to play pranks for no good reason, and as long as they were married, Matt couldn't have the ranch.

Of course, if Corinne were no longer around...

His heart flopped and his breathing grew shallow. No. Matt hadn't the gumption to take out his wife. Matt might be a braggart, but that's all he was—a talker.

Surely.

And yet...

Light flickered dimly in the cabin's windows. Slightly reassuring.

To the left, a shiver of movement arrested his attention again. He slowed as he scanned the area. "Mickey?"

Hadn't Corinne taken the dog with her?

No black mutt bounded out of the overgrowth, but a shadow crouched not far from the cabin. Too big to be insignificant, but what—

It moved.

He squinted, his heartbeat on the uptick. If only the cloud cover wasn't so thick.

If he didn't check it out, he'd worry all night. He steeled himself and trudged into the brush to assure—

Zip.

"Ahhh!" Nolan landed flat on his back, his false leg yanked out from under him. "Ooof."

He groaned at the ache pounding in his head where it had hit ground. The rock jabbing him in the back was uncomfortable, but he lay unmoving. What on earth?

He tried to move, but his leg was caught up in—

Wait, where was his lamp? He snapped his head to the side, thankful to discover its outline rocking back and forth in the dark as it settled to a stop, its flame extinguished. Fighting a grass fire wouldn't have been fun right now—or even possible. What was he tangled in?

"Who's there?" Corinne's voice sounded from near the cabin.

A strong light pierced the dark.

What kind of lamp did she have that was so bright? The light moved closer as he attempted to push himself into a sitting position, struggling against whatever had hold of his leg.

"I said, who's there?" Her voice turned menacing.

"Me," he called back, and then grimaced at the ringing bouncing around between his ears. He reached up to feel if he was bleeding somewhere on the back of his head. "Nolan."

"Why are you tromping through the brush at this time of night?" She came up beside him, her light blinding, making him wince. "That snare wasn't meant for you."

A snare? "Who was it meant for?"

"The coyotes." She set down her lamp and grabbed whatever invisible wire had him tethered. "I'm glad it worked though. I've not set one before."

"I guess I should be happy I helped you figure that out?" Though his head certainly wasn't.

Instead of releasing his foot, she looked down at him and shook her head. "What were you doing out here, anyway?"

Turning her lamp so it no longer blinded him, he noted the brightness came from the curved mirrors she'd fitted inside the lamp's housing. He aimed the beam of light toward this evening's nemesis, a stump with broken branches piled on top of it. "I forged into the brush to be sure that stump knew I would have none of its shenanigans."

"What?" She turned to see what he'd illuminated.

"That stump waved its leafy arms at me, threatening your very life, if you can believe it." He tried to sit in a more dignified position, but she hadn't loosened the snare. "I was going to teach it a lesson, but instead you taught me one. Never underestimate my wife and her contraptions."

Though the light barely illuminated her face, he could make out her grin. "Sorry."

"Don't be." He relaxed when she started working on releasing him from the wire. "Are you worried about coyotes?"

He tried to sit up again, but with his inability to flex his leg, he gave up and leaned back on his elbows.

"Not worried for myself, but the chicks. We don't have a rooster anymore to alert us—not that he did last time."

The tension on his leg disappeared, and it fell to the ground with a thud.

"So you set up a snare out here?" How would that help the chickens?

"I figured there was too much open space around the coop for a coyote to get snared there." She leaned down and grabbed hold of his ankle.

He turned the lamp toward her so she could see better.

"Thanks." She worked on loosening the wire and pulling it off. "The coyotes come up here, though. Figured if they were going to make a nuisance of themselves, I'd make them regret it."

"What would you do if you caught one?"

"Get one of the men to take care of it." She pulled off the snare and sat back to look at him, staying in a crouch.

Was that a smile on her face? The shadows were too harsh for him to be certain.

"Of course, you're not a coyote. At first, I thought I might've caught your cousin."

"So you're worried about him, too?"

Corinne shrugged then stood and held out her hand as if he were a woman in need of assistance.

For a second, he considered scrambling up on his own to preserve his one last shred of dignity, but the temptation to hold her hand was too much. Once on his feet, he held on, testing if his false foot had twisted in the fall.

It felt fine enough, but he didn't release her. He looked down, wishing he could see her eyes in the dark. "Thank you."

"Thank you?" She jerked back. "I was expecting a lecture."

"Nope." With her this close, he could smell something floral and clean wafting from her. He groaned. How could she smell this good after a full day's work?

"Are you hurt?" Her free hand ran up his arm and over his shoulder.

Was it wrong not to answer, to let her hand continue to wander?

He closed his eyes. He'd not known his body had been craving touch this badly—or maybe just her touch.

When she dropped her hand, he blew out a breath. "I don't think anything's hurt other than my pride."

She stepped back. "I'm rather embarrassed about that. If I set any more snares, I'll let you know."

"Please do, and tell us all." He turned to pick up his lamp, hoping not to find broken glass. Luckily, his light had landed on a thick clump of vegetation.

"Are you worried about Matt?" She picked up her own lamp. "Being out here?"

"I wasn't until I started walking to check on you. He's never been one to think highly of women and your very existence ruins his plans."

"You mean...?" She quieted as she matched her stride to his. "Surely not. What about his fiancée? Don't you think he thinks highly of her?"

"Of her savings accounts, yes—not to mention she's pretty. Whether they actually get along, who knows?"

"I like how we get along," she said softly as they approached the cabin's front door.

He slowed, not sure how to respond—how to tell her the truth without scaring her off. Because he more than liked how they got along. He wished they got along better—much, much better. "Uh, me, too."

Well, that wasn't exactly brilliant. But she'd outlawed anything romantic-sounding, so what could he say but the unvarnished truth? "You're certainly nicer to have around than Matt."

She gave him a playful push and then stepped in front of him to enter the cabin. "Did you two ever get along?"

He followed her in. "When we were little, maybe. But ever since that first summer after I lost my leg, we've been competing for my father's affection, and I always lost."

Taking a seat on a stool, he readjusted the strap holding his leg as best he could through his trousers.

"Let me tidy up, and I'll walk back with you."

As she moved about organizing her tables, it was clear she was not interested in talking anymore.

Was last night's kiss plaguing her as much as it was him? If only he were certain she'd not shut him down if he tried to talk about it. Had he done something wrong?

No, he'd simply kissed her. Whereas she'd offered to be intimate without even so much as an "I love you."

And why did that bother him anyway? Would he have been able to utter those three words to her?

The moment he'd thought Matt might kidnap Corinne—or worse—the anxiety that had gripped him wasn't because he feared losing the ranch, but his wife.

His first thoughts upon waking were of her. If he could find an excuse to be closer to where she was working during the day, he took it.

She was everything a sane man wanted. If Matt so much as laid a hand on her, he'd fight him, even knowing he'd likely lose.

If he dreamed about sleeping with her once, he'd dreamed it a hundred times.

And after she'd kissed him, the times he'd wanted to ask her to allow him to do so again were too innumerable to count.

She couldn't do or say anything that would ever compel him to ask for a separation. And it wasn't just because he was lonely.

What was there left to believe but to consider himself in love?

And love wasn't what she wanted.

But then, after hearing how her father and fiancés had treated her, she likely didn't know what love could be like. Not that he did either really, but what he felt for her…

He knew how it was to yearn to be loved but give up on it to avoid inevitable anguish. He'd done everything he could to make his father happy, but it hadn't been enough.

But he'd vowed to love Corinne as Christ loved the church. Though he hadn't promised to love her as a man loved a woman, he could still love her. Nothing could stop him from putting her needs above his—

"Are you ready?"

He startled to find Corinne beside him. He took a quick glance around and realized she'd blown out all the lamps in the cabin except her own. "Am I ready?"

She nodded, her eyebrows tweaked up at his silly question.

But it wasn't a silly question.

Was he ready? Not in regard to leaving the cabin, but to loving her sacrificially, knowing he may never gain her love in return.

She stood waiting, an unspoken question in her eyes.

"Yes, I think so."

Or rather, he had no choice.

And what was wrong with loving a woman he'd promised to live with for the rest of his life? If he'd married for love, and his bride became frail or sick, he'd not stop loving her. He'd love her in the ways she could be loved.

So he'd do that. Love Corinne in the ways she could be loved.

"Let's go." He picked up his dead lamp and limped quickly for the door, so he could hold it open. "After you."

She ducked under his arm and started off into the night.

He didn't want to scare her away, so for now, he'd say nothing about his feelings. But as for actions? He could love her without saying the words.

For he already did.

CHAPTER TWENTY-NINE

Two weeks had passed since her snare knocked Nolan to the ground, and her skin was tingling with electricity every time he came near.

Didn't matter if they were alone, or like right now, sharing Sunday supper with friends, she knew exactly where he was, how close, how far, without even seeing him.

She nodded at something Annie was saying across the table, but it was as if her ears had ceased working the second she sensed Nolan walking closer. She braced herself for the feel of his fingers that would trail across her shoulders as he passed. Bracing, and yet, at the same time, eagerly awaiting.

Every time he walked by now, whether at church, in the barn, or on their way to their separate rooms at night, his touch would light upon her, skimming softly, as if he didn't even realize his fingers were magnetized to her.

He'd also been doing a lot of whispering lately, leaning close, his warm breath stirring the curls she let hang loose.

He kept taking her hand, too, especially in town. Of course, that was for show, to keep the townsfolk from realizing their marriage was in name only, but lately he'd continue to hold her hand after everyone had walked away.

As expected, the tips of Nolan's fingers grazed across her neck and down her shoulder as he finally moved past her to hand the bowl of raisins to Spencer.

She failed to keep from shivering as hot and cold sensations rippled through her body at his touch.

Yet, despite all his attentions, all his touching, he'd not kissed her once after that first time.

Her heart dropped into her stomach like a stone. She'd known better than to ever hope—

"Corinne, are you sure you don't want to share that gravy with us?"

Annie's amused tone made her snap to attention. "What?"

"The gravy." She pointed in front of Corinne.

She looked down. Seemed she'd ladled out half the contents of the gravy boat onto her mashed potatoes. She clinked the ladle back into the boat and shoved it to the right toward Celia.

She'd almost forgotten the girl sat next to her with how her body was so attuned to Nolan on her left.

He put his arm around the back of her chair, and his thumb lightly grazed the top of her shoulder. And now he was making circles against her skin through her blouse. Did he even realize he was doing that? He was likely subconsciously mirroring Jacob and Annie across the table—but his absentminded caress was nothing her former fiancés would've done except behind closed doors. They'd never shown her affection in public.

Was this affection? No, it was just … just…

Well, maybe it was affection of a sort. She hadn't met a kinder man than Nolan. That's what it was. This was just kindness.

"Pepper?"

A hard tap to her shoulder jolted her thoughts away from the thumb Nolan was circling against her skin.

"Huh?" She turned to Celia.

The young lady looked at her like she was crazy. "Spencer wants the pepper."

It took a second, but she realized she was holding the pepper with a death grip. And she didn't even like the spice. "Oh." She pushed the shaker across the table so the boy could grab it.

She couldn't bear to look down at her plate, where she'd probably sprinkled everything with pepper, including the canned pears.

Jacob glanced from her plate back to Nolan. "Do you want me to take your scythes home with me to sharpen?"

"If you don't mind, we can't sharpen blades as well as you can."

Nolan's hand moved off her arm, and she released her breath. When his fingers skimmed across the skin above her dress's high collar, she shot up. "Anyone want dessert?"

Spencer's eyes lit. "We get dessert before we're done eating?"

Annie made a noise that resembled a choked chuckle. "Not you, but that's an advantage of being grown up. You can eat whatever you want whenever you want."

Jacob piled green beans onto his plate—which was still full.

The amount of time she'd thought passed evidently hadn't. She looked at her own plate, swimming in peppered gravy. "Uh, I just thought I'd ask since I have to set it out."

Which was the stupidest thing she'd uttered so far, considering dessert was blackberry pie. Jacob had already stolen a pinch of the crust.

"The cream, I mean." And now she was obliged to put out cream … hopefully they liked warm cream.

She had to get out of this chair. If she didn't, Nolan might slide his fingers down her back or, heaven forbid, rest his hand atop her thigh, and she'd probably squawk like a chicken.

Jacob took a glance at Nolan before returning his gaze to her. "I think we'd all like cream with our pie—once we're done."

She gave him a sharp nod and then nearly tripped in her effort to get out of her chair.

Gah! How much more of a fool could she make of herself?

In the kitchen, she took a second to catch her breath, and

then headed out the back door to get the honey-sweetened whipped cream from the cellar.

On her way, she pulled a rag off the clothesline. Inside the musty little cellar buried under an earthen mound, she dropped to her knees and pulled the cream from the ice water she'd set it in to stay cool. She wiped the jar with the rag and pressed the damp cloth against her neck.

Could cold water make a blush disappear?

How was she going to go back and sit next to Nolan without instructing him to keep his hands to himself so she didn't end up choking on her food?

She couldn't without making a scene—and she certainly didn't need to make another.

She sucked in several deep breaths. She could do this. She just needed to keep her attention on dinner and their guests. Not Nolan.

Squaring her shoulders, she pushed herself off the ground and forced herself back to the house.

She had an entire plate of gravy to choke down.

Jacob pushed his plate away before he'd finished his pie. Nolan took another bite of his. He'd rather have had cream, but Corinne had brought it in so early it'd melted. Poor girl, one thing after another kept messing up the dinner she'd worked so hard to prepare. But even without cream, it was good. Maybe Jacob didn't like blackberries.

His friend picked up his napkin and wiped his mouth. "Why don't you and I get your scythes so we can head out?"

He was ready to leave? Nolan looked out the window. The sky was still bright. "Sure, they're in the lean-to."

Annie popped up from her chair and took her plate to the sink, her pie also half-finished.

Spencer, however, seemed in no hurry. His dessert was swimming in melted cream, and by the way he licked his spoon after each bite, he'd probably lick his plate, too, if his momma wasn't looking.

Jacob stood and Nolan looked around. Had he offended them at some point during dinner? He got up and headed for the back door, glancing over his shoulder to be sure Jacob followed. As soon as they stepped outside, he turned to his friend. "Did I do something to upset you?"

Jacob's brow furrowed. "No."

"Good." Nolan descended the stairs before continuing, "Before you leave, could you help me stretch my leg so we can skip tomorrow?" Weeks ago, he'd gotten Jacob to agree to help him follow the doctor's order. Three times a week wasn't enough to make Doc Ellis happy, but it was something. He did what he could on the other days, but with Jacob and Annie leaving to consider buying polo ponies from a ranch in Nebraska, he needed to get one last good stretch in.

"Why would you want me to do that now?" Jacob looked even more confused.

"Why wouldn't I, considering you're leaving the day after tomorrow?"

He slowed behind him. "Annie and I figured we ought to head home as soon as dessert was over."

But they hadn't actually finished. "Why? I was hoping for a chess rematch."

Jacob cleared his throat. "Uh, we gathered your wife wanted alone time."

Nolan shook his head as he started for the lean-to again. "She spends hours alone every night in her cabin. She's not so desperate for quiet she'd pass up visiting with your wife. Besides, you and I—"

Jacob smacked Nolan's shoulder. "Alone time with you, you dolt, not Annie. Have Corinne do your stretches."

Nolan cocked his head. Corinne had certainly been out of sorts this evening, but she'd told him several times how much she'd looked forward to Annie's visit. "Remember, her hands aren't strong enough—"

Jacob let out a disbelieving puff of air. "Who cares if she's any good at it?" Then he looked at Nolan as if he were trying to shoot some message into his brain by narrowing his eyes at him.

"But, the doctor—"

Jacob's eye roll stopped him.

Oh, Jacob thought...

How was he going to explain without actually explaining? "I think you've misunderstood." What had Corinne done to make them think she wanted to be alone with him?

She clearly didn't, as evidenced by her leaving a room as soon as he stepped into it. "She and I ... well."

Goodness, he couldn't explain. Her reasons for remaining platonic were not his to tell. And that she'd said they could be intimate if he remained unfeeling toward her—he wasn't going to tell anyone that, no matter how good a friend.

"Don't worry about us." Jacob laid a hand on his shoulder. "We aren't upset to cut dinner short. If the honeymoon's just started—"

"But it hasn't. She's not interested." How he could tear his tongue out! Why had he said that? "I mean..."

What could he tell Jacob? He'd say nothing to besmirch her reputation. But if he could frame it as his own failure... "It's that she uh, doesn't enjoy herself romantically."

A small groan escaped him. That had sounded worse than he'd expected. "The thing is, I won't put her through something just to, uh, please myself, so we ... are..." Why on earth was his mouth still running! But if he ended in the middle of a thought, Jacob might assume something even more unflattering. "So, for the foreseeable future, we're nothing but business partners."

Jacob shook his head as if he didn't believe a single word he'd heard. "What I saw during dinner was not business partners."

Nolan looked away and shrugged. "I'm not going to pretend

she doesn't drive me insane whenever she's near, but if pushing for more makes her miserable, I've promised—"

"Are you willing to do whatever it takes to make her happy?"

Nolan looked back at his friend. "Of course."

"Then what's keeping you from doing so?"

"It's not me. She's … she's closed down."

The silence between them got awkward as Jacob sized him up.

Jacob usually had good advice, and something inside him wanted to know every thought his friend was thinking. Yet the agony of receiving advice he couldn't implement might drive him even further toward madness. "Look—"

"I was lucky." Jacob's voice wasn't loud enough to cut him off, and yet, his softly spoken words and the way he fidgeted made Nolan's heart thump harder.

His friend cleared his throat and looked past him. "As you know, Annie was married before. We've only talked about this once because I wasn't interested in the details, but her first marriage started as you're describing. She didn't … enjoy herself. Evidently, they were at odds for the first few years because of it."

Goodness, and he'd thought the beginning of their conversation had been awkward.

With redness crawling above Jacob's collar, it seemed he wasn't the only one feeling they were treading dangerously toward sharing too much information.

And yet … was there hope? "So, that's not a problem anymore?"

Jacob's droll grin made Nolan's stomach sink. He'd probably never have reason to sport such a sloppy expression.

He fisted his hands. He had no right to be jealous of his friend's marital bliss. Corinne was doing everything he'd requested of her.

Jacob's lips wriggled a bit. "I'd say she's quite happy now, but I was lucky—as I said. Evidently, it took Annie and Greg years to figure out how she could be happy, in that regard."

"Years?"

Jacob shrugged. "After she got desperate and confessed her unhappiness to Leah, some advice Leah gave her helped turn things around. Why don't you have Corinne talk to Annie or Leah, whoever she's more comfortable with?"

What was he supposed to say? *Corinne, pudding pie, I think you should talk to Annie about the marriage bed. Jacob says she enjoys it.* If his cheeks had been hot before, they were hot enough to fry an egg now.

Ducking into the lean-to to retrieve the scythes, he turned to hand the first one to Jacob, shaking his head. "I doubt Corinne would ask anyone about that."

Jacob took the implement from him. "I could suggest Annie bring it up."

"Please, don't." He could barely force the words out of his mouth, his throat was so dry. If Corinne found out he'd even hinted to Jacob about her reasons for not marrying in truth, he could kiss any hope of returned affection goodbye. "I mean, she'd be embarrassed to find out I talked to you about this. If the right time presents itself, I'll encourage her to talk to someone, but that might never happen."

Jacob stared at him for a moment, then let out a noisy exhale. "I don't think I can share much more without my own wife being displeased." He gathered up the three scythes. "I'll get these sharpened before we leave for Nebraska and leave them in our lean-to since we won't be out this way again before we go. You can pick them up whenever you want."

He turned and headed for the house.

"Hey, wait," Nolan called out. "Could you…?"

When his friend looked back, he couldn't finish his request for Jacob to reconsider stretching his leg tonight. "Never mind."

He'd run out of options. Either he had to accept his wife's

help, or hire that nurse he'd always told his father he'd rather have than a wife.

How wrong he'd been.

CHAPTER THIRTY

Corinne buckled up Buttermilk's breeching, finishing off hooking the horse to the wagon, and looked out the barn's wide open doors.

Nolan was riding up from wherever he'd gone this morning, clearly in pain. He likely had no idea she could see him, hence why he wasn't trying to hide his grimace as he adjusted himself in his saddle.

She patted Buttermilk on the neck. Her hands hadn't hurt for days. Occasionally, she'd poke and press them, thinking she was too busy to notice how they felt, but beyond some numbness, her hands were mostly back to normal.

But the doctor had said Nolan's leg might always hurt, even without pressure or friction sores, mentioning something about choices made during surgery.

Yet ever since the Hendrixes had come over for supper last week, Nolan had seemed determined to work twice as long, which likely meant his leg hurt twice as bad. From the look of him, that was true.

He'd told her Jacob was helping him stretch and massage his leg, but perhaps no amount of massage would make up for the strain he was putting on his leg lately.

She should've told him days ago she thought he was working too hard, but she would've had to remain longer in his presence, and lately, he'd been too hard to be with.

Every polite question about her day, every offer to get her a drink, every sincere thank you, light touch, long look, and tipped smile would make her wish she could get closer to him. She longed to spend more time asking him what he was thinking, but how could she without stirring up the attraction she was desperately trying to squash?

Despite the doorframe being a good six inches above his head, Nolan ducked as his horse entered the barn. He slowed, clicking in soft tones amid the quiet hisses that indicated his discomfort, but when he spotted her, he rammed himself upright. "I thought you'd be in the cabin."

She would've been, but she'd found herself feeling guilty in light of how much he'd worked lately. Sure, she'd redesigned the coop and kept the house and took turns cooking for the hands, but as much as she tried to tell herself that was enough, he was working five times harder. Now that her hands were nearly back to normal, she couldn't let him outwork her. "I needed to go to town."

Nolan dismounted, obviously trying to disguise a limp.

In the dim light, she allowed herself to look at him longer than she usually did. The tension in his jaw strained his features. It was too dark to see his eyes, but she could imagine how he was looking at her—the way he had for weeks, a soft look that roamed over her face as if cataloging every freckle.

Her hand rose a fraction of an inch, the desire to run her fingers through the curl behind his ear maddeningly strong. She tucked her hand away in her pocket. "Have you seen the doctor lately?"

He stopped. "Haven't needed to."

She pressed her lips together. If anyone was going to tell him he was wrong, it seemed it was up to her. "I think you do. Whatever Jacob's doing, it doesn't seem to be helping."

Nolan ran his hands through his hair like he did whenever she asked personal questions. "I suppose I could see the doctor whenever I get to the bank, but I didn't want to make a trip in for just that."

"Well, then, why don't you go with me?" And now her hands grew clammy. Too late to retract her invitation. Her insides fluttered at the thought of sitting beside him for a couple of hours. On the other hand, driving to and from town was far less intimate than spending time with him behind four walls ensconced in lamp light. "I'm already going, and we've not had much time to talk lately. I've missed that."

His eyebrows winged up.

Of course he'd be surprised at such an admission, considering how she'd been making every excuse to be somewhere other than near him.

"I suppose I could go along."

"Good." She pivoted and checked Buttermilk's harnessing as if this were an ordinary occurrence. "I'll make sure everything's hooked up if you need to get ready before we go."

"No, I'm good."

The tone of his voice and the way he was looking at her made her think he meant something other than having no need to retrieve anything.

Once he put away his horse, he came to her side of the wagon and held out a hand to assist her.

She hesitated, not because a piece of her melted at how attentive he was, but because he was in pain and she could've managed on her own.

To keep from offending him, she accepted his assistance but flinched when his other hand cupped her waist when she stepped onto the wheel spoke.

That hand trailed down her side as she climbed up, from hip to thigh. Against so many layers of fabric he couldn't have felt a thing, yet one might think he'd grazed her bare skin by the amount of heat blooming in her face.

Once she seated herself, his other hand squeezed hers. She looked down, and he smiled up.

Then he walked off—as if that smile hadn't been warm enough to cook her insides.

Seconds later, he hauled himself up onto the seat and started driving. Once they were out of the gate, he gave the horse some slack. "Mr. Lansing caught us near the back forty and paid the stud fee he owed me. What do you want me to do with your share?"

"My share?" A breeze pulled at her bonnet and she held it tighter against her head.

"Of the profits."

"I thought I'd only be paid when the cattle were sold. You don't have to—"

"As a businesswoman you know profit is profit. Sales generate most of my income, yes, but it's not the only way the ranch pays for itself."

"Oh, of course." Then the profit from the butter she was intending to sell was partially his, too. "If I sell the butter I'm taking in today, what do you want me to do with your share?"

He encouraged Buttermilk to get back up to speed. "Put it toward whatever you see fit."

She squirmed on the seat beside him. "If you're splitting Mr. Lansing's payment with me, then I don't think it's right I spend your part of the butter proceeds without direction."

"I'm not worried—"

"What if I chose to spend it all on gumdrops?"

He turned slightly, one brow raised. "I guess I'd be eating a lot of gumdrops."

She crossed her arms. "You can't tell me you wouldn't chastise me first."

He shrugged. "Maybe, if that was the only thing you ever bought—"

"You just said we agreed on splitting the profit."

"Yes." He had the nerve to look confused.

"Then why wouldn't you care if I spent your money on gumdrops?"

"Because money from butter and eggs is nothing but icing on the cake. I'm happy to let you have it."

She blew out a frustrated breath while shaking her head. "I thought I was marrying a good businessman."

His expression froze, yet he didn't defend himself.

The wagon tilted into a rut, the movement sending reverberations around inside her chest—where her heart ought to have been.

"I'm sorry." Once the wagon got back on flat ground, she summoned up the courage to grab his free hand and squeeze it. "Whether you're a good business man or not, you're a plain good man, and I'm honored you trust me."

His expression softened as he squeezed her hand in return. He began to pull away, but she held on, then looked away toward town, keeping his hand firmly in hers.

Once they reached the outskirts of town, Nolan extricated himself.

She tried not to frown. She'd enjoyed being connected to him without worrying it might lead to more.

But then, what if it did lead to more? What if she allowed herself to be free to fall in love with him? He'd been kind to her before he'd needed anything from her, whereas Kurt and Randolph had only appeared kind because they wanted something. Though Nolan had certainly needed her to save his ranch, he'd given her a portion of it—forever.

And Gerald? Well, being abandoned for her younger sister because she kissed better couldn't ever happen again. If Nolan didn't enjoy kissing her, well, he could just choose not to. He'd said he'd counted the cost when marrying her—that it was her or no one.

She twisted her hands in her lap, trying to keep herself from leaping off the seat and running. A part of her wanted to flee this desire to mess up a good partnership because there was no guarantee they'd end up pleased with each other. Yet another part wanted to grab Nolan by the lapels and kiss him whether he liked it or not.

"Good afternoon!" Frank Dent tipped his hat at them as they drove past, shocking Corinne back to the fact they were already in town.

After returning the deputy's greeting, Nolan turned to her. "That stepladder you're working on? Should you pick up something to help you build it?"

She put a hand against her abdomen. Though neither running or kissing were possibilities right now, her stomach seemed intent on the former, even if it meant leaving her behind. She let out a long, slow breath, trying to formulate a response. She did need hinges. "We could stop at the livery to see how much it'd cost for him to fabricate something for me before we head to the bank."

"Sounds like a plan." He turned in that direction.

"What are you doing with the money you're depositing today?"

"Leaving it in savings."

She played with the folds of her skirt. If it hadn't been for her, his bank account wouldn't need replenishing. She'd suffered twinges of guilt when she'd asked for that hundred dollars, but now that he saw to her every need, pushed her to do what she loved, worked harder than her... "Never mind about the livery. I'll put mine in savings, too—half into your savings, half to send to my brother-in-law. I'll do that until the money I took is returned."

"Those aren't the terms we agreed upon."

"True, but I *am* a woman." She gave him a shy side glance. "I hear we like to change our minds regularly."

And boy was her heart trying to change her convictions completely right now.

"Then change your mind back. You should make the stepladder. Every invention I've seen of yours looks like a worthy investment. I'm sad every time I'm in the coop and your covered waterer isn't in the corner."

She stiffened. She hadn't shown him that. "When did you see my waterer?"

He kept his gaze on the road in front of them, but reached up to pull on his collar. "My curiosity got the better of me when you left behind some of your sketches. You should get what you need to make that, too."

She wanted to be mad at him, but if he thought it was good … no, that didn't matter. "I'll have plenty of time to make those things after I've paid back your one hundred dollars."

"What about getting ready for the ladies' fair?"

"They'll likely have one another year."

"I don't feel right about you putting your dreams on hold to pay back something you aren't supposed to." Nolan slowed the team to a stop in front of Doctor Ellis's. "It's your money to do with as you please."

"I know." Why did he appear so grim? Maybe he was in more pain than she'd thought.

He shook his head but handed the reins to her. "All right, then. Why don't you check on Leah while I see the doctor?"

If she didn't go in with him, how likely was it he'd inform her of what the doctor said? "I wanted to ask Mrs. Ellis if she's pleased with Leah's work before I do so." She trusted Leah, but what else could she talk to Mrs. Ellis about?

His jaw worked, but he nodded and started down his side of the wagon. She was on the ground before he had a chance to help her and nearly flinched at the frown he gave her. Didn't he know she was only trying to keep him from hurting himself?

Besides, the more he touched her, the more aggravated she was for telling him their marriage could be nothing but convenient.

Except it already wasn't. Yet if he was happy right now, he deserved to stay that way. Because if she loved him…

She swallowed and looked to the dirt at their feet, nearly overwhelmed by the sudden rise of emotion.

Was there an *if* to contemplate? Was there even an *if* about it? What was love if not a desire to make someone happy? Just because she feared she couldn't, didn't mean she didn't desperately want to.

She let out a shaky breath. She could very well be in more trouble than she'd thought.

Mrs. Ellis stepped out onto the porch to empty a dustpan. "Hello, you two!"

Corinne clamped her hands against her sides, as if that might settle the sudden bout of jumping frogs wreaking havoc within her.

The older lady smiled at the two of them as Nolan started up the stairs. "How's married life?"

Corinne glanced up at Nolan, who was taking the steps slower than usual. Hopefully the doctor could give him something to help with the pain he must be in. She followed him up and gave Mrs. Ellis's arm a squeeze. "Your husband's prescription to marry wasn't as bad of a suggestion as I thought. My hands truly are better now."

"Good." Mrs. Ellis gave her shoulder a friendly pat and they headed inside.

"Nolan?" The doctor had just stepped out of the stairwell. "You here to see me?"

Nolan held the door open for her and Mrs. Ellis to crowd into the waiting room. "Yes, sir."

After the two men disappeared into an examination room, Corinne turned to the doctor's wife. "While we're here, I wanted to check if you were happy with Mrs. Whitsett's laundry service."

"She's doing fine. Come." Mrs. Ellis took Corinne's arm. "Let's quilt while you wait for your husband. I've got everything set up."

"Well, I…" How could she admit she'd planned to eavesdrop on their husbands since she doubted hers would tell her anything? "I don't think Nolan's going to be that long."

The old woman frowned. "Probably not, but I'm excited about how my newest top turned out. Come see it, at least."

The log cabin design was certainly pretty in dark browns, pinks, and greens. The white, even stitching was beginning to take shape atop the pattern. After the obligatory compliments and politely turning down the offer to come into town to quilt in the evenings, Corinne headed back downstairs in time to see Nolan leave the exam room.

The doctor pulled the door shut behind them. "Now, I mean it. Rest that leg more often."

"I will." Nolan's voice seemed resigned. Enough to do as ordered or just resigned to hear that particular advice over and over?

"Have Corinne do more stretches with you. You're losing too much range of motion."

Nolan nodded and headed out the door. Had he forgotten to tell the doctor Jacob was doing his stretches?

She followed her husband to the wagon, though he didn't seem to realize she was behind him.

"Nolan?"

He startled. "I'm sorry. I thought you were visiting with Mrs. Ellis."

"I was, but I finished." She climbed into the wagon before he could reach her. "Give me a ride to the laundry?" It wasn't far, but if she didn't ride with him, she'd not be able to ask about the doctor's orders until later. And if she didn't ask now, she had a feeling it'd be harder to pull out an answer. "What did the doctor say?"

He circled around the horse and wagon. "Nothing I didn't expect to hear."

"Which was?" She tried to busy herself with rearranging her skirt so he'd not catch that she'd overheard the doctor's instructions.

"I'm on my leg too much, and I need to follow orders. Same old, same old." He climbed up and called for Buttermilk to giddyap.

So he wasn't going to tell her about the increased need for stretching? She sat quietly, wondering if he'd open up, but they were in front of the laundry within minutes.

He pulled to a stop, and this time, she waited for him to come help her. Once she was on the boardwalk, Nolan gave her a peck on the cheek.

Her knees barely held up. Had he just done that in public?

He stepped back, stuffing his hands into his pockets. "I'll be back shortly." With that, he turned to leave.

Once her head cleared, she watched him walk away. The townsfolk he greeted might not notice how he was trying to disguise his pain, but she did. That limp was not a good one. Had he not asked the doctor for anything?

She crossed her arms. He'd ask for help if he really needed it, wouldn't he?

Maybe she was wrong. Maybe his limp was more exaggerated on some days than others. Once she lost him in the crowd, she turned into the laundry.

Spencer's tousled head popped in through the door that led to the back. "Mrs. Whitsett!" He called behind him. "Miss Stillwater's here!"

"Mrs. Key, you mean," Leah's voice responded.

"Oh, I forgot." He half-walked, half-jogged up with a handful of folded linens. "I'm sorry, Mrs. Key. Been working here *all* day. But we're almost done!" He hefted his small armful onto the counter with a huff. "But don't worry, I'm doing it for free, ain't making Mrs. Whitsett pay me nothing."

Leah came in and swatted him playfully with the towel in her hand. "He's not exactly free since I've got to feed him. He puts away more than a full-grown man."

Spencer shrugged. "I'm growing."

"I'm watching him while his parents are gone; however, they

didn't warn me how much his 'free help' was going to cost me."
Leah put her hands on her hips and exhaled as if exasperated,
but the twinkle in her eye gave her away. "I might have to take
out a loan to keep him fed."

"How long will the Hendrixes be gone?" They'd not
mentioned they were leaving when they'd been over for dinner
last week. Of course, they'd seemed in a hurry to leave—probably because she'd made such a fool of herself with the gravy
and cream.

Spencer climbed the counter halfway, perching himself on
the hidden shelf. She forced herself not to tell him to get down
since this wasn't her place anymore.

"They left after we were at your place, and they're not
supposed to be back for a looooong time. But they said Mrs.
Whitsett shouldn't have to watch me every day so I'm going to
have to be with Celia on the weekends." He frowned deep
enough for dimples to show.

She looked to Leah. "They've been gone for a whole week?"

"Yep." Spencer answered for her, jumping back down. "And
they might be bringing back lots of ponies. But then they'll be
gone even loooooonger."

"But…" She shook her head.

Nolan must not have had his leg stretched or massaged at all
this past week.

Did her nearness bother him so much he chose to suffer in
silence? Of course, she could kind of understand—lately, she'd
been nearly out of her mind whenever he was close for very
long.

"Are you all right?"

Leah's question dragged her back to the laundry.

Seemed at some point she'd started hugging herself. "Yes,
yes. Just wanted to check on you. Everything good?"

She finally looked around. Spencer was correct. Considering
the amount of neat stacks and empty bins, he'd helped her
catch up.

If only months ago she'd offered to feed Spencer after school, maybe she could've gotten things under control and retained possession of her business.

And yet, she didn't want to return.

Leah swiped a damp tendril off her forehead. "I'm doing well. I've got a big order from the boardinghouse coming in tomorrow, so we'll be busy."

"Good, well, I'm sorry to come in and head back out, but—"

"Go on." Leah shooed her toward the door. "We've got it covered. Tell Nolan hello."

Corinne somehow made it out onto the porch and to the wagon to wait for her husband.

What was she going to do with him? He had to get that leg massaged and stretched.

"It's either business partners or lovers."

Corinne blew out a long, shaky breath. Business partners didn't force massages on one another, so she'd have to let it go.

…Or not.

Business partners also didn't kiss.

She closed her eyes and took a deep breath. No matter what happened, unlike the men before him, Nolan wouldn't turn his back on her. He'd vowed to protect and provide and had done so. He truly planned to split his money with her. He did what he said he'd do.

He deserved more than a business partner. But would she be enough?

CHAPTER THIRTY-ONE

Corinne frowned up at the kitchen ceiling as Nolan thumped around upstairs.

He'd hardly spoken to her on the way home after they'd stopped at the bank. He'd disappeared after unhitching the wagon, leaving her to peel potatoes alone. But that had been fine. It had given her time to think about what she needed to do about him.

Her heart was urging her to disregard all fears, but her head kept reminding her of all the other times she'd allowed herself to love a man.

Nolan had said if they didn't want to be with one another, they could live separately. What if she handed her heart over one last time, and months down the road, he asked her to move out per their agreement?

It could happen. No matter how nice he was, she had no assurance they'd survive as lovers. She'd loved Kurt, and that hadn't been enough.

Nolan came thumping down the stairs on crutches, and she shook her head at him. Unlike Kurt, this maddening man, who gave her everything she needed and wanted—asked nothing of her.

She looked up at him as he came into the room. "Why didn't you ask me to get your crutches for you?" If his leg hurt enough to switch to crutches, he should've asked her to go upstairs for him.

"You were busy."

"I could've gotten them quicker."

"Doesn't matter."

"It does. You don't ask me for anything, and I need to earn my keep—my thirty-five percent. So, please, what can I do to help?"

The furrows in his forehead deepened. "I can't come up with anything you don't already do."

She drummed her fingers on the counter. Was he not thinking about his leg, or had he decided he'd never ask for her help with that? "I think I understand now why your father insisted you marry. Not because he thought you incapable of running the ranch, but because you need someone to look after you since you refuse to do so yourself. Maybe he loved you too much to see you—"

"Please." He slashed his hand at her. "Don't say any more."

She clamped her mouth shut, but her foot tapped a swift staccato. She tossed her knife onto the counter and blew out a breath. Why was she so upset at his thick-headedness, anyway? She'd accepted his marriage offer because he *hadn't* required much of her.

But he was supposed to be a good business partner. And how could she trust a man to run his part of their business if he did a fool thing like hurt himself by working too much? And for what reason? Pride?

How dumb.

"Excuse me?"

Had she said that out loud? Good.

Or maybe not, considering that hadn't been kind. She closed her eyes and huffed. Why was she losing her head around him so often lately? She really, really wanted to go over and shake him … all the while hoping he'd stop her by grabbing her around the waist and kissing the daylights out of her.

Oh, where had the sensible woman who'd married him gone?

"I'm sorry. I shouldn't have said that." She turned and picked up another potato.

"All right, do you want help with dinner?"

The lump in her throat grew thick as she shook her head, keeping her back to him so he couldn't see how close to tears she was. She'd insulted him, and he offered help. "No, thank you. Why don't you go rest?"

When he left, she stopped peeling potatoes and rubbed at her eyes.

She had warned him not to fall in love with her, and here she'd gone and fallen in love with him.

But maybe that wasn't such a bad thing. Many people found joy after disappointment, didn't they? Maybe this time, with an honest-to-goodness wonderful man and the approval of God, she'd find hers.

She couldn't let the fear of reliving past disappointments keep her from the chance of discovering a joy she'd never known.

The silence in the parlor ticked on as Corinne's knitting needles clacked steadily, as if she needed to finish her scarf tonight despite cold weather being at least a month away.

Nolan closed the newest copy of *The Prairie Farmer*—which pain and sheer exhaustion had kept him from focusing on anyway—and tossed the periodical on the floor. "I'm heading upstairs."

He hesitated a moment before pushing himself out of the chair. He did need help with his leg … but just couldn't ask. He took up his crutches and bid her a soft goodnight.

She'd been right earlier—he needed her. But at no time during her impassioned speech had she mentioned needing him.

She had said she needed to earn her keep, but now that he knew how smart she was, she would've figured out how to save the laundry on her own. Once she sold one of her inventions for good money, she'd realize she didn't need him at all.

And yet, he'd still need her.

At the top of the stairs, he paused for a short rest.

Dad had been wrong to force him into a marriage to be sure someone was there to take care of him. Hiring a nurse, as he'd always insisted, would've worked much better. Because a wife? She'd be around forever. And he didn't want to be her burden, her project, her patient.

After getting ready for bed, he attempted his stretches as best he could.

A light tap on the door made him pause. Was that a knock?

"Nolan?"

He sat up on the mattress and slipped under the blankets. "Yes?"

She pushed the door open, the glow of the lamplight golden amid her loose blond hair.

She was too pretty by half.

"Leah told me the Hendrixes have been out of state, looking at polo ponies."

He froze.

"Which means you haven't had anyone do your stretches for a week now. Why didn't you ask me?"

He crossed his arms and sighed. If Dad were still alive, he'd have been right behind Corinne, arms crossed like his, calling him out for being stubborn.

Was Corinne right? Had Dad forced him into marriage, not because he believed him incompetent, but because he loved him?

Dad could've just simply said so. Although Corinne's theory might explain his father's crazy will, that didn't make it true. If

Dad had only once told him he loved him, once said he was proud of him—maybe he could believe the man had forced him into this because of love.

Corinne stood in the doorway, clearly exasperated with him.

Love didn't drive her either, profitability did, and his well-being was a part of that. Craving love from his father had only made him miserable, so he shouldn't do the same with Corinne.

"All right." He huffed. "Would you please help me with my leg?"

Considering he'd nearly fallen asleep taking off his boots, her hands shouldn't have an effect on him.

"Good." She slipped into the room and closed the door. Yet, she didn't come closer. Why did she appear conflicted all of a sudden?

After a few moments, she walked over. "You need to lie back and come out from under the covers."

He did as instructed, pretending he was answering to Mrs. Ellis in one of the doctor's rooms lit by noonday sun rather than in his bedroom filled with candlelight while Corinne looked like an angel at his side.

The moment she touched him, he closed his eyes and imagined himself flat on a hard examination table.

Ouch! He tried his hardest not to flinch. Her fingers were about as unforgiving as Doctor Ellis's. She'd evidently paid close attention to his instructions, and now that her hands were feeling better, she must be able to press harder than the last time.

Though the doctor always insisted it was better if he relaxed, his every muscle tensed. He breathed through his teeth to keep from making any noise that would make him sound weak.

After about twenty minutes, he was trying to calculate how many days were left until Jacob's return. He'd been much, much gentler.

Either that, or he'd been too easy on him and had done him little good.

With one final push, Corinne lowered his shortened appendage and covered it with his blanket. She patted his leg lightly. "How does that feel?"

He kept his eyes closed. His leg was in more pain than it had been in all day. But it was a good pain, hopefully. "It's fine. Thank you."

She moved to sit beside him. "Nolan, I..."

He took her hand and gave it a gentle squeeze. "If it seems I'm hurting more than I did earlier, don't worry about it. After the doctor gets through with me, I feel just like this. It takes some time."

She fidgeted. "What I wanted to say was I'm sorry I got angry at you earlier about being stubborn. Since you've been so good to make sure I can do as I please, I want to be sure you can, too."

"I understand. I'll try not to be so hard-headed about it in the future." He squeezed her hand again and closed his eyes with a contented sigh. She was indeed the perfect wife.

"Goodnight, Nolan." Her free hand pressed against his chest, and then her lips lighted upon his.

His eyes startled open for a second, his body frozen.

She pulled her other hand from his grasp and placed it against the side of his face. With the same tenderness he'd kissed her with weeks ago, she moved her mouth against his.

He relaxed and combed his hand into her hair, letting himself enjoy her sweet kiss.

Maybe he wasn't just another one of her projects. Maybe one day she'd not offer to endure making love to him. He only had to be patient.

When she broke away, he smiled, his hand still entangled in her curls. "Goodnight, sweetheart. And thank you."

She didn't reply, but leaned back down and kissed him again

—and this time, sweet was not the word to describe it. Her lips and hands explored with a hunger.

His heart rate ramped, his lungs worked double time, and his hands took on a mind of their own.

Then she got closer—much closer.

She didn't pull away until he was drunk on the feel of her.

How were they supposed to live under the same roof after that? "I want ... more," he breathed, unable to suppress a shudder.

Though she responded without words, he was left in no doubt she wanted more as well—much more.

CHAPTER THIRTY-TWO

Nolan's breathing had slowed, deepened, and now rumbled with the soft rattle of sleep.

With imperceptible movements, Corinne wriggled herself closer to the edge of the bed and out from under the covers. Sitting up, she let her head sink into her hands.

What had she done?

Gathering up her clothing, she held them against her and slipped out of the room.

After walking down the hallway and closing her bedroom door as quietly as possible, she sank onto her bed and let silent tears fall.

What a fool she'd been as a young woman. Kurt had declared his undying love without the commitment to prove it true, and she'd fallen for it. He'd promised her the world and never delivered in any way. She'd played wife in every sense, trying her hardest to make him happy until her heart couldn't take it anymore. Once she'd let her dissatisfaction be known, Kurt was done.

From then on, he'd felt free from trying to make her happy. Finally taking the easy way out by looking for someone who'd be happy without asking for more than he was willing to give.

But Nolan? She'd married a man who'd committed to her without a profession of love. And in one night, he'd proven he loved her. Not by successfully making her body react as she'd once hoped it would, no—that hadn't happened. But because he'd spent time trying.

Even now, her body felt warm with the memory of the gentleness of his caresses, the wonder in his eyes, the time he'd taken to express how lovely he thought she was.

She wrapped her arms tight around herself.

Despite the pain wracking his leg, despite the fact he could've taken what he desired and gone to sleep—Nolan had spent time doing what she could only describe as cherishing her. Without saying a word, it was clear he loved her.

Did he realize it yet? Or was he trying to honor her wishes by not turning this marriage into a romance?

Perhaps she was no good at determining whether a man loved her or not—she'd once thought Kurt and Randolph had. Though whatever Nolan felt for her right now was ten times closer to love than whatever those two had shown her.

And yet, though she'd told herself not to expect anything other than what she'd experienced with Kurt, she had hoped things would be different when she'd climbed into bed with Nolan. Her mind, her heart, her everything longed to sing, but like so many years ago, her body's reactions did not match up with her desire to enjoy a man's—and this time an honest-to-goodness husband's—intimate embrace.

She had nearly cried at the disappointment. Her heart might've been moved by his attentiveness, but her body had been frustrated, like a child who'd finally been taken to the fair only to realize she wasn't allowed to do anything but sit behind a booth and watch everyone else have fun.

If her heart had been broken after Kurt's kind of love had grown cold after he'd realized she didn't respond to his touch…

She burrowed under the blankets on her bed and pressed her face deep into her pillow. She couldn't stay up all night trying to figure out what to do when there wasn't anything she could do. She'd learned that full well when she'd done everything she could to respond as Kurt had wished all those years ago.

The chiming of the clock downstairs marked off the half hour, and she willed herself to fall asleep before the hour chimed again.

After two hours passed, her pillows, despite being plumped and re-plumped and flattened and rolled, were simply unbearable.

She stared out the window, waiting for the subtle glow of orange and pink to take over the black of night. A few times her eyelids felt heavy enough to win the war, but her brain kept pestering her back into consciousness.

The moment the shadows lightened enough to outline her furniture, she tossed her blankets and punched her arms into the sleeves of her dressing gown.

She could shut off her mind better if she were cooking breakfast, polishing silverware, organizing spices, making lots of coffee—something other than lying here trying not to think.

At least one good thing had come from not sleeping, she'd be downstairs before Nolan awoke and realized she hadn't stayed beside him.

In the kitchen, she tied back the curtains despite the lack of sunlight, fired up a few lamps, and looked at the clock. She couldn't start breakfast now or it'd be cold by the time the men came in. Since Nolan tended to sleep longer than most, the men did lots of chores before eating.

Sitting down with the silverware, she began to polish. She placed them in piles as noiselessly as possible so as not to wake Nolan.

When dawn overtook the sky, she caught sight of Timothy leading his horse out of the barn, the dog at his heels. She packed away the triple-polished utensils and forged out into the crisp morning to get eggs and cream for breakfast.

When she left the cellar, the muffled voices of Rascal and Abel in the barn, mixed with the nickering horses, initially drew her attention, but then the subtle clomp of hooves and the crunch of wheels made her walk to the barn's other side to see who was traveling on the road this early in the morning.

In the rosy eastern light, a buggy was silhouetted against the sun, now shining horizontally across the expanse of swaying prairie grass.

Hopefully Matt wasn't returning with his fiancée. But who else drove a buggy this far out of town? A neighbor would be riding up fast this early on a lone horse, possibly a wagon, but not a buggy.

The horse and conveyance rolled up to the house, and a hefty man who somehow seemed familiar stepped down as he muttered to his horse.

She'd definitely not met this man before, but yet something…

She walked toward him, tying her wrapper tighter. She should be better dressed to greet their visitor, but she wasn't about to let this stranger out of her sight.

The morning light was enough to make out his fine suit, shiny shoes, and watch chain. His hat looked stiff and new.

A lawyer Matt had sent up from Denver?

Her heart fluttered. What other possibility was there?

The man brushed his suit and turned, startling upon seeing her. "Oh, good morning. I didn't see you come out." He straightened his shoulders and looked her up and down. "I'd heard Nolan married, but I'd not expected you to be as good looking as you are."

She narrowed her eyes at him. "I don't think we've met."

"Matthias Key, Sr. at your service." He came forward and tipped his hat, his well-tailored suit coat stretched across his broad chest. "I'm your uncle."

Hadn't Nolan said Matt's father liked him more than his own son? Yet this man had been surprised Nolan had married a decent-looking woman. Maybe Nolan had more than one uncle. "Are you Matt's father?"

He stiffened, his smile disappearing. "Yes." He sniffed and looked up at the house. "Is Nolan up yet?"

"No." She gestured to the front door. "We can go in and wait for him, if you'd like."

"That'll be fine." His confident steps indicated he'd indeed been here before.

She tried not to scowl at his back as she followed him through her own house. It was obvious now where Matt's high-handed manners came from. Matthias Key, Sr. hadn't even asked her name.

When they entered the kitchen, she skirted around him to set down the eggs and cream. "Shall I get you coffee?"

He shook his head while taking a seat at the table, leaning back in the simple chair as if it were cushioned.

"I'll go see if Nolan—"

"Stay." He held up a hand. "I want to talk to you before he comes down. For a woman to have convinced my nephew to marry, he'll undoubtedly praise you to the heavens. But I'd like to make my own assessment."

As bossy as that had sounded, his tone was certainly less condescending than his son's. A hint of warmth had even colored his voice, as if he expected to find her praiseworthy.

"Do you mind if I start cooking breakfast? Have you eaten?"

"As a matter of fact, I haven't. Nolan makes the best biscuits and gravy, and I was hoping to catch him before he started cooking so I could request that."

She'd intended to cook sausage with the eggs, but it wouldn't be too hard to change plans. "I can make biscuits, but I don't know how Nolan does his gravy. I've had it twice now, and you're right, it's good. I'll go get him."

"Don't bother." Matthias sat back in his chair. "We can wait. No need to rush the genius."

The genius?

"Or maybe it's you I have to thank for inspiring him. When he sent me his drawings, he wrote about them pretty humbly. Uncalled for modesty. I've been peddling wares for more than twenty years, and everything he sent me could potentially reap him a bundle—especially his waterer."

Her heart clunked to a stop. His waterer? "You said he sent you *his* drawings?"

"Yes." Matthias reached inside his suit coat and pulled a paper from an inside pocket. He unfolded it atop the table.

She walked over somehow, barely aware of anything but that paper.

Those were her designs—not drawn by her hand.

"This,"—Matthias tapped his index finger against the sketch of her water cover—"should make you two a nice profit once we find someone to put it into production."

She scanned the paper looking for anything indicating these were her drawings, but her heart quivered, stalled, then sank to the floor.

Her name wasn't anywhere.

"I don't know what Nolan's told you about me, but I'm in charge of distributing wares to mercantiles in the northwest. Our catalog is number two in selling farm equipment." He smiled as he leaned back. "I've got connections to several investor types, but we've got to get things patented and produced before—"

Chuckling, he waved his hands in front of him. "I'm sorry, my dear. You don't need to look so stricken. I should've realized the technicalities wouldn't interest you. But whether or not you understand anything about business, you should turn that frown upside down. Within a few years, I suspect you'll be able to buy all the new china and curtains you want."

She clenched her hands at her sides, but that was a mistake, because now she felt like punching him—and Nolan.

How could he?

"You might even be able to fix this place up nice enough for my son's fancy fiancée to be jealous. Especially if Nolan has more good ideas like this, as he says he does."

"I—" She clamped her lips back together. She'd been about to tell him she had no desire to play host to Lilith again, but what did that matter?

What mattered was that Nolan, a man she'd let herself care for, had stolen her ideas just like her father had, and was using it for his gain—without her knowledge.

He must not have realized how quickly his subterfuge would be exposed. "Why didn't you write Nolan back about these?"

"I'm on my way to Billings. A few men I'm meeting there might be interested in something like this. We don't have much time before final decisions are made on what goes into next year's catalog, and I'd like some of Nolan's things in it…"

Matthias's jovial chatter faded from hearing as her heart beat a rhythm of betrayal in her ears.

She'd thought Nolan had encouraged her to make prototypes because he'd wished to see her happy.

Instead, he'd been plotting to steal her ideas out from under her.

Oh, he might make up an excuse about passing off her inventions as his because it'd be better for business. Or even that he intended to split the profits per their agreement. But to not even discuss it with her? To sell them out from under her?

And he'd acted as if her father stealing her paint formula had been egregious.

"Enough of all that," Matthias's words broke into her thoughts. "I can see I've started talking over your head again. Why don't we get back to you?"

Corinne nodded, but only because she couldn't trust her voice to answer. She headed back to the counter and grabbed an onion.

"What family and town do you hail from?"

With her body trembling in either a surge of rage or a need to cry, she couldn't look at him. She picked up the kitchen knife and whacked off the ends of the onion. "I'm from the Chicago area. My parents are no one of importance."

"How'd you meet Nolan?"

She ripped off the skins and threw them in a pile. "It's a long story. Perhaps you'd rather hear it from him."

She took the knife back up and chopped with more vigor than necessary.

Though her knife pounded against the cutting board, it didn't drown out the sound of Nolan's thumping gait on the stairs.

She smacked the knife flat on the counter. It was best she not have a weapon in her hand when she saw him next, because she might be tempted to thrust the blade through his heart, like he'd already done to hers.

CHAPTER THIRTY-THREE

The smile Nolan had sported since he woke died under the glare his wife was giving him. He stepped off the last stair into the kitchen and hesitated. That certainly was not the look he'd hoped to see this morning.

She turned back to chopping the onion in front of her, the sinews in her neck tight and stiff. What was wrong?

A creak to his left swung his gaze to his uncle.

His uncle?

"Uh, good morning, Uncle." He forced his feet forward to shake hands with his favorite relative.

Matthias sported a large grin, his grip on Nolan's hand warm and affirmative. "Good morning, Nolan. I've met your wife."

"I see." Nolan took his hand back and looked to Corinne. He'd thought she'd like his uncle once she met him, but perhaps he'd been wrong. Matthias was blunt and arrogant sometimes, but he wasn't as hard to endure as his son. "What brings you up here? Did we miss your letter?"

"No letter, it was a last-minute detour."

Nolan tried to keep his smile up, but maybe that was why

Corinne was acting as she was. Perhaps she, too, had been hoping they'd have the house to themselves this morning. He'd toyed with the idea of sending his men to go dig up a fence on the back forty for no reason—as long as it took them all day.

Matthias's chair creaked as he sat back down. "I hope you don't mind my dropping in, but I'm on my way to Billings and thought I should come see you beforehand."

"Of course not, you're welcome any time." He wanted to mean that, so he plastered his smile back on. Corinne would be here every day for the rest of their lives, so he could wait until nightfall to have her to himself again.

He turned to give her an anticipatory wink, but she still didn't appear happy. When he lifted a brow in silent question, she gave him the look his mother had whenever he'd displeased her.

Corinne went back to whacking the onion.

He walked toward her, careful to stay far to her right. "Do you need help with breakfast?"

"I was hoping for biscuits and gravy," Uncle called over.

"That's what I'm making," Corinne said tightly as she kept chopping.

He frowned at the tiny slivers of onion bouncing around on the counter with each thwack. He was afraid to mention it, but... "I don't put onions in my gravy."

Corinne smacked the knife down. "Fine, you make it." Then she brushed past him, yanked out a chair from the table, and sat.

Uncle looked at her for a moment, then to Nolan, his expression likely mirroring his own bewilderment.

Nolan shrugged. He had no idea what had gotten into her, but now wasn't the time to probe. He began moving things aside to work on the dough. Thankfully, the oven was already hot. "Why don't you tell us what brought you to town while I cook?"

Wait. If he'd come about Corinne's ideas—

"Uh, are you here to drag Matt home?" With any luck, that

would steer Uncle onto another subject. "He's in danger of getting himself roughed up for being too good at cards. Maybe you could encourage him to move to another town."

"I want nothing more to do with my son."

Nolan stopped measuring flour. "What?"

"The boy stole money from my business to invest in schemes he didn't tell me about—until they failed. Then he had the gall to get angry when I got upset. He thought I'd be fine with his embezzling."

Nolan expected a shock to have rippled through him, but his subconscious must not have been surprised at such a revelation. He brushed the flour from his hands and added the salt and baking powder. "Have you pressed charges?"

"No." Matthias scowled, turning to stare out the window. "Didn't want my business partners to know. But he's out. He'll have to make it in the world without my money and influence. His luck with cards will run out, always does. Hopefully, he'll actually try working at some point."

Corinne sat in stormy silence.

Nolan forced himself to finish the dough despite wanting to pull Corinne upstairs to talk instead of discussing Matt. But it wasn't too surprising his cousin was the center of attention even when he wasn't around. "From what I've heard, the money's coming easily—too easily. If he doesn't find somewhere else to play, he might end up losing his life to someone who doesn't take kindly to being fleeced."

Earlier in the week, Rascal had shared that the saloon goers were beginning to think Matt was counting cards.

His uncle sat looking out the window, stone-faced.

The kitchen went silent, all except for his biscuit making and the noise of Corinne's leg shaking under the table. If she was that agitated, why did she stay?

After he slid the baking sheet into the oven and set the pan on the stove, he could no longer ignore the black cloud enshrouding his wife. "What's wrong, Corinne?"

She startled, then pushed herself away from the table. "Excuse me, but since I'm not needed, I'll head upstairs."

And with that, she stood and stomped off.

Nolan watched her until she disappeared into the stairwell. Not once did she look back.

He turned to glare at his uncle. "What did you say to her? She's acting as if she's been offended."

His uncle's head snapped back. "You know I wouldn't insult a woman—to her face, anyway."

"Did you say something she could've taken as an insult?"

"Women do twist every word a man says."

"Corinne doesn't." Though his late aunt had made a mess of his uncle's life with her deception, he wouldn't lump all women into the same category as Aunt Edith.

Matthias rolled his eyes, as if Nolan were a naïve boy. "Every man's convinced his woman's different—until she stabs him in the back."

Nolan shook his head and turned back to fry up the sausage.

His late aunt had cheated on Matthias decades ago, but his uncle always acted as if it happened yesterday. Matthias's second son, the late Lionel Key, with his red hair, green eyes, and delicate bone structure, had turned long-held suspicions into assurance upon his birth. He had been the spitting image of Matthias's former warehouse manager. Years later, when Nolan had learned of the affair, he'd been surprised his uncle had remained married, especially since he and his aunt never got along.

"You haven't been married long, right? Could be your wife's one of those moody types."

Nolan pulled himself back to the present, quickly scraping the pan to keep the gravy from burning. "I can't say I know everything about Corinne, but after last night—" He stopped himself by clearing his throat. "I, uh, thought she seemed fine. So something must have happened since she awoke. Are you sure you didn't say anything to upset her?"

If last night had gone as well for her as he'd thought it had…

"I did say I was surprised you snagged such a pretty woman. I hadn't expected it after talking to Lilith at the station. I assume Matt wrote to her after meeting your wife."

"Actually, Lilith was here a couple of months ago." Nolan thwacked his spatula against the pot's rim.

"Really?"

"Yes." He didn't want to get into that mess. Now that his marriage was real in every sense of the word, he no longer had to worry about either one of them. "What exactly did Lilith say about my wife?"

"I only talked to her in passing, but with the disdain in her voice, I figured Matt considered the match far below you."

"She was the town laundress."

"Ah, that explains it. But now,"—Matthias reached into his suit's inner pocket—"for the reason I came."

Nolan shook his head though it didn't surprise him his uncle wasn't worried about Corinne. The man cared little about women's feelings.

Matthias unfolded the paper he'd pulled from his pocket. "These are really good, Nolan. In your letter, you alluded to having others. If they're half as good as these, we might make ourselves a pretty penny."

Nolan shoved the pan off the heat and crossed over to the table. If his uncle had come all the way here for this, he must think Corinne's ideas were good.

"The men I'm visiting in Billings will probably be interested in what you have here." Matthias tapped the sketch of the waterer. "I can help you with the distribution, but you're going to need investors. I need to know what else I can present them."

Nolan's heart shuddered. "You think they're that good?"

"I wouldn't be here if I didn't."

Corinne would be ecstatic. A shrewd businessman not only

thought her ideas were good, but so good that he wanted to pitch her other inventions sight unseen? "There are more that would likely interest you. A stepladder especially, but these aren't my designs."

"What? You led me to believe—"

"No. I only asked your opinion." He got up to check on the biscuits.

"Then which of your men do I need to talk to?"

"Not a man. A woman."

His uncle frowned and pushed away the drawings.

Nolan came back to turn the paper around. "That reaction is exactly why I didn't tell you whose they were in my letter."

"Your new wife, I assume."

"Yes."

Matthias's posture softened a touch. "Well, that's not too difficult. Have her draw up the ideas and we'll decide which ones have merit. She'll need to make prototypes to prove they work, you'll patent them—"

"She'll patent them."

Matthias shook his head. "To an investor—"

"Doesn't matter. They're either good, or they're not."

"Son."

A lump in his throat formed. As much as he wanted to keep his uncle's favor, his wife was more important. "They'll be patented under her name, or no name."

"But—"

Nolan held up his hand. "I know you don't hold women in high regard. Yet only minutes ago, you thought these would sell. Nothing's changed about them since."

He grabbed the ad copy he'd clipped from the newspaper when he'd realized it was the same one Corinne had shown Annie. "Look at this." He handed Matthias the square scrap of paper. "This is some lady's iron handle-swapping thing. A woman sells these."

His uncle barely glanced at the advertisement. "Just because she paid to put her name on an ad, doesn't mean she's selling any. It could be she hadn't enough sense to listen to someone who told her to keep her name off it."

Nolan huffed. This was more of a fight than he was hoping for. "But you could sell these irons?"

"Maybe." He shrugged and leaned back in his seat. "But it's household goods. This Mrs. Potts isn't trying to sell stepladders and farm equipment. Does your wife invent kitchen stuff, beauty tonics, that sort of thing?"

He frowned and stuck out his leg. "I don't know what's all in her notebook, but she did fashion this new leg for me."

Matthias huffed. "That isn't any better. You'd need a doctor's name to sell that."

Nolan kept his mouth shut on that one. Even Corinne had been discouraged when she'd seen the brochure and realized who her competition was. "I think she's working on a laundry stain remover for grease."

"Now, that's more like it." His uncle nodded slightly.

"But you can't tell me you're more excited about a stain remover than this chicken waterer."

He shrugged. "I'm excited about anything I could sell."

The stairwell echoed with Corinne's heavy tread. She'd gotten dressed, but she still wore a blank expression.

Surely this news would put a smile back on her face. "Hey, honey, my uncle stopped in because he's interested in the things you've come up with. The waterer, the wire nest, and possibly your stain remover."

Her expression changed from blank to confused. She glanced at Matthias, then back at him as if he'd said something unintelligible.

Of course, he'd skipped the part where he told her he'd sent his uncle her ideas. "You see, I sent a page of your things to him."

If only his uncle had sent him a letter before he showed up, he wouldn't have to confess he'd sent her ideas off without her permission. If only he'd believed in her abilities enough to tell her to patent them first, and then ask Uncle if he wanted to join their venture.

She took a step forward, holding her head cocked as if wary of walking into one of her own snares.

"He came in hopes of doing business with us."

"Us?" Her voice dripped with disbelief.

"Yes." Why was she acting as if that was the wrong way to put it? Hadn't they discussed splitting everything? Of course, they'd only talked about the ranch's profits before they'd married—he hadn't known she could do this. "Can you show him what else you have? He's thinking his friends in Billings would be interested in investing if you could give him more things to show them."

She nodded woodenly. "I suppose after breakfast." And with that, she abruptly turned toward the oven, taking out the biscuits he just realized smelled done. She had probably come down to rescue them.

"How many of these do you have prototypes of?" Uncle sat up, obviously eager to eat now that the smell of buttery dough wafted through the room.

"I don't have any, but—"

"No matter. I can get preliminary feedback with these drawings to see if it's even worthwhile. But I'll need prototypes to get anybody to sign on, considering. Do you think you could have some done when I come back through next week?"

"Next week?" Corinne's face screwed up as she set the hot baking sheet down. "I doubt I'll have time."

"Sure you will." Nolan jumped up, joining her at the counter to get plates. "She can spend all her time working on whatever you'd like to see first."

On the back porch, the clomping of his men scraping their

boots sounded. Seemed they were as eager for biscuits and gravy as Uncle.

The door creaked open, and Rascal's nearly toothless grin wrinkled up his face. "Mr. Key! I'd wondered who that buggy belonged to."

Matthias got out of his chair to shake the hand of his brother's long-time ranch hand. "Rascal, you look as worse for wear as ever."

Rascal thumped him hard on the back. "You're looking quite old yourself."

Sal took off his hat and hung it on his usual hook behind the door. "What brings you up?"

"Mrs. Key's chicken waterer, apparently."

"Oh, did you come up with something new?" Timothy practically slid across the floor and up against the table. He spun the paper around so he could see it. "Looks like it'd work."

He then flopped into his chair, draping one lanky arm over its back and gesturing toward Uncle with the other. "You should take a look at the chicken coop. Best chicken coop for miles around, I'd bet."

"You improved a coop?" Uncle cocked an eyebrow at Corinne.

She shrugged as she handed Sal the napkins and silverware to set out.

"Don't let her shrug fool you." Timothy took the napkins from Sal and tossed them around the table. "She had us do a complete overhaul. Took us two weeks to get done."

"Nothing you can pack up and show anybody," she said quietly.

"Oh, does he want to show off something you've done?" Timothy chimed in again.

Nolan shook his head at Timothy's mouth running off with him. For some reason, his youngest ranch hand was more talkative than usual.

Timothy poured himself coffee. "She came up with a new stepladder while working on the coop with me."

"It's not done either," she responded as she set the creamer on the table.

Matthias eyed Timothy. "Do you not find it abnormal for a woman to be telling *you* how to rebuild a chicken coop?"

Timothy's eyes widened. Seemed he'd finally realized Uncle didn't think as highly of Corinne's talents as he did. "Uh, sir, I take my orders from wherever they come."

Nolan laid the biscuits on the table. He needed to keep this conversation going in a positive direction, especially with Corinne here. "My uncle was only wondering what you thought of Mrs. Key's ideas. He's interested in investing."

"Oh!" Timothy's face cleared up. He turned to smile at Corinne. "That's right good, Mrs. Key." He then turned his mischievous grin toward Nolan. "Us average men can't aspire to women who've got money, so if we can't marry money, getting a woman who can make you some is smart going."

"Average men?" Rascal grumped. "You're still a tenderfoot."

"I beg your pardon. I grew up out here. You're just jealous because you ain't ever got you a woman."

"Hey, now." Sal clinked his spoon against his mug. As foreman, he never allowed the men to stray too far out of line— especially Timothy, whom he treated like the son he never had.

"A toast!" Timothy held up his mug. "To the new Mrs. and the money she'll bring in to get us all the cattle this ranch can handle."

Nolan grinned at Timothy's antics and held up his mug in silent assent, though perhaps cattle weren't what they'd be buying.

Corinne raised her glass of milk halfheartedly, her eyes clearly missing the levity Timothy was trying to infuse into the room.

Nolan tried not to deflate at her lack of cheer. Whatever anger she'd harbored earlier had likely intensified after learning he'd sent off her drawings behind her back. Did she not feel ready to put her things out into the world? But even if one of her ideas failed, surely another was bound to take off and give her some much-needed confidence.

He certainly believed she was something special, and he ached for her to believe it, too.

CHAPTER THIRTY-FOUR

In the cabin, Corinne gave her notebook one last look and handed it across the table to Nolan's uncle. She turned her back, as if not seeing his face when he opened the pages would make it easier to allow someone such free access to her thoughts.

She'd never handed anyone her notebook. Nolan didn't even know all that was in there—though perhaps he might. He'd taken it from her at some point, although the page he'd copied had fallen out a few times.

But even if he'd only seen that one page, that didn't absolve him.

She busied herself with making an empty spot on her cluttered table as Uncle Matthias looked through her drawings. He uttered one or two grunts of what sounded like appreciation, amid others that definitely suggested he found her ideas wanting.

Which many of them were. She couldn't be miffed at the man for thinking the same as she.

A familiar slight dragging sound indicated Nolan was coming out to check on them. Within seconds, his frame filled her cabin's little doorway, and she restrained her scowl.

He had come clean with his uncle about the inventions being hers, but then, he didn't have much choice since Matthias had surprised him in person.

If his uncle hadn't shown up, would Nolan have patented her ideas and sold them without her knowing?

She shoved a metal bowl out of her way, letting it clatter.

Matthias made a half-grunt that sounded more positive than any of the other noises he'd emitted so far. Nolan walked up to his uncle with a huge grin on his face and a quick wink for her.

Didn't he realize she wasn't happy about this? Matthias only had her notebook in hand because her husband had essentially lied to her.

She'd always been honest with him. She'd thought him the best sort of man—and yet he did something so underhanded.

The way he'd treated her last night…

She'd been jittery at the thought that he might love her—no, she had believed it. But now?

She tossed another scrap of metal into her junk box with more force than necessary.

His smiles, lingering touches, and what she'd assumed was Nolan putting her interest above his own had broken the chains she'd put around her heart for a very good reason. She shouldn't have unlocked them.

A soft whump sounded behind her. Her notebook fluffed up dust where Uncle Matthias had dropped it on her workbench.

"I think we can generate interest in several of these." He walked around the table to her vats that contained strips of soiled fabric. "What about your stain remover? Does it take out more than grease? It'd be better if it removed everything."

She barely refrained from rolling her eyes. If it could remove everything, there'd likely be no cloth left either. "I'm afraid it has only lightened the stains, so I'm trying something else. If you're interested in soap, I'm attempting to make one for a friend with sensitive skin."

She handed him the nearly fragrance-free bar that had

turned an ugly yellow. "This got the clothing clean, but the real test is if it causes a rash. If it doesn't, plenty of women should be interested."

Matthias sniffed the soap then frowned at it.

"What about the stepladder?" Nolan took the soap Matthias handed over.

"I don't have what I need to start—"

"We can go into town tomorrow and put in an order for whatever you need," Nolan interrupted.

"I need hinges. Special ones I'm not sure the town's blacksmith has the skill to make."

"How many and what kind?"

She opened up her notebook and pointed at the drawing she'd finalized last week.

Nolan glanced over his uncle's shoulder. "They're awfully long."

The better for stability. "I doubt the blacksmith could get them done before your uncle came back through."

"Oh," his voice descended a touch.

"I might be able to get you the wire basket aerator in time, maybe the waterer."

Matthias's face looked more thoughtful than miffed.

"Boss?"

Sal poked his head into the cabin. "Could you come with me, please? We've got a situation."

"Sure." Nolan pushed away from the table. "Excuse me a minute."

She frowned as she watched her husband leave with their foreman, but since she wasn't needed, she turned back to Nolan's uncle.

Matthias peered over the top of his reading glasses at her. She crossed her arms and stiffened her spine. After a second, he sighed and took off his glasses. "Some of your ideas are really good."

She tilted her head. If that was true, why the sound of

resignation?

"I know your husband insists you take credit, but I see you are an intelligent young lady. And I think both you and I know that if you want to make money, you have to keep your investors and buyers from having a lick of doubt in your product."

She narrowed her eyes at him. He'd not had a lick of doubt when he was under the impression Nolan had drawn these.

Considering the fatherly look he was giving her, she braced herself for whatever unarguable advice he was about to dole out.

"Nolan may have duped me into thinking these were his contraptions, but once I learned they were yours ... I can't say that your being female can be overlooked."

"What do you mean, 'duped'?"

"He never outright said they were his, but considering he wrote the letter and these sketches were in his hand, I assumed so."

She chewed her lip. Maybe Nolan had good reason to approach his uncle that way. Maybe he hadn't been trying to steal anything from her.

That still didn't excuse him from deceiving them both.

"I'm afraid most men won't believe in you like Nolan does. Love makes men blind—not that he's blind to what you have here." Matthias tapped her notebook. "But he is blind to the fact that not everyone's going to ignore your sex. Women don't patent much. The man of the family usually—"

"I'm familiar with that process, and no, Nolan will not be patenting my inventions in his name." The hard edge to her voice should end any further discussion to that end.

"Since Nolan seems amenable to that, you can do as you please, but though he has the ability to run a ranch well, he's not familiar with these kinds of investments like I am. I know you ran a laundry, but you don't know the art of selling a product.

It's best if you put down your pride and let Nolan take the credit. You're bound to sell more, get further faster. It's simply business."

She wanted to tell him to keep his unsolicited advice to himself, but she couldn't ignore her husband had a relative who could get her inventions on a mercantile shelf quicker than she'd ever dreamed. "Are you unwilling to show your friends my inventions in light of the fact that the patents will belong to me?"

He rubbed the bridge of his nose. "I'll take the paper Nolan sent me and see how they react to those three. You work on getting that covered waterer made. Make sure it works." He looked at her intently. "I suggest you think about changing your mind."

"There's nothing to think over."

He shook his head, but the set of his mouth indicated he'd finally resigned himself—and that he thought her too stubborn for her own good. "Then I'll need prototypes of everything before I can get anywhere with them. How soon can you get me that stepladder?"

"Out here?" She arched one eyebrow. Did he forget where they lived? "I don't know if the in-town blacksmith and cabinet-maker have the talent and time to fashion what I need. It could take months."

Matthias started cleaning his glasses with his shirt, shaking his head. "If we have any hope of getting them into next year's catalog—"

"He-lllo, Father," Matt's slurred voice accompanied him as he stepped inside the cabin and knocked into the table under the front window. He shored himself up against the wall and crossed his arms. "I heard you were in town, not planning to see me."

Matthias's frown hardened. "Nonsense, I've told no one that."

"But you didn't ask where I was now, did you?"

Matthias didn't answer, just looked at his son as if a reproving stare would answer Matt's question.

Corinne scrunched her nose at the rank odor of aged alcohol.

"Why'd you come out here, anyway?" Matt stagger-stepped to her table and picked up one of her failed washing dollies. He frowned at the plunger-like contraption, undoubtedly having no idea what it was, and tossed it to the floor.

What right did he have to come in here and throw her things around?

Nolan hustled in, not even trying to hide his limp. "I'm sorry." His voice was breathless. "I tried to get him to wait."

"Why?" Matt pivoted toward Nolan, somehow keeping himself upright. "What's in here I can't know about?" He scanned the room, his disdainful sneer growing wider. "It's all just junk."

He turned to his father. "What are you doing out here in the junk shed?"

"It's not junk." Corinne retrieved the washing dolly and set it back on the table with a decisive thump. "It's my workshop."

She shook her head. Why was she wasting breath arguing with him?

Matt shrugged and took a swaggering step toward her. "What is it Nolan has that you want? He doesn't need you anymore. He's got the ranch."

"Now, son. Look here." Matthias placed himself between Corinne and his son.

"Oh, I'm looking." Matt pulled up short and glared at his father. "You think Nolan's got it all together, do you? Did you know his father didn't want him to have this ranch and practically disowned him like you did me? Nolan ain't no better than me, and you ain't no better than Uncle Lewis."

Matthias glanced over his son's shoulder toward Nolan with a questioning look, but Nolan didn't notice because he was grabbing for Matt's arm. "Let's talk about this elsewhere. We ought—"

Matt yanked himself from Nolan's grasp. "Don't touch me."

Nolan put both hands up in surrender, but moved to place himself in front of her, next to his uncle.

She moved closer to Nolan.

Matt scanned the room as if he'd found himself in a garbage heap and gestured at his cousin. "Why were you so dad-blamed determined to keep me out of this place?"

Matthias harrumphed. "Probably because he knew you wouldn't react well to the fact I'm going to be investing in a woman's ideas before I lay another penny on you."

Corinne cringed—though under different circumstances, she might have crowed a little. Matthias's reservation over whose name was on the patent wasn't a deal breaker after all.

He really thought she had something.

"What's she got that you want?" Matt's disdain suddenly drained away, and he turned to glare at her like a fox that had spotted its next meal.

"What I've wanted you to have your whole life—gumption, stick-to-it-tiveness, and plain ol' work ethic."

Matt shrugged. "I bet I made more money this past week than she did all year. Nolan told you she's just a laundress, right?"

"And she'll likely make me more money this upcoming year than what you embezzled from me last."

Though this was her cabin, perhaps she shouldn't stay in it any longer. She took a step around Nolan, but he held out his arm and tucked her back behind him.

Matt flung out his arms. "You've always said it takes money to make money. That's all I was doing."

"And I've also always said principle before profit." Matthias huffed and did a quick turn to face Nolan and Corinne. "Excuse us." He took Matt's arm.

But his son wriggled out of his grasp as he had with Nolan

earlier. "What makes the two of you think you can manhandle me?"

"Get out of here, Matt. They don't need to be involved in this."

Matt took one last glance around before stomping out of the cabin.

Seemed she ought to put a padlock on her shopping list.

Matthias sighed and followed his son out.

Once the men exited, Nolan put his hand on her shoulder. "I'm sorry. Sal tried to redirect him, but evidently he started throwing things. Once Matt figured out where Matthias was, he wasn't about to sit in the parlor. Unfortunately, he walks faster than me, even intoxicated."

Corinne glanced out the doorway where Matt was marching ahead of his father. "Is he often drunk?"

Nolan shook his head. "Not that I'm aware of, but apparently he lost a good deal of money last night. I shouldn't have told him Uncle was here."

"It's all right."

He took her hand. "But is it? You haven't seemed yourself this morning. This isn't how I'd envisioned today."

She extracted her hand. "No, I suppose you wouldn't have expected your uncle to show up and reveal you sent off my designs without permission."

He stepped back, his face tense.

"How could you snoop through my sketches? I told you they weren't done, they weren't good enough—"

"You need to stop saying that. I apologize for sending that paper off without your knowledge, but I was afraid to get your hopes up. Your opinion about your ideas is already low enough. I didn't want any criticism from my uncle to stop you from continuing."

She lifted her chin. "You redrew it. I saw the page. You were passing it off as your own."

He had the good sense to look sheepish. "I figured if he

knew they were your inventions, he'd not even look. My aunt did him wrong, and ever since, no woman starts out with a clean slate with him. I'm sure once he gets to know you he'll be able to see past his prejudices, but that'll take time. I thought I could get his opinion before he knew they were yours, so we could speed up the process if he were interested."

"Why not wait until I was ready? Are we hurting for money that badly?"

"No, but we definitely don't have enough money to help you with any of this. It might take years to save up enough to manufacture and sell just one of these things, so I was hoping Uncle could help. You've upended your entire life to save my ranch, so I just hoped to arrange something to make your dream a reality sooner rather than later."

Nolan's heartbeat had ramped up with their first real fight, but less because of her ire, and more because he was mad at himself. Their chance at convincing his uncle to work with a woman was likely short-lived. What if he'd messed up her biggest opportunity by pushing her into it too soon?

Corinne only stood there staring at him.

Uncle must have told her before breakfast that he'd sent her inventions to him—and yes, he deserved the fiery darts zinging out of her eyes right now, but with Uncle being willing to work with her, surely she'd forgive him. "I believe in you, Corinne. I only wanted—"

"Corinne?" Matthias pushed open the cabin door but didn't come in. "I want you to be ready to go with me to Denver when I come back through. Unless we want to lose a year's worth of potential revenue, we need to get prototypes made in time to convince my friends they should invest. Denver has everything you need. I can call in favors with my manufacturers and get you the chemicals you require and anything else that you'd have to order if you stayed here."

Nolan couldn't move anything but his eyelids.

He had hoped his uncle would help her achieve her dreams sooner rather than later, but to leave within days? To be gone for who knew how long, after…

He turned to look at his wife. She appeared interested.

Not uncertain. Not unwilling. Not like a woman too in love to leave her husband behind.

"I…" He couldn't push any more words out.

They were close enough to the three-month mark no one would be suspicious of a newlywed bride heading off to visit a relative, especially when they learned of the opportunity his uncle was affording her. He'd told her she'd be free to live her life, but would she come back? If Denver would be that much better for making prototypes and talking to investors and working with manufacturers…

"I suppose you two should talk it through. I'll be at the hotel until nine tomorrow morning." Matthias ducked out, shutting the door with a soft click.

"Well?" She looked to him with a newly blank expression. Was she trying to hide how eager she was to say yes to Uncle's offer?

He swallowed hard. "It's up to you. If you think it best to go to Denver…" How could he tell her not to go when he was the reason Matthias had offered this? "Uncle's right, it'll take you much longer to get things made out here."

Her face was unreadable as she picked up her notebook and hugged it to her chest. "But I don't know your uncle, any more than I—" She shook her head.

Know you, she likely meant to finish.

Considering how she was clutching her notebook as if to keep it safe from him, any trust he'd earned the past couple of months was gone.

His heart dropped to his toes. She likely had no desire to

hear anything that sounded like romantic nonsense from him now, but he could tell the truth. "I trust you to make wise decisions, Corinne. I believe you've got what it takes to do well. If you think you should go, I'll support you."

Even if it broke his romantically inclined, nonsensical heart.

CHAPTER THIRTY-FIVE

Nolan walked toward Corinne's cabin, a bowl of stew and a canister of water in hand. He was tired of limping, but his leg hurt from a long day's work. None of which he'd had to do. But considering Corinne would be out here until nightfall again, busily rethinking designs and coming up with new ones, he hadn't wanted to sit in the house alone any more than necessary.

Matthias was due back on Sunday, and he'd hardly seen his wife since his uncle left.

She hadn't told him yet whether she'd decided to go with Uncle to Denver, but since she'd done nothing but work on her inventions this past week, he couldn't help but resign himself to her going.

Their night together hadn't brought them closer—or if it could have, sending off her drawings weeks before had messed everything up.

So why was she having such a hard time forgiving him for that? He'd explained his intentions, and he'd won her an opportunity she would never have gotten without him. Plus, he'd taken over her chores so she could spend her every waking moment in her cabin.

He was proud of her.

If he'd told her once, he'd told her thrice—but only thrice, because each time he mentioned it, she got quieter.

With each compliment, wink, and encouraging squeeze he gave her, she turned further into herself.

He stopped midstride and sighed. She *was* leaving him.

He'd hoped her lack of enthusiasm since the day Matthias had proposed the plan meant otherwise, but she'd also not once kissed him goodnight again.

Why wouldn't she tell him of her plans? Was she contemplating staying in Denver forever? Did she not want him to talk her out of it? Would he only ever see her again if he visited Colorado?

No, he was being too pessimistic, but then, why wasn't she talking to him? Hopefully she'd answer his questions tonight. He couldn't sit and worry about it any longer.

The sound of feminine laughter sounded from Corinne's cabin, and Nolan shook his head. Apparently he'd been too lost in thought to have noticed the Hendrixes' wagon.

He paused just short of the cabin. Should he bring out another bowl of stew? Though if Annie wanted some, he could go back for more. It was unusual for her to drop by around supper time, but it was nice to hear Corinne laughing.

A strange slapping sound seemed to make the women laugh again.

Nolan stopped in the open doorway. His wife and her friend were crouched beside a wooden duck toy, their backs to him.

Annie tugged the string attached to the duck's breast, and its wooden wheels, with what appeared to be embedded leather feet, smacked against the planks, making the duck's head bobble on its spring.

Annie laughed again, picked up the duck, and sat down on the floor. "This is great. My kids never had such a toy."

"I'm glad you like it." Corinne tapped the duck's head, making it nod wildly. "It's one of the better things I've come up with this week, and I had the material to make it. Too bad your baby's not born yet. I could've tested it out so I had some feed-back for Nolan's uncle on how well it might sell."

"You don't need a baby to tell you if this toy will sell. It's the parents who'll buy it, and I certainly would."

Corinne slumped to sit on the floor beside Annie, staring toward the back wall.

Annie put a hand to Corinne's shoulder. "You don't seem excited to be going to Denver."

Nolan fidgeted in the doorway. He likely ought to announce himself, but would Corinne tell Annie what was wrong? She certainly wasn't telling him.

"I am excited." But Corinne's voice sounded flat.

"I don't think I believe you."

"It's just … some things, though you expect them to make you happy … can't."

Annie put her arm around Corinne. "True, you can't expect any *thing* to make you happy. Joy comes from within. If you're missing that, you should pray—"

Corinne harrumphed. "I can't ask God for help with this."

"Why not?" Annie's voice sounded as confused as he felt. "God knows everything and—"

"God wouldn't—I mean, He hasn't before. It's just that I thought…"

Nolan turned back to lean against the outside of the cabin, his heart sinking with how his wife seemed so sad and resigned. Had he known the light would've gone out of her by getting his uncle involved, he'd have never sent that letter.

"You see…"

He closed his eyes, as if that might help him hear her softly spoken words better.

"Nolan and I, we were…"

He couldn't help but lean closer.

"Well, we were … *together*, for the first time last week. And I shouldn't have let it happen. It didn't go at all like I'd hoped."

If his heart hadn't already sank earlier, it wouldn't have survived the fall.

A rush of cold swept over him. His wife was talking to someone else about how disappointing he'd been. His best friend's wife, at that.

"Oh, honey." Annie's voice held sympathy, but also a touch of amusement—as if what Corinne had said was cute.

He pinched the bridge of his nose. With a quick shake of his head, he pushed off the wall.

Abandoning the stew and water jug on a nearby stump, he marched off, but only made it to the next tree. He stopped to lean against it and stared blankly at the house up ahead.

So she'd kept her distance not just because he'd betrayed her trust, but because he'd disappointed her in every way a woman could be disappointed.

He'd tried. Really tried. He'd known her history, and Jacob had told him patience was key. So he'd been careful to pay attention to her while trying to show her how he felt. It wasn't like he knew what he was doing.

But to be worse than expected?

He'd not bother to ask her to stay. He didn't want to hear whatever half truth she'd tell him to spare his feelings.

Annie gave Corinne's shoulder a comforting squeeze.

Now that she'd spilled her entire history, she couldn't look up at her friend.

The older woman nudged her chin up. Annie's eyes were still bright, but the twinkle Corinne had assumed was amusement earlier now looked more like understanding.

"Thank you for entrusting me with that." Annie took hold of Corinne's hands, letting them lie between them, where their knees met on the floor. "But honey, what you experienced is not God punishing you for your past choices. You've asked His forgiveness, and because He's promised He will completely forgive, He's done so. If we can't trust Him to forgive, then there's no reason to trust Him to do anything else He's promised."

"Well, yes, but there are consequences."

"You've been forgiven, you've chosen never to sin that way again, and now you've entered into a God-ordained marriage. God wants marriages to flourish. Trials aren't punishment."

"But…"

"Think of my daughter. She's apologized to Leah for her part in the accident that left her permanently scarred, has finished her court-appointed service to the community, and is showing by her actions that she intends to stay on the straight and narrow. What would you think of me if I kept punishing Celia?"

Corinne wilted. "That you were vindictive."

"Does the Bible paint God as vindictive?"

"No, but I understand why He didn't bless my relationship with Kurt, but with Nolan … I thought things would go better. I'm sure at some point, like Kurt, he'll—"

"Now, hold up. I'm not sure you can say your less-than-wonderful experience with Kurt was a sign God was with-holding a blessing. He wasn't withholding pleasure from Kurt now, was He?"

"Well, no."

"Do you think Kurt deserved pleasure and you didn't? That you were the only one sinning against God?"

She looked down and shook her head. It would be unfair to only punish her for the moral offense they committed together, but then why? "I guess I'm broken, then."

"I doubt you're broken." Annie squeezed her hands.

Stealing a hand back to swipe at the tears spilling down her cheeks, Corinne refused to look at Annie again. Why had she told her anything? Talking with her friend only confirmed what she'd already known. She shouldn't have gotten involved with any man.

She knew being with Nolan wasn't wrong, and yet, if intimacy would be no different than with Kurt, how could their marriage avoid the bitterness and resentment that had shattered that relationship?

As much as she should be ecstatic right now about the opportunity to have an entire catalog page of her own inventions for sale next year, the thought of living apart from Nolan made her depressed. Yet, it was probably for the best. How could she survive his discontent when Kurt's had devastated her?

She had to keep her heart shuttered.

But she'd caved, she'd fallen, and now she'd trapped a good man into a lifetime of disappointment.

"Corinne." Annie's whisper was too pointed to ignore.

She glanced up.

A rosy glow colored her friend's cheeks. "I know this isn't something polite ladies talk about, and I won't go into detail unless you ask, but years ago, Leah gave me advice about enjoying intimacy, and I can share if you'd like. You see…"

It was now Annie's turn to stare at her lap. "My first husband and I had problems like yours. He never laid the burden of pleasure solely on me, but we'd become frustrated. First Corinthians seven says husbands and wives should not deprive one another and the key is 'one another.' God doesn't just say don't deprive your husband. He also says don't deprive your wife, and if a wife isn't supposed to enjoy marital relations, well then, what is a husband depriving you of? Marital intimacy should not be one-sided. He created wonderful things about women that demonstrates He never intended for you to feel as you do."

Corinne closed her eyes and her heart lifted a little. Could she really believe that?

"Sometimes there's a problem He never designed us to have

to deal with. Other times it just takes time and advice. There's a reason some older couples are happier than newlyweds." She winked. "They've learned a thing or two."

Corinne tried to smile, but what if Annie was wrong? Or what if she was indeed a woman who had a problem that could never be fixed?

Annie jiggled Corinne's hands. "First thing to do is pray."

"Pray?" She couldn't stop herself from widening her eyes. "About this?"

"Certainly. God created sex and called it good. Therefore, it is. Second, you need to stop thinking negatively. God *wants* you to experience the lovely things of this world within the boundaries He set up, otherwise, why do they exist? He saved you so you could not only have life eternally, but abundantly."

"I'm tempted to hope so, but you can't tell me every child of God gets everything they want."

Annie looked to the ceiling, her mouth scrunched in thought. "I can't promise you'll get what you want, no, but there's joy. James says, 'Count it all joy' when you face trials. You can't find the joy if you're focused on the negative. We're to set our minds on whatever's lovely and pure and praiseworthy. If you're not hoping for the good God wants for you, how can you pursue it?"

"And if you don't find it?"

"He doesn't promise the journey won't be frustrating, and sadly, sometimes what we find at the end of the journey is not what we hoped for. But when your focus is on believing God has good things in store for you, if you follow Him—seeking His kingdom first—He can bless you with joy."

"Nolan's a blessing I already don't deserve."

"He's a good man. I doubt he'd be unwilling to seek God's blessing with you."

"No, I can't imagine he'd not want to try." Though could she find joy if things didn't turn out as well as Annie thought?

It was easier to believe God was still punishing her over how badly she'd once failed than hope for joy where she'd only ever felt disappointment.

In order to believe God wanted the best for her, to believe she deserved His goodness—she'd have to change her frame of mind.

No matter how awkward she might feel praying about this, she'd do so. For what other hope did she have?

CHAPTER THIRTY-SIX

Plumping his pillow for probably the seventy-eighth time, Nolan flipped over in bed and stared at the shadowy shapes outside his window. The downstairs clock chimed three. If only the bells were louder and rang every quarter hour. Then maybe the constant noise would drown out the conversation his mind wouldn't stop playing over and over…

"We were together for the first time last week. And I shouldn't have let it happen. It didn't go at all like I'd hoped."

"Oh, honey."

Nolan wrapped his pillow around his head, as if covering his ears would muffle the words ringing in his brain.

"We were together for the first time last week…"

Ugh! He threw his pillow across the room and flopped back onto the bed. Closing his eyes, he forced himself to listen for the branches scratching against the house. He'd count each and every time they scraped. That should bore him to sleep.

But something was off about the scratching. It sounded more like crackling.

The vegetation must be drier than he thought. They'd been through droughts before, but things must be going downhill quickly if——

Smoke.

He sat up and sniffed the air.

Tossing his blankets onto the floor, he hopped to the window. With the cloud cover, the moon wasn't bright, but to the right was a faint glow.

Was the old barn on fire? A flit of a shadow passed the bunkhouse as he threw up the sash.

If one of his men was already running around, they likely all were racing to get out there, but without knowing what was burning—

"Corinne!" he hollered as he hopped to the closet. Grabbing his leg, he scowled. Putting this on would eat up precious minutes, but crutches would do him no good fighting a fire.

"Corinne!"

Hopefully it was the dilapidated barn—nothing in it but junk—though Corinne probably could've repurposed the stuff. If it wasn't the old barn, what could it be?

As he started unclasping his leg's straps, Corinne staggered sleepy-eyed into his bedroom. "What's wrong?"

"Fire."

Her eyes widened and her posture lost its slack. "Where?"

"I'm guessing the old barn. The building with the broken plows. The glow's coming from that direction."

"Oh, no." She shook herself and stumbled backward, her footsteps heavy but fast down the hallway. "I'll get the wagon and the ramp for water."

After he finished making himself ready, he hobble-ran down the stairs and out the back door, the night air thick with smoke. Arriving at the garden shed, he grabbed buckets and threw burlap sacks over his shoulder.

Lord, bless us with enough water and no wind.

He returned to the front of the house, meeting Corinne as she pulled the wagon up. After tossing the buckets on top of the ramp in the back, he launched himself onto the bed. "Go!"

She drove to the rain barrels and they both quickly

hammered lids on. Working together—though awkwardly—they rolled the barrels up the ramp and onto the wagon.

After the third barrel settled alongside the others, his heart was beating double time. Without his wife's ramp, the two of them never would've gotten them up there. He turned to give her a thankful smile, but she was already climbing up to the driver's seat. He launched himself into the back to hold the barrels in place while she raced toward the glow, definitely coming from the old barn. The flames weren't terribly high, but every second felt like an eternity.

Corinne stopped the wagon so hastily the barrels nearly knocked him out of the back. He tossed the ramp to the ground and slid off the wagon, scanning the area around the barn.

Where were his men? Hadn't he seen—

"Move." Corinne pushed him aside.

"Sorry." He helped her put the ramp into the notches she'd cut into the wagon bed. "Did you knock on the bunkhouse door before you came for me?"

"I didn't." She huffed as she forced the last board into place. "You should've told me to."

"I thought I'd seen one of them running out here." He held in his groan. It had been hard enough for the two of them to roll these barrels in. Now they had to get them out without losing water. "Do you think you can get the barrel moving enough on your own to get it onto the ramp?"

"You're going to catch it? By yourself?"

Though he wanted to snarl at her for believing him incapable, he was just as uncertain. "We don't have much choice."

She hesitated, looking into his eyes as if she could see him despite being backlit by fire. But before he could insist, she hopped up into the back.

Slowly, agonizingly slowly, they got the barrels onto the ramp and rolled them down. He ignored every stitch of pain as they set three full barrels of water onto the ground.

With his lungs short on air, he assessed the increasing flames. Should they get the men or start fighting the fire?

With the crowbar, Corinne opened the first barrel and had a bucket filled within seconds.

"Go hit the biggest flame with that. I'll wet the sacks." He dunked the burlap, surveying the barn. It should be easy to contain the fire to the structure considering they'd let the cattle graze down the grass here last week.

"What next?" She raced back, her breath short.

He frowned at the swirl of her nightgown. What had he been thinking to send her off wearing loose clothing? "What shoes do you have on?"

She skidded to a stop, a crease in her brow, but lifted her gown and stuck out a foot. "Your father's boots."

He puffed out a breath. "Good." The soles were wider than lady's boots'. "See where the fire is crawling slowly against the wind to the north?" He pointed to the curved line of flames, no taller than three inches. "Go rub it out with your boots, but gather your nightdress as high and tight as you can, and here."

He took the bucket from her and refilled it with water. Dropping to his good knee, he grabbed a handful of ruffles and dunked the wadded cloth into the pail. "Turn."

"What do you mean rub it out?" She did a quarter turn as he dipped more of her skirt into the water.

"Twist your sole on it until it's snuffed. Then walk the line doing so, holding your gown out of the way. I'll work on the bigger flames." He pushed himself to stand.

"Are you sure?" She grabbed his arm and held on until he was steady on his feet.

"Yes." He had no time to explain. "Go now!"

She bent over immediately, pulled her skirts up around her legs, and ran out to the growing circle of flames.

Flinging a wet sack over each of his shoulders and a full pail in both hands, he scrambled to the spot she'd thrown water at earlier. Hopefully he could minimize his water usage because he certainly wasn't as fast as she was at running with a heavy pail.

Even if he had two intact legs and all his men helping, he wouldn't be able to save the barn. Just like he couldn't stop Corinne from leaving him—his best was simply not enough.

Smacking the larger flames, he drove himself by swatting to a tempo, despite how much his shoulder protested.

Corinne ran back. "That's done. Now what?"

Taking the chance to breathe, he rewet his bags. "Can't save the barn." He huffed. "We can keep it contained though." He pushed the damp hair from his face. "But if a wind comes, I'm in trouble, so go get the men."

"I don't want you—"

"Woman! My handicap is less of a problem than your skirts. My arms work just fine."

"That's not what I was going to say!" She yanked him by the shoulders, but he resisted. "Promise me you'll be safe." She stepped around to look him in the face. "The ranch is not worth your life."

He shrugged. "With me gone, you'd have all the profit."

"Why would I want that?"

"You don't need me."

"What are you talking about?"

A gust of wind blew in, twirling the loose hair about her face.

The fire on the side of the barn jumped a foot. He stepped back and grabbed a sack. "I've got to—"

"Nolan." She grabbed his arm, her fingers digging into his muscle. "Be safe. Promise me!"

She only waited to see his nod before rushing off.

As the rattle of the wagon faded behind him, he whapped the flames.

Whapped, and whapped, and whapped.

Why not let the fire take him?

Would that be worse than facing her disappointment? Facing

the day she'd write to him from Denver to tell him she wasn't coming back? That he wasn't worth coming back to?

Gritting his teeth, he marched back to the bucket.

He dunked his sacks in and sloshed out more water than he should have then headed to the tree the wind was driving the fire toward.

He knew he shouldn't have gotten married.

The love his father had had for his mother had waned. Why had he thought it'd be any different for him?

He drove himself forward, smacking down not only the fire, but every stupid hope he should've never let himself entertain.

Whap. Whap. Whap. For an eternity. *Whap. Whap.*

Sweat trickled into his eyes and the world turned dark. Had the smoke choked out all the light?

The wind rushed across the back of his neck, making him shiver despite the heat. He wiped his face and scanned his surroundings.

The fire was out.

The barn was gone, charred black. The boards' edges glowed orange, but they were no longer licked by fire.

He let the wet, crispy sacks slip from his fingers and onto the ground.

He'd done it. Without anyone's help.

See, Dad?

He glared at the sky. "I did it without you!"

The muscles in his shortened leg took that moment to cry out in pain, but he gritted his teeth to rail more at the sky. "See? You don't leave people behind because they can't do everything you think needs to be done! I don't need you! I don't need them! I don't need her! I don't need anybody!"

He staggered back.

"I don't." He lowered himself to the ground, his voice choking. "I don't."

Swallowing hard against the rise of tears, he squeezed his eyes shut and slumped over his one bent knee.

What a lie.

Behind him, the rattling of the wagon bumping over unseen pasture grew louder. The voices of his men barely registered over the erratic beat of his heart and heavy breathing.

Corinne pulled up, and Timothy jumped off the wagon before it stopped.

He jogged toward Nolan. Only one of Tim's suspender straps was hooked to his pants, his shirt buttoned up cockeyed. "From the way your wife was going on, we thought this was going to be worse."

Sal sauntered up, his hair standing up on one side of his head. "What started it?"

"Don't know." Nolan swallowed past the clump in his throat, his limbs shaking more than expected.

Sal surveyed the damage, hands on his hips. "Have you noticed any static lightning? Is it dry enough for that?"

Timothy shook his head. "I haven't, but it's too dark to figure out anything tonight."

Sal clasped the young man's shoulder. "We might as well go back to bed."

Tim didn't need any more encouragement and headed back to the wagon where Rascal and Abel hadn't even jumped off.

Sal came over to offer him a hand up, and he took it, considering his one good leg was nearly mush now. But with the men dangling off the back of the wagon, that meant he'd have to sit up front with Corinne.

He waved them on. "I'll walk back."

"Then I'll walk with you." Corinne set down the reins. "Sal, you drive."

Nolan held up a hand. "That's not necessary."

She clambered down before he could stop her, and Sal vaulted himself up into the driver's seat.

Nolan groaned. He didn't want to be alone with his wife right now. No matter what she chose to talk about, how could he ignore the fact that she was only walking beside him out of duty?

Suddenly his foot thumped straight down into a hole, and a crack of lightning burst through his ankle. "Ah!" His hands instinctively shot out as he fell.

"Nolan!"

He rolled over on the uneven grass clumps and clamped his hands around his ankle.

Stupid cattle!

Stupid him!

He hissed sharply. He knew better than to walk in freshly tromped pasture without watching his step.

The sharp jabs stabbing his ankle were not good, not good at all. A sudden bout of lightheadedness made him reel for a second, and then the pain came back in full force. He couldn't hold back a growl through gritted teeth.

"Hold up," Corinne called to Sal. She whistled high and loud then crouched beside him. "What happened?"

He'd twisted his ankle. His one good ankle. That's what.

After all his self-congratulations on how he'd put the fire out all by himself, he did this. "I need to get up."

He tried to put weight on it, but ended back on his backside, letting out another angry growl. Maybe this was far worse than a sprain.

"What's wrong, boss?" Timothy was already beside him. The young man undoubtedly had jumped off the wagon again without waiting for it to stop.

"He twisted his ankle." Corinne kneeled. "Help me get him up."

She slipped her hand under his arm, but he batted her away. "No, I'll get up on my own."

But he fell once again, scrunching his face hard to keep from tearing up. For a minute, he was afraid he was going to lose his dinner on his wife's boots. He tried not to double over as he pulled in a few long breaths until the nausea passed. "Fine, I need help."

Timothy came around to his other side. "You gotta be careful walking in the dark."

If his hands weren't necessary for putting pressure against the throbbing, he'd have been tempted to slap the boy upside the head. He hadn't been the one to jump out of a moving wagon twice now.

"Just help me up and keep any further advice to yourself."

"You should put ice on it right away," Timothy said as he slipped a hand under his arm.

Had the boy not heard what he'd just said?

Abel joined them on Nolan's other side, and once he was on his feet, he tried to hobble forward, but gave up and let the men lug him to the wagon.

After Nolan slid up onto the bed, Abel lifted Corinne to sit beside him. She put a hand on his shoulder. "After we get the men to the bunkhouse, we're going to the doctor."

He shook his head.

"Don't fight me. We can't have you losing the use of your other leg."

Those words might as well have been a bullet to the heart.

If Corinne's inventions didn't work out, this place had to float them. He'd promised her that. But a man needed legs to run a ranch.

If he lost the use of his other one?

He never should've gotten married.

Hours later, Nolan laid his head on the hard, flat pillow on the bed in the doctor's convalescing room. He gritted his teeth as Doc Ellis probed his ankle. The burn on the backside of his arm rubbed painfully against its bandaging.

"I can't determine whether there's a break under all that

swelling, but with the amount of pain you're in, it's possible." He set down Nolan's foot and sighed, his eyes heavy with sleep. "We'll have to wait and see."

"What if there's a break?"

"All depends on how it heals."

"And if it heals badly?" His ankle felt as if it were shattered and both his leg and arm felt on fire. He'd never hurt himself worse than this—besides the one time...

"We'll wait and see."

"What does that mean?"

"Exactly as I said: we'll wait and see." Doc raised his eyebrows in that annoying way he did whenever he felt his expertise was being questioned. He grabbed a pillow and thrust it under Nolan's foot, starting anew another round of painful sparks.

"You can stay here for the day, or go home if you promise to lie down in the back of the wagon with your foot elevated and you keep it that way until the swelling goes down."

"I'll make sure of it."

Corinne's voice startled him. He'd thought she'd disappeared into the waiting room.

"I'll stay here." He gritted his teeth as he scooted up to sit, trying his best not to jar his foot. He'd not let her witness him writhe any more than she already had. He especially didn't want the townspeople watching him get carted home on the flat of his back. "I'm more of a burden than—"

"No, you're not."

He couldn't look at her. "You can't tell me I'm not." He nearly yelped when the doctor laid the blanket back over his foot. "It's as plain as day."

"A temporary one, maybe."

Right. A temporary one. He'd never heard of anyone losing the use of a leg over a turned ankle, but if there were breaks, and those breaks were bad, others had at least one good foot to make up for it.

Corinne walked over, her brown eyes dark and glistening with worry. How did she have the audacity to look attractive right now—with her hair mussed and soot smeared across her cheeks—while looking at him as if he were a lame horse the cowhands would have to put down later.

He looked away.

How foolish he'd been hours earlier, thinking he'd done something on his own. His men might not have helped with the fire, but Corinne had driven him out to the barn and made the ramp for the rain barrels. Without her contraption, he'd have had to awaken his ranch hands—with their two good legs—to lift those barrels into the wagon.

And even then, if God hadn't blessed them with no wind… He'd essentially accomplished nothing on his own. Who did?

So why was he so driven to prove he could? Because he was missing a leg?

Seemed only right for God to have made him take a tumble to set him straight.

"Are you thirsty?" Corinne sat on the edge of the bed, making the matress give. He hissed so loudly, she jumped off, which led to him releasing a full-out groan.

"I'm so sorry."

He couldn't answer with more than the shake of his head. If he tried to respond, he'd likely emit more of a whine than a string of words—and none of them would be good words.

She leaned closer. "What if I…?"

"Uhhh." He was seconds away from either crying or passing out because of pain, not only in his ankle, but from the raw heat emanating from the burn on his arm.

"I'm sorry, let me—"

"Just leave."

Her body stilled. "Are you sure?"

The uncertainty in her voice almost made him relent. But he nodded, keeping his jaw clamped tight, his body stiff. He'd not whimper again.

She stood, heaving out an exasperated breath.

Once her footsteps retreated and he noted the doctor had gone as well, he grabbed a pillow and bit into the fluffy mass, muffling a bellow.

After vocalizing until he couldn't breathe anymore, he lay back and tried to remain as still as he could. He let himself breathe even and deep until he could call for the doctor without sounding like he was about to cry. The medicine was not working. "Doc! I need something more for the pain."

"I'm working on it already," came the muffled reply.

As he waited with his fists clamped, he shook his head slightly. He couldn't end up bedridden. Corinne might not want him as a husband in truth—but that hadn't been why she'd married him to begin with. She'd married him to provide for her, and he'd have to do that, no matter what.

But to do so in a wheelchair?

Could sheer force of will cause a bone to heal correctly?

She'd have to go to Denver and stay as long as it took her to do well. Perhaps forever. Her life there might give her more than she'd ever hoped to get out of their pretend marriage—freedom, time to tinker, money for her projects, patents under her own name, no disappointment of a husband.

Being separated from him wouldn't break her heart.

He'd not allow himself to think of what it would do to his.

CHAPTER THIRTY-SEVEN

Running her hands atop the neatly folded piles of linens and pressed shirts, Corinne couldn't help but marvel at how different the laundry looked from the last time she'd been in. "You're doing such a wonderful job. Seems only right I left this place to you."

Leah gave her a playful shove as she walked past to set down another neat pile. "Before your hands got in the way, you were doing as well as I am."

Corinne flexed her fingers, still amazed she was free of constant pain. Some days her hands reminded her she wasn't taking enough breaks, but never with the constant cry from every muscle and tendon. "I still chose the right person to take over. Thank you."

Leah's laughter sounded more like a coal miner's than the soft feminine chuckle Corinne remembered, but it was still good to hear her happy.

"It's I who should thank you. I'd not realized how dire our finances were until Bryant was sent away. And without him…" She stopped folding a pair of trousers to look at Corinne, her eyes more compassionate than usual. "I should've had more sympathy for you when you were running this place on your own. My son-in-law doesn't make much, but I was never in danger of being homeless. But you…"

Leah's lopsided smile practically beamed as she laid a hand atop Corinne's. "I'm glad you're married now and have financial security."

And then Leah's smile went limp. Was she thinking about Nolan's accident or Bryant's incarceration?

As much as it'd be nice to believe marriage could guarantee they'd face no want, every woman dealing with wayward husbands, illnesses, natural disasters, bearing more children than they could afford, and other such problems, warned otherwise.

Nolan would do all he could to make their ranch prosperous, but if he ended up in a wheelchair? The ranch would then be at the mercy of the best men they could employ, which required the best pay to attract them.

She leaned against the counter. She had to be practical. She had to use the head for business God had gifted her with. Which meant she couldn't ignore Uncle Matthias's offer. He was already leery of her because she was a woman. If she appeared too weak to jump on an opportunity when it was hot, he might not attempt to work with her again—especially if she insisted on taking credit for her inventions.

Leah leaned across the counter from the other side, her head dipping to catch her gaze. "Something seems to be weighing you down."

Corinne nodded. No use denying it.

She wasn't exactly upset about having to go to Denver, but rather, why didn't Nolan seem to care?

He'd been surly at the doctor's office and the day after when he'd endured the ride back home—but she'd attributed that all to pain. Since then, he'd gone quiet—as if he didn't care if she left or not.

She looked through the window to the empty wagon.

Nolan, with his turned ankle, hadn't been able to ride in with her, so she'd brought Timothy. But even if her husband's foot had been in perfect shape, she wasn't sure he would've come. His mood was so dark lately. She'd attributed it to wounded pride, yet despite his pain abating, he still seemed discouraged, which probably meant he was worried they were in a mess he couldn't get them out of.

She took a deep breath. It was time to ask Leah what she'd come to ask. "Would you be willing to keep the laundry going for the rest of the year? I know Bryant's due back before then, but I've an opportunity to go to Denver with Nolan's uncle to see about putting my inventions in his catalog. With Nolan's injury—well, if he doesn't get better and my inventions don't gain traction, I might need to return to work."

"Oh, honey, we'll pray that won't happen." Leah's warm hands encompassed hers.

"I pray that, too, but as you know, things don't always go as we'd like."

Leah nodded, her one sloping eye twitching slightly. "I've thought for a while now I'd like to continue working here even after Bryant gets back. I can finish out the year."

Corinne's lungs collapsed with relief. "Wonderful. That will buy me more time away so I can…"

Leah shook her head harder with every word Corinne uttered. "Are you sure being gone so long is a good thing?"

"With the uncertainties we're facing, I need to be prepared to stay as long as necessary." Corinne's throat tightened. It hurt too much to admit they'd only married to do exactly what she was planning—taking care of their financial needs in the most profitable way possible.

"Time apart isn't good for a marriage—that, I know." Leah's expression lost its sparkle. "It's not helping mine right now, but I have no choice. You do."

Corinne dropped her gaze to the counter. "We do what we must to keep our families afloat, yes?"

"We do." Leah's usually warm voice felt a little chilly.

The bell above the door clanked behind them as Timothy

walked in. He took off his hat, letting his shaggy hair fall over his eyes. Too bad his errands hadn't included a haircut, though maybe he liked his hair long, considering it covered his blemishes.

"Are you ready to go, Mrs. Key, or shall I see if someone's willing to play checkers at the store?"

"No, I'm ready." She turned to Leah and grabbed her hand, giving it a squeeze. "Thanks for keeping the laundry going for me in case we need it."

"I'll pray you don't."

She smiled. "And I'll pray those prayers come true—and for you and Bryant as well."

Taking Timothy's arm, she walked out of the laundry. Just as she was about to step into the street, his arm tensed under hers.

She glanced up quickly, worried she'd misjudged traffic, but the only thing approaching was Miss McGill and her brother's young lawyer friend, arm in arm.

Mr. Wright tipped his hat upon seeing Corinne.

She nodded and was about to keep walking, when Miss McGill caught sight of her and the young woman's smile widened. She began pulling Mr. Wright straight toward her.

Gwendolyn McGill had never given her more than a polite acknowledgment before.

"Mrs. Key? Good morning!"

So the young lady's smile truly had been aimed at her. "Good morning."

Miss McGill sashayed beside the lawyer, making a show of being attached to his arm. "Isn't the breeze lovely?"

She hadn't noticed, not with being worried about Nolan's mood and Leah's potential response. "I suppose it is."

"Mr. Wright here was just disagreeing with me, saying there wasn't enough wind considering this humidity. But it's not tugging at my hat and mussing up my hair, so I say it's lovely."

Corinne glanced at her suddenly cold arm. Timothy had

released her and was now slinking down the stairs and then slipped into the shadow by the hitching post.

Mr. Wright laughed, his eyes dancing with amusement. "I know I shouldn't argue with a woman, but I can't help myself. She's entertaining riled up."

Miss McGill gave him a playful slap on the arm. "I should've known." She turned back to Corinne. "He and my brother find it amusing to say things to get my dander up."

Corinne nodded politely, but worked hard not to fidget. Why had Miss McGill pulled her into this conversation?

"Excuse me a moment, Mr. Wright." Slipping her arm from his, Miss McGill crossed over to Corinne. Her lips lost their flirtatious smile and her forehead wrinkled.

She pulled Corinne a couple of steps away. "I've been meaning to commend you for helping Mrs. Whitsett. That was kind of you."

"Leah?" Of course Miss McGill knew of Leah's misfortune, considering Bryant had worked for Gwendolyn's disgraced father, but she couldn't imagine they'd been close.

"Yes. Out of all the ladies in town, she shouldn't have to beg for help. I wish I could've assisted, but I'm glad you stepped in."

"Leah is actually doing *me* the favor, but you're right. If one lady in this town deserves to be helped, it's her."

"True." Miss McGill's expression brightened back up. "Goodbye, Mrs. Key. I'll see you around."

She returned to Mr. Wright, took his arm, and said something to him that Corinne didn't quite catch as they walked off. Whatever she was saying made the young man's face bloom with a matching smile.

Still standing in the shadows, his gaze locked onto Gwendolyn's retreating figure, Timothy didn't seem to realize Corinne was coming down the stairs to meet him.

She stopped short of poking him to remind him of her presence.

What had Timothy said that day Uncle had dropped in?

Something about how an average man had no hopes of marrying a woman with money, so Nolan was lucky to marry a woman who could make some?

She turned to watch Gwendolyn walk away, laughing with Mr. Wright. Seemed Timothy had not only set his cap for a woman with more money than he'd ever make in his lifetime, but one who hadn't even acknowledged his presence.

With the McGill name sullied, could Gwendolyn really believe Timothy was unworthy of her notice?

Of course, she herself had been shocked Miss McGill had spoken to her just now. She was likely the only woman in town Lilith would've been pleased to dine with.

Despite her father's crimes casting a shadow over his children, her brother was chipping away at the townsfolk's animosity by fairly redistributing the property his father had stolen. After enough time passed, his sister would likely be able to make a good match.

She turned back to Timothy, who was still staring after the wealthiest young lady in Armelle. Attaching herself to a hired hand was not something Gwendolyn would do willingly. Though it seemed the woman had a heart under her flirty ways, she was all curls, flounces, and porcelain skin. The pock-marked son of a poor homesteader couldn't help but know he'd set his sights too high.

She laid a gentle hand on his arm.

He snapped his gaze off Gwendolyn and straightened, his face a mask.

"Time to be going."

"Of course, Mrs. Key. I'm sorry you caught me woolgathering. Don't know where my head was."

If only she could tell him there was a chance Miss McGill would look at him twice, but if anyone knew dreams didn't always come true, she did.

And if Leah and Bryant's marriage fell apart—the kind of

relationship many in Armelle had aspired to before scandal hit—what hope was there for anyone?

She shook her head at her gloomy thoughts as Timothy helped her into the wagon. Once seated, she turned to look back at the laundry. Leah's silhouetted form was already hard at work scrubbing something against a washboard.

Seemed happy marriages weren't always a given, even when they started off like a fairy tale.

Corinne rearranged her skirts that had bunched beneath her. Her marriage had definitely not started out like a fairy tale—she hadn't even wanted it to. But then, she'd begun to hope...

And that hope had been dashed.

Plus, with how Nolan had insisted this morning that everything was going to be fine, that he'd find a way to provide as soon as he was back on his feet...

Did he regret marrying her, thinking he might still lose the ranch and then be unable to do what he'd vowed? If she knew one thing Nolan hated, it was not keeping a promise.

However, she could lift that burden from him by going to Denver and making enough for them to live on. And yet, she didn't want to leave.

Which was silly. Money and security were what she'd wanted from this arrangement, and Matthias was offering her an opportunity to obtain exactly that. Plus, her hands were better, and the world would soon know her name.

Timothy turned onto the dirt road leading out of town. She tried to summon the desire to strike up a conversation to fill the time, but what could she possibly talk about when her brain was numb and her insides empty?

CHAPTER THIRTY-EIGHT

From his wheelchair, Nolan threw the last of his biscuit onto the plate at his feet. The after-church picnic lunch with his uncle had been tense, and his wife and Leah had abandoned him for more companionable conversation.

He'd been rude. Not only today, but this past week. And yet, he hadn't the heart to act like everything was fine. Though the doctor thought his foot injury was a bad sprain, a hairline fracture hadn't been ruled out, and he worried how it might heal if he didn't stay off of it.

Nolan looked to where Corinne was talking to Leah's oldest daughter while holding the woman's infant. He'd been trying hard not to glance that direction, trying not to think of how good she looked with a baby in her arms.

"You sure she hasn't told you her decision yet?" Matthias had returned from his trip to the necessary and lowered himself to the blanket with a groan.

"I'd tell you if she had." Nolan looked away lest his uncle chide him again for allowing 'his woman' to decide rather than telling her what to do.

"I haven't time to stay past tomorrow. I've business that won't wait."

"She knows."

Matthias had already told them twice that morning, but he understood his uncle's frustration. Why hadn't she told them her decision? On more than one occasion she'd acted determined to go, but then she'd wobble ... and he'd hope...

If he'd learned anything since the fire though, it was that he controlled nothing. During the two days he'd been stuck in bed, staring at the ceiling, all the ways God had provided for him and the people he'd relied on for the entirety of his life had paraded through his mind.

He'd been a fool to have railed at God about needing no one.

The meaning of the verse that taught that a person only ought to say, 'if the Lord wills,' when planning to do one thing or another, had struck him hard. He never should've promised Corinne that he could provide—for it was entirely up to God whether he could or couldn't.

His uncle grunted as he forced himself back to his feet. "I'm going to get more food."

Nolan acknowledged his comment with an imperceptible nod.

"And find some non-gloomy Gus to talk to."

Nolan shrugged, though he should've apologized for his poor company.

"If you don't want her to go, tell her she can't."

He shook his head, despite his guts trembling at the thought of actually doing so. "No, she should go."

"Well, then, I don't know what your problem is." His uncle hobbled for a few steps before finding his rhythm.

Nolan ran his hands over the smooth wheels of his chair.

He knew what his problem was—he didn't want Corinne to go, and yet, he would let her pursue her dream. He'd have to rely on God to heal him and keep the ranch running without her. He'd also refrain from thinking about how likely she'd turn him down once he did request to court her, considering what he'd overheard her say to Annie. And yet … what if he could say something that would let her know how he felt that wouldn't scare her off, maybe even entice her to return?

Matt ambled toward him with a slick smile on his face.

Nolan tipped his head to look at the sky. *Isn't Corinne leaving enough of a trial for me to face today?*

Best to start the conversation and force it in a direction he might be able to endure. "Good afternoon, cousin."

Matt stopped beside him, looking down at him in his chair. "How are you feeling?"

"Ready to dance a jig. Yourself?"

"Fine, right fine." He smoothed his muttonchops. "I received some good news recently."

What was Matt going to rub in his face now? "You found a ranch to purchase far away from here?"

"Nope, my ranch is right outside Armelle."

Nolan's heart sank. So Matt would be around indefinitely—hopefully clear on the other side of town. "Well, congratulations. I hope Lilith can stand it."

"She will once renovations are made. In fact, she's how I got my good news. You know, she never did like your choice of wife."

He bristled but held his tongue. Why bring up Lilith's disdain for Corinne now?

Matt raised both brows. "You're woefully lacking in curiosity."

"I suppose I am."

"You should want to know though, considering it has to do with what Lilith found out about Corinne."

Nolan froze. He couldn't think of anything his cousin would look so smug about other than…

His fingernails dug into the armrests of his chair.

Matt's grin turned up a slimy notch. "Seems your virginal bride wasn't so virginal."

He kept his gaze hard. If Matt thought this information

would persuade him to set Corinne aside and hand him the ranch, his cousin's smile would be short-lived. "I know that. Besides, I've already married her."

Matt's brows winged upward, but his smile didn't fade. "I admit, I'm surprised you knew, considering how much of a stickler you are for keeping vows and such, but then, I wonder who else might know." He paused, as if waiting for Nolan to give something away.

They weren't playing poker. "Doesn't mat—"

"Let's count." Matt held up a hand and ticked off fingers. "I know. Lilith knows. Her informant knows. I wonder what my father will do when he knows."

To keep from telling Matt where he could go if he so much as uttered a word, Nolan clamped his jaw hard enough to crack a tooth. Threatening him might make the fool even more eager to tell his uncle. "We both know he wouldn't like it. But she didn't cheat on me. Her situation is completely different than what your mother did to your father."

"I don't think he'd see it that way."

Nolan sat as still as he could with his mouth pressed shut. Any minute his uncle could appear.

Matt cocked his head. "You know, since the day you brought her to the ranch and got all prickly about me pointing out she wasn't worthy of the Key name, I figured anything I said that would paint her in a bad light would make you defensive."

If he could stand right now, Matt would've learned the truth of it. "Stop playing games and say straight out what you're getting at."

"The ranch. For my silence." Matt shook his head as if pretending to be pained. "Or else the whole town learns your wife used to be a married man's mistress."

"What?" Nolan's face scrunched of its own accord. "He wasn't married."

"Oh, no?" Matt's expression brightened. "Guess I do know something you don't."

Slipping his hand into the inside of his jacket, Matt pulled out a paper. He unfolded it then cleared his throat, holding the paper out as if reading a proclamation. "'Kurt Stone, tried for bigamy in 1879. Married Myra Croft, 1866'—that'd be eight years before he took up with your Miss Stillwater—'in Allentown, Pennsylvania. Took his young son out West, leaving twin newborn daughters behind. Married a Josephine Carter in 1877. No children.'"

Matt slipped the paper back under his jacket. "From the information Lilith obtained, Corinne was cavorting with a married man from 1874 to 1875."

Nolan rubbed his temples, less because of how his uncle would react, and more because if Corinne learned of this, she'd only heap more guilt upon herself. She'd been duped, not only into giving away her virginity, but to a man who'd never been in a position to make her an honest woman as promised. "He lied to Corinne, in more ways than one, apparently." He looked up at Matt, hoping to see a speck of compassion in his eyes that he could appeal to. "She wouldn't have known. Doesn't know."

"Whether she knew or not," He glanced at Nolan's legs. "You're still going to lose the ranch."

"Wrong. I can work harder on my hands and knees than you can with two good feet." He clenched his fists. How hard it was not to fall back into vowing things he couldn't fulfill.

Matt flicked his hand as if tossing that boast out a window. "Be that as it may, you didn't follow your father's wishes. You don't get the ranch."

"What are you talking about? Just because she's not the kind of woman you'd marry—"

"But you didn't really marry her, now did you?"

He straightened as tall as he could in his chair. "Nonsense."

Matt pulled another paper from his coat pocket while glancing in the direction his father had disappeared earlier. "I asked your town's lawyer what loopholes would get me the ranch, but he said as long as you followed the will, you get it. But you haven't fulfilled your father's wishes—not if she's your business partner."

The world suddenly turned frigid.

The second Matt unfolded the letter, Nolan's heart seized, recognizing his own handwriting.

"This declares you to be business partners. With a thirty-seventy split."

Where had he gotten that old contract? Nolan racked his brains to remember where he'd placed it, cursing himself for not burning it. "How dare you go through my stuff while a guest in our home!"

Matt's smile kicked up a notch. "You mean my home."

Nolan spluttered. "It … it doesn't matter what the previous arrangement was, we're married legally and in truth—"

"Oh, I'm afraid even if you've fallen madly in love with her, Lilith's lawyers are far better than any you'll be able to afford. And *I* say, you married to defraud me of my rightful property. What happened afterward is of no consequence. If you fight this, it might be necessary for me to explain to the court what kind of woman Corinne really is, since women like her are the kind to willingly participate in fraud."

"We didn't—" Agh! What use was there in arguing with a cheat, an embezzler, a man who believed he was better than everyone else despite evidence to the contrary.

Was there anything he could do to shut Matt up?

His cousin was right about one thing—he'd do whatever it took to protect Corinne. If that meant giving up his ranch … could he?

He turned his head, unable to continue looking at Matt.

On their wedding day, he'd vowed to provide, he'd vowed to give her a share of his profit, but he couldn't do either without a ranch.

God, what should I do?

He couldn't allow Matt to shame her publicly in a town where gossips like Mrs. Tate resided. For how, then, could he ask her to stay with him on the ranch where she'd be shunned every time she went to town?

He might get a charge of blackmail to stick, but it's not as if the court could muzzle his cousin—Matt could ruin Corinne in a second.

Plus, the accusations aired in court would not only be detrimental to Corinne but to the ranch. Under oath, he'd have to acknowledge the truth of the agreement Matt found. Since he'd always touted his integrity, if people thought he'd intended to defraud his own cousin, who'd do business with him anymore?

His whole body went limp. He'd have to give up the ranch.

He summoned up the strength to glare at Matt. "You're despicable."

Matt shrugged. "I'm not as bad as you or Dad think I am. But since I've lost his favor and didn't have enough time to shore up my coffers before he kicked me out, I have to start somewhere. I don't get Lilith's money until we marry. So here's what I'll do." He crouched beside Nolan and put his hand on the wheelchair's armrest as if he cared.

"I'll let you buy the ranch from me. You give me what it's worth, and I'll be out of your hair."

As much as he wanted to spit in Matt's eye at his so-called generosity, Nolan spoke through gritted teeth instead. "No good. I don't have enough money."

"A pity." Matt's frown looked genuine. He likely would've preferred the cash. "Then it seems you've only got this week before your three months are up and I get the place. Whether or not you want to fight me over the ranch, why don't you think about divorcing her? Then you won't be stuck with a woman you only married to keep the ranch from me."

"No," he spat. "A vow is a vow."

But what if she wished to be free? Why would she want to remain bound to him if he had nothing she wanted?

"Let me remind you, if you contest the obvious evidence I have of you defrauding me, I'll tell the world who Corinne is.

I'm sure you know as well as I do that when Dad finds out, he'll no longer be interested in working with her. If he informs his investors—which you know he will—she'll never sell a thing."

He patted Nolan's leg, and it was all Nolan could do not to sock him in the head.

"Or you could sign over the deed, and I'll be nice and keep things to myself. Then you can ride your wife's coattails in Denver—hopefully her little projects can keep you afloat."

"How magnanimous." Nolan gripped his chair harder to keep from launching himself at his cousin. "And how do you propose I explain why I'd do such a thing?"

Matt pointed at Nolan's bandaged foot. "Your injury plus your wife's golden opportunity made you realize you shouldn't hold on to something you can't handle."

Nolan caught Corinne looking at him from over Matt's shoulder, a worried furrow marring her brow.

Matt glanced behind him, likely seeing Corinne was about to head over. "I'll leave you to think things through. But don't take too long, cousin, or I'll be forced to share what I know with others." Matt stood, patted Nolan's shoulder as if they'd had a good talk, and walked off.

Corinne watched Matt walk away before coming over.

Nolan tilted his head back and let out one long breath. He needed to collect himself before she—

"What were you and Matt talking about?"

How could he tell her? "He was being his usual, arrogant self."

"You look tired. Do we need to go home?"

"No, enjoy your time with friends. I just … I shouldn't have left the house this morning." Not that doing so would've stopped any of this.

"I did want to talk to a few more people before I … I leave with your uncle."

A dagger sliced through his abdomen. Why had that hurt so badly when it was now exactly what she needed to do?

Corinne's eyes looked uncertain as she chewed on her bottom lip, so he nodded to let her know he'd heard because he couldn't trust his voice.

A minute passed, making him afraid he'd have to attempt to say something, but then she let out a loud exhale.

"I suppose I'll say my last goodbyes and get us home so I can pack. Matthias is insisting we leave tomorrow and I could be gone for weeks. He wants to get the tickets early, and so…"

Nolan closed his eyes, listening to her rattle off a well-planned itinerary along with a list of things she needed to take with her to Denver. No declaration of how she'd prefer to stay, that she'd miss him, that she wanted him to come along—no hint of any romantic feelings.

Her no-nonsense practicality should've made him happy. He'd married her specifically because she was this way.

And he wouldn't beg her to reconsider. He wanted her to be happy, and if that didn't include him…

Her chatter faded, and he opened his eyes. She seemed to be waiting for him to respond.

Hoping his voice wouldn't waver, he forced out words. "I trust you to do whatever needs doing."

Her chest heaved. "All right, I'll let Leah know I'm going and say my goodbyes." Corinne nodded, stood, and then marched over to Leah.

After listening to Corinne for a few minutes, Leah glanced over at him, but turned right back to Corinne and gave her a hug before his wife headed into the crowd.

Leah started his way, a frown marring her scarred face, and he braced himself.

"Mr. Key, may I have a word with you?"

"If you'd like, Mrs. Whitsett, but I'm afraid—"

"I know I don't know you very well, but I'm beholden to your wife for what she's done for me. I want what's best for her, so I'm worried about her going off to Denver with you two only be married a few months. It sounds like she intends to work there for quite a while."

He looked up into what he could see of her eyes, hooded by drooping eyelids. "I understand your concern, but—"

"It's hard enough to be separated when you've been together for decades, but considering how you two married so quickly, I just want to be sure you know what you're doing."

He couldn't look at her any longer. She was likely right, but what could he tell her without divulging more than he ought?

Only God could help them out of this mess. But then, was that not true all the time?

God knew Nolan would lose his leg. He knew Dad would force him to marry. He knew Corinne's hands would convince her to give up the laundry. He knew to what lengths Matt would go to get the ranch.

He'd have to trust God to do as He saw fit—which right now seemed to require him to give up all he'd ever wanted. "As I said, I appreciate your concern, Mrs. Whitsett, but this seems the best way forward for us at the moment."

Leah laid a hand on his shoulder. "I'll pray for you."

He reached up to squeeze her hand. "Thank you."

After she walked away, he bowed his head.

No matter what I'd thought before, Dad was right. I'd needed someone.

Maybe it wasn't a wife. Maybe what I'd needed all along was a good kick in the head—or ankle—to make me realize that no matter how well I've compensated, I've needed to trust you instead of me. That no matter how much blood and sweat I spill, if you don't will it...

In my own way, I'm no better than Matt. I've thought myself far more capable than I am.

He needed to free himself from his foolish vow to personally provide for Corinne and seek out how God would have them survive. He could give up the ranch without a fight if it meant Corinne escaped unscathed, but he'd have to cling to God's grace to get them by.

And in case Matt didn't keep his promise, it'd be best if Corinne was far, far from here.

God, please keep Matt's mouth shut. Corinne's already going to suffer financially because of me. I couldn't bear being responsible for her losing her reputation and dreams, too.

CHAPTER THIRTY-NINE

"I'll take that, ma'am."

The porter held out his hands after tossing the last of Uncle Matthias's luggage to the other porter waiting to shuffle off their items to the baggage car. Corinne handed him her large carpet-bag, keeping the smaller one in hand. Though the platform was crowded and the train was chuffing, the silence was crushingly heavy.

Beside her, Nolan said nothing, quiet like he'd been all week. And yet, his silence had somehow amplified since yesterday's picnic.

It was as if he were cutting all ties, even vocal ones.

Matthias clamped a hand onto Nolan's shoulder. "I'm sure you two would like to say goodbye without me around. I'll see you inside, Corinne."

He took a step but scowled.

She looked over her shoulder and spotted Matt departing the depot, satchel in hand. She was tempted to scowl, too, despite Uncle Matthias already telling him he wasn't welcome to sit with them. How inconvenient to have Matt choose to leave on the same day they were.

Matthias remained rooted where he was as his son mounted

the train's steps. Before Matt entered the car, he turned to give Nolan a look, as if asking a silent question.

She turned in time to see her husband nod, his expression more submissive than annoyed.

What was that about?

She might've asked, but she doubted Nolan would answer with anything beyond the "don't worry" he'd been parroting lately.

The train let off steam with a deafening whistle.

"Don't be long." Matthias gave Nolan a slight wave before lumbering off across the platform.

For some strange reason, Nolan pushed himself up out of his chair.

"What—"

He held out a hand to stay her comment or maybe to ward off help as he struggled to stand upright. He took a shuffle step toward the low wooden wall bordering the platform and leaned against it.

She shook her head at him. He shouldn't be putting weight on his foot, and yet, it was nice not to be looking down at him.

His eyes held a mountain of words he seemed unwilling to share.

She furtively wiped at the corner of her right eye. He'd at least tell her goodbye, right?

His throat worked, but the silence continued.

"I guess this is it." She fiddled with her bag's handle, unsure how to take leave of him. They'd worked so well together, but these past few days, it felt as if he'd set her on a raft and pushed her to sea.

Nolan looked ready to cry, but surely not. She was simply reading in emotions she wished were there.

If only it weren't unladylike to give him a good, swift kick to the shin. How dare he force her to stand here and yet say nothing that made her want to stay.

She nodded, and he nodded back, finally seeming to stir.

317

"Godspeed, Corinne. I'm sure you'll do better than fine in Denver." He reached over and touched her arm. "Don't worry about what happens here."

Would he give her nothing more than an arm squeeze? Only weeks ago, he'd trailed his fingers across her shoulders, rubbed her arms, and put a hand to her lower back so often she'd been driven to distraction.

Seemed he was severing himself from her completely, body, mind, and soul. Would he not even tell her he'd miss her?

She sniffed hard. "Goodbye, Nolan. I'll write to let you know how things are going."

He nodded and she couldn't look at him anymore, so she took off across the platform.

Marching down the train car aisle, she blinked away the blurriness, trying to remember what Uncle was wearing since the sea of men was merging together in a watery mess. She would not cry in front of Uncle. He'd send her back if he thought her weak.

Catching a glimpse of Matthias's gray felt hat, she forged forward and took the seat directly across from him since the rows all faced each other in sets. Hopefully she wouldn't get ill riding backwards.

The windows were all open, stirring the sticky, gritty summer air, but she could barely breathe.

Nolan was still leaning against the platform's wooden border. His eyes latched onto hers the second he saw her, his hands clenched at his sides.

If she hadn't known better, she might have thought he was glaring at his mortal enemy. But standing was likely making his pain unbearable. He shouldn't have gotten out of his chair.

His chest heaved, but his stiff posture returned quickly.

Had she only imagined he'd moved?

When the train blew its departing whistle, he didn't flinch, nor look away, even when steam enveloped him.

"Don't worry, sweetheart. He'll be waiting for you when you come back."

She tore her gaze from the hazy platform. "I'm not so sure. He'll be at his ranch, yes, but waiting for me?"

Uncle pshawed. "Of course he will. If Nolan's one thing, he's absolutely rigid when it comes to promises. If he makes a vow, he'll keep it—unlike other people I know."

"That's not—" She clamped her mouth shut. Nolan hadn't promised to be waiting. He'd promised she could live her life as she wished, but Uncle wouldn't believe that.

Matthias leaned over and patted her knee. "Don't worry your pretty little head. As much as I chide him for his rigidness, it's a good thing, especially for you."

The steam dissipated as it rolled out over town, and she caught sight of Nolan again, still standing, watching as the train chugged haltingly forward.

When they moved far enough away she could no longer make out his eyes, she could still feel them, more than she did the sway of the train as they gained speed.

What message was he trying to impart? Why stand there so long if he hadn't had anything to say to her?

Of course, what if he couldn't say it?

Absolutely rigid when it comes to promises… She'd made him promise to forgo all romantic nonsense, and he'd agreed.

What if he'd been afraid she'd view whatever he wanted to say as a broken promise?

Though he was now only a speck, he still stood rooted in that spot.

"Excuse me, I see a fellow I think I know. I'll be back." Matthias sidled out into the aisle.

She nodded her acknowledgment, then looked down at the handle of her carpetbag, which she was gripping too hard.

Nolan loved her—after that one night, it'd been clear—but their relationship had taken a tumble the next morning. She'd been angry at him, his uncle had upended their world, and then the fire and his ankle. He'd let her make all the decisions, and yet now he stood rooted to the platform as if he would literally be right there, waiting, until she came back.

She tucked more of her skirt beneath her, despite the extra cushioning doing little to make her comfortable on the hard seat. How was she going to survive the hours to Denver? If only she could've left Nolan on better terms.

Pulling out her notebook to distract herself, she flipped the pages, looking for a blank sheet. A folded piece of paper and a thick envelope stopped her progress.

Her fingers trembled as she unfolded the letter, recognizing Nolan's handwriting. Perhaps he'd been silent because he'd said what he wanted to in a letter—which only made her heart pump all the more. If he couldn't say it to her face…

Corinne,

I'm having difficulty knowing where to start, but I apologize for the strange place I've put us in. I know you're uncomfortable with what this pretend marriage has turned into, and I'll harbor no ill will toward you if you choose not to return to me. As I promised when I proposed this arrangement, you can choose how you live.

She pinched the bridge of her nose to keep from crying. She'd hoped he'd cared enough about her that he wouldn't want to be parted for long.

But did he wish to be parted forever?

She breathed in, trying to fortify herself to continue, for she wasn't certain she could bear to read the rest.

…I want you to know I have faith in you. Uncle will soon realize he was a fool to ever think your being a woman was any sort of detriment. I'm including an envelope of money for you to invest in whichever endeavor you think has the most promise. No matter what happens, please send me that first catalog containing your inventions, circling them so I can talk up your products to whomever I meet.

Please don't let your vows to me hinder you from doing great things. For as long as I'm able, thirty-five percent of my profits are yours, but I'm afraid all you can count on to finance your dreams may be what's inside the envelope—though you'll likely not need it. You don't need a man to help make your dreams come true. You'll find a way no matter what happens. Which should come as no surprise to anyone if they've taken the time to get to know you. Uncle's a bit hard-headed and might try to talk you into seeing things his way, but I trust him to do right by you, just stick to your guns. If he doesn't treat you fairly, write me and I'll call him out.

She let out a sad little chuckle, certain he would if she wanted him to.

I eagerly await that catalog,
    Nolan

With a shuddery breath, she set his letter aside to check the envelope. Her eyes widened with every bill she counted. If she recalled correctly, everything in his savings account was now in her hands.

She stared at both the letter and cash in her lap. Why did he write as if he were resigned that she'd leave him? As if their pretend marriage—which wasn't so pretend anymore—had been a mistake? Was this his way of letting her know he didn't wish for her to return?

The only thing that had made her put one foot in front of the other this morning was the thought of returning and fixing whatever was wrong between them once she'd given Matthias and his investors what they needed to start manufacturing—if they even chose to back her.

But what if nothing could be fixed? Nolan wrote as if this were the end.

A tear rolled down her cheek, and she smudged it away.

Oh, to go back to the morning after they'd spent the night together and do everything differently. If only she'd not let her past trauma color her reaction to Nolan betraying her trust, if only she'd said…

Said what, exactly?

Her hands shook as she rubbed her hands along the letter that had made her feel both cherished and abandoned. The emotions she'd suppressed these past three months for a man she'd never wanted to have feelings for nearly overwhelmed her. She pressed her fingernails deep into the flesh of her palms. She would not break down in the middle of a train.

"You look a mite flustered."

Well, one good thing about Cousin Matt, he came in handy for drying up tears. "I'm not in the mood to talk. Besides, your father said you were not invited to sit with us."

"He's in the dining car."

As if that made disregarding his father's wishes all right.

"Why the long face?"

She made the mistake of looking at him. His smirk was wicked and all too knowing.

Her anger turned to ice. "I have a feeling you know—considering the way you looked at Nolan before you boarded."

She wrapped her hands around her husband's letter, crinkling it. "You know if we separate before our three-month anniversary you could try to take the ranch, but that won't happen, no matter what you do."

He settled onto Uncle's bench seat, smoothing his muttonchops as if he'd heard what he'd wanted to hear. "Actually, I know more than that. I know everything is already over because the two of you committed fraud."

Her body flashed back to fire.

He pointed to the letter in her lap, which she immediately flipped over.

"I suggest you quietly accept Nolan releasing you from your felonious arrangement so as not to cause you both embarrassment."

"I don't accept it." Her voice had wavered far more than she'd intended.

What evidence of fraud had Matt conjured up? Evidently enough to cause Nolan serious distress.

Matt shrugged. "Then you'll have to deal with the consequences. And though you deserve whatever happens to you since you colluded to steal the ranch from me, it's best you not fight."

He pulled a paper out from under his jacket, and her eyes grew wide at the sight of the agreement Nolan had drawn up before they'd married.

Once he noted her recognition, he returned the paper to his interior pocket. "I'd only hoped to steal a few of your drawings to sell to the highest bidder, but instead, I won the pot. Evidence that you two married to thwart me from inheriting what's mine. Lucky for you, I've decided to be nice. I'm letting Nolan hand over the ranch quietly and you get to continue to work with my father unhindered."

"But since we've married, we——" Her cheeks heated at how she'd almost explained to Matt why they were no longer business partners.

Matt's knowing gaze made her stiffen. "Oh, I know all about your escapades. Do you realize how poorly my father would look upon you once he finds out you're a loose woman?"

She blinked hard. *Loose?*

"I'm afraid Lilith didn't take too kindly to your haughtiness."

Her haughtiness?

"So she was rather willing to use her family's connections to help me find out who you are exactly."

A porter walked the aisle, hand up. "Red Buttes in five minutes."

Once he passed, she shook her head. "What do you mean, who I am? What does that——"

"Lilith found out Nolan isn't the first man you've sunk your

claws into. I know about Kurt Stone, but my father doesn't…"
He looked at her as if hoping to watch her squirm.

Regrettably, she gave him the satisfaction.

"Let's just say, you don't want my father to know about your
past unless you wish to give up everything he plans to give you."
He leaned toward her, lowering his voice. "My father wouldn't
back a woman like you if he knew what you were, and any
investor already interested will change his mind once my father
informs him he's no longer supporting you."

"I'm sure what you're doing constitutes blackmail."

He shrugged. "I'm not buying your silence. If you decide to
tell the world what you are, I still get the ranch. But I'm willing
to do things quietly if I'm given what I'm due. It's nice of me,
really. Oh, and Lilith found out something else. Seems you
burned down your last laundry playing with fire."

"I don't play with fire—that was…" Why was she even
arguing with him?

"Investing in a woman inventor is risky enough. And you are
not only a moral risk, but a physical risk." Matt stood as the
train slowed to a stop and picked up the satchel she'd not realized he'd brought with him. He stepped into the line of passengers waiting to deboard. "I'll leave you to think about how it'd
behoove you to accept this and move on."

"You're getting off already?" She squinted up at him. "Why
were you on this train?"

"To make sure you knew what you're up against. Now, be a
good girl and make my father proud, heaven knows I can't. You
wouldn't be able to either if he knew the truth. So consider my
silence a gift to you in appreciation for your share of the ranch.
It's a generous gift, considering my father and his friends can get
your things on every mercantile shelf west of the Mississippi."

She gripped her seat as Matt inched away in the line of
disembarking passengers.

Could he get away with it?

Considering Nolan's letter, her husband thought so. His

words had hinted to there being nothing to come back to. Would he capitulate to Matt, so she could succeed?

Matt didn't look back, just detrained, head high, shoulders erect. Her shoulders, on the other hand, deflated. If Matt told his father about her past...

Her inventions weren't earth-shattering enough for Matthias to ignore the truth.

When had Matt gotten that paper? She rubbed her forehead trying to remember what she'd done with it. She'd shoved it into one of her file boxes, maybe? She should have cast it into the fire!

Fire... She closed her eyes tight. Hadn't she chastised herself the day after the fire for leaving her cabin in more of a mess than usual? Well, not that it wasn't always a mess, but she'd had trouble finding things in her perfectly arranged chaos when she thought she knew where they were. Had he set the fire to go through her things? Had he been trying to steal her ideas to sabotage his father?

She rubbed her forehead. Was there any way to prove it, if he had?

If they pried too much into his affairs, would that not spur him to ruin her immediately? If they fought him in court, how would that help? She would have to admit to the truth of his accusations in front of witnesses.

If they lost both the ranch and Uncle's favor, they'd be up against the same dismal future they'd married to escape—with shame piled upon them for good measure.

She couldn't do that to Nolan.

CHAPTER FORTY

Sweat trickled down Nolan's forehead as he fingered one of the leather scraps Corinne hadn't cleared off her workbench. He should roll his wheelchair over and open the windows and prop open the door farther, but he hadn't the desire.

Corinne had left without uttering one word of "romantic nonsense." That shouldn't have hurt as much as it had, but he'd hoped to hear something to assure him she'd return, that no matter what happened while she was away, she'd care…

He huffed and flicked the leather piece across the table and onto the floor. It was probably best she'd said nothing. Once Matt stripped him of everything he owned, she'd need to stay with Uncle as long as possible.

Picking up a piece of curled leather that looked like a smile, Nolan ripped it apart. If only he could've done that with the smug expression Matt had worn when he'd boarded the train to return to his conniving fiancée.

But instead of chasing after Matt to smack the smile off his face, he'd bowed his head, letting Matt know he'd won. He'd asked Matt earlier to schedule a court date to obtain an official ruling that might make Corinne less curious about why he'd signed over the deed without a fight.

Surrounding him were all of Corinne's odds and ends, none important enough to pay to ship to Denver. Should he try to save any of it? Leah might let him store it in the laundry's back room again. Maybe he ought to see if he could have Corinne's old upstairs apartment.

If things were different, he'd be headed to his uncle's, but how awkward would that be? How would he even begin to explain to either of them how Matt now possessed the ranch? And then to ask his uncle for a separate room—

"Knock, knock," Annie's soft voice interrupted his melancholy as she stepped through the cabin door. "Your men thought you might be out here."

He brushed the clingy bits of soft leather off his hands. "I am."

She walked over. "You look miserable."

He shrugged.

"You love her, don't you?"

The breath he drew wasn't so he could respond, but to stall. Corinne ought to hear how he felt before anyone else. Not that he planned to tell her any time soon—or maybe at all. He didn't want her to feel any more unwanted obligation toward him than she already did.

He sighed. "You know as well as I do, Corinne wants nothing to do with me as a husband. The best thing I can do for her is to let her go."

Annie sat on the stool beside him. "Now, why would you think I believed that?"

He picked up another leather scrap to keep from looking at her. "I overheard."

"Overheard what?"

"The two of you. I know what she told you." He closed his eyes. Why had he even brought this up? "About the night we spent together."

Silence reigned for a moment before Annie spluttered with laughter.

He glanced over at her. How was that funny?

Her cheeks were pink, though her eyes kind. Her face reddened as she fretted her lower lip. Then she looked away, sobering. "Goodness, I don't know what to say considering this isn't an appropriate topic for you and me to engage in. It'd probably be best to have Jacob speak with you, but then I'd have to tell him…" She suddenly sat up straight and peered down her nose at him like a mother about to lecture a wayward child. "The short of it is, you shouldn't have eavesdropped."

"It's better that I know——"

"You'd have known more if you'd listened longer, apparently."

He crossed his arms. Not knowing everything was a blessing.

"You ninny." She poked his arm. "She told me about how things went with Kurt, and I told her that with time there was hope she could one day enjoy every aspect of her husband's attentions."

He kneaded the back of his neck. "So she doesn't wish she'd never married me?"

"No, and let that be a lesson to you about eavesdropping." She jammed her finger into his arm again. "Corinne was concerned you'd not want to stay married to her if she couldn't make you happy. Seems that's why she'd been against marriage all along. She doesn't want to hurt someone she loves."

He couldn't do much more than blink. Did Annie mean Corinne loved him, or had she meant that hypothetically?

Annie rested a hand on his shoulder. "Corinne cares deeply for you—more than she's likely letting herself feel considering how scared she is you might not love her back if she can't … fulfill your expectations."

He blinked against tears, and his body lost half its tension. So Corinne hadn't found him unpalatable after he'd tried his best to show her how he really felt? "Thank you for telling me."

She stood, giving him one last squeeze. "I'll excuse myself now."

"I'm sorry, what did you come for?"

"I was going to ask you over for dinner so we could tell you about our trip, but we can do that another day." She waved and was gone.

As he stared unfocused at the cattle grazing outside the window, his body began to shake at the thought of signing over all these acres of rolling plains to Matt.

When he'd thought Corinne had no real attachment to him, the loss hadn't seemed so significant, but if she was coming back...

Yet, the ranch was nothing compared to her. Dragging her through the mud to keep this place wasn't worth it. If he had a chance to win her heart, he couldn't allow Matt to stop him.

He might not be able to provide much without this place, but he could serve and care for her wherever they found themselves. And though Matthias would certainly help Corinne in order to profit, his uncle didn't believe in her like he did.

Why hadn't he gone with them?

Shoving away from the table, Nolan scanned the room, trying to judge what Corinne might want saved.

He'd have to get a job in Denver. He may not know much about Uncle's business, but he'd proven he could run a place profitably without resorting to shadiness. Surely his uncle could use him in the mailroom or something.

He wheeled over to grab a sturdy crate and started wrapping her flasks of chemicals with old newspaper.

Would it be too much to hope Matthias wouldn't lose respect for him when he showed up without a penny and asking for a separate bedroom? But he needed to be there to support Corinne—not push her for more than she wanted to give.

Plus, without the ranch, it might take time to prove he wasn't like her father, wanting to profit off of her work without doing any of his own.

The jangle of Mickey's collar drew Nolan's attention back

out the window. Timothy was walking the fence line, the dog running beside him.

"Timothy!"

The young man turned, scratching his head as if he was uncertain he'd heard his name called.

"In the cabin!"

Timothy jogged over and poked his head in through the door. "Yes, boss?"

Mickey ran past him to jump into Nolan's lap.

Nolan gave him a brisk, playful petting, jiggling his ears back and forth. "Round up the men to come help me pack. Tell Sal to go into town to rent me another wagon. I've got all the furniture in the hou—" He couldn't let Matt have everything, but what would he do with it all? "Maybe don't do that yet, but definitely pull my wagon out here. Corinne will want some of this stuff."

"Wh—why are we doing this?"

"I'm afraid the ranch will soon be under Matt's ownership, and I need to take some of this to Colorado."

Timothy didn't move. "Come again?"

"I'm leaving."

"Why?"

"We have to do what we must to win over the love of our lives, right? Means I'm going to Denver."

Timothy tried to smile, but it was weak. "Well, I don't know that there's much one can do if the lady hardly knows you exist." He sighed then shrugged. "But your woman's definitely worth running after, especially since she don't think herself better than others and has more than fluff and feathers upstairs."

She certainly wasn't a woman with a head full of nonsense. Though she was smart enough to think herself better than others, she didn't put on airs. She was certainly the best woman he'd ever met.

"I didn't realize you two had a falling out."

"Not exactly, but … sort of. Anyway, go get the others."

"Sal ain't going to like this. I don't think he'll stay on if your cousin's boss."

"I don't like it either, but as hard as it'll be to let go of this place, it's not worth destroying lives to keep it."

As much as it pained him to admit—his father had been right all along. He'd needed the companionship of a devoted wife—a true helpmeet in every sense of the word—more than he'd ever needed a ranch.

He'd needed Corinne.

CHAPTER FORTY-ONE

Unclasping her largest bag, Corinne forced herself to pull out the clothes she'd left packed away since arriving in Denver. Her maid was growing more adamant each day that Corrine allow her to unpack things, but she'd kept putting her off.

Not because the guest room Uncle Matthias had given her didn't satisfy. The furnishings were polished and plush, the ceiling tall, the windows large, but she might as well have been put in the root cellar for all the joy these accommodations gave her.

Before she finished emptying the bag, she sank onto the bed and stared out the window at the townhouse roofs across the street.

The clattering of horses and the shouts of drivers below helped drown out the constant barrage of thoughts, but not enough.

Could she let Nolan give up everything for her?

But if she didn't, her disgrace would become his disgrace. He didn't deserve that—at all.

A soft knock on the doorframe dragged her attention off the pale sky and to the hallway.

Uncle stood in the open doorway, his forehead furrowed.

"Miss Inglebird is concerned you don't like your room. Would you like to choose another?"

"No, the room's fine." Considering it was the size of two of the ranch house bedrooms and quadruple that of her laundry apartment, she had no complaint.

"Are you all right?"

"Yes."

Even she wouldn't have been convinced by the flat sound of her voice.

"You certainly don't sound so." Matthias walked in and pulled the rocker from the corner of the room to sit. "What can I do to cheer you up? It's not the maid, is it?"

She shook her head. She'd never had a maid. Miss Inglebird brought her tea, shushed the house servants so she could have enough silence to "create," and pulled down the covers of her bed each night. Who wouldn't have felt blessed to have such things done for them?

However, blessed was far from what she felt.

"You miss your husband? You should be proud he believes in you. What other man would allow you to leave your duties behind and come all this way to follow this unusual dream?"

Exactly. What other man?

Since he was such a man, he deserved to know how she felt. If he felt as she did, but hadn't been able to say so because of the ridiculous vow she'd forced him to make to follow her stupid rules, he shouldn't have to spend another minute believing she felt nothing.

But what if he was gone by the time she returned? If he'd meant to hand the ranch over to Matt and come live here, he'd have said so. But he'd said to send him a catalog. Where did he intend to go?

Matthias stood, then dragged his chair back to its place. "Come with me to the parlor."

"Oh, no. I think I'll stay here. I'm just…" Maybe she shouldn't be such a troublesome guest, because if she couldn't return to the ranch and needed to support herself, this place offered—

"Corinne?"

She startled and turned for the door. "I'm sorry. I'm coming."

In the middle of the hallway, he stopped, gesturing for a maid to come to them. "Get Mrs. Key a seltzer, something to liven her spirits."

"That's all right, I—"

He put his arm around her shoulders and pulled her along. "I know it won't make everything better, but it'll help."

"I'm sorry to seem ungrateful—"

"Don't worry about it any longer. I can see what the problem is now."

"You can?" She looked up at him, but he was still looking forward as he led her down the hallway.

"Of course. I should have asked Nolan to come along. I'm afraid it's been a long time since I've been besotted, and in the years since, I lost my head with the opposite feeling toward the woman. I should've realized how the separation would affect you." He jiggled her shoulder. "But no need for such melancholy. He can visit whenever he wishes."

"I'm not sure he can." With all the money he gave her, what Matt had threatened, and how Nolan never asked for help… "He's so set on proving he can provide, I can't imagine he'd come here. What man would want people thinking he had to live off his wife?"

"You're talking in riddles, Corinne. Why would visiting you make anyone think that?" He'd stopped a foot inside the parlor and stared at her.

Unable to hold his gaze, she moved to the window, though the glass was too coated with grime to see out well.

What should she tell him?

Since Matt had left her reeling on the train two days ago, she'd played over every possible option. Going back to Armelle in an attempt to save the ranch would likely destroy one or the both of them. But if she remained in Denver, they had a chance at staying solvent—as long as Matthias continued to support her.

"If something's wrong, I can't help you unless you tell me about it."

The maid came in and handed two glasses of seltzer to Matthias. He crossed the room to hand her one. "Sip on this and tell me what you're worrying about."

What would he do if she told him? She moved to sit in one of the upholstered chairs facing a small table with a chess set and set down her glass. "How good are my inventions?"

He moved to lean against the wall. "They're good. Some are nothing more than that. Others have a chance at making you decent money. I'd still prefer you to allow Nolan to put his name on them, but if you insist…" He sighed. "I can still sell them."

"But what if, at one time, I was … well—" She should quit this conversation right now and buck up.

Yet how could she allow Matt the power to spill her secrets whenever he wished? "The fact of the matter is, Nolan didn't marry a virgin bride—and it wasn't because I'd been widowed or forced."

Matthias stiffened, his brows nearly meeting in the middle. He scratched his cheek for a moment, but then shook his head. "I'm aware you know about my late wife and how information like that would not make me think highly of you."

She dropped her gaze to her lap. "I know."

"Then why on earth would you reveal such to me?" His voice was hard and heated.

Would he kick her out immediately? Oh, how she should have held her tongue. But it'd do no good to stay silent now. "Your son found out."

"Why does that matter?" Matthias set down his glass and crossed his arms.

She put a hand to her cheek, hoping to hide the heat

blooming there. "He thinks me a loose woman, but I was seventeen and naïve. I'd believed Kurt when he said he'd make an honest woman out of me. When he betrayed me, and then Randolph after him, I swore off trusting another man ever again."

"Yet you married Nolan?"

Her cheeks heated even more. "It was a business arrangement—no different than when a family arranges a marriage to consolidate wealth, power, or any other reason besides love."

"Why? What did you have that would entice Nolan into marrying you?"

"Your brother's will said Matt would get the ranch if Nolan didn't marry within three months after his passing."

"It said what?" Matthias cursed under his breath. "Lewis was always too hard on Nolan. My son doesn't deserve that ranch."

"Nolan didn't think so either, so he decided to marry. Since he and I were the two people most adamant about not wanting to wed, he figured we could arrange this like business. Split the ranch's profits, lead our lives separately, no hearts involved."

"I'm not sure why any of this matters."

"Because Matt knows all about that, too. He riffled through our things and found the paper Nolan had written up delineating our marriage agreement. Matt says he can prove we defrauded him of his inheritance. If we don't fight him, he claims he'll refrain from revealing what he knows of my past—especially to you, since he expects you'll quit aiding me once you know what happened before I met Nolan."

She laid over the chess set's king. "So in exchange for not telling anyone about my indiscretions, he asked Nolan to quietly hand over the ranch."

Matthias cursed again. "I don't know yet how I'll end up thinking about you, but I do know what I think of Nolan. I'll take care of this."

He stood abruptly, righted the king piece with a definitive thunk, crossed the room, and pulled a bell rope.

She slid to the edge of her seat. "Please don't do anything that'll reveal my past to the gossips in Armelle. Not for my sake, but I don't want to hurt Nolan anymore than I have. I did tell him about Kurt, but not before we married. I didn't think it necessary since we were only pretending to wed."

"Oh, that won't matter when I'm done."

The butler came in, somber of face and rigid of posture. "You rang."

"I want you to contact Peters, Carlson, and Tabor. Find out the soonest they can see me."

"Would Tabor be at Capital Bank today?"

"Yes, and the other two are likely at their office on Thirteenth."

"Very good, sir." The butler turned on his heel and left.

She gripped the armrests. What was he going to do? Buy Matt off?

As much as she didn't want him to—for how would they ever be able to repay him—she couldn't tell him no. She'd do anything to help Nolan keep his ranch.

"When you've figured out how much it'll take to purchase Matt's silence, let me know how many of my ideas you'll need to patent under your name to reimburse your expenses." Her words felt wooden, each one had been harder to get out than the last. But what else could she do? Nolan was more important than anything she had or might ever possess.

Matthias returned to her and pulled her up from her chair. "We're not buying him off. My pride kept me from pressing embezzlement charges, and I thought I was doing him a favor by kicking him out. I didn't realize doing so would hurt you and Nolan—or anyone else for that matter. I was only thinking of saving myself the public embarrassment of such a son."

"How will pressing charges help?"

"Your marriage with Nolan isn't purely business anymore, is it?"

She started wringing her hands like she used to when they constantly ached. "I don't know."

"What do you mean you don't know?"

"I mean, no, it isn't. But I'm not sure he…"

"He what?"

Oh, why hadn't she said it wasn't business anymore and left it at that?

"I'm not sure he wants me," she whispered. "Not after how I've messed up his life."

He took her by the shoulders. "Go pack your things. We'll leave on the next train to Armelle. I'll take care of Matt, and you'll straighten things out with Nolan. If you two decide you want my lawyer's help in annulling your sham of a marriage, I'll take care of that, too."

"What?" Her chest heaved hard with the solitary word, and she went numb from nose to toe.

He chucked her chin up gently, his expression semi-soft. "That's what I thought."

Spinning her, he nudged her toward the hallway. "Don't forget who your husband is, Corinne. That boy never vowed to do something he didn't intend to follow through with. Why you're so unsure of him, I have no idea. Maybe it's because he needs to know you're not interested in business any longer."

CHAPTER FORTY-TWO

Pulling on his string tie, Nolan sat behind the small table in front of the courtroom and looked back toward the gallery where a few townspeople sat. Did they not have enough stuff to do? Thankfully there weren't as many spectators as the hullabaloo this past spring when the mayor had been convicted of several crimes.

Nolan glanced at the clock again. It had barely moved since the last time he'd checked.

Once he'd decided to travel to Denver to be with Corinne, he'd been tempted to sign over the deed and leave immediately. However, Jacob and Sal had convinced him to stick around to make sure Matt's case held water.

Nolan tugged on his string tie. Matt had promised not to bring up anything against Corinne—but now that he wasn't simply going to hand over the deed, would he stick to the facts of the case and leave her out of it? If not, hopefully word wouldn't spread as far as Colorado. He glanced back at the people in the courtroom. No one present was known for gossiping, but that didn't mean they refrained.

As to what his uncle would think … the faster he got to Denver, the faster he could point out that nothing Matt accused

Corinne of changed the kind, hardworking woman she was today.

He scanned the room. Where was Jacob?

His friend had offered to loan him money for a lawyer, but it hadn't mattered. Mr. Wright had left to go home for a visit, and it was too short notice to get another. But his friend had volunteered to do the best he could.

As hard as it had been to bring someone into his mess, to see how vulnerable he was, he'd needed Jacob's help.

What if he had admitted his needs and weaknesses to Corinne before she'd left? Would she have remained behind?

Of course, he wouldn't have wanted that. She needed to be as far away from this circus as possible right now, no matter how much he wished for her presence.

Nolan spotted Sal in the back corner. The man's jaw was set as if he could intimidate the judge into siding against Matt. But who was the man in the crumpled coat, scraping dirt from under his fingernails with a pocketknife? A drifter looking to sit a spell out of the summer sun?

Maybe he could ask the court to remove people who had no need to be privy to his financial affairs. The fewer people who heard what Matt said, the better.

The back door opened and Matt walked in with the man who'd showed up on the train yesterday, carrying a briefcase in one hand and a cane with a shiny gold topper in the other.

Mr. Driscoll, the big-city lawyer Matt had hired, was the talk of the town already, so smooth in tongue he'd talked the barber into a free shave and Mr. Ivens into extending him an invitation to his private poker game—an invitation Matt had wanted for months.

Whereas Matt thought himself a smooth talker, his lawyer truly was. Not a comforting thought.

Especially since the judge trying this case was Judge Morrisey. Though he was generally fair, he tended to flout procedure, speak frankly, and was a bit eccentric. He'd roamed the western territories for decades, basking in the freedom of an untamed land which mirrored his unpredictable rulings.

Jacob strode in, shoved his way through the little half door at the front, and sat in the chair next to him. His friend was breathing as if he'd run all the way into town.

Matt eyed both of them before leaning over to whisper something in his lawyer's ear.

Nolan leaned to do his own whispering. "Do you think we have any hope?"

He turned. "I got Judge Morrisey to allow a few last-minute witnesses, but he's unpredictable. I can't tell you what's going to happen."

His heart tripping anew, Nolan turned to see Annie seat herself in the corner opposite the man in the hard-worn clothes. "I don't want—"

The door to the judge's chamber swung open and a blond man walked out stiffly. "All rise for the honorable Judge Morrisey."

A few chairs screeched across the floor as the judge, who never wore the normal black robe but a caramel-colored duster, came out and flapped his hand at everyone in a "be seated" gesture.

No one sat. All waited for the bailiff to tell them to do so.

The judge's silvery mustache drooped far below his chin, lush and full, and Nolan couldn't help but glance over at his cousin. He stifled a smirk at the self-conscious way Matt was running his fingers through his sparser muttonchops.

Judge Morrisey dropped a folder onto the solitary desk at the front and sat. "I've decided I want the defendant to come up first."

Nolan grabbed his crutches that the doctor had only approved this morning to keep his healing ankle from bearing all his weight, circled his little table, and stood to the judge's right. After being sworn in, he tugged on his suit coat. He wasn't going to lie, but to tell the whole truth and nothing but the truth?

He shouldn't have caved to the men's prodding to stay. What if Matt's lawyer forced him to say something that would make Matt blab everything?

"Did you write this paper Matthias Key Jr.'s lawyer submitted to me earlier?" The judge held up the paper Matt had flashed at him days ago, containing the agreement he'd proposed to Corinne.

"I did, Your Honor."

"Any questions for Mr. Key?" The judge looked at Mr. Driscoll and Jacob, but neither nodded.

"You may be seated."

Nolan raised his brows at Jacob. Shouldn't he have been cross-examined or something? And yet, the shorter the hearing, the less chance Matt had to besmirch Corinne.

"Mr. Hendrix, you wanted to call witnesses?"

Jacob stood, ignoring Nolan's attempt to catch his eye as he maneuvered back into his seat. "Yes, Your Honor. I'd like to call Sal Towers, Nolan Key's head foreman."

Nolan's heart quavered. He trusted Jacob, but witnesses would only goad Matt into defaming Corinne.

Once Sal was sworn in, Jacob moved around the table to question him.

"Were you aware that your boss made an agreement with his wife to split the ranch's profits?"

"No." He cocked his head. "But that's none of my business. Though it does sound like something Mr. Key would do. And considering Mrs. Key worked hard from day one, she'd be worthy of it, unlike others I know." Without turning his head, he glared at Matt.

"You say it sounded like something Nolan would do. How's that?"

"He gives us ranch hands a say in what we're doing. When we had good years, he convinced his dad to give us a bonus at Christmas. I imagine he'd talk through how to split things up with anybody he brought on board permanently."

"Brought on board? Is that how a man speaks of a wife?"

Sal shrugged again. "We were surprised Mr. Key married at all since he seemed against the institution. But it'd make sense he'd change his mind if he found a woman who wasn't hard on the eyes and had a head for business."

"So you didn't find it odd she didn't stick to the usual women's work?"

"We might've been irked in the beginning, but we got over it. I'm sure if we complained though, Mr. Key would've listened. He even listens to Timothy, and he's not yet twenty. I stay at the Key ranch because, unlike other ranches I've worked, Mr. Key listens to his workers. He takes everyone's opinions into account and attempts to do what's best for more than himself. I don't see why he'd not enter into marriage the same way—setting it up so things were fair for the both of them."

"Thank you."

Jacob returned to his seat and Matt's lawyer took his place. "Mr. Towers, have you ever heard of a woman asking for a share of her husband's profit? Wouldn't a wife *in truth* expect to benefit from the entirety of his profits and possessions?"

"That's how it should be, I guess. But some men turn out to be scoundrels, and a woman with a head on her shoulders might—"

"Answer the question, Mr. Towers."

"No, I don't know of any other wife with the same arrangement. However, I'm not privy to everyone's matrimonial affairs."

"Thank you, Mr. Towers."

Annie was called next. Her cheeks were suffused with red, more than the summer heat could account for.

Her husband walked up beside her, his face blank as if trying not to show any kind of relationship to the witness. "Can you verify the marriage between Nolan Key and Corinne Key was real—in every way?"

Nolan closed his eyes and stifled a groan. Considering the

blush she'd sported on the way up, Annie had known before-hand what Jacob was going to ask her.

Thankfully Corinne wasn't here.

"Yes."

"How do you know?"

She looked up to the ceiling, her face turning even redder. "Women talk."

Judge Morrisey pointed his gavel at Nolan. "You verify this?"

Was that all it would take to turn over Matt's charge against him? "Yes, we've fulfilled my father's will in truth."

"I was told from the opposing party's lawyer you were considering dissolving the marriage. That your wife had separated from you."

His heart began beating so fast at the thought, surely the judge could hear it. "She's attending to business with my uncle in Denver. I have no intention of divorcing my wife."

Mr. Driscoll turned to the judge. "We don't question Nolan Key's intention to officially stay married, Your Honor. The problem lies in why they did it in the first place and how they plan to live thereafter. And considering the woman he chose—that's the real evidence for why this marriage doesn't fulfill Lewis Key's will."

Nolan gripped the table as Mr. Driscoll called Matt to the stand.

Matt shot a glare at Sal and Annie, as if they were at fault for being called up as witnesses.

"Tell us, Mr. Key, why do you doubt your cousin's integrity in fulfilling his father's wishes?"

"Because he's a stickler for everyone being righteous and trustworthy, but the woman he wed is anything but."

The sounds of chairs creaking and people sniffling ceased.

Nolan was about to burst out of his skin. Why had he believed for a second Matt would keep this to himself?

"How do you know such about the woman in question?"

"Can we object?" Nolan asked Jacob loud enough for the whole court to hear.

"My fiancée discovered Corinne Key lived with a married man eight years ago, a Mr. Kurt Stone. She wanted his money, and once under his employ, seduced him, and became his mistress."

"Hearsay!" Jacob called out amid the gasps coming from behind them. "He's assigning motivations——"

"Quiet." The judge shook his head at him. "It's not your turn."

Jacob stood. "I'm sorry to point this out, Your Honor, but we rarely follow correct court procedure when you're presiding."

Judge Morrisey tilted his head with a half shrug as if Jacob had a point, but shook his finger. "Don't interrupt like some four-year-old. And why, Mr. Driscoll," The judge turned back to the lawyer. "Is this relevant?"

"My client knows Mrs. Key is not the kind of woman who'd entice his cousin into marriage under normal circumstances. A woman like her, however, would willingly join a scheme to defraud a man as long as it was to her benefit—as the paper you possess proves."

The room got even quieter. Jacob and Mr. Driscoll stared at each other as if sizing each other up, and Annie's face had turned paler than cream, making her freckles stand out.

While his smirking cousin returned to his seat, Nolan tried to keep his face expressionless. It would've been better to have handed the deed over and let everyone think him a fool than have Corinne's past dragged out for all to hear.

Jacob called a Mr. Agee.

Nolan frowned, unfamiliar with the name, and watched as the man who'd been scraping his dirty fingernails came to take the stand.

What did this man have to do with his ranch?

Matt shrugged as if Mr. Agee were inconsequential, but he

noticeably stiffened. Mr. Driscoll leaned over to ask him something, and Matt shook his head.

"Mr. Agee, how do you know Matthias Key, Jr.?"

"I don't know him from Adam, really."

Jacob ran a hand through his hair. "I mean, how are you acquainted? What has been your involvement with the man seated at the plaintiff's table?"

"It's the same as what I told you and Mr. Dent last night."

"Please tell the court what you have against Matthias Key, Jr."

"Objection, Your Honor." Mr. Driscoll stood.

Judge Morrisey smacked his gavel. "Mr. Hendrix, Matthias Key is not on trial here."

Jacob raised a hand. "Mr. Agee's testimony brings Matthias Key's creditability into question, along with the evidence he's presented against Nolan Key."

The judge swung his gavel halfheartedly as permission to proceed.

Jacob couldn't hide the big breath he took before returning to his witness. "Sorry about that, Mr. Agee. Please inform the court what you told me and Deputy Dent last night. Start with how you're acquainted with Matthias Key, Jr., if you would."

"I play cards when I'm not working the railroad. That gentleman over there has been at the gaming tables a lot lately." He pointed at Matt. "He flaps his gums an awful lot, 'specially when he's had a pint. Mentioned a time or two he was going to take back the Key ranch, though he never said how. One time he did say he was going to poison the man's stock or something, but we figured he was just distracting us so we didn't notice what he was doing card-wise because he's awful lucky. I mean, who'd just outright admit to crimes like that? But we never could catch what he was doing."

"About how many men could attest to that?"

"Half a dozen maybe." Mr. Agee crossed his arms over his chest and leaned forward. "Last week, he was really getting on our nerves. Started boasting about how he was getting his ranch back by the end of the month, cockier than he'd ever been. He started playing sloppy, so I took advantage. Won a hundred and fifteen off him. He didn't take kindly to that. After he cut his losses and knocked the table over, he started slandering me. My boss at the railroad heard and fired me. I wanted the deputy to help me get a cut of Key's new ranch, considering he's the reason I'm out of a job."

Mr. Driscoll's face was blank, but Matt wasn't even trying to hide the glower he directed at Mr. Agee.

Jacob stepped closer to the witness. "How did the plaintiff slander you?"

"He told my boss I was a cheat and that I'd been sleeping with his wife behind his back."

"And are you?"

"No!" Mr. Agee straightened in his chair. "Have you seen my boss's wife? No offense to the lady or nothing."

"Your witness, Mr. Driscoll."

The lawyer stood, but didn't approach. "I have no reason to question a bum who's trying to get a cut of what he heard my client was soon to inherit after finding himself unemployed. He knows nothing about this case."

Mr. Agee turned to frown at the judge. "Others heard what he said about me, and can tell you it ain't true. Shouldn't I get something?"

"I'm afraid, Mr. Agee, that you'll have to press your own charges if you want to take him to court for restitution."

"Aw, you mean I have to come back here again?"

Jacob encouraged him to return to his seat upon his dismissal, and Mr. Agee stomped away, grumbling loudly about how he'd been brought in for nothing.

With a knock of his gavel—most likely to startle Mr. Agee out of his muttered tirade—Judge Morrisey addressed the few in attendance. "I've no need to take a recess. The terms of the will, provided by the defense, appear to have been met. Nolan

Key maintains ownership of the ranch." He pointed toward Matt. "I'd suggest you, young man, find a way to earn your living rather than fleece it from others.

"And Mr. Agee." The judge gestured to the man who'd plopped into his seat. "If you hope to get anything from this man, you better press charges before he high-tails it out of town. Court's adjourned."

Nolan blinked.

He'd won!

God bless Judge Morrissey. Plus, Jacob and Sal for forcing him to stay. He turned to smile at his foreman, who tipped his hat at him.

Matt rushed off in a huff, his lawyer following.

"Congratulations, Nolan." Jacob gripped his shoulder, and Annie walked up with a pleased expression, her cheeks no longer aflame.

No soul in the courtroom looked toward him with anything reminiscent of pity or disgust. So they were all going to chalk up Matt's testimony against Corinne as slander, like what he'd invented to ruin Mr. Agee?

"I told you." Jacob shook his shoulder. "Never give in to a thief. They get their comeuppance sooner if not later."

He could only muster a half-smile—it didn't feel right to rejoice over his cousin's downfall. "Thank you, both of you. I was certain I'd lost everything. I shouldn't have underestimated the friends God gave me."

After a round of hugs, Jacob and Annie left and Sal came up.

His foreman gave him a quick handshake and put his hat back on. "Seems I still need to stop at the feed store and pick up corn for the missus's new hens. Anything else you want me to get?"

Nolan sagged in his seat. Just an hour ago, he'd thought he was heading to Denver, the ranch no longer his concern, but now...

He had a profit to make so he could split it with Corinne—as promised.

"I'll come with you."

Sal about-faced and Nolan grabbed his crutches to follow him out. Funny how little elation he felt at being able to return to the ranch.

With the cattle soon to be sold, it'd be a while before he saw Corinne again.

And though Annie had convinced him his wife wasn't looking to leave, Corinne's drive to succeed and eschew romantic nonsense meant she'd not cotton to him abandoning the ranch at this critical time. Especially not to ask her face-to-face if he could court her, considering they'd be separated indefinitely.

With a sigh, he headed to the feed store. He likely had a better chance at winning her heart by doing as she'd requested, no matter how badly his arms ached to hold her again.

CHAPTER FORTY-THREE

Taking off her bonnet, Corinne spotted Nolan sitting on the parlor sofa, staring out the side window toward the evening sky. He must be doing some serious thinking to have missed hearing her come in.

The room seemed bare. Crates were stacked behind the furniture. Had he been packing up before the court case?

She couldn't help but smile knowing the ranch was safe. She'd seen Annie in town, and the woman had nearly run to welcome her back and share the good news from this morning.

Uncle Matthias and his lawyer had taken the sudden change of plans well. After they found Matt and delivered the summons to appear in court for embezzlement, they planned to find hotel rooms for the night and return to Denver on the morrow.

She'd rented a horse and rode straight home.

Why was Nolan slumped? Was he still in pain? She looked around for his wheelchair, but only saw crutches. Was he on the mend or pushing himself more than he ought?

She took a step forward and her heartbeat clattered at the thought of reciting the speech she'd rehearsed on the train ride here. She stopped and took a deep breath.

She had pursued financial security and patents for years and finally had success within her grasp. But validation paled in comparison to what she really wanted—what she'd assumed God would never permit. She wanted a man to whisper romantic nonsense in her ear and she wanted to let herself believe it.

She'd never get that chance unless she told him she loved him.

Dropping her bonnet on the chair, she forged into the room, letting her feet thump to stir Nolan from whatever he was daydreaming about. "What are you doing?" she asked gently.

With a jerk, he straightened in his seat and turned. His face lit for a fraction of a second before his mouth fell open. "I—I was trying to decide what to do. I was asking God about it."

"What was God saying?"

He shook his head, his eyes wide like a lost child's. "I didn't feel like He was talking to me at all. But since you've shown up…" He glanced over at his crutches for a second, but turned back to her. "Why *are* you back? Did something go wrong with my uncle?"

"No, but I…" She took another step closer. "I heard about Matt. Annie caught me at the train station and told me about the court's ruling. I'm glad he didn't get what he wanted."

"Me, too. I think."

He wasn't glad? She closed her eyes and shook her head. She'd not get sidetracked. She needed to spit out what she could remember of her speech before her courage flagged. "I came back because I didn't get what I wanted, either."

He frowned. "How's that?"

"The day I left? You didn't say very much to me at the train station."

His face scrunched with confusion, and he ran a hand through his hair. "I didn't want to say anything that would've stopped you from pursuing your dream."

She pursed her lips and slowly exhaled. "So it wasn't because you were afraid you might let some nonsense slip out?"

He blinked. And blinked again, one eye sort of twitching. "I'm confused."

"Did you want to tell me something but felt you couldn't?" She moved to sit beside him, then leaned over, nearly brushing his ear with her lips. "Do you want to know what I should've said?"

He let out a shaky breath.

"I should've told you I'm no longer interested in being your business partner."

He tensed.

"That I've cried myself to sleep thinking there's nothing special enough about me for you to break your vow to keep all romantic nonsense to yourself. I was hoping before I left that you'd tell me you wouldn't be able to breathe without me, or that you'd be cold without a woman as lovely as a summer's day at your side, or... or... I don't know." She sat back and played with the seam of her glove. "I tried to come up with something sweet you could've said—things that only months ago would've made me roll my eyes, but now..."

She chanced a look at him. He still sat rigidly, but his eyes took in every inch of her face, as if trying to determine whether what she said was truth or a trap.

"Of course..." She gripped the back of the sofa to keep herself from scooting away. "If you don't feel like saying anything like that to me, you don't have to pretend you do—or ever will. You'll need to tell me plain though. Because somehow, I need to rid myself of this longing for you that's stuck inside of me. I'm uncertain about how you feel, and I can't promise..." She placed a hand against his chest.

He grabbed her hand and held tight.

"I can't promise I'll be able to make you happy in every way, but I want the chance to try."

He remained silent so long her heartbeat began to falter, but then he scooted closer.

"It's more that I can't breathe with you near." His voice was hushed. "So afraid I'll say something that'll push you away from me forever."

Her heart tripped. "I'd never do that."

He pressed his forehead against hers, and his free hand buried itself in her hair. "This week, I was ready to launch a thousand ships just to be near you again, though I was certain they'd all sink. But I'd have happily gone down with them if it meant your dreams would come true."

"Why?"

"Because you're special." The hand holding hers squeezed harder. "I didn't realize how much so when I asked you to marry me. No one else had either, otherwise somebody would've launched those ships ages ago. But if my leg doesn't heal well … as I said, I'll go down with the ship if it means you'll be happy."

"That won't make me happy."

"I can't promise being with me will, either."

"True."

His breath caught. After a second, he lifted his head from hers.

She reached up to keep him from moving farther away. "Expecting you or anything else to make me happy is bound to fail, but I can practice gratefulness. I can thank God for what He *has* given me—meaningful work, someone to love. For now, my inventions can wait. My ideas don't have feelings. You do."

She played with the hair that curled behind his ear. "You've put my needs and wants above yours since before you proposed, and I want to put your needs and wants above mine, too."

"But with Kurt," His words were breathy. "That didn't work out. You ended up deeply unhappy."

"Because he didn't put my feelings above his. Selflessness needs to be mutual if a relationship's going to work, don't you think? And if I'm in Denver, how can I claim I'm loving you more than I'm loving me?"

"But if you don't go—"

"I have no doubt you'll find plenty of other ways to put my

needs above your own. Every morning." She traced his jawline with one finger, then skimmed across his bottom lip. "Every night."

His breathing stuttered. "And if things don't go as hoped?"

"Since God meant marriage for our good, I bet we can find some if we look for it. And right now, distance isn't going to help us find the good. Perhaps next year we can go to Denver together. Or maybe my dreams will change by then. But I don't want my aspirations to trample on your happiness in any way."

She moved in to kiss him lightly on the cheek, then sat back to trace her fingers along his hairline. "What would make you happy, Nolan?"

He took hold of her shoulders, as if afraid she might run away. "You. To be mine—in all ways. To spend my life figuring out how to make *you* happy." He pressed a kiss to her forehead, then moved to whisper against her temple. "To know you'll be by my side even if I lose the ranch and every last one of my limbs."

"I've already chosen to stay." She moved in closer and wrapped her arms around him. "That's why I'm here."

He tucked her in tight. "Then I will love you—now and for the rest of my days."

"Only if I get to do the same." She kissed him lightly, then talked against his lips. "As best as I'm able anyway."

He moved back a little and gave her a wink. "With your intelligence and determination, I'm sure you'll be able to figure out how to love me beyond my wildest dreams."

She leaned in to kiss him again, nearly shaking over the fact he was keeping himself in check instead of kissing her back like he had that one night. "Shouldn't we get to experimenting then?"

The side of his mouth curled up slyly. "Scientifically? With variables and all that?"

She shrugged. "Science comes in handy sometimes."

He shook his head. "I have a feeling we'd be better off without it. Something more like … this."

He bent his head so slowly, she couldn't help but whimper a complaint. His eyes twinkled for a second before he brushed his lips against hers, smoothly, tenderly, leisurely…

What was he trying to do to her? She dug her hands into his hair, and he finally lit like an oxygenated flame. She'd relived their handful of kisses often in her dreams, but how had she forgotten how heady they could be? If she could only learn to kiss him back half as good as he kissed her, surely he could be content to survive on kisses alone.

Minutes later, he pulled away, leaving her dazed. She let out the biggest sigh of her life.

With a grin, he pulled her closer. "I love you, Corinne."

And then he tucked her in tight, whispering the most overly sweet, romantic nonsense he could make up as he plied gentle kisses from her temple to her neck—until there wasn't any more need for words.

EPILOGUE

Two months later

After turning her lamp wick up again, Corinne started another chapter of the novel she really shouldn't be reading. Her eyelids were so very heavy. But now that the hero's brother had revealed himself as the bad guy, how could the good guy possibly stay alive, subdue his brother, and deliver the gold on time?

She'd come out to the cabin to rework her idea for a bobbin winder, but she'd been unable to resist the urge to start reading the dime novel Nolan had given her for her birthday.

She only had two chapters left.

The door's hinges whined behind her, and in a flash, she slipped in a bookmark and shoved *The Luck of a Ranger* aside.

Nolan stepped in, his gait back to his normal limp. "I was beginning to wonder if you'd fallen asleep."

As nonchalantly as she could, she pulled one of her rejected drawings from a stack and laid it on top of her book. "You know how easily I lose track of time when I'm … working." She glanced at the clock and her eyes widened. How had she been out here for four hours? No wonder she was tired.

"You got a new idea? Something for Uncle?"

"No, nothing's ready for him yet." She shut her notebook in case Nolan remembered what he'd seen of her drawings yesterday and realized she'd added nothing to it.

"You don't have to quit now." He shut the door behind him. "I can wait to walk you home."

She shook her head at herself for making him keep his leg on this long. After she'd told him about the laundry she'd burned down in Rapid City, he wouldn't take his leg off until she was safely inside the house for the night, likely in case he needed to come to her rescue.

Last week, Timothy had informed her how often Nolan sneaked away from work to make sure her cabin wasn't on fire. Seemed now that he was no longer babying his foot, he had focused his anxiety on her.

He covered for it well, though. She only knew how much he worried because Timothy had been amused by the amount of times he was ordered to check if the cabin was still standing.

"I love you." She couldn't help but smile at him and the words that so easily left her lips. Nothing romantically nonsensical about those three words at all—just simple truth.

He glanced at where her novel lay half-covered and winked at her. "Love you, too."

He pressed a kiss against her hair then headed to the old sofa he'd scrounged up for her. "I'll wait over here for you."

She shook her head at his retreating back, knowing she'd been caught. And yet, he'd likely sit patiently, as if it wasn't past their bedtime and she was doing something important.

And what she ought to be doing was important. She reopened her notebook and with blurry eyes flipped through her newest drawings. She'd sold the design for her stepladder and chicken waterer to one of Uncle's investors, earning enough money to buy a new bull for the ranch, and Matthias was eager for new ideas to pitch.

Giving up on patenting stacks of ideas and marketing them herself hadn't been as hard as she'd thought. After she'd told

Nolan exactly how she felt, spending the amount of time away from the ranch necessary to make such a venture successful no longer tempted her.

The day she'd returned from Denver, Nolan had told her he was confident she could find a way to love him beyond his wildest dreams, and she was certainly trying. Nolan, however, had already succeeded. For her fear that the tingles of attraction might be all she could ever revel in were melting away deliciously, day by day.

Never had she been so thankful to God for a season in her life and the people He placed in it.

So for now, she'd let Matthias sell what ideas of hers he could while she helped Nolan with the ranch, as promised. Besides, learning the ins and outs of production and warehouse catalogs weren't nearly as tempting as the handsome, patient, romantic man sitting across the room from her.

Pushing away both the notebook and the novel, she unscrewed the cap off the scent she'd been working on to add to lotion and dabbed some on her neck before heading over to Nolan.

That quick kiss to the top of her head hadn't been nearly satisfying enough.

Taking a seat next to him, she kissed him just enough to warm him up, but not enough to get him too distracted, then snuggled into his chest. Her body relaxed, as if knowing that cuddling with her husband meant sleep was only minutes away. "I'm sorry I was out here so late," she whispered.

"If that's how you start off apologies now, I'll complain more."

She yawned and shook her head against him. The weight of his arm around her and the rise and fall of his chest called her to nestle in. "No, you won't."

He rested his head against her hair. "You're right. I've got too much to do to waste time complaining. Like all those nest boxes you want me to build for all those chickens you want to go broody."

"More chickens, more money." She yawned again, trying hard to calculate how many chicks would be hatching next month, but for some reason, the math in her head became a muddle.

"...I've got to get the barn doors fixed, too, but I'll have to get more nails if I want to finish those. And didn't you want something from the smithy? I could get that while I'm..."

With the way Corinne's arm rolled down his chest and her ribcage moved rhythmically under his hand, he craned his head to confirm her eyes were closed. Her mouth was slightly open, puffing soft, warm air against his neck. He pressed his lips against her hairline again and breathed in the scent of her shampoo, along with some other pleasant smell he couldn't place.

He pulled her in tight. And as he often did when she fell asleep first, he began whispering into her ear all the romantic nonsense he'd come up with throughout the day that wasn't polished enough to save for nights he wanted to entice her away from tinkering—which thankfully wasn't hard to do.

She didn't hear any of these half-baked, sappy sentiments, but hopefully, she felt the love behind them deep down in her heart.

I hope you enjoyed *Pretending to Wed*!

If you did, please take a moment to share with others. You can do so by posting an honest review wherever you purchased this book and also on Goodreads.

Also consider mentioning *Pretending to Wed* on any social media, especially where you talk about reading! Word of mouth is the number one reason people pick up unfamiliar books, so I'd love your help in getting the word out. Every review and mention helps!

More stories in the *Frontier Vows* series are being written. In the meantime, if you'd like to read Jacob and Annie's own marriage of convenience romance, check out *Romancing the Bride*, which is the first book in this series. If you've already read that one, you might like to start another of my series to hold you over while you wait for book three! If you enjoyed Corinne, perhaps you'll like another of my heroines who's not afraid to dabble in a man's world. Charlotte Andrews can't quite keep herself from besting Harrison Gray in shooting competitions even though that makes falling in love a bit complicated... Check out *Engaging the Competition*, a novella that starts off my *Teaville Moral Society* Series!

To keep up to date with my book releases and special events, subscribe to my newsletter at melissajagears.com

AUTHOR'S NOTE

As a teen, I enjoyed reading Christian romances because I did not have a good marriage modeled for me growing up. I am super thankful there were many healthy relationships portrayed in the Christian romances I read (not all, mind you—all books, all authors, have their flaws). These sweet romances helped me see how relationships could be. However, some made it seem all too easy. If you were in love, got the "tingles," and had Christ in your life, a happily ever after was guaranteed. When I decided to write romance, giving back to the genre that gave me so much, I wanted to be sure I never fell into the trap of making marriage seem as effortless as some Christian romances portray, and so that's what I strive to do.

What I really wanted to drive home with Corinne's story for my single readers is that the world's advice of "You must find out if you're sexually compatible before marriage" is a lie. Don't fall for it, single ladies and gentlemen. Don't give up your virginity because you feel pressured to be sure you're meant for each other sexually before they commit to you. Untethered by vows, I doubt many would put the time needed into the physical side of the relationship if you end up having an issue like Corinne. Also, playing the field and becoming experienced guarantees you *absolutely nothing* in regard to being able to make your future spouse happy—or even yourself for that matter. Every person is unique.

To the married women who feel as if you're broken and your husbands are at a complete loss at figuring out how to make you happy—seek advice, as uncomfortable as that might be. If you have no one you're comfortable talking to, I'd suggest checking out the website, To Love, Honor, and Vacuum (https://tolovehonorandvacuum.com/). This resource is Christian-based and very candid. There is hope—if you're both committed to taking the time to work with each other for as long as it takes. May you find joy together!

ACKNOWLEDGMENTS

Ah, writing! The thing I haven't the time for, the thing I can't keep from doing! And I've had a lot of help doing it. Thanks to Myra Johnson and Naomi Rawlings for giving me such good input on this story, working with me despite their own crazy writing schedules.

Plus, I cannot thank my beta readers enough! I'm so glad they give of their time to catch things that bug readers that I've grown blind to after so many drafts. They are the wonderful Cara Grandle, Sarah Keimig, Stephanie McCall, Natalie Monk, Amy Parker, Andrea Strong, and Anne-Marie Turenne. And to Judy DeVries for such quick proofreading turnarounds!

Thanks to Najla Qamber for your graphic expertise with this novel's cover and gracefully dealing with the perfectionist author who asks for so many nitpicky things.

Thanks to my agent, Natasha Kern, for being one of the best people to have on your side when life is just not being kind. Her belief in my writing and her love for me and my family is not something I take for granted.

The people that deserve the most acknowledgment for having to deal with the crazy that is a writer is my family. This last year has not been easy, and yet none of you suggested I hang up the author hat and clean the house. Thanks for your belief in me.

Thanks also to the readers who occasionally email me out of the blue and ask if I'm writing another book. You might have wondered if I consider that pesky, but I want to assure you it meant the world that you were waiting for another book by me when there are so many out in the world to choose from. Thanks for being loyal readers.

May God be pleased with the offering presented with the talents He's given.

ABOUT THE AUTHOR

Much to her introverted self's delight, award-winning writer Melissa Jagears hardly needs to leave home to be a home-schooling mother and novelist. She lives in Kansas with her husband and three children and can be found online at Facebook, BookBub, Pinterest, Goodreads, and melissajagears.com. Feel free to drop her a note at author@melissajagears.com, or you can find her current mailing address and an updated list of her books on her website.

To keep up to date with Melissa's news and book releases, subscribe to her newsletter at melissajagears.com

- facebook.com/melissajagearsauthor
- twitter.com/MelissaJagears
- pinterest.com/melissajagears
- bookbub.com/authors/melissa-jagears

Library of Congress Cataloging-in-Publication Data

Names: Jagears, Melissa.

Title: Pretending to wed / Melissa Jagears

Description: Wichita, KS: Utmost Pub., 2020. | Series: Frontier Vows

Identifiers: LCCN 2020906852 | ISBN 9781948678056 (pbk.) | ISBN 9781948678063 (ebk.)

LC record available at https://lccn.loc.gov/2020906852

Cover design © Qamber Designs and Media

Author represented by Natasha Kern Literary Agency

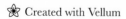 Created with Vellum

Made in United States
North Haven, CT
21 January 2022

15055726R00224